CROWLEY'S TOMB

"Even Heaven Has Rebels"

By Casey Moore

Library of Congress Control Number: 2014916455

Printed in the United States

ISBN 978-0-692-27784-3

DEDICATION

First and foremost I want to thank the fans across the globe for your unwavering support. Without you my visions of Crowley's Tomb could not have come to fruition. To my best friend and life partner, Kim Moore, thank you so much for your sacrifice, dedication and devotion. I love you; I thank you for supporting me while making my dreams as a writer come true. Your organizational, editorial, and web design skills are second to none. A very special dedication to Mickey Botjer who brought me back from the dead with true friendship and financial support that helped turn my life around. I am eternally grateful and indebted to Anne Glowacki who brought me back to earth emotionally and re-established "hope" into my life through counseling. Your life coach skills helped me discover my passion and writing career, not to mention you enforced in me that "all things are possible". A very special thanks to public relations and technical advisor Dawn Santillo, who kept me on the right path professionally. I would not be here today without the emotional support and guidance of Ron Rollband and Ron Robey (aka Stoney), I thank you from the bottom of my heart. Thanks to my dog Tootsie for your patience and love. This would not be complete without thanking all my Facebook friends and groups for support.

Crowley's Tomb was brought to life by three talented artists: Anne Marie Thies, Vinnie Plzak, and Vanessa Henke: your visions truly inspired me and I am so thankful for all of your creative hard work and ideology.

I wanted to specially thank all of the Rock-N-Roll artists over the years that have touched the lives of many. This fable is dedicated to you with the hopes we can once again conjure up, salute, and bring back our Rock Gods; putting rock-n-roll back on top of the mantle where it belongs. I do not own the music. I only wish to shed light on those who may not have experienced the best music of all time.

I dedicate this book in loving memory of my parents Charles & Dorothy Leonard, my brothers Tim Akins and John Honeyman, and all my Pomeranians (my kids) who loved me unconditionally through the years. I may have rescued you from the shelter, but it was your unconditional love that truly gave me the meaning of life. I miss you and love you all: Misty, Molly, Pickles, Nini, Foxy, Roxy, CiCi, Max, Mookie, Martha, Precious, Niko, Caesar, Blackie and Fluffy. And let me not forget my cat Mesu and Ferret Gizmo. I will meet you all once again in time at the "Rainbow Bridge".

Visit me at www.crowleystomb.com or on Facebook.

ARTIST ACKNOWLEDGMENTS

Ann Marie Thies: Born in 1989 in Longmont Colorado, Ann grew up with the love of art. Her father was an inspiration to her being blessed with a talent for painting. When she was 11 Ann's father took her to their first oil painting class. From then on, Ann pursued her career in art. Ann believes to be successful in life you must do what you love. People are blessed with certain talents in life, and it's those talents which make you happy. Pursue your talents, and you will never be let down. As an artist, she believes there is always room to grow with every brushstroke or drawing achieved.

Ann can be reached at blissfulbrine@gmail.com

Ann created the following illustrations: Front/back cover, Cemetery Boys Intro, Animal, Beast, Chief, Ghost, Magic, Maverick, Medicine Man, Ninja, Preacher, Raven, Shadow, Wolf, Zombie, Cheech & Chong, Delilah, Demon Lady, Giants, Langley/Parks/Bloom, Night Man/ Gabriel, Nuns and the Wizard.

Vince Plzak: After transplanting from the southwest suburbs of Chicago to sunny Florida many years ago, Vince continued to utilize his illustrative and fine art skills to private residences and local businesses. Discovering new techniques and enhancements in subject matter, he has always found that working with his clients' friends and partners producing art that appeals to the public to be greatly gratifying. Vince mainly favors doing fantasy and/or contemporary oriented styles of art, but also found traditional work to be a strong valued asset. Attention to detail and clairvoyance is what he always strives to achieve in his work.

Visit Vinny's website at www.vinceplzakart.webs.com and Vince Plzak on Facebook.

Vince created the following illustrations: Asylum Kids, Battle Scene at Tree House, Bloody Mary & Baby, Boogieman, Crowley's Tomb and Crowley's Backyard, Flooded Graveyard, Four Horsemen, Graveyard Scene, Hot Rod Hearse, Ice Cream Truck & Clowns, Pirate Ship, Purgatory, Quarry and Tree House.

Vanessa Henke: Vanessa Henke is an extremely talented fantasy artist. She can be reached at vhenke@live.com.

Vanessa created the following illustrations: Elite Killer Monks, Father Blackwell, Gothic Girls, Hanging Lady, Pig Man, Satan/Hitler/Manson and the Tall Man.

TABLE OF CONTENTS

CHAPTER ONE: VILLAGE FOLKLORE

Journals by Sheriff Langley

Over the years, I heard more than my share of eerie tall tales of Crowley's Tomb. Myths passed on from generation to generation. Rumors, sightings, and frantic calls flooded the police station in waves about evil monks in black robes chasing the local kids around the cemetery. In every case it turned out to be a hoax. Did you hear me? Every single case! Anytime there were reports of missing kids, runaways or murder the village community shamelessly linked the cemetery, blaming Crowley's Tomb. The police station would get reports about vandalism, markings of pentagrams spray painted on the walls of buildings; yet the neighborhood immediately associated the crime with the occult of Crowley's Tomb. Panic one year was so out of control the Mayor forced the local authorities to launch an investigation and an extensive search attempting to locate Crowley's Tomb. Oddly, it was never found; there was not one single shred of evidence that Crowley's Tomb ever existed.

The only actual fact was that of a group of teenage misfits called the Cemetery Boys who hung out in the legendary cemetery. Media reporters speculated these were the culprits of criminal activity. The neighborhood watchdog named Wizard fought tooth and nail disclaiming the reports. The police department did an inquiry on each of the boys. Later background checks were run but the Cemetery Boys' reports all came back clean as a whistle. No arrests or charges were ever filed against the teenage suspects. The closest thing they were guilty of was being different. Suspicion never left their notorious reputation. Still the town's unwilling story of Crowley's Tomb would not die off. The media constantly kept it alive selling fear to the public. Like clockwork, during the kids' summer break from high school, the media would ramp up the traditional hype of Crowley's Tomb.

The villainous Crowley's Tomb was treated like a celebrity on Halloween. After a record breaking long hot summer, missing kids were being reported at an all time high. Then events transpired in October that rocked an entire community as Hell came calling. First was the breaking news report of the disappearance of the Mayor's daughter that ignited the fuse. Then an eruption occurred at the high school when another student's dead body was discovered. That broke the Village's disgruntled back as Hell came rushing home. With the disappearance of the Mayor's daughter and the murder of a high school student, the order was sent down to crack the whip using all necessary means to solve the mystery. Tensions were brewing in the Village; the unwelcomed worldwide media coverage and pressure was beginning to mount for investigators. Lead Detectives Parks and Bloom were given the case. With desperation coming from the Chief of Police, no clear suspects, and the trail drying up, frustration was at an all time high. Media reporters once again found another opportunity to point their fingers at the obvious scapegoat, only it wasn't Crowley's Tomb, it was the weird dressing kids named the Cemetery Boys. The local and national media seemed to have a conspiracy theory. News reporters were on a mission of their own. The media investigation focused directly on the teens once again as suspects. Hunting season was in full force, the game was about to begin, and the Cemetery Boys had a bulls-eye on their backs from mounting pressure. The real challenge was trying to sort out the hunter from the hunted. The tragic events that unfolded on that Halloween night, along with the aftermath, troubled the community for months. Something in their minds just didn't add up. Nobody believed the story or conclusion handed down from the Shadow Government. The tension in the air was like a ticking time bomb waiting to go off.

Then one day out of the blue, the Village got their wish as media outlets across the globe dropped a bombshell. That shelling would have dire consequences for the fates of many. The official chronicles exploded onto the scene about the teenage juveniles known as the Cemetery Boys. Events were uncovered in documented separate journals from the Cemetery Boys themselves. For many it was closure but for others it left doubt. I honestly think the Village never wanted to let go of its own folklore of Crowley's Tomb, nor that of the Cemetery Boys' own fable. The truth finally shed light on the events that killed off the town's dubious past, so I thought. Today the Village in the Forest is a multi-billion dollar tourist attraction featuring the *"Urban Legend Tour"* of the cemetery and Crowley's Tomb. You can even buy souvenirs from the countless gift shops. As for the journey and fate of the Cemetery Boys, I can only tell you it was mystical in life and legendary in death. What did or didn't occur depends on who told the story. I've always said, "It's better to hear it right from the source's mouth." Now for the first time you can read the journals for yourself and form your own opinions. Be forewarned of its heart-pounding events, graphic details, violent nature, and disturbing characters. The riveting journals have no bounds in the minds of madness. I learned the hard way that horror has no end.

In the aftermath I began my own independent investigation. I had confiscated some of the information, while also making deals through other channels. Luckily I was able to get my hands on Detectives Parks and Blooms' old notebooks, case files, and the key piece of evidence in a large box from a friend of mine down at the police station who worked in evidence named Finelli. Sometimes it paid off doing favors back and forth between departments. Many times I stuck my neck out for Finelli. It really didn't seem to matter anymore. The case was over, while many officials were promoted because of its notoriety. My big break came one day when I was rummaging through the box; at the bottom I found a ribbon tied around four journals. I didn't think much of it at the time, but decided I would compare my notes with what I thought were police journals. Later that night I started reading the journals one by one. I couldn't put them down; it was like that one mesmerizing book you just couldn't stop reading. I was excited on one end, yet sick on the other. I realized this was a bombshell. My daughter Delilah was even mentioned in the journals. I needed to sit on this information, compare notes and talk to a few key witnesses. I also needed time to think and clear my head. The next day I spent time talking with my daughter, but I also wanted to learn more about the Cemetery Boys without her getting suspicious. Delilah, for better or worse, worshipped the ground they walked on. She unknowingly gave me a wealth of information. Later that night after I gathered all the facts, I started piecing together the chronicles of the Cemetery Boys. I began writing my own journal. It started with Detectives Parks and Blooms' notes.

My Case Notes

The kids grew up in a poor, violent, mixed ethnic neighborhood. Through their trials and tribulations together they became thick as thieves. The kids formed a tight unbreakable bond with each other. With each passing year they ventured farther off into the dark paths of the cemetery. Creating the brotherhood meant each member signing a scroll in their own blood. Honor codes of the covenant were designed as a pledge to one another by a secret oath. All the members had a branded scar on their left palm of a star. The star represented the meaning of life as "blood brothers" sanctioned by nature. Nature apparently was the God they worshipped. Sunday's forced Bible shows by parents, along with school teachings of Greek mythology only motivated the Cemetery Boys' own vanity. The God forced onto them by others was not their God nor would it ever be. Father Aleister Blackwell was the local priest who was hailed by the parents and hated by the kids. He was a fanatical believer. The boys would mock the priest by singing a song called "Mr. Blackwell" by the band Kiss. The boys were always in conflict over beliefs and ideology. The Cemetery Boys would seek out answers to questions only to have Father Blackwell give the same old duplicated answer over and over again. That answer was "faith". The Cemetery Boys could not accept a God who at times seemed to be a hypocrite.

Father Blackwell once said in the aftermath, "The Devil enticed the youths by dangling out his playground in the cemetery only to play a cruel trick on their souls." The war between God and Satan is well documented. The Cemetery Boys conceded that God should get all the glory for his creation yet at the same time he should also be responsible for all of his creations; that meant being accountable for creating Satan. What I discovered for myself was the teens were twisted, but in their defense they had very viable points when dealing with religion. We can't teach onto others what we ourselves can't live by. I understood and even related to their struggles because I myself resisted what the profit man was selling. In the minds of these young warped boys, faith was for the weak. The boys' vanity had them believing the strong seek out the real answers at the cost of death and fate. Over the past couple of summers the legend of the Cemetery Boys only grew stronger. The kids reminded me of Samurai Warriors; they were extremely disciplined and constantly honing their favorite crafts such as fencing, knife throwing, martial arts, grappling, and archery competition. Physical training was an everyday occurrence. In their minds they were not meant to live an ordinary life, but an epic one remembered in the annals as martyrs. Adversaries called them rebellious, deranged rock-n-roll music junkies that worshipped the Devil. Personally I think they were all heroically insane. I only tolerated them at the time because of my daughter's love for one of them and her admiration for all of them.

The kids stood out of the crowd like a sore thumb. They always dressed in the same colored black leather vests, jeans and combat boots. The Cemetery Boys' nicknames resembled the characters painted on their war faces at night. The vests had their logo on the back and the same with their famous jackets. Most significant were their jackets, which were very distinct and well recognized, though they resembled cloaks which most found odd. By design the jackets were reversible with hoods (black on one side; white on the other). They were intricately handmade with embroidery patched symbols on the upper right and left fronts which represented significant meaning to each one's life. On the back in big bold red letters the embroidery read "CEMETERY BOYS" with a red cross above the headstone and their nickname written on the gravestone. Symbolic jewelry was also an important part of their wardrobe. Each member wore the same rings on each finger with different meanings. Personally I think they wore the rings much like bikers did so they could damage their opponent in a fist fight. Leather wristbands contained diverse animal symbols. Around their necks was the distinguished "Necklace of Karma" comprised of eight deeply sacred symbols etched on small black stones and strung together with a black string. Last, and most important, was the "Life Pouch of Remembrance". Throughout their life journey, each member had to collect small, meaningful items of their life and place them in the pouch so upon death, their soul's powers could be fulfilled in the afterlife. Everything they did in their own minds had a cryptic symbolic significance. You almost had to be a psychology major to understand the insanity.

The Cemetery Boys consisted of thirteen high school juniors. The neighborhood sometimes referred to them as "The Chosen Few." Looking back, maybe thirteen wasn't a very lucky number. The kids came from various ethnic backgrounds and beliefs. One thing that was universal was they believed in each other more than they did in their own immediate families. The tribe designed rituals and beliefs of their own free will. They rebelled like fallen angels, especially at the heckling and forced opinions of others. The tribe fought vigorously with the new Shadow Government (aka the SG). Political and religious leaders were using brain-washing techniques through the media and the whole world was buying it like candy, with the exception of the Cemetery Boys. The kids not only loathed the SG, but also the greedy corporations and the Bible's own cast of characters as well. With a lack of trust all were considered public enemy number one. Any sense of established dictatorship became a villain to the kids.

The forgotten promises in the Bible only fueled their anger. The biggest disappointment was God's lack for real time along with his broken promises of the unfinished war of the apocalypse. It was a reminder that the world needed new voices and heroes for the people. The misunderstanding of a higher being's hypocrisy drove them over the edge. The Cemetery Boys witnessed not only religion's manipulation and the greed of corporations, but also the shocking SG's betrayal of the people that they were meant to represent. In the minds of the boys the establishment known as Big Brother was nothing more than a corrupt two-bit thief. Dictatorships of any kind were branded immediate enemies. God, Satan, demons, angels and the figure named Death were a mere hypocrisy to the Cemetery Boys' wrath. Chief, the leader of the Cemetery Boys, believed no heaven or hell on earth should have servants. Servants were slaves by their definition. The thought of taking responsibility for someone who created the universe and Satan was unacceptable. God was perfect (so He said), just not through his actions: Satan cast out of Hell, Adam and Eve ate the forbidden fruit, Jesus died sacrificing for our sins, and mankind was left to follow the impossible laws of the Ten Commandments, yet the Maker himself couldn't follow the rules and left the people to suffer for it. Meanwhile, Satan was given all the liberty to continually destroy the world, which was not a welcome theory. The principle of "do as I say, not as I do" wasn't going to fly in the teens' way of life. The Cemetery Boys would not bow down to false idols or anyone who self worshipped themselves. Self worship was believed to be evil, so was control and manipulation, even through the good book. Preacher's (another member of the Cemetery Boys) parting words to Father Blackwell in public were, "Profit leads no kingdom to the wise, just destruction of mankind." Those words of venom left Father Blackwell extremely bitter. The war between the parties never ended. TV reporters got wind of the comments then chastised the Cemetery Boys through the media.

Greek mythology impacted the Cemetery Boys' own twisted beliefs upon death; placing two tokens over the eyes of the dead for the boatman so he could take them to the gates of Heaven only to be met by the gate keeper who then placed the bodies in a final resting place. This was significant and could not be understated in what they believed. Their Heaven was believed to have no servants, no bowing down to any self worshipping higher beings, just a world of compassion, acceptance, and peace.

If you had a bone to pick with one, you had a bone to pick with them all. Many found the kids to be morbid; some even called them confused demented sociopaths. They reveled in being called names from the establishment. For them it was a compliment that planted a seed; unlike in the Bible, the boys never offered the other cheek. Their mentality was "us against the universe" and they lived by the phrase "eye for an eye and tooth for a tooth". Attacks on the tribe meant war. Newspaper clippings from the media always poked fun at the Cemetery Boys. The media made them out to be monsters involved in black magic. It was outlandish and couldn't be farther from the truth. Inside the cemetery playground, the teens didn't have to watch or listen to the media's ignorance. The boys were all musically talented - maybe that was their common bond, I really can't say for sure. The kids all had one thing in common: they were society's poor and unwanted. These boys came from either struggling hard working families or broken homes. No matter what, the boys always helped provide for each other regardless of legal means or not, taught by nature it was survival of the fittest.

The Cemetery Boys all lived in a place called the Forest; it was a suburb of what most called the City. Their passion was adventure and for them it came from the cemetery. I think they thirsted for the unknown. Looking at them from afar they were junkies thriving on the adrenaline rush. The kids' only true ambition in life was to be forever remembered in the annals of history. That ambition gravely impacted and changed the lives of many that summer. The Cemetery Boys consisted of a band of brotherhood. They all danced to the beat of a different drum but together they were like synchronized harmony. Their nicknames were "Chief", "Medicine Man", "Ninja", "Zombie", "Shadow", "Ghost", "Maverick", "Beast", "Raven", "Animal", "Magic", "Wolf" and "Preacher". I don't really know the story behind the nicknames, but I knew the real story of their fate. They were right about one thing: the world does need more heroes. You can make your own conclusion, as did everyone else when the truth broke. I only forwarded the files and journals to a trusted personal friend in the media so the true story could be revealed and my own daughter could have a sense of closure.

Information gathered through additional sources (Including Delilah Langley)

The Cemetery Boys hung out at an old small diner called Bishop's. The owner's name was Mel who gave my daughter a job there as a waitress. Delilah met the Cemetery Boys when she was in high school. Some of her friends hung out with them as well. Interaction was commonplace at the diner. Bishop's had a jukebox with rock music, served chili to die for and cold "near beer". All the kids consumed it because it made them feel cool. None of the kids were of legal age to drink real beer, so it was either near beer or soda pop. Bishop's was located right across the street from the cemetery's front entrance gates. The boys were movie fanatics and the quickest way to get to the theater was walking through the cemetery. It was the largest cemetery in the world. It was an enormous maze; one wrong turn could cost you your life. Unsavory characters hung out there such as homeless vagrants, gangs, criminals, confused souls, paranormal activity and of course ghosts. The cops patrolled the cemetery on a regular basis. There wasn't an evening that would go by that the station wasn't flooded with calls or complaints. The local police bitched at the Boys all the time because of it. It seemed everyone was pointing fingers playing the blame game for one reason or another.

Another favorite hangout was Dewey's Famous Hamburger Joint. Dewey's was located on the opposite side of the cemetery near the movie theater. The joint also had a jukebox and was best known for rock-n-roll karaoke parties for the teenagers. Every weekend you would hear secondhand stories about the Boys' exploration into the cemetery. Rumors would bounce around from one village to another. The tales always became exaggerated and bigger depending on who told the foolish myth. Make no mistake; they knew the cemetery better than anyone in the Village. The Cemetery Boys' thirst to explore and quest to conquer was a drug they just couldn't kick. They were troubled, highly intelligent, talented, misguided, and a little crazy: crazy being prevalent. The weird thing was that they were adored and loved in our community and the surrounding villages hailed them like famous outlaws. Naturally, the churches, authorities, governments, media, and establishments thought they were juvenile delinquents who should've been locked up in a loony bin long ago. In Delilah's words, the Cemetery Boys were misunderstood.

While Bishop's was the Cemetery Boys' main hangout, their "adopted home" was Wizard's place. Wizard was well respected throughout the Forest and certainly the most feared. He was the mentor and father figure everyone respected and loved. If you caused any mischief in the neighborhood, or were in any kind of trouble, you had to go see the Wizard. He made it his mission to make sure the village kids (especially the Cemetery Boys) stayed the course growing up. He cooked amazing homemade food. You never had a choice at Wizard's house other than to eat. Nobody went there after dinner because he would just force you to eat again. He would often give the boys a lecture on life and death using riddles like a Chinese prophet. Wizard was a practical joker who loved playing pranks on the Boys. The Wizard was old as molasses, small in stature, had a scruffy white beard, always in a white cloak, world-class drinker, and a classic chain smoker who was constantly on his porch. He always seemed to have a different pipe when he smoked. Wizard even smoked pot. The neighborhood believed he had the ability to hypnotize people. On the other hand, he had a very loud voice with a short fuse and the temper of the Devil himself. If anyone did something unethical in the neighborhood or at school, the chances were he already got wind of it. That was a fact of life as aggravating as it was. If at fault, you would have to go to what was known as "the meet" at Wizard's. He loved putting everyone on trial and listening to them argue their point as he played the Judge, Jury and Executioner. He absolutely got a bang out of the back-and-forth debate. Teaching was how he got his rocks off basically.

Wizard was well known as the neighborhood watch dog that seemed to have a bionic ear. It was either that or the birds throughout the kingdom tattle tailed with tweets. Not only would the parents whisper to him, so would Father Blackwell, who had it in for the Cemetery Boys. It was frustrating but at least Wizard for the most part had an open mind. You couldn't escape the Wizard. He was like a ghost floating around in your head; Preacher actually believed Wizard had telepathic powers. He enjoyed riding those boys harder than most. He was also a ball-breaking prick to the establishment. Arguments with Chief were of epic proportions. Those two argued like cats and dogs. The more he could get under your skin by stirring the pot, the louder the laughter. Chief had a penchant of falling prey to Wizard's goading and banter. Eventually, one or the other would blow up like a volcano. Chief's classic temper could match Wizard's, it was comical to watch. Arguments between those two seemed like a daily occurrence. Wizard also had a talent of getting information out of you subconsciously and that got under Chief's skin. The old man saw himself in the Boys and I believe that gave him an abundance of life. Make no mistake, the Cemetery Boys immortalized the ground he walked on even during heated disagreements. Every weekend was the same routine over and over again. The Boys would pass by Wizard's house waving, then go hang out at Bishop's. Later it would be off to the cemetery for adventure, a quick pit-stop for a shake at Dewey's and on the way home a meeting with the Wizard was unavoidable. Wizard always wanted to socialize and have a few laughs. Wizard's place was closest to the cemetery and Bishop's, so the Boys had to pass his place whether they wanted to or not, and he was always outside on his porch waiting. Wizard was like a king in exile; he enjoyed his perch and notoriety. His drug was the Village while his pets were the Cemetery Boys.

Folklore at the high school had it that anyone who entered Crowley's Tomb to sneak around was normally chased by monks in dark cloaks. If attempts were made to disturb the mausoleum where Crowley was rumored to be buried, they ended up in the hands of evil monks who forced them to kneel on glass while chanting. It is alleged they would be tortured and forced to a life of slavery, never to return. The gossip from friends of friends was, "No one ever made it back alive from Crowley's Tomb." This was never more evident than on Halloween where countless kids would venture from the neighborhood to find Crowley's Tomb only to vanish without a trace. Police were so undermanned that most times it was filed as a missing person or written off as a runaway. Authorities always scoffed at complaints of monks or the mention of Crowley's Tomb. They refused to take it seriously until it was too late.

The institution of Crowley's Tomb was feared by many. They say there was treasure to be had in the Burial of the Tomb. Surrounding villages even agreed that black magic was likely practiced at Crowley's Tomb; rumors boiled over that the cemetery was an unholy land ruled by a satanic cult. The neighborhoods believed it existed somewhere deep in the cemetery but it could never be proved. Authorities never could find Crowley's Tomb and after a while it was just dismissed as a myth. For those who would not let it die off, they continued to believe it was buried somewhere deep into uncharted territory in the cemetery. Rumors still swirled with stories of those who discovered Crowley's Tomb only to be left with cries of help that fell on deaf ears while being chased by relentless monks. It was also said if you needed help from a higher power you might as well have sold your soul to the Devil. There was never a rumor of Jesus or his Father ever attempting to save anyone. Basically, it meant you were shit out of luck.

The Cemetery Boys witnessed things through firsthand experience in the cemetery. Delilah would hear stories constantly at the diner about things they encountered. To me it was fictional hearsay out of a tabloid paper. The rumor mill was beginning to explode about their ambition to go to the forbidden city of Crowley's Tomb. Fables of the famous tomb were celebrated by many and for years Crowley's place would always be the most popular chatter among the public's gossip. The Cemetery Boys were overshadowed by this renowned tale and tired of Crowley's always garnering all the attention. It was just a matter of time before ambition and jealous curiosity would clash with this immortal tale. The Wizard had knowledge of Crowley's Tomb yet rarely ever talked about it. The few times he did his infamous temper would come out. He continuously warned the Village that no one shall ever journey off to the forbidden city of Crowley's Tomb. The Cemetery Boys clashed with the Wizard over this rule. Wizard hated talking about it and Chief's lust for immortality pushed Wizard's buttons to no end, just as Wizard would get under Chief's skin for a variety of reasons. I think Wizard knew deep down sooner or later it was an inevitable journey; one he tried venomously fighting with the boys to avoid their own fate.

The boys had solved so many mysteries before that I think several villagers wanted to know the truth about Crowley's Tomb. They were counting on the Boys to find the answers since they were too scared to risk their own lives to find out. No one else had explored such an array of cemeteries around the Forest and near the City as the Cemetery Boys. Those boys were constantly on a mission to conquer not only their own cemetery but neighboring ones as well: they had their eyes on the prize of the largest cemetery in the world with the greatest story ever told. The temptations could not be overcome. So at the end of the school year, that summer a decision was made that changed and altered the lives of many forever. The story of Crowley's Tomb and the collision course of the Cemetery Boys started in the beginning of the summer. Evil was about to come face to face with this young band of brothers. The battlefield began at "The Bridge and Afterlife Cemetery", and the war never ended after that. The great conflict of war between good and evil carries on today, even in the hereafter.

So in another time and place, a legendary tale from the Village broke out about a band of brothers better known as the Cemetery Boys. Here is where the true story of the Cemetery Boys begins.

CHAPTER TWO: THE TRUTH HURTS

Journals by Preacher

How do you explain a place that has no remorse? The Devil has a goal and his demons won't stop until evil has accomplished the dirty deeds set forth. Cries of help have fallen on deaf ears to those who believe in God. Miracles of the past are left for the Bible thumpers. Christ died for the sins of the Creator, while everyone else was left to suffer in Hell. At Crowley's Tomb there is no way of separating the dead from the living. Those of the righteous and those that live by the sins are merely a contradiction. There is an end in Heaven but there is no end in Hell! Crowley's mystery is in the Devil's clues. Are you prepared for the Devil?

With each passing day the media was turning us into monsters. Local reporter Marilyn Jenner was the biggest bitch in the world, not to mention a major pain in our ass. That lady was clueless as to who we really were or what we believed in. Her news reports were a joke. She fabricated more bullshit that instigated enough trouble for us than we could have ever imagined. It was her fucking garbage that started a firestorm. Unfortunately, we later learned the extent of how far the media will go to force their own agendas. The media's misuse of power manipulated the opinion of viewers with the accuser passing down judgment before ever hearing the side of the accused. So much for the slogan: "fair and balanced" from the media, radio stations, and public opinions. She was throwing mud at us down every avenue, for some reason, it was sticking. Other media outlets were jumping on the bandwagon like bullies. So, one day I decided to start a journal just to keep track of my sanity. Over time I did it to document our journey to Crowley's Tomb. I encouraged the others to do the same. In the end only a few of the guys wrote journals. So between the four of us we documented our tribe's adventures – good and bad. Me personally, I put it all out there, for better or worse. I figured if anything ever happened to me, I'm taking everyone down with me. The truth was in the pudding.

Growing up, life was never normal in our crazy neighborhood known as the "Village of Brotherly Love" in the Forest. Powerful outside influences began to force change. A new political agenda was sweeping not only our town but the country. It was called the Shadow Government, a secret government. Their forces worked behind the scenes like ghosts. They consisted of the elite four thousand wealthiest members from around the globe. The right and left wing politicians were nothing more than overpaid puppets on a string. The SG let greedy corporations run people like slaves for a financial kickback to the government. The SG wanted more than just money; they wanted to control the world by blindfolding the people through the media. They began squeezing villages financially by all means necessary. One of their biggest goals was putting the World Slave Trade back in business. The slaves in their eyes were the entire population underneath them. Business was booming for the SG.

It began with the bankers in the financial district then moved like a snake through the government, corporations, military and media. Hell, they were even changing the currency all on their own. They were behind the drug empire business, which was exploding and making the select few even richer. Unfortunately greed is never satisfied, they were now moving towards controlling Mother Earth. Water was like liquid gold. The secret society was rapidly multiplying. They dangled out carrots to the people only to betray them. People always envisioned an invasion from another country dropping from parachutes; the truth of the matter was the enemy was always right here in our backyards. The SG used any means necessary: false pretenses, brain washing through the media, payoffs, dirty deals, murder, you name it. Hell, they were also behind the religious empire known as the occult; the business of selling fear for profit was expanding all over the world! Even the Vatican Empire was cashing in as they moved full steam ahead in bed with the SG. Selling fear was an amazing money maker, not to mention the control and influence it had over the people in the world. They eliminated the entire mob so they could control all the assets. The SG was even behind the sex trade. No way were they going to stop this trade. Sex was selling; shamefully the entire world was in line buying it. No stone was left unturned in the sex trade. Not even the priests or nuns could control their same- sex desires. Somehow the church industry leaders found a shortcut, avoiding the line to get their share by attacking our youth. The media, churches, governments, and Hollywood darlings were sending a message that it was okay to become pedophiles. I could see it a mile away but for most they were blinded by the concept of a "dream of prosperity" that didn't exist. Homes were being invaded by technology, while constitutional rights were being manipulated. They might have been fooling the masses, but we were not fooled. In our eyes the SG was truly "Public Enemy Number One." Control the financial districts, the governments, world military, media, and you have an evil dictatorship. I kept saying to myself, "Power to the people but the power's corrupt."

Church goers waited for the war of the apocalypse that never came. A burning question always ran through my mind, "Where was the people's champ that went by the name of God?" I sat through years of religious persecution listening to the witnessing of miracles, self worship, and fear. The only ones that appeared to be doing well were the profit man known as Father Blackwell, the SG, and the renowned over-glorified "Angel of Light" known as Satan. This elite faction had the best of everything. All the material possessions money could buy. Yet, I only witnessed fear, hunger, slavery, death and the absence of parents who were working twice as hard to put food on the table. The strain of hunger was common for the people while the wealth of religious leaders, corporate CEO's, government officials, and the SG only grew stronger wealthier.

My own father was a fallen priest; a victim of alcoholism. Instead of help from the church or the God he loved so much he was abolished from his own kingdom. Where was the compassion and forgiveness preached throughout the Bible? Meanwhile the swine Father Blackwell was promoted by the SG to run the church. It was a travesty. I was not angry because Blackwell replaced my father; it was the hypocrisy of not only the church but God himself. Father Blackwell was full of excuses for God's religion. Oh man did I hate looking at him. He had these dark lifeless eyes as if he was inhuman. When he came near you there was always this sense of dread and fear. His eyebrows were long, his skin pale, and he was always dressed in all black. He gave me the creeps with his greasy black hair. Blackwell had no personality at all. It was like looking at a person who was never there. That dreadful smell of cheap cologne made me want to vomit. He enjoyed staring you down with those crazy volcanic eyes. It bothered me to no end he gave me shivers down my spine. I felt the presence of evil whenever he neared. The only time he came alive was at the church altar during lackluster sermons and the passing of the offerings. God forbid you disagreed with him; he would quickly get agitated with his tyrant temper. He hated us because we wouldn't bow down, back down, or agree with him or God himself. In my opinion he wasn't one of God's soldiers. I think personally he was batting for the wrong team; I just needed the right opportunity to expose him somehow.

Matthew 23:9 Jesus states: "*Do not call anyone on earth your father; for One is Father, He who is in Heaven.*" Basically it warns not to have reverence for any other man as Father, yet that is exactly what the Catholic religion practices. Yes, I know it is pretty fucked up.

First Timothy 4:1-5 states: *"Now the spirit expressly says that in latter times some will depart from the faith, giving heed to deceiving spirits and doctrines of demons, speaking lies in hypocrisy, having their own conscience seared with a hot iron, forbidding to marry, and commanding to abstain from foods which God created to be received with thanksgiving by those who believe and know the truth. For every creature of God is good, and nothing is to be refused if it is received with thanksgiving; for it is sanctified by the word of God and Prayer."* Sounds to me the churches misunderstood the passages in black and white. No one said the truth would be easy to swallow. This was just a small sample of a more sinister and powerful being manipulating mankind so he could destroy us all in the end. I call it blinded by the light.

I was tired of all the chatter about God and religion. I was choking on the hypocrisy. Religion, Satan, and God had spilled more blood than anyone in history. The world was murdered in a flood. Who created the flood? That crime scene was a slaughter. Who created his most beautiful angel in his own words? Who should be responsible for that creation? Who ate the fruit from the tree of life? Not me! Where are those miracles I have read about, but not in the world of today? When I would question God I got the typical answer from Blackwell, "Faith! Never question God! God is perfect! You're a sinner! Satan has a hold of you!" I didn't create the Ten Commandments, I only read about God and Satan breaking them. God always said, "Forgive thy neighbor." Why didn't he forgive Satan? Better yet, why didn't he just kill the sick fuck like he eventually did to the dinosaurs or at the great flood? What about all the animals he murdered in the name of sacrifice? When Jesus was tortured and later killed, God used his own vengeance killing those involved. Yet I am to give my own vengeance to God, as he does nothing. Jesus came from Heaven, I did not. If I really knew such a place existed and someone really had such powers it would seem like an easy sacrifice, would it not? Again for us, we are asked the impossible from someone who knows no sense of time nor lives the life of a mortal man. Why do God and Satan have this fascination with self worship, control and manipulation? Are they that vain? The world is already full of slaves through laws, governments, religions and corporations. Yet God talks about servants in Heaven. Servants are slaves to the rich and powerful. Why would I want to go to Heaven to be a slave again?

Asking these questions would only be excuses by the establishment to brand us as Satan followers. It was a joke! The world was ready for new heroes in our eyes. A person who never came when you begged, saying He was our Father, just wasn't cutting it. Hell, for most of us we already had a father who disappeared and didn't take responsibility for his actions. I certainly didn't need another nut job. The Bible told of a God who promised the great apocalypse war that would put an end to suffering as we know it. God's excuse that he doesn't work in time is no longer acceptable, maybe there is no end. Typically, the priests always had an excuse or lame answer for him. How fucking convenient! My original message to God is simple, "You're too impressed with yourself. You better get your fucking clock fixed pal! Just maybe it's time to fulfill some of those broken promises you made to mankind." There was no doubt imperfection represented Angels. I think God was too busy worrying what the jealous Angels might say. God forbid, we don't want to inconvenience the angels who originally questioned God to begin with! If I remember correctly, that is who and why the war in Heaven started in the first place. The Angel's jealousy of mankind began a war with apparently no end in sight. The Angels fucked the Heavens up, now Satan and the fallen Angels decided to do the same to Mother Earth along with their greedy puppeteers known as mankind. We would not let the hypocrisy of rulers or rules ever govern us in this life or the next. We were the Cemetery Boys, who were willing to live and die in honor for a true cause. If we were to end in Heaven, Hell, or Purgatory, so be it. All we ever asked in return was to be "remembered." Maybe it's time a higher being take note!

Besides our disgust with religion and the SG, we were so sick of everyone glamorizing Crowley's Tomb. Everywhere you went it's all anyone ever talked about. The Police Chief went on record saying that it didn't exist. Funny thing about it all was kids continued to disappear at a rapid rate through the summer and fall. We had explored many of the cemeteries yet we never came upon the famous monks. Because authorities said it didn't exist gave us more reasons to search for it ourselves. I don't think they really knew where to look, or even cared. Honestly, I don't think they put much effort into it. With the rumors of treasure buried in the Tomb of Crowley's it gave us additional motivation. We knew if we could shed light on Crowley's Tomb and prove it actually existed, we would be heroes forever. Crowley's was being hailed, yet no one knew if it existed, and that pissed us off. The neighbors are a fickle bunch; the villagers themselves only told the tales but none had the guts to go find it on their own. Nobody wanted to risk their own neck, nobody wanted to spill their own blood for what treasure might or might not be found. I guess it's why they will never be remembered. For us glory was the biggest prize of all but for a few dollars more Chief said, "The risk was worth the squeeze." Whatever the hell that meant. The village was terrified of death; we on the other hand readily embraced it.

The man that rides the pale horse better known in the Bible as Death lays hidden in the biggest cemetery in the world, which includes Crowley's Tomb; fortified by hundreds of cemeteries that span over 20,000 acres. Your new friends here are the morticians, grave diggers and caretakers. This is the place to which you are escorted on the last ride by the famous black hearse. Your new place is home to millions of permanent residents after meeting Death himself. Next is "Judgment Day" where you supposedly get the opportunity to be judged by your creator. Depending on the Maker's decision, you get to go on a thrill ride through the gates that either goes up, down, or remains stationary. Once situated, your stay will be cozy; highlighted with caskets, mausoleums, headstones and fresh flowers. You will also be excited to know that as a permanent club member in a pine box, you will be visited by frequent guests from spirits of the dead, ghosts, demons, maggots, worms and paranormal activity. It's important to remember your secrets are well kept and your story soon forgotten. Also in the confines of your new home, entertainment is free. You'll get the pleasure of witnessing the timeless classic of the "Seven Sins" over and over again. Special features include murder, violence, turf battles, drug deals and unsavory characters spitting on your grave. For an added bonus, movie night is now 24 hours a day, seven days a week. Another gift from your God will allow you to never talk again or lift a finger. For some very lucky stiffs, your old body might even experience necrophilia. All this can be yours for the low, low, low, low discounted price of death; but since God is running a special today we're only going to take your soul. There are no choices, refunds, or second chances. If you read the contract, in small print it states, "God promised you death, misery, and taxes." Well, at least you will be forgiven for all your dirty deeds I guess. We were not so convinced on these wild tales and double standards of the universe. So we concluded it would be best to find out on our own and come to our own conclusions about the Bible, Death and Crowley's Tomb.

For most people they either feared the cemetery, the Bible, or Crowley's Tomb, but like fools, we embraced it. We were adrenaline junkies hooked on fear and so was the cemetery. It was a high like no other. When we walked towards it I could feel my heart pounding from the anticipation. Nearing it there was this foul odor and the smell of death in the air. The entity had an array of tricks up its sleeves with mind games as its favorite. When entering the jaws of the graveyard's front gate, lights faded to black, Death came cruising, and the cemetery would come alive. The thing about the cemetery: it's a living/breathing entity all its own. Much like the lottery, you never know when it's your turn. Staring into the empty eyes of the cemetery was like staring at the Devil himself. It was a supernatural force. The cemetery and Crowley's Tomb were one in the same. It was an entity of pure evil. You could feel the goose bumps crawling all over your skin while the tingling sensation went up and down your spine. Fear was like blood in the water, if the entity sensed it, you were a dead man. The entity lacked mercy, unleashing hell on its victims. It was a freak of nature. This ruthless element was a terribly bad seed, and a mighty opponent. I never forgot the echoes around me, hearing the high-pitched screams of others throughout its lands. I had many nightmares of others screaming while fighting and pounding in a lost cause. I remember the first sight of blood splattered all over the ground, watching the last breath fade away from the life of your best friend, witnessing its appetite for destruction. That emotion of loss frightened me most while waiting for my turn next. I never ran from it again. We had ventured off into the cemetery hundreds of times, even made it back from Crowley's Tomb once. But, the last time thirteen of us went into the cemetery, none came out; Crowley's druids took all by Hallows Eve Night. Anyway, we delivered revenge on a plate to our renowned enemies. I only ask whoever discovers my journals one day that you deliver the final plague, so that it may kill any and all remaining tyrants of evil. Our names deserve to be forever engraved in the annals of history. We have shed our blood for the greater good of mankind.

The cemetery not only turned out to be God and Satan's favorite playground, it was ours as well. The game played was rich in tradition called "Hide and Seek." Eventually we all play it whether we want to or not. Our adventures were no dress rehearsals, certainly no picnic. Life in the cemetery was an addiction. We couldn't kick the high, like all junkies sooner or later you pay for it. Evil ruled in the darkness while the light of goodness was merely a spectator most of the time. If you were waiting for intervention from the Good Book you were in for a rude awakening, it was nothing more than an afterthought which we paid no mind. At night, walking into the pale moonlight the cemetery was calling our name, it enticed our morbid lifestyles. Its gloom and doom nature, its suspense and mystery, the crimes of its grisly characters and its endless special deliveries of the dead were all part of the misunderstood addiction of a junkie. It was a place like no other and certainly not for the faint hearted.

The hearse delivering the dead scared me most. The hearse is like the spirit that walked through the valley of the dead alone and owned the cemetery as king. This ancient battlefield is nothing more than a continued war zone. We believed that "time travel" was possible through the gates of the cemetery. We concluded this possibly could be the secret to the Tenth and Final Dimension. Inexplicably, we experienced traveling this dimension by astrophysics through a wormhole or some form of unseen black hole in the cemetery; it brought great skepticism from the village. We experienced things most would never dream possible. We believed in our own minds that all things are possible, only a fool would believe differently.

We were closer with each other than our own families. We all met in grammar school. Through martial arts we all started hanging out together. Wherever we went growing up, our rumored reputation spread through the village like the disease of Crowley's Tomb. We all walked to the movies together. Through our journeys, we learned that going through the cemetery would save us considerable time. So, when we got brave enough, one day we went through the cemetery and it changed our lives forever. It didn't take long before we started to experience strange anomalies there. The fear and laughter became an obsession, even an addiction. Over the years we noticed the cemetery began to take on a life form of its own. Crime, drug deals, murder and the constant turf battles with rival gangs began to invade the cemetery. We would all be tested that summer and beyond. I was so tired of the chicken shit paper pushers bitching at us all the time for things we didn't do. If I got money for every time a cop bitched at us, I would have bought the sons of bitches a lifetime supply of day-old wieners along with stale donuts to make them happy again. The establishments accused us every time something went wrong. The same thing could also be said about the village population, who always credited Crowley's Tomb for any and all incidents. Like anything, sooner or later the two sides were bound to collide. No one could have predicted the events that transpired or the outcome. The secrets of Crowley's Tomb changed the lives of everyone involved forever.

CHAPTER THREE: NEW FOES EMERGE

Journals by Preacher

We were celebrating school being out that summer with a trip to the movies, but first we stopped at Chief's basement so we could talk tribal affairs. "Schools Out" by Alice Cooper was playing on the radio, how appropriate. We danced around the table like little kids lip syncing, just cutting loose having fun. Chief lived in the basement of his Aunt's house by himself. His parents were killed in a car accident when he was really young. His Aunt Rose never bothered us; she was rarely home anyway, but she always left Chief with money in his pocket. During the winter months we would all go around the Village shoveling snow to make a few bucks. Nobody was rich by any means, unlike the other kids we didn't work in the summer months. The summer was our time to explore the cemeteries, hang out, and chill with one another. Father Blackwell from the church reluctantly gave us odd jobs from time to time for a little extra spending cash. Of course we had to listen to his creepy lectures, which was a drag.

Wizard would occasionally put a few bucks in our pockets as well. We saved our money throughout the year mainly to blow it in the summer time. Over the years we prided ourselves on the Robin Hood theory when we were short on money. Hell, the rich always stole from the poor so we thought we would return the favor for the better good of the Village. We only targeted the rich corporations and the SG officials' houses. Taking back from the rich made it a lot easier affording supplies. The Bible says, "Thou shalt not steal." We didn't quite look at it as stealing, more like returning to the rightful owner, which turned out to be us. If you want to get technical, we permanently borrowed from the rich. Our motto was, "Do unto others that was done unto you." We were playing the same game the Financial District was playing with the Village. The Financial District had a license to steal, we didn't. We just played a different financial game with the same concept they did. I never witnessed God punishing those rich bastards for stealing from the Village. The Financial District came up with a scheme in the real estate market that eventually blew up the economy. The Ponzi schemes also backfired on the Financial District. They had gambled with the country's money and lost with some coupon plan. Their solution was getting a reprieve from the government by taxing the villages across the country with a bailout scam and introducing new currency. Why didn't our fathers or other companies get the same offer? Gamble others' money away and ask the government to fix it. The SG had no conscience.

Chief's basement was where we always had our secret meetings before walking to the cemetery. Chief had an old antique roundtable that was reminiscent of royalty. We always sat in the same seat as if we were the knights of the roundtable. We voted on everything; each person got one vote and majority ruled. Having thirteen people made it convenient because there would never be a tie to our affairs, just a precise outcome to always move forward, unlike the selfish corrupt politicians who only repeated history like Groundhog Day. Chief commenced our meeting. It was time to vote on whether to seek out Crowley's. Chief began, "Stand up and speak your vote now with either a yes or no vote on exploring Crowley's Tomb." The vote always rotated clockwise from Chief, which was me. Chief said, "Preacher start the vote." I voted yes, Medicine Man no, Ninja yes, Shadow (always voting the opposite of Ninja) with a no vote, Maverick yes, Ghost no, Beast yes, Raven no, Animal yes, Magic no, Zombie no, Wolf yes, and last but not least was Chief. Ending in a tie it came down to Chief's vote. All eyes were on Chief as he held the answer to our fate on that hot summer night. The room was silent; you could've heard a pin drop. The moment was tense, all eyes were on Chief. I would have thought it would be a quick yes vote but Chief looked as if he had doubt in his eyes. I was stunned it was taking so long waiting for his vote. Chief glanced around the room with a straight face then stared at each and every person. He then nodded his head up and down answering, "Yes."

The room erupted in excitement. Ninja blasted the radio to the song "Keep Your Hands to Yourself" by Georgia Satellites. Once again we were dancing around the table taking turns lip syncing while playing air guitar as the party was coming into full swing. I can tell you when the vote is in, that's it, for better or worse, everyone is all in. There were no back stabs, cries of foul, behind the scene deals or bribes. As a tribe, we didn't believe in politics, only in a majority vote of living in the moment. Chief walked around the table passing out an agenda as he said, "This entitlement shall pass. So enjoy every moment as if it was your last. We will leave two months from today. In the meantime we need to scout the area, draw maps, build a new camp, set traps around the fort for a defensive stronghold, train like we are in boot camp and gather all the food and water we can. Building a camp in the Dark Forest gets us closer to the Land of the Dead." I spoke up, "Chief, I don't think that's a good idea; I think we should stay at Five Points." Chief responded, "Look, the Dark Forest is a better area to defend, close enough to Crowley's Tomb and it gives us plenty of escape routes." I stood there with a dumbfounded look on my face asking, "How do we know this for sure? We have never stepped foot in that area." Chief answered, "Me and Wolf secretly scouted out the area last summer. Take my word, the Dark Forest will serve us well." Standing up in anger, Zombie interrupted, "You have to be out of your fucking mind! Christ that place is haunted!" Chief's facial expressions reminded me of a lunatic as he responded sarcastically, "Yes, I am out of my mind. Call me insane! Insanity is a higher self than reality. When this is over your reality will be your insanity I promise you! Now, let's go to the movies and celebrate at Dewey's for dinner." Maverick stood up towering over the table, asking, "I've just got one question before we adjourn. What if the Wizard finds out? If we don't tell him, he'll find out, you all know that. He will have our asses!" Chief answered, "Before we go, I will set up a meet with Wizard and tell him personally. Now let's get the hell out of here."

Before passing through the cemetery we walked by Wizard's place waving at the old man; he waved back while watching us walk off into the sunset. As we neared the cemetery Wolf suddenly raised his hand, motioning us to stop. Walking behind, Chief asked, "What's wrong?" Wolf answered, "Someone is watching us." Chief scanned across the street toward the cemetery and said, "Well I don't see anyone." Wolf replied, "I suggest we take the long way around the cemetery tonight." Pissed off, Animal yelled out, "Are you fucking crazy? That will take us twice as long, we'll miss the movie!" Chief said, "Animal's right, we're not pussies!" Wolf continued to walk across the street with the tribe following behind him. The guys were joking with each other when we reached the gate fence. Chief said, "Keep your eyes open and your voices down." The gate fence had to be about 8-10 feet tall with sharp metal spikes on top. So we all carefully climbed over the fence. I could hear music blaring from Bishops. The song was "Bridge of Sigh" by Robin Trower. We walked toward the road leading to the east side of the cemetery. It's an indirect route which eventually leads you south to the other side of the cemetery. This was the most peaceful area of the cemetery with the least amount of excitement normally. You could say boring described it best. The landscape was mainly flatlands, a few trees, loads of short hedge bushes and colorful flower gardens; thousands of headstones lined this part of the graveyard. Raven said, "Man, I can't believe how quiet tonight is, the weather is groovy man."

Wolf replied, "I think you talked too soon bro." Walking in the pitch dark, the howling of the wind seemed to be a warning sign we ignored. I remember looking up into the night sky; the stars seemed lost in the blackness, the graveyard echoed of lurking animals in the background. You could hear that summer buzzing noise coming from insects. Sweat was dribbling down my face. An avalanche of lightning bugs glowed around us as frogs croaked and dogs barked in the far distance. The zoo in the cemetery seemed to be getting louder with every step. Zombie whining to the sounds of owls hooting was always a precursor of very bad things to come.

As we were coming around the bend we were blinded by bright beaming headlights, our ears rang from the sounds of a rumbling stock car engine, then witnessed a speeding vehicle rapidly coming straight toward us. Music blasted from the car stereo. Magic yelled, "That's a badass tune!" The song was "Running with the Devil" by Van Halen. Wolf screamed, "Get the hell out of the way!" We all scattered from each side of the road hiding behind gravestones except Shadow, who decided he was going to play chicken with the car by standing in the middle of the road. Well I can tell you the car never flinched; Shadow on the other hand at the last minute dove towards the side of the road as the speeding car passed by us. Suddenly we heard the screeching of the car brakes. It scared the Jesus right out of me. We all turned to see what was going on; the car, which looked like a black hearse, came to a screeching halt. Go figure, the hearse's music was louder than hell. I could feel my heart pounding through my chest. Magic whispered, "Well this is a first." Freaking out, Zombie asked Wolf, "What the hell are we going to do?" Ninja yelled, "Quiet!" The hearse was just sitting there; that minute seemed like eternity. Suddenly the hearse did a burnout, tires slipping while putting on a smoke show on the pavement. Wolf yelled, "Run!" So the smaller tribe ran east following Chief towards the fence, while the rest of the larger tribe got stuck following Wolf moving west.

Wolf again yelled, "Get down!" So we hid behind some short hedge bushes lying on our bellies watching intently to see what the hearse would do. The hearse backed up to where we were hiding as the brakes continued screeching before coming to a full stop. The hearse sat there for a couple minutes, then suddenly the tinted windows slowly came down as a cloud of smoke floated out from the inside of the vehicle. The music was exploding like at a rock concert; you could hear UFO's live album playing "Love to Love" from the speakers. Raven said,

"This cat is unbelievable man, he must be smoking a big fatty. That shit smells amazing. I think it's Hawaiian pot." Magic and Ghost laughed quietly as they covered their mouths. The driver's window was only cracked open a hair so we couldn't see who the driver was. Without warning, like a bat out of hell the hearse peeled the tires, speeding off in a straight line like a dragster only to turn around. In disappointment, Zombie yelled, "Fuck! He is coming back in our direction. Typical, this is our God damn luck!" Wolf yelled, "Run!" Again we took off running further west in a panic.

Chief's group ran like the wind through the flowered gardens led by Maverick in front. Chief's boys had the shortest way to go as they neared the east side fence by the street; we on the other hand had nothing but endless shitty acres to lose this crazy maniac in his rock-n-roll hearse. Wolf yelled, "Hit the dirt!" So we all hit the grass crawling towards gravestones. Again we heard that fucking hearse getting louder as it rambled towards us. Music still blaring played the song "Mississippi Queen" by Mountain. Annoyed, Wolf yelled, "Stay down, keep fucking quiet!" We watched as the hearse passed by us again. Becoming impatient Ghost asked, "Who the fuck can this be? This God damn clown is getting on my last nerve!" Ninja yelled, "Shut up for fuck sake!" As luck would have it, we could hear the music as the lights beamed back towards us; Wolf yelled, "Stay down!" The hearse, racing at high speeds, abruptly stopped screeching the brakes while sliding in a 360 degree angle. Zombie asked, "Who is driving that fucking hearse?" I answered, "He drives like a pro."

The hearse was on a street east of us so I knew we couldn't take the shortcut to get out of the cemetery. As the hearse roared up and down the streets stalking us, without warning the bastard came to a dead stop, brakes screeching as the hearse slid, just missing a statue of the Virgin Mary. Music was detonating from the hearse which was now parked right in front of us at a standstill. I mumbled, "Just our fucking luck!" I kept imagining Pusher (the resident drug dealer) and his demented drug-running thugs getting out of the hearse trying to kill us. I figured maybe Pusher carjacked the hearse. Then we heard a deep loud voice from the hearse window yell in a drawn out voice, "Hey little piggy's come out and play! Piggy, Piggy, there is no escape piggy's. Come out, come out wherever you are. Come out now you rotten, filthy, fucking pigs!" That was not Pusher's voice, certainly creepy nonetheless. The voice sounded like a record playing at slow speed. I had tingles down my back. Scared shitless we looked at each other not knowing what to do, I could feel the adrenaline rush racing through my veins traveling at the speed of light. Nobody made a sound.

Raven, who was always playing his own obnoxious harmonica whispered, "That God damn harmonica coming from the hearse is driving me crazy, man." Looking back at Raven while making an odd face, Ghost whispered back, "You got some fucking nerve to be complaining about someone else playing harmonica!" Raven had a habit of talking through his harmonica by playing sad melodic music. Ninja sternly whispered at both in frustration, "Why don't you both shut the hell up? Pay attention dickheads!" The song was "Train, Train" by Blackfoot. We stayed silent even though we were scared as hell. "Fortunate Son" by Credence Clearwater Revival jammed next from the maniac's hearse. After a few minutes the hearse slowly pulled away; I was relieved hearing that rumbling engine move away from us. Wolf said, "Okay, let's move." Magic asked, "Where are we going?" Wolf answered, "We have to go through the Bush of Thorns. It's the fastest way out of here." In disgust, Raven said, "That sucks man! We're going to get bloody dude. That way is a pain in the ass." Wolf answered, "We can't go east, that's the direction the hearse went, and whoever it is knows that's the fastest way out of the cemetery." Standing in front of Wolf, Shadow asked, "Why don't we just hunt down this jerk-off?" Wolf replied, "With what? Shadow you never were very smart. We have no idea who we are dealing with or how many there are. Did it ever occur in that thick skull of yours that they might be packing guns?" So through the thorns we went. Raven fired up a fat joint. Smelling marijuana, Ninja looked back at Raven yelling, "You fucking burn out! Are you seriously a freak or what? You could give our position away!" Raven tried handing the joint to Ninja, who pushed his arm away then turned back around shaking his head yelling, "You're unbelievable, you selfish bastard! Your indulgence is going to get one of us hurt, if not killed one day." Laughing, Shadow said to Ninja, "Why don't you leave him alone with all your hocus pocus." We slowly kept moving through the thorn bushes as the trash talking continued. The constant poking from thorns was an extremely painful reminder of what a sacrificing path this was. There was no one in their right mind that would follow us through this bloody gauntlet. Nobody escaped without getting poked or scratched up. Zombie whined like clockwork the entire time, only this time, he wasn't alone.

Eventually we reached the other side of the cemetery; I couldn't be happier to see street lights in the distance. The sound of heavy traffic on the street was music to my ears. I could also see the mall in the distance. Magic began arguing about music with Shadow. I asked myself, "How could these two assholes start bickering over music with all this shit going on?" This wasn't the time or the place, for Christ sake. Magic was a cocky, self worshipping pretty boy who had a rock star image to protect. Believe me he certainly acted the part. Momma's boy was busy trying to fix his long, straight, girly blonde hair. I have to admit Magic always got the hottest girls, with Raven a close second. Magic was skinny; he looked like he never ate. His mom spoiled him rotten when she was home. The prick was so confident and obnoxious that it made me sick personally. In his defense he was a great singer and a historical buff when it came to music. Chances are he was probably right in his dispute with Shadow. Time was precious at this point. He was a diva but I can say when push came to shove he was the first to stick up for you while mouthing off at the adversary. As the two continued disagreeing about who was the best drummer of all time, I was busy pulling a thorn out of my left hand. It hurt like a son of a gun. Wolf was scanning the area when he abruptly said, "Okay, listen up, the cemetery fence is about forty yards from here. Is everyone okay?" We all answered back in soft voices, "Yeah." Wolf said, "I think our best chance is to run like hell and get over that God damn fence. There is a road about ten yards from the fence; so there is a chance the hearse could drive near us. Does anyone have a better idea?" Whispers went back and forth then a unanimous answer of "No" came from several voices.

Wolf said, "Okay then, on the count of three let's haul ass." So Wolf counted, "One, two, three", then we made a mad dash for the fence. I could hear the sounds of heavy breathing and pant legs rubbing against the other, while Ghost giggled as others yelled at one another to keep moving. We were closing in toward the street when fate would have us colliding with the maniac one last time. I could see the car lights flashing out of the corner of my eyes. I yelled, "Hurry up!" The sound of music was getting closer and closer. We all heard the distinct engine roaring in our direction. I passed the road with less than ten yards to sprint to the fence. As we climbed the fence the hearse was in the vicinity - maybe 10 to 15 yards away - when it came to a screeching halt sliding near the fence. Wolf, Ghost and Ninja were already on the other side of the fence; Raven and Magic just jumped over it while I was on the top of the fence. Zombie, on the other hand, was the last guy still stuck on the other side of the fence lagging behind. The hearse door opened quickly; the music was so loud I think the hearse was trying to wake up the dead by playing the Rolling Stones "Sympathy for the Devil." I jumped over the fence watching intently as a tall, ugly, old bastard emerged from the rock-n-roll hearse; he ran faster than I anticipated he could toward the fence armed with a spiked club in his hand. That moment seemed like forever.

At the same time we yelled impatiently at Zombie to hurry up. He was at the top of the fence when the Tall Man struck his club towards Zombie's feet. Magic threw a couple of rocks attempting to distract the Tall Man, then yelled, "You fucking pussy! Leave him alone God damn it!" Wolf yelled at Zombie, "Jump you moron!" As Zombie attempted to jump, his bottom pant leg got caught on the spike as he crashed into the fence hanging upside down. Luckily for him, his momentum ripped his pant leg as he hit the ground. The spike cut his ankle pretty good. Well at least he made it safely to the other side. We grabbed Zombie and ran like hell. The Tall Man stood at the fence watching. Magic turned back raising his middle finger at the Tall Man. The Tall Man's face was against the fence as he yelled in a loud angry voice, "Piggy's stay out of here or I will slaughter you all!" I could hear the old bastard laughing in the background. From that moment on I could never get the Tall Man or his rock-n-roll hearse out of my head. Nightmares haunted me from that point forward.

We were too late for the movie but figured we needed to get to Dewey's to meet the rest of the tribe, so we ran across the busy intersection toward the mall. When we got to Dewey's the others were impatiently waiting for us. We walked inside Dewey's when Chief asked, "What took you guys so long?" I could hear the song "Midnight Rider" by Greg Allman playing on the jukebox. Wolf explained to Chief what had happened. Drinking a near bear, Medicine Man asked, "Do you know who it was?" Anxious to answer, Ghost said, "Hell yes! It was the Tall Man." Animal asked, "Who the fuck is the Tall Man?" Shaking his head, Magic answered, "He is one ugly, nasty, old bastard with evil black eyes." Animal responded in disbelief, "That's bullshit!" Zombie yelled back in anger, "Look at my ankle, you fucking asshole! The Tall Man was an old crab ass, pale like the dead, and taller than a fucking giraffe!" Beast yelled, "Bullshit!" Zombie answered back in excitement, "I'll tell you something else, the weird old fart jams to the same head banging music we do!" Chief said to everyone, "Calm down and relax." Wolf said, "I got to admit, I think he is from the next place." Animal shook his head in doubt replying, "That's total bullshit! Okay Wolf, what did he really look like?" Wolf answered, "Animal, we finally found someone who is uglier than you." Laughter broke out as Animal responded, "Whatever!" Wolf said, "Seriously, I can speak for all of us, this psychopath has grave intentions. I don't know who he is or where the fuck he comes from, but God damn, I am thirsty as hell for a cold near beer!" Medicine Man hopped onto the small stage singing karaoke to the song "Hot Legs" by Rod Stewart.

Ordering cheeseburgers at the counter, Ghost turned around and asked Chief, "How are we getting back? The Tall Man will be waiting for us." Chief answered, "Let's eat, we can take the long road home outside of the cemetery fence tonight." Zombie blurted out, "Thank Christ! That takes a load off." The rest of the tribe ordered cheeseburgers and drinks from the waitress. Chief asked Zombie, "How's the ankle?" Zombie replied, "Just a scratch." But as Chief scanned our tribe, he noticed we all had scratches and cuts from the thorns. He could see trickles of dry blood on our clothes and skin. He knew from firsthand experience about the rough terrain leading through the Bush of Thorns. Maverick said, "You know, I haven't experienced a hearse chasing us before. We need to deal with this asshole before we wrestle with Crowley's Tomb." Chief replied, "We will, he only ups the ante." I don't know why I felt compelled to interrupt the conversation by showboating to the crowd standing on the table quoting the Bible. Mockingly, I shouted in a loud obnoxious voice: "I pursued my enemies and crushed them; I did not turn back till they were destroyed. Then you must destroy them totally without doubt! Make no treaty with them, and show them no mercy!" In a sarcastic tone, Magic yelled "Hallelujah! We believe Reverend! Can I give you a dollar for your show? Now sit the fuck down, hotdog!" The room broke out in hysterical laughter as I bowed to the crowd. On that note, we were convinced by the Tall Man and his rock-n-roll hearse from hell to take the long walk around the cemetery on a hot, shitty, summer night. I can't say all the boys were thrilled with the decision not to go back into the cemetery. It felt defeating for some of the ego maniacs. Nobody liked eating their pride; regardless, I think hiding underneath all that testosterone everyone was relieved to walk around the cemetery that night.

Walking home across the street from the cemetery at three o'clock in the morning, which by all accounts is the beginning of the witching hour, Shadow pointed in excitement yelling, "Guys, check that chick out!" As we all looked across the street, a woman in a long wedding dress was walking along inside the cemetery fence. Exhaling, Zombie said in disgust, "Oh boy, here we go again." Maverick replied, "No worries, I'll go talk to her, I got the big sausage." Everyone chuckled. So we all followed Maverick across the street while Magic sang "Time of the Season" by The Zombies before he quickly shut up. Maverick stopped in his tracks. We halted right next to him staring at the girl in the wedding dress; she then waved to us all. Excited we all waved back. She had her veil on so we couldn't see her face. As we got closer to talk with the mysterious night walker she removed her veil smiling at us. She had long white hair, pale skin, and her eyes were missing. The look on our faces had to be priceless. Frozen stiff, we stared at her face long enough to be petrified in horror. I think we were all in disbelief. It all seemed like a weird dream. The woman began laughing at us then slowly opened her mouth as a big black snake slithered out falling to the ground. In terror, Zombie took off running down the street screaming deliriously. It took us a minute to comprehend what we just saw. When it finally hit us we took off running scared out of our minds trying to catch up with Zombie. I turned around to get another look at the Night Walker but she wasn't there. She somehow just disappeared. I then put my feet in high gear and motored out of there like no one's business trying to catch up with the tribe. Zombie stopped running. Maverick asked, "Why are we running from a woman?" Shouting in sarcasm, Zombie replied, "Because of that ugly nut case you wanted to screw! She is a fucking demon! I didn't realize you were into necrophilia!" Laughing, Maverick answered back, "Well at least it's legal for Christ sake." Chief with a grin calmly said, "I don't know about the legalities of that, but aren't all women the Antichrist?" The tribe burst out laughing. So our first night of summer ended stranger than it began. None of us had answers, I was just glad we were almost home.

CHAPTER FOUR: THE HUNT FOR TALL MAN

Journals by Zombie

The next evening at Bishops we were arguing over the hearse incident that forced the long cowardly walk home. Animal ranted, "The other night was a bitter pill to swallow; our pride took a spanking. That shit will never happen again." Shadow remarked, "Oh well." Animal responded back, "Fuck you Shadow!" Delilah joined her friends sitting at a table across from us after her shift was over. A few of the boys lost their focus while flirting with the girls. "Spirit in the Sky" by Norman Greenbaum played on the jukebox when Beast pounded his fist on the table in anger. Animal said, "Now that's what we at home call an attention getter." The tribe quickly unfucked themselves and refocused in on the discussion. Sitting at the end of the table, Beast asked, "What the hell are we going to do about the Tall Man?" Chief answered, "We're going back there tonight." My face went from all smiles thinking about the scent of pussy, to a quick frown full of fear. Pissed, I asked, "Why tonight?" Beast yelled, "Don't be a fag you little twerp!" I yelled back angrily, "Screw you buddy, I almost lost my leg last night!" Rolling his eyes, Ghost said, "Stop being a drama queen." Mel, the owner of Bishops, yelled in a stern voice from the kitchen, "Watch it boys, keep it down! I am only going to warn you once."

Chief sucked up to Mel with an apology then informed us, "We're going back tonight." Sulking, I responded, "I fucking hate you Chief!" Angered, Chief said, "Look, me, Preacher and Wolf have devised a strategy to deal with this notorious speed racer. We're gonna break off into three tribes tonight. Tribe one will consist of Preacher, Shadow, Medicine Man and Magic, you guys will set the chained spikes. Tribe two will be me, Beast, Animal and Ninja. We will be on the lookout till you guys set the traps. When the traps go off our tribe will give Tall Man a night he will never forget. Tribe three will be Maverick, Zombie, Ghost and Raven. You boys go to the base camp at Five Points, get the weapons and back us up. Wolf will take the point by himself as the bait drawing the hearse into the traps." Irritated with the plan, I asked, "Are you sure we want to do this tonight?" Animal screamed, "For fuck sake, will you grow a pair of balls!" Wolf yelled, "Knock it off, now get in your tribe, get ready and make sure you bring your balls!" Laughter broke out. Chief ordered, "Let's get ready to move out."

As we began to gather in our groups at Bishops, Chief put a coin in the jukebox, letting me choose a few tunes. Naturally I selected "Living Dead Girl" and "Dragula" by Rob Zombie. Chief gave me a dirty look shaking his head. We always had this unwritten rule that you couldn't play two songs by the same artist. What a crock of shit! Chief yelled at me, "You're a real pain in the ass, dude!" I laughed, danced, and mocked the music as we took turns in the bathroom putting war paint on our faces. It always freaked people out. It felt like we were part of the Kiss Army. I loved the shock value. Delilah, with her own motives glanced at Chief, winked with a smile then selected the song "I Want to Know What Love Is" by Foreigner on the jukebox. It was a subliminal message to Chief, I guess. Those two in their own way communicated through music. Chief waved goodbye to Delilah as we strutted out the door. Ninja gave me a lecture for playing back to back songs from Rob Zombie. Shadow asked, "Hey man, why don't you leave him alone? I thought the song selection was cool, so fuck off!" Ninja walked up to Shadow's face within a nose hair threatening, "One of these days, we are going to settle this little feud of ours!" Shadow grinned as he replied back, "The only feud is your head hitting the pavement pal!" Furious, Chief stepped in the middle of the squabble yelling, "Knock that shit off you pukes! Save your energy for the real enemy, the fucking Tall Man! He is out there waiting for us. Pack your cover and let's get the fuck out of here!" We had a tribe rule that we could never physically fight with one another. Wizard would've had our ass anyway if something like that ever occurred. Shadow and Ninja were really pushing the envelope. All of us could feel the tension in the air between those two.

Approaching the cemetery it never seemed to matter weather wise, the wind always made that eerie howling noise. I could always feel the goose bumps popping all over my skin. It felt like bites from army ants as I walked. I wasn't sure what was going to happen; I just knew we were in for an eventful evening. My panic always set in at the front gate. It seemed spooky, as if I was being watched. Reluctantly I climbed over the fence last; I could still hear "Wheel in the Sky" by Journey on the jukebox from outside of Bishops. I said, "That song's fitting for tonight." Medicine Man replied, "I agree with you Zombie. I feel a bad spirit in the air." That put me in double panic mode. Beast asked, "Okay Medicine Man, what does the spirit smell like tonight?" Medicine Man answered, "The Spirit of Omaha." Beast remarked, "You are so full of shit. The only thing I smell is your BS man." Wolf warned, "Omaha is no bullshit. I wouldn't take that spirit lightly."

Maverick asked, "Who is Omaha?" Wolf answered, "Native Americans believed Omaha was the evil spirit which attempted to snatch the souls of the dying." Animal chirped, "What a crock of shit!" Shadow said, "The moral of the story tonight boys: there is nothing to worry about if you don't put yourself in a position to die." Chief barked, "Time to give the Tall Man a big kick in the pants!" As each tribe went their own way I could feel the goose bumps multiplying as my heartbeat raced faster with every step.

Wolf disappeared into the night; I was left only to wonder what it was like to be in his footsteps alone, dangled as the bait. Wolf came from a proud family tradition of professional trackers, a skill he learned at an early age. He ran like a fucking cheetah with an innate skill of invisibility in the blink of an eye. Wolf was always in great physical shape. He had long hair that bore a resemblance to what Jesus is thought to have looked like. He had this thing about always wearing bandanas on his head. I admit he looked cool. His skills for animal tracking, primitive survival skills, knowledge of tracks, behavior characteristics of animals, and the ethno botany of plants always came in handy. His hunting, fishing, trap setting and problem solving skills were second to none. The crazy bastard had a knack for making weapons, including pipe bombs. Wolf was always into Zen, yoga and meditation. Wolf enjoyed teaching us the basic human needs of food, water and shelter in the wilderness. It was a huge advantage we had over most in the cemetery. He was more of a philosopher than a religious person. Chief relied on him heavily for planning strategies and executing them to perfection. He was well respected by the guys. He always seemed to find a way to break the ice by making people laugh under duress at the worst of times. I truly admired Wolf. He was intelligent, followed orders, and without a doubt could have led the tribe better than Chief; he just never had the interest of really leading (other than the task at hand). Wolf just enjoyed being one of the guys.

Later that night Wolf covered a lot of ground trying to find the hearse. We had about a 45 minute walk to our base camp at Five Points. Raven led the way flashing his flashlight in the distance. The cemetery enjoyed playing with my mind and vision. I would see things that weren't really there. Creepy shit, what can I say? Five Points was a very active area, especially at night. During the day the landscape was beautiful. The trees and the amazing sculptures made of stone were a sight to behold; at night it became the paranormal intersection of the dead. Five Points is the center of where the five main cemeteries meet.

The circular drive is made of bright white stone that glows at night. Our base camp sat in the center of the circle up in the trees. We built a tree house fort at its highest point. The leaves and moss hid our camp well. The tree house consisted of three levels. The top level was where we had a lookout area along with zip lines for escaping. The mid level was where we stored our water, food, utensils, tools, ropes, medicine kits, personal items, blankets and weapons. The bottom level was the main living quarters. I think the Swiss Family Robinson would have been proud of us. So as we approached the opening of Five Points we raced to the tree house to get first dibs on the snacks. I mean who didn't like cookies or candy? So we all had a little treat, then Maverick yapped out orders, "Choose a weapon, we gotta go!" I grabbed my two pellet pistols, Maverick picked up two small clubs, and Raven chose the homemade bow set made by Wolf, while Ghost put the sling shot set in his pouch. Staring at his watch, Maverick said, "Shit! We are late, we need to haul ass." We bolted towards the Bush of Thorns to meet Wolf.

Meanwhile, Wolf roamed the cemetery in an attempt to locate the Tall Man when he realized he needed to meet tribe three at the Bush of Thorns. On his way Wolf heard something in the faded background. He would stop, pause for a minute, so would the noise. As he continued to walk he could hear a resonance as if something was stepping on small sticks behind him. Wolf suddenly jogged in a zigzag pattern in front and behind gravestones. He vanished behind a gravestone that had taller bushes surrounding it. He waited to see what might pass in front of him. Out of nowhere he heard the sound of demonic chants that echoed near him. To his surprise, he heard something in front of the stone he was hiding behind. Wolf briefly heard an angry hiss noise, then a strange gargle. Wolf stayed still; he could not figure out what could make such a bizarre noise, then it just stopped. Wolf quickly made a mad dash further into the woods. Behind schedule, he ran like the wind to the meet-up point at Bush of Thorns.

Wolf was making his entrance when he spotted the tribe waiting for him. He walked toward the tribe relieved, stating, "Am I ever glad to see you guys. Sorry I'm late. I think something's following me." Maverick asked, "Do you think it's the Tall Man?" Wolf replied, "I don't think so, I don't really know; whatever it is, isn't from this planet. I heard something strange, nothing I have ever heard before. We better get to the traps." In full panic mode I whined, "The spirit is hungry tonight, I can feel it. We need to get out of here sooner rather than later. I can feel something bad is going to happen tonight." Raven responded, "Calm down man, you're freaking me out bro." Suddenly we heard music behind us. It was "Sunshine of Your Love" by Cream. I slowly turned around towards Muskets Path when we met terror face to face. Blocking the pathway stood a rival gang called the Skeletons. Ghost quickly glanced over the weirdos and asked, "What the hell is this shit?" It was a creepy gang that dressed like skeletons with a twist. In the dark they looked true to form. Some of the gang sported German army helmets with gas masks on while others looked like skeleton officers of the Third Reich. Raven said, "My God, are they intimidating man." Maverick replied, "Let's go kick their ass!" Ghost asked, "Are you crazy? They have us out-numbered almost three to one." That was definitely our signal to get the hell out of dodge. Wolf suddenly yelled, "Follow me!" So we took off running through the cemetery heading toward the road. Some of the guys were laughing while others (like me) were freaking out.

The skeletons were farther behind us trying to catch up. We could hear each other screaming trying to outrun the freaky German hit squad. Wolf was in front of the pack with Maverick a step behind him; the rest of us were a little bit farther behind. I fucking hated running! I was slower than most girls. Wolf yelled, "Split!" So Wolf and Maverick raced for the left path hiding in some bushes; I followed the other two heading for the path on the right. The skeletons of fifteen all went right. My shitty luck of course! Wolf and Maverick sprinted out of the bushes then quickly followed the lagging skeletons from behind. Wolf and Maverick became the hunters as they chased down the slower skeletons falling back further from the pack. Wolf tackled the slow fat skeleton from behind while Maverick hit him in the head with one of his clubs. The second to last skeleton swung with a haymaker, Maverick ducked while Wolf round-house kicked the second skeleton in the head, knocking him to the ground. The third and forth skeletons came rushing toward them, Maverick leg-swept one of the oncoming skeletons, then smashed him in the face using his elbow. The other skeleton jumped Wolf; they grappled on the ground. The two continue rolling around when the skeleton punched Wolf in the face; as he went to swing again Maverick grabbed the skeleton's neck from behind and with brute-force broke his neck as the body plummeted to the grass. Maverick looked at Wolf and said, "They fight like pussies." Wolf replied, "The costumes are scary. Remind me later, we need to deal with your anger issues." Maverick laughed. Wolf said, "Come on, we've got to help the others."

Raven, Ghost and I were running for our lives headed toward the street. The Third Reich was gaining ground, maybe a couple arm lengths behind me. Crossing a wooden bridge over a creek I could hear "War Pigs" by Black Sabbath blaring. The headlights were blinding as the car was approaching. Raven and Ghost darted across the street while I was tiring out. Ghost yelled, "Hurry up!" I began crossing the street with the skeletons directly behind me. The car rushed towards me, so at the last minute I dove off the street head-first; the car hit three skeletons in pursuit. I heard high pitched screams followed by a violent collision. Ghost yelled, "God damn, I actually feel sorry for those dumb bastards!" Raven replied, "Fuck'em man!" Apparently it didn't register right away to the guys that maybe I got hit. When Ghost finally realized I had disappeared, he yelled out, "Zombie!" The boys were about 15-20 feet past the street.

I stood up near a bush waving when Raven yelled to me, "Look out!" Two skeletons tackled me from behind. A melee broke out just as six more skeletons were running across the street towards me. As me and the two skeletons wrestled, I rolled over, drew out my pellet guns and shot the skeletons. I hit the spooky Third Reich officer right between the eyes; I shot the wacko in the gas mask in the neck several times. I might be small and whiny but I can shoot the pimples off your nose. The next two ran towards me; all I heard was the wallop of an arrow impacting a skeleton in the chest as he fell backwards to the ground from Raven's bow. The next sound was another thump from a skeleton being hit in the face by Ghost's slingshot. The other four skeletons were smarter than they looked because they turned back around running towards the other side of the street. Within seconds, before the skeletons could make it to the other side I heard screams, then silence, followed by their bodies being crushed underneath the hearse. It was disgusting to watch, let alone hear. Again the hearse had run the gang over like it was an ordinary drive-by occurrence. At least the Tall Man didn't play favorites. The sick bastard was jamming the song "Roller" by April Wine. The Tall Man left no doubt in my mind that he was a maniac who had no conscience. We were dealing with a cold blooded killer. This scrapper reminded me of a great white shark who roamed around stalking its prey showing not an ounce of mercy in its actions. They both had the same characteristics of playing the game with the constant taste for killing. Neither could survive without it.

Ghost screamed out, "Oh shit! The Tall Man's turning around!" By this time, Wolf and Maverick were on the opposite side of the street. Raven yelled, "Come on man, the maniac is coming back!" Wolf and Maverick dashed across the street. The hearse swerved toward Wolf then came to a screeching stop crashing into the bushes. The hearse's horn was steadily honking when I screamed at the Tall Man, "You piece of shit!" Wolf yelled, "Run!" We ran toward the east side of the cemetery. I could hear the hearse roaring up and down the streets, rapidly getting closer. I couldn't run any further; I was exhausted. I kept hearing the sounds of a fucking stock car; those screeching brakes gave me a heart attack every time I heard them. The Tall Man was rocking out to Metallica's "Enter Sandman." He was hunting us down as if we were livestock. I actually admired the maniac's music jams. He was causing us to become adrenaline junkies with his addictive cat and mouse games. Laughing, Ghost said, "The rush was better than any needle I could stick in my vein." Raven replied, "Speak for yourself, man." It was an incredible high, one that I can't describe or explain. The madness was better than the reason.

Then all of a sudden I heard, "Get down!" We all dove to the ground. It was Chief giving the order. He then shouted, "Where the fuck have you guys been? You're a little late." Chief was getting on my last nerves. I yelled back, "We have been a little busy running for our fucking lives! What the hell do you mean where have we been ass wipe?" Wolf yelled, "Shut up!" I could hear the hearse getting closer and closer. I said, "The roar of that car sounds like the Devil himself." Shadow said, "The Tall Man might just be the Devil." Chief yelled, "Quiet! Zombie, are you okay?"I answered, "My heart is about to come pounding out of my chest, you fucking toad!" Frustrated, Preacher said, "He has been everywhere except in the God damn traps! What the hell?"

Shadow impatiently stood up, yelling, "Piss on this turd! I'm tired of this shit. I am going to draw this monkey to the traps." Medicine Man said, "I'll go with." Magic replied "No, you're too slow, you're more valuable here. I will go with." Chief approved then said, "Let's give this old turd a taste of his own medicine." The boys were all giggling in the background. On the east side of the cemetery, streets and headstones go in a north/south direction with an average of every 20 yards of graves between each street. Jogging away, Shadow and Magic faded in the distance. The hearse searched from behind rambling viciously up and down the streets. The maniac should have been a race car driver. That rock-n-roll hearse had some balls. Ninja said, "He must have a rocket engine in that baby." Medicine Man answered, "I am telling you, he is not from this place." Beast said, "Jesus Chris, Medicine Man, enough with that spirit world Indian bullshit!" We all laughed out loud when we heard the song "Thirty Days in the Hole" by Humble Pie coming from the hearse. I said, "I told you guys he jams to our music." The Tall Man's rock-n-roll hearse must have had state-of-the-art stereo equipment. We admired the loud crystal clear music and the rumbling engine, which seemed to talk to you. I admit the combination was lethal, and badass. I was even jealous of the old man's hearse. I would have liked the opportunity to drive that bad boy. Out of the blue, we all heard screaming in the distance when I witnessed Shadow and Magic running for their lives toward the trap. The hearse was about twenty yards behind and closing in. It was a scary image to watch, one I will never forget. From that point on my vision was like a blur. Music cranked the song "Run to the Hills" by Iron Maiden as the hearse was closing in on them. Chief yelled, "Get the hell out of there!" The hearse was now directly behind them. The tribe could only watch helplessly. Magic was on the left side of the street curb near the grass rushing towards us, while Shadow was on Magic's outside shoulder. The hearse was now within a couple of yards; all of a sudden Shadow jumped on Magic and their momentum carried them crashing into the grass near us. As the hearse sped past us, it swerved trying to hit Shadow and Magic but missed. We saw that the driver's window was wide open; in slow motion the Tall Man stuck out his finger giving us the bird. He was rocking out to the song "Stuck In The Middle With You" by Stealers Wheel. It was almost comical. Just as the hearse hit the chain spike trap, it vanished into thin air. I yelled, "What the fuck?" I felt like I was in a movie. I couldn't believe my own eyes.

Beast yelled out, "Holy shit! Did you guys see that shit? That was a '67 Cadillac hearse I think!" I screamed, "Who gives a shit? Oh my God! Oh my God! What are we going to do? He really is the Devil!" Animal asked, "What the hell did we just see?" Panic was going through our entire bodies, fear now our reality. Medicine Man answered, "Tall Man is not from here." Shaken up, Ghost asked, "Where is he from then?" Medicine Man answered, "The spirit world." Animal asked, "Are you really expecting us to believe your native bullshit about the spirit world?" Chief yelled, "Knock it off!" Ghost asked Wolf, "Do you believe that shit about the spirit world?" Wolf replied, "Yep, I believe in the spirit world shit. I am not sure what the hell I saw either. What I do know is the Tall Man isn't from this place." Beleaguered, everyone turned their head to Preacher for answers. In a concerned voice Ninja asked, "Preacher, what the hell is the Tall Man?" Preacher nonchalantly answered, "Don't look at me; my best guess would be a demon if you believe in it. What I know is we need to get across that fence and get the hell out of here. I need to go see the Wizard; maybe he can explain this shit."

Preacher was considered the brain among us all; most would describe him as a macabre individual, an avid reader, straight-A student and very knowledgeable about the Bible, being an ex-preacher's son. Preacher's father used to be a Reverend by day and a drunk at night. He was kicked out of the church, later replaced by Blackwell. Preacher dealt with the whole situation by withdrawing from the congregation, becoming a bookworm. He read every book he could get his hands on. The subject never mattered. He spoke five languages, was a steady honor student, and already had scholarship offers coming in all directions. Like Chief, Preacher got his nuts off by hanging out in the cemetery. Preacher and Medicine Man were the tribe medics. Preacher also was the co-strategist for our adventures and plans. He loved being one of the guys. Most kids called him a nerd. They were just threatened with their own lack of knowledge. Preacher had a distain for the in-crowd; they made him sick to his stomach. If you asked me, the in-crowd was overrated, immature and terribly insecure with themselves, especially the jocks and cheerleaders. I hated both. I had no interest in sports or wasting my life away watching it. I preferred chasing the girls, yet Preacher played that shy card all the time. It worked for him too. It was so easy for the shallow people to make fun of weaker kids. I never paid attention to their shallow behaviors. We hated those type of rich jerk-offs.

Preacher, Medicine Man and Ninja always searched for enlightenment. Personally, I thought that was a waste of time. Preacher usually had a calm demeanor; he loathed getting mad because it reminded him of his father's famous temper. Preacher himself had a crazy dark side of his own. He was tall, lanky, with long brown wavy hair. His only vice was his undying loyalty to the Cemetery Boys. He aspired to go to medical school; unfortunately his father always insisted he become a Pastor of God. We all respected his old man even though he could be abusive to Preacher. Some say his father's disease of being an alcoholic killed him, they were all so wrong. What killed his father was being expelled from the fellowship. I will admit, like Preacher, we all clashed like titans when it came to the Bible. Preacher's pop had stringent old-school beliefs, versus Preacher's more analytical ideology. Preacher always had a fascination with blood for some reason. That was what always scared me about him. When he got really mad he had a dark side that had no resemblance of the person I knew.

We walked home from an unbelievable event at the cemetery mentally drained and physically exhausted. Confused would be an understatement. Nobody knew what to make of the Tall Man's Houdini act. This might have been the most silent the tribe ever was. We had walked around the cemetery from the east side of town. As we walked north near our own village, I could hear music coming from Bishops; it was "Voodoo" by Godsmack. I kept wondering to myself, "Could the night get any creepier?" Some of the boys wanted to go have drinks at Bishops; as for the rest of us, we just wanted to go see the Wizard.

So as the two groups split up in different directions, we walked past the front of the cemetery across the street, goose bumps recurring all over my skin like multiplying fleas. I looked at the cemetery's front gate. I couldn't help but stare at the entrance sign which read "The Bridge and Afterlife Cemetery", with statues of a Gargoyle on one side and an Angel on the other; my mind was racing in circles. I kept wondering about the statues. Did they represent a battle between good and evil? I was spacing out, just staring at the gate, when I noticed a being walking in slow motion toward the closed gates. I squinted, trying to get a better look in the dark. Just like that, he walked through it like it wasn't even there. He wore a red cloak. I couldn't see his face but his necklace was bright silver and it had a huge pentagram on it. I was frozen stiff, I couldn't move, I couldn't yell. I was hearing a weird sound as it got closer – some sort of demonic chant - and as it approached I could hear some kind of hiss. Just as he got in front of me, Wolf tapped me on the back, I about shit myself. Wolf said, "Hey Zombie we gotta go, we almost left you behind brother. Are you okay?" I was confused and shaken; it felt like I was in a trance. I snapped out of it answering, "Yeah, let's just get the fuck out of here." I had experienced many things in the cemetery, just nothing of this magnitude. We were starting to fall on black days over the summer.

Turning down the street I could see a figure sitting in a rocking chair on his porch smoking a pipe. The scent of cherry tobacco from the pipe floated in the air as we got near. I heard music coming from the

Wizard's stereo in the house. Laughing, Wolf asked, "Can you believe the Wizard is listening to 'The Pusher' by Steppenwolf? That's awesome!" The music summed up our mood. I personally felt like I was strung out on drugs. Wizard asked, "Did you boys have fun tonight?" Chief responded, "What do you mean?" Wizard said, "Must have been an exciting night to answer my question with a question." Chief asked, "So, what did you hear?" Laughing, Wizard answered, "The little birds around here tell me everything." Beginning to have a panic attack, I asked, "Everything?" Wizard stared directly at me, answering, "Every fucking thing! Would you like to tell me about what happened in the cemetery?" I made a gulping sound as I explained to Wizard about our events in the cemetery. He listened with great intent.

I slugged down Wizard's whiskey then asked "Who is the Tall Man?" Chief refilled Wizard's drink. Wizard carefully watched our reaction, paused then answered, "He doesn't exist." Confused, I asked, "Are you trying to tell us what we saw never happened?" Voicing concern, Preacher also asked, "Are you trying to tell us it's all a fabrication?" Wizard responded, "Your imagination is your reality." Chief, in a very agitated tone asked, "Are you fucking kidding me? You're going to sit here and tell us we just made all this shit up?" Wizard laughed so hard he almost choked trying to catch his breath. Wizard loved getting us riled up; he always enjoyed poking and busting our balls, especially Chief because he knew how pissed off he got. With a laugh, Wizard warned, "I know everything about everyone." Chief rolled his eyes at Wizard and sarcastically replied, "Oh you do? Tell us what happened out there since you know so much." Wizard chuckled, looked us all in the eyes again, hesitating while taking a long sip of his drink, stated, "Use your head, but live in your heart." Chief asked, "What kind of bullshit is that? Okay boys, let's go. Let's call it a night." We all got up from the porch steps, walking away when Wizard pointed to Preacher and yelled at Chief, "You two come here tomorrow!" Wizard covered his mouth while shaking his head laughing for a moment, then had another drink, lit up his pipe and said, "Good night boys."

So as we walked each other home one by one, Chief, steaming from the ears about the night's events was rambling on about the Wizard. How could anybody blame him? Chief just didn't understand what happened, he didn't have any answers, nor did the rest of us for that matter. As we continued to walk each other home, it was down to just me and Chief. Luckily I was spending the night at Chief's place. I couldn't wait to go to sleep. I needed sleep in the worst way so I could make sense of all this. Tonight was even more troubling than last night, just mounting questions that had no answers. In the back of my mind I knew there had to be a logical answer for all this shit. If the media got wind of this story there was not a doubt in my mind we would be branded total nut bags.

CHAPTER FIVE: PRANKS

Journals by Preacher

The next day Chief and I again went to see the Wizard. As usual the Wizard was drinking and smoking his pipe, this time I swear it smelled like pot. Upon approaching the front porch stairs, Wizard asked, "Do you boys want something to eat?" Not that we had a choice in the matter. The Wizard brought us food and drinks. The mostaccioli, meatballs, and Italian sausage were to die for. Wizard asked Chief, "Have you cooled off yet?" Chief answered, "Please don't start this shit again." Wizard asked, "What have you boys learned?" I answered, "I think we ran into a demon last night." Chief asked again, "Wizard, who is the Tall Man?" Wizard replied, "It is said Crowley was cast out of Heaven along with others who questioned God. He was one of many giants that were punished by God." Chief remarked, "So, you have heard of him." "Oh, yes", replied the Wizard. Chief asked, "Then why didn't you say that last night?" I asked, "What do you think happened to Crowley?" Wizard replied, "Satan warped Crowley's mind through the occult. He was the original caretaker ordained to bring the souls to the Devil." Chief, scratching his head asked, "What happened to him? I don't understand." Wizard answered, "Son, you can't kill evil. Crowley descended down a ladder to Hell only to ascend back up in the form of a demon, a gift granted from Satan. Crowley roams the underground and between worlds."

I yelled, "I knew it, God damn it, I knew it!" With a confused look on his face, Chief asked, "How could Crowley's hearse disappear into thin air?" Wizard answered, "Black magic, a whole lotta black magic. Don't underestimate Crowley's powers. He plays inside your mind. That is the real battlefield. You must never fear in the mind. Fear is what dooms all mankind. The media uses it like a master magician. When there is a breaking news story, it is only used to draw your attention to the story so that the real story can disappear with no attention. Control and manipulation is used for an illusion. Once you understand this, your eyes will be reborn to the world, also to the here and now. Never let the true moments of life slip away. True power is not in seeing, hearing, or even believing; rather it is in the subconscious that will expose the truth. Call it the intuitive state." I attempted to speak when Wizard interrupted and said, "Boys, I know you like the adventures of the cemetery world but some things aren't worth exploring; you might not like my answer - leave it be. Why don't you find a new place for adventure? Let this one go. The cemetery is a place for the dead to rest. Let go of Crowley's spirit. Move forward with your lives." Wizard hesitated then said, "The cemetery is a gateway to other worlds and dimensions. In our own time, we all make that journey. So blaze a different path in this lifetime. There are only two roads in opposite directions, you either go down the road to good or the road to evil. It's not an option once you choose. There is no turning back once you choose. One walks you to eternity, while the other walks you into misery. Bottom line, it's your choice to make."

Excited I asked, "So, you are saying it's possible to travel through another dimension into time in other worlds and to see spirits, right?" Wizard answered, "Oh yes boys, and much more. You have somehow unlocked the spirits to you." Chief asked, "How did we do that? Are you saying the Tall Man is a haunting dead spirit?" Wizard answered, "You boys are walking on sacred ground. This is one spirit better left alone. Crowley was pure evil and he still is today! You've read old ancient books about spirits, ghosts, and demons; yet you beg sitting here asking me what you already know. Now, I have a question for you boys based on rumors I am hearing around the neighborhood; are you going to Crowley's Tomb?" Chief answered, "Yes, we are. We were planning on telling you before we left." In an angry tone, Wizard said, "I have forbidden you to go there! I've known you boys since you were little, each and every last one of you. I realize you are going to go regardless of what I say at this point. I will only tell you, you will not come back, none of you! You will only bring back evil in yourselves. Before you ask about treasure, let me answer it for you. Yes, but it will not be the treasure you seek from this world. I will not stop you, for I am just an old man, but what you will find is your own reality, journey and destiny - that of death. You will only bring doom to yourselves. Here are my last words to you: your best defense and weapon is your own mind. I have spoken, now leave me be." Chief said, "I don't understand your riddle, Wizard. On one hand you're saying Crowley's alive and on the other hand you're talking as if he is a spirit. Which is he?" Wizard answered, "Some say Satan is alive; others believe he walks the earth in spirit. Which is it, and how? Once you unlock that mystery, the truth will be told. I assure you, the answers you uncover will not be worth the sacrifice, I promise you that! Now go home and rethink your position."

In the meantime, the rest of the tribe brought everything they could to our base camp at Five Points. The tribe made trips all day long.

Apparently listening to AC/DC's "Hells Bells" made each trip easier. The boys brought much more stuff than needed. You name it, the camp had it. It sucked to be reminded we still needed to bring supplies to the new base camp in the Dark Forest. The Dark Forest had many hills, muddy trails, tons of enormous trees, and the terrain was rough. It had long been rumored that trees in the forest of that region talked to one's soul. Some of the boys were spooked about the area.

Over the next four weeks, during the day we worked on building our new base camp. Moving the supplies again from Five Points to the new camp in the Dark Forest was a pain in the ass. We all hated that most. Wolf worked on drawing maps and setting traps all around the camp's perimeter. I drew up the sketches for Beast and Animal to execute the construction of the new tree house. Our original tree house at Five Points took us over six months to build. We didn't have the same luxury this time; we had less than a month at best. Chief wanted small platforms built all around the trees at its highest point with a zip line system that could get us from one platform to the other. He also wanted an emergency zip line with escape routes. Animal was in charge of building the camp along with his brother Beast, both excellent at carpentry. They had their hands full with the task at hand. Ninja and Magic were the tree monkeys diligently crafting a zip line system so we could escape from one place to the next through the trees. The rest of the guys did the grunt work for whatever needed to be done.

The following month we all practiced reading maps, zip lining, and hand-to-hand combat. If that wasn't time consuming enough, we spent more time rehearsing escape drills, target practice and survival tactics. Chief spent time imitating a drill instructor during training to get us in top shape. Pushups, sit ups, and running were an everyday regiment. By all accounts, I think Chief really was a jarhead in his previous life. He pushed us to the edge physically. Some days I just wanted to punch him in the mouth. Weapon training was endless. The long days were exhausting. The boot camp environment, while necessary, was a fucking grind. We were at Camp Zip day and night hustling against time trying to finish the camp. How the Wizard knew everything was surely up for debate. I wondered if Wizard was really telling us the truth about Crowley or fabricating the whole thing, being the ball buster that he was.

We were now less than three days from making the trip to Crowley's Tomb. Tonight, we were hanging at Wizard's eating, drinking, and listening to music. I remember "Old Man" by Neil Young was playing in the background; normal conversation took place when Wizard yelled at Animal, "You got one ball!" We all looked at each other laughing. Wizard again glared at Animal shaking his head saying, "You got one ball!" We were laughing at the time wondering if maybe Wizard knew something we didn't and that maybe Animal really did only have one ball. I was thinking to myself 'how would he know that?' Wizard looked at Animal again, pointed towards the bathroom and said, "I think you better go check." I laughed so hard I almost pissed myself. Others were brought to tears, while some were kind of stumped at the whole thing. Animal got up answering, "I better go check." The room erupted with laughter.

Animal confidently came back from the bathroom yelling, "I have two balls!" Wizard again argued, "No you don't, you only have one ball." The laughter stopped as Wizard became more serious. The argument continued as we kept looking at each other in confusion. The room went silent when Wizard yelled to everyone, "You all better go check because you all have one ball!" You could hear the tribe groan when Medicine Man said, "Damn Wizard, you almost had us believing that shit." Wizard was humped over hysterical, knowing the joke was on us. He laughed so hard he couldn't catch his breath. Chief stood up pissed. Shaking his head in disbelief, Chief asked, "What was the point in that?" Wizard answered, "Never trust what one says no matter what they look like." Annoyed, Chief replied, "Yeah, okay, whatever."

Wizard staring at us with a serious face said, "I know where you boys are going, so with that in mind, I wanted to give you all a going away present." Suspicious, Animal glanced at Wizard asking, "What kind of bullshit are you up to now?" Beast also asked, "What's the gift?" Wizard answered, "You are all going to lose your virginity tonight." Some of the boys were really excited; I of course was not one of them. Wizard said "I have a bunch of professional girls coming over, so I need you boys to undress in the bedrooms." Wolf skeptically replied, "This is bullshit." As he pointed, dividing us in half, he directed, "You six go in the van downstairs and wait for my brother to drive you to a special place where the other girls are." So Shadow, Magic, Medicine Man, Wolf, Ninja, and Ghost went to the van. His brother Zoe met the boys at the van, asking, "Are you boys ready for a night to remember?" Wolf, rolling his eyes, sarcastically replied, "I can hardly wait," as the van pulled away.

At the same time, Wizard paired Animal and Beast together, demanding, "Go into my bedroom down the hall to your right and get undressed because the girls don't have a lot of time." He then paired Maverick and Raven, pointing to go to the bedroom down the hall to their left. Wizard gawked at Chief and Zombie telling them to go in the bedroom by the kitchen and undress. He then gaped at me and promised, "You're going to undress right here and I am going to watch." Everyone burst out in laughter. I thought Chief was on the verge of pissing his pants he laughed so hard. In all the rooms you could hear everyone continue to laugh; on the other hand, I was about to cry. This was a bad dream for me; I had no intentions of Wizard seeing me naked, let alone watching me with a girl. I begged Wizard, "Come on! Let me at least have my own room." Wizard responded, "Well your shit out of luck! There are no more spare rooms. Well?" I replied, "I'm not doing it, man! There is no way I am going to let you watch!" Wizard again in a harsh voice said to me, "I have someone very special for you! You are going to get Wanda, she is going to give you the 'around the world' and I am watching." I asked, "Who the hell is Wanda and what the hell is the around the world?" I had no idea sexually what he was talking about. With the thought of Wizard watching me, I began turning pale, I felt dizzy, almost ready to pass out. Wizard enjoyed every minute of my misery.

The boys in the other rooms were giggling so hard later they would tell me they had tears rolling down their faces trying to catch their breath. At the time I struggled not to have a heart attack. Suddenly Zombie came running out naked yelling, "I am all warmed up, let's go!" Laughter erupted again from the other bedrooms. I had to admit that was funny as shit, it probably helped me prevent that heart attack. Wizard shouted, "Get back in the bedroom, tiny, and shut the lights off, the girls are coming." My heart began to race again. Zombie ran back into the bedroom. Wizard said, "Okay boys, I am coming to make sure you are naked so I can divide the girls up." I kept arguing with Wizard but he reiterated while he yelled at me, "Yes you are! I have handpicked Wanda for you and she is going to give you the 'around the world' and I am gonna watch." Laughter again broke out. The boys were enjoying my misery and arguments with Wizard. I knew then I was never going to live this down from the guys. In that moment I stared right into the eyes of the Wizard; I felt as if I just saw the devil himself. I was nearly in tears. I thought I'd never live down this hell and humiliation. Wizard stood up, walked away from me then began knocking on the doors asking in a long drawn out voice, "Are you boys ready for a night to remember?" You could hear shouts from the other side of the doors answer, "Hell yes, bring on the girls, hurry up; let's go for Christ's sake!" The rooms went silent, the anticipation was a killer. Wizard hesitated for a moment, knocked again on the door then sudden opened it, yelling "Surprise!" Wizard was standing alone in the doorway. I remember that moment vividly, the boys were disappointed and very pissed off not to see any girls; instead we all realized we just fell into another one of Wizard's fucking pranks. I fell to the floor in relief, yelling, "Thank God!" In that same moment everyone else was extremely angry. Zombie came running out naked asking, "Can I at least get Wanda?" That broke the ice for everyone as we all laughed again. Beast yelled to Zombie, "Go put your clothes on, you fucking turd! Put tiny away while you're at it." Fuming at Wizard, Chief asked, "Did you get your rocks off? What the hell was the point?" Wizard answered, "You must learn to trust no one, not even pussy! You boys would have fallen for temptation had I been a woman! Learn from your mistakes and stop bitching."

Still trying to overcome his disappointment, Zombie sat in the corner pouting. I can tell you, Zombie was a natural comedian that could make you laugh with his whinny behavior and horny demeanor. He just had no shame; don't get me wrong, the kid would stand up to anyone. He wasn't the strongest in the tribe unless you put a gun in his hand, then he was the most lethal one of us all. Zombie was an expert marksman who could have made the Olympics, he just didn't have that type of ambition. On the other hand, he had no problem sharing his opinions with you. He was the classic underdog you rooted for. He had great foster parents. Zombie had a resemblance every time I looked at him of Layne Staley in my mind. Zombie was a genius at mathematics, whiny and a big pain in the ass. He was a classic worry wart. Everyone loved the whiny turd even though he was a drama queen. He had a real niche for getting under anyone's skin.

Still in the van Ninja asked Zoe, "When are we going to get there?" Zoe rolled his eyes answering, "In a few minutes, kid." Ghost searched channels on the radio to tune in to the song "Dreams I'll Never See" by Molly Hatchet. Anyone could see the boys were aggravating Zoe with their music and questions. Frustrated, Wolf asked, "What kind of bullshit is this? We are right back at Wizard's house." Zoe parked the van around the back alley. Zoe glanced back at everyone and said "Okay kids, get behind me and follow me back up to the house." As the back door opened, everyone yelled, "Surprise!" I heard more disappointed moans and groans outside the back door. After the Wizard and his brother swapped stories of the boys' reactions, the tribe joked about it except for me. I was traumatized, but in time I eventually got over it. Medicine Man said to me afterwards, "God damn, pal! You look like someone shot your dog. Are you alright?" I answered, "Yeah, the Wizard about had me shit my pants telling me how he was gonna watch me and Wanda. I should have known better, tonight was a lesson well learned from that son of a bitch." Laughing, Medicine Man said, "One of these days we need to pull a prank on the old goat."

Later that night things calmed down. Medicine Man played guitar while Magic sang an old tune called, "The Wizard" by Uriah Heep. We chatted later on when Wizard said, "I think you boys should go see Father Blackwell." I asked, "What the hell for?" Wizard replied, "For prayer and confession before leaving." I yelled, "No fucking way! There is something wrong with that crazy fool!" Wizard responded, "I don't like him much either, but don't make the will of God personal because of Blackwell or your father." Angered, I answered back, "My father has nothing to do with it nor does God! My beliefs and opinions have changed; the stories in the Bible are just fables. God is as guilty as mankind or Satan with his own actions. As for Blackwell, rumors continue to fly around about sexual abuse." Wizard yelled, "Dear God, listen to yourself Preacher! You are misguided. How could you say such things about a man of God?" I answered, "That's my point, he isn't a man of God!" Things were getting heated when the boys interfered and Medicine Man said, "Wizard, you're right. We'll go see Blackwell tomorrow." I ignored the Wizard the rest of the night. My father's death was still fresh in my mind. For the rest of my days, pops was always on my mind.

WIZARD

CHAPTER SIX: BETRAYAL OF INNOCENCE

Journals by Preacher

The next morning we walked block to block gathering the boys. On his front porch steps, Medicine Man played "Sunshower" by Chris Cornell on his acoustic guitar while Magic sang. When they were done we walked together to the church's lair. Every time I ever walked into a church I got the feeling of gloom and doom. The sight of the creepy windows, hand painted pictures framed in gold, the old uncomfortable benches, and the stench of mildew in the air just didn't feel warming in my opinion. The large crucifix above the stage always had that unwanted feeling of death and suffering. What bothered me most was the gross sight of reliving a murder scene over and over again. A man hanging there in excruciating pain while dying in my mind sent the wrong message. As a kid it gave me nightmares. I would hear the awful sounds of stakes driving through a man's flesh as he cried out in agony. The terrible screams never left me. My dreams would repeat the sight of dripping blood down the cross.

It wasn't until I was older that it subsided, I just never let go of the vision in my head. My anger and rage were building from this unnecessary act of cruelty. I listened more carefully to the words they preached, I comprehended the stories being told, when finally I came to my own conclusions. I refused to have someone else's assumptions stuffed down my throat. The Bible had a very simple message, "compassion". It draws a very simple line of either good or evil. After that is where it gets messy. You're not to kill but if it is in the name of God, I guess it is okay. So we bent the rules by fighting evil as God did. We also used every means necessary just like the angel known as Satan. It would appear God had lost the balls to fight such a worthy enemy; it was obviously easier to bully mankind around. So that is where we come in to fight at the same level as our antagonist opponents would. Church is where evil hides out the most. Evil wears an incredible mask. Whatever happened to being fed the "words of wisdom from God" without the signs of the profit man? They bought the best of everything then would justify it by preaching words like, "It's God's will. God should have the best of everything." Last I looked, God didn't play musical instruments, drive fancy cars, sleep in mansions, own boats, or enjoy the material possessions of the church. I remember Blackwell preached one Sunday about the offerings. He complained about someone putting only five bucks into the bucket. I wanted to kill him on stage for his greedy behavior. The profit man had taken tithing way out of context. If I had my way I would burn every profit man to the stake.

Entering the front of the church, Raven said, "Hey Preacher, the door is locked." I answered back, "It shouldn't be." Chief walked up and rechecked the door, it was locked. Shadow volunteered his services to unlock the door but I yelled, "No way!" We went around back, same thing - the door was locked. This was highly unusual because someone was always at the church. I said, "Let's sneak in by the Sunday school window so we can scare the shit out of Blackwell." Everyone agreed. The window lock had been broken for years. One at a time we all went through the window. Beast was like a little kid as he hurried off in front of us. Without knocking, he foolishly opened the church office door. I heard chaos inside the office. I ran to the door first, Beast was fighting the entire church hierarchy. Animal quickly jumped in the fracas as things were getting way out of control. It took three of us to separate Beast from Father Blackwell. The rest of the tribe had to drag Animal out of the room. Bishop Benedict, very upset yelled, "You're all going to Hell!" Chief rolled his eyes. Not that I knew what happened, but I yelled back, "I don't think so pal! We will be in Elysium, where will you be?" Brownstone, who was a Deacon yelled, "You boys stepped over the line, by God! You have killed yourselves this time!" Shadow answered, "I don't think so dick!" Chief realized technically we were trespassing so we needed to get control of the situation by getting out of there.

As we walked back to Chief's place Ninja asked, "What the hell happened in there?" Still hyper from the incident, Beast answered, "Those sick fucks were sexually abusing a kid in there!" I said to Beast, "There was no kid in the office." Beast said, "I walked in on the three of them, they abused a young boy." Beast might be hyperactive and overbearing, yet this was way out there even for him to make up. This was a serious accusation against the church leaders. We all heard rumors before involving Blackwell, but not of other church members. Ninja said, "It isn't possible; there is only one way in or out of the office." Animal yelled, "My brother would never make that shit up!" Shadow immediately asked Ninja, "Did you ever think just maybe there is a trap door? I have an even better question for you, what if it's true?"

Chief yelled, "Everyone calm down! Let's go tell Wizard what happened, then we need to get things ready for the party." We were throwing a little going away bash that night so this put a major damper on things. This was truly a very serious problem. The SG anointed these three fools to represent the church. We already had our hands full going to Crowley's Tomb, so this was an unwanted problem. We went to Wizards and as I suspected, it didn't go well. He was busy cooking stuff for our party. Before we could even tell him, he told us. He was pissed at Beast to no end. Wizard wasn't a big fan of Blackwell but he had great respect for elders in the community. If the information leaked out, the Village would become hysterical over this shit. On the other hand he knew Beast wouldn't lie to him, the story itself was so hard to fathom. I think that was the first time I saw Wizard stumped. I knew when we got back from our adventure Wizard was gonna make a big ordeal regardless, just so he could put on one of his famous "meet" sessions. It was so annoying to realize how much he loved to play judge, jury, and executioner. While he enjoyed debates, we didn't. This was a severe issue not easily swept under the rug. Wizard was generous enough to let us enjoy our party. Behind the scenes, I'm sure he was doing some serious talking to his spy birds. For us it was "party time"!

CHAPTER SEVEN: THE JOURNEY

Journals by Preacher

We left for Crowley's Tomb at 7pm. I heard the song "Hair of the Dog" by Nazareth as we climbed over the gate. The long awaited journey began through the forgotten worlds. I heard about all the rumors surrounding the evil monks. I couldn't wait to find out if that shit was true or not. Silence didn't last long on a hot summer night. Mosquitoes were in full force sucking our blood like vampires. Out in the distance I heard screams near our former base camp at Five Points. We jetted toward the camp where we came upon a station wagon parked, the engine still running. The headlights beamed toward us while the radio jammed "Black Hole Sun" by Sound Garden. Raven turned his flashlight on as Wolf stuck his head in the driver's window. He jumped back shaken as the boys glanced inside. Ghost said, "Jesus Christ, the kid's head has been decapitated!" Hysterical, Zombie asked, "Oh my God, who could have done something like this?" The station wagon was the sight of a butcher shop. Fresh blood soaked the entire inside of the car. Shocked, Wolf yelled, "God damn, the girl in the back seat is Gina Taylor from my math class!" She had gouges all over her body with a gaping hole in her front neck. Raven walked around to the back of the car noticing a hook embedded in the rear glass window. Medicine Man asked, "Do you think the Tall Man did this?" Raven answered, "I have no clue man." Magic said, "We better call the cops." Chief answered, "No way! There isn't anything we can do for them at this point." Zombie yelled, "There is a fucking killer loose!" Chief replied, "I don't give a shit. Nothing will stop our destiny with glory. Let's get the fuck out of here!" That massive warning sign should have been enough for us to turn back, we just couldn't. I felt guilty leaving them like that.

The world's largest cemetery had five main cemeteries which also branched out to hundreds of smaller ones. We had names for them all. There was the Gateway Cemetery, which we called "The Gates of Hell". It whispered the supernatural elements of evil. Topping it off was an old creepy wooden church just after the gate. It was at the top of the point leading south. Clockwise was the Plantation Maze Cemetery, known as the largest maze in the world. It spread over 100 acres. Between the two locations further up near the southern edge was an area referred to as "The Dark Forest". Riverside Cemetery consisted mainly of mausoleums. It reminded me of a toilet because of the constant flood problems. Next was Groves Cemetery, by far the creepiest; it was popular for ghost sightings but best renowned as the "Killing Field". Last was Resurrection Cemetery; the Devil's playground. This was the local favorite used for murder, a serial dumping ground for disposing bodies of evidence. If you were looking for trouble, this was the place. It was a welcome home site for dopers, drug dealers, gangs, and criminal activity. It also was an open house filled with vagrants and strange characters; even runaway kids found refuge there. At least it was constantly filled with action. The police patrolled it consistently. We called it "Wasteland Cemetery".

We were grabbing some gear at Five Points when unexpectedly Shadow noticed a car pulling up flashing a spotlight around. Shadow yelled out, "Get down, it's the cops!" We hid behind the bushes; regrettably a few of the guys were stuck up in the tree house. The patrol car drove around Five Points. The cops pointed their spotlight towards the gated entrances to the cemeteries. We stayed quiet when the patrol car spotted the station wagon and abruptly drove off to investigate the vehicle. I whispered with a question, "What are we going to do now?" Zombie frantically whispered, "We're going to fry for this!" As we gathered our things the police car came rambling back up the road with the spotlight pointed in the bushes, this time they spotted us sneaking across the street. Wolf screamed, "Follow me to the Maze!" Most of us made a mad dash for the entrance. We attempted to climb over the gate. The rest of the tribe, stuck in the tree house, turned the radio up to "Barracuda" by Heart trying to distract the cops. The squad car came to a halt, an officer jumped out then rushed towards the tree house. The squad car came roaring in front of the gate; the cop quickly got out of his vehicle and yelled something. We were too busy hauling ass to listen to the dip shit officer. Shadow did stop long enough to give him the finger. Shadow laughed and quickly disappeared into the giant bush maze.

The other muppet attempted to climb up to the first level as he yelled, "Stay where you are!" Three of the boys climbed to the top level. Meanwhile, Animal threw a box of miscellaneous goods at the cop: bam! The box nailed him right in the head, knocking the slug to the ground. The cop car peeled out towards the tree house. Animal rushed up to the top and yelled, "Let's zip line to the maze baby!" Beast went first, followed by Medicine Man, and then Magic. The other cop rapidly made his way to the third level of the tree house. Animal escaped just as the cop tried to grab him. The cop watched him zip across into darkness. The boys patiently waited for Animal at the tree platform. Animal came zipping across in laughter. Beast yelled, "Hurry up!" They could see two flashlights beaming from the tree house. The cops decided to chase the boys by using the zip line. The zip line made a very distinct noise; it is hard not to enjoy the euphoria gliding in the air. The cops in hot pursuit, yelled as they got closer. Animal, laughing in dismay, asked, "Can you believe these muppets are actually coming after us?" Medicine Man took out his tomahawk, chopping the zip line. Their screams were met with a loud thud. Beast yelled, "Let's get out of here." We stopped running in the maze when Wolf asked, "Where are they?" Shadow replied, "They got stuck in the tree house." Ghost asked, "Do you think they got busted?" Shadow answered, "I don't know." Chief belted out orders, "Wolf, take Ninja and Shadow; go to the platform, see if they zip lined over. We will meet you guys at Camp Zip. Good luck. Now move out." Later into the night the rest of the tribe made it to Camp Zip without incident.

The morning came; Ghost singing "Some Kind of Wonderful" by Grand Funk Railroad woke everyone up while he made breakfast. Quickly Magic got in on the act as the two sang back and forth. Of all people, Chief joined in by singing "I'm Your Captain" by Grand Funk Railroad. Raven, still up in the tree, changed songs singing "Inside Looking out" also by Grand Funk Railroad. One of the worst singers among the bunch, Zombie jumped on a tree stump and sang "Taking Care of Business" by Bachman-Turner Overdrive. Before long the entire tribe was marching and singing along with him. We were having a gas when Chief crashed the party, gathered everyone together and said, "Listen up, there's only two ways to Crowley's Tomb from here. I'm sure there might be other ways, but these are the only two I know of." Drawing in the sand Chief informed us of our options, "The first way is to follow the river bank that leads out to the sea; unfortunately none of us have a boat. The second way is to travel through a small portion of the Gates of Hell, which also leads us to the Land of the Dead." Concerned, Zombie replied, "You have to be joking! That's suicide and you know it! We will never make it out of there alive. Why didn't you tell us this before?" Chief answered, "It's the only way. I knew if I told you there would be unnecessary panic. We need to stick together on this, especially you, worry wart." Zombie yelled, "You son of a bitch, you misled us, you lied!" Chief answered, "I played the hand that was dealt. My leadership in this tribe includes using every means possible to get the job done." Zombie yelled, "The only job you have accomplished is driving us straight down to hell!" Zombie shook his head, while walking away angry mumbled under his breath, "I really hate this fucking peasant!" Comforting Zombie, Shadow said, "Come on bro, you're the most dangerous shot out of us all, no worries, I'll be right by your side." Zombie got a pat on the back from Shadow when he replied, "Ah, fuck it dude."The tribe was disappointed that Chief lied to them, but the truth be told we all would have gone anyway.

Medicine Man asked, "How far is it from here?" Chief answered, "It will take us several days to get there." The boys stopped in their tracks staring at each other in disbelief. We always messed around in the cemetery, just nothing of this magnitude or distance. We had a plan, I guess Chief left out a few details. Ghost popped off, "Several days! Jesus Christ, Chief! Why didn't you say something? That is pushing it, don't you think?" Chief responded, "Do you want to be legends or cowards? You guys make a choice right here and now! If you want to go back, I suggest you get a move on it." Medicine Man replied, "I think I can speak for all of us, we all voted, and we're all in this thing together, Chief. Don't blame anyone for their opinion especially considering that you left out a few major details!"

We could have had a mutiny on our hands; luckily cooler heads prevailed. Chief shook his head in agreement then continued drawing in the sand, instructing, "We will camp near a crumbled old church before entering the unholy land at Crowley's Tomb. There's an old bridge crossing with a few large sphinx sculptures; it has two old canoes tied under the bridge. There are several buildings that are fortified with large bushes around them. It can be confusing in there so we have to be very careful. Near the tomb there's a replica of Stone Hedge. I saw it from a tree last summer. It also has a large wall around that area. The only way in is through the pyramid. There are signs posted everywhere that also lead to a quarry. I didn't have the time or firepower to go down to investigate it." Shadow asked, "Did you see monks? Did you or Wolf go inside anything? How did you guys not get caught?" Wolf calmly answered, "We were as scared as you are right now. We didn't see anyone outside. For all I know this might not even be Crowley's Tomb. We didn't know what to make of it. We went camping for a couple days last summer when out of coincidence noticed this hidden place. The place looked abandoned. We really weren't prepared to explore it. We had to leave it to beat nightfall. Truthfully, this little trip of ours is nothing more than a hunch at best. Nobody lied, we just didn't know, so there was no point in mentioning anything. Now you all know what we know. So take it easy and let's have some fun exploring it. This time we're prepared."

Chief said, "Listen guys, we are the Cemetery Boys; we don't get caught. No, we never made it inside, that's where we have to improvise, adapt, man up, and grow a pair." Magic sarcastically replied, "That's great! Just what we all needed, my balls are swelling by the minute." Wolf cut in on the conversation, "Hey, we all voted on this and we're all in, baby. Remember why we're here, let's solve the riddle, grab the loot and go home to be heroes. Now man up and gather your gear. Oh, yeah one last thing, don't forget to bring your loaded balls." Laughter broke out as Wolf smiled.

That morning we followed Chief through the Dark Forest. I had never seen such large trees before. The farther we walked the bigger the trees got. I would've thought we were in the Redwood Forest. I got that eerie feeling the trees were watching our every move whispering throughout the forest. The tree branches inter-connected with one another. The sun wanted to come shining in, the trees had other ideas of their own. The trees blocked the light out on purpose it seemed. Normal trees obviously shade the area from the sun. These tree soldiers were far different than most, their kinship enjoyed the cold, black darkness, apparently. It only allowed the sight of small speckles of light which resembled snowflakes. While it was daytime, it appeared like nightfall in the winter time as if it was snowing. I called it the "beautiful scary".

I swear hours felt like days walking through the darkness of the forest. Magic was singing the song "Lay it on the Line" by Triumph trying to pass the time as others joined in. Gradually a blinding light came upon us. We couldn't see anything in front of us - it was that bright. I thought we might be entering Heaven. We continued to walk through the light when our vision slowly came back. Unknown to us, we came upon the outer edges of the Gates of Hell. I caught up to Chief who stood still gazing in the distance. I remember hearing an eagle screech out as it echoed through the sky. Wolf asked Chief, "What's wrong?" Chief pointed as we all stood looking down the road. You could see hundreds of vultures circling in the sky around a tree. Raven said, "Man, I hope that's not what I think it is." We walked down the hill to investigate. My heart began to race, I was as anxious as the next to find out if our eyes were playing tricks on us. Slowly we approached a woman who was hanging from the trees, the smell was foul. It was the saddest thing I ever saw in my life. I couldn't believe my eyes. I wished I could take back the images of the woman hanging there; that might have been the only time I wished I was blind. Several of the guys were on their hands and knees vomiting. It was a grisly discovery.

Chief said to Ninja, "Cut her down." Ninja climbed the tree cutting the rope, the body came crashing down. Flies were buzzing all around us. Medicine Man examined her first, he said, "Someone cut out her eyes." He opened her mouth and said, "They cut her tongue out as well. You might want to check this out." He held up the ace of spades. Chief said, "The death card. This poor girl was tortured and murdered but someone obviously wanted to send a message." Medicine Man also noticed dry blood stains on the front of her ripped gown near the stomach area; as he lifted the dress he got spooked. Wolf took a peek, quickly glancing at the pentagram etched in her stomach. Chief asked Wolf, "How long do you think she's been here?" Wolf replied, "Maybe a day or two. By the marks on her body, the vultures just recently discovered her as well." I took a closer look at her body, I could tell she had been beaten, severely tortured and strangled. I said, "Whoever killed this poor girl wanted to make sure the last image she ever saw was his face. He enjoyed seeing the twinkle in her eyes as her life faded away." It didn't take a rocket scientist to figure this out. Somebody with enormous rage really worked her over. If that wasn't bad enough, the turkey vultures had been pecking away at her.

Animal asked, "Fuck me, who would do something like that?" Zombie answered, "I don't know, but she is deader than the earliest mother of mathematics Hypatia." Chief said, "We need to bury her." I put two tokens over her eye sockets, wrapped her up in my blanket and prayed for her to the Gods of Nature. The boys placed her body in a small hole they had dug up with their hands. Magic sang the song "Angel" by Jimi Hendrix as a tribute to the dead woman. Medicine Man rudely interrupted and said, "We need to report this one to the police." Shadow answered, "No fucking way! The police are gonna think we are serial killers. We did what we could, now let's move on." Medicine Man yelled, "This isn't right!" Ninja asked Shadow, "Where is your fucking heart man? This girl has been through hell! Someone needs to be held accountable." Shadow yelled back, "Look man, I'm not going to jail for something I didn't do. Use your head; the cops are gonna point the finger at us. They probably already think we killed those kids in the station wagon!" Ninja and Shadow continued getting in a shouting match when Maverick intervened. Wolf said, "There's nothing more we can do for her, she's dead. At this point let her rest in Elysium." Shadow said to Ninja, "You're lucky the tribe saved your ass again. You were about to get a severe beating!" Ninja walked away laughing. I couldn't help but wonder what the poor woman must have went through. My next thought was 'what sick sadistic fuck would do something like this?' It was a heinous act by some psycho still on the loose. One thing was becoming evidently clear: everywhere we went murdered bodies were popping up around us at an alarming rate.

We continued on following a dirt path with gravestones on both sides of us. Bushes also formed in an endless line that you could see for miles. The tribe was tiring from the hills. Chief raised his arm up motioning for us to stop. We heard a trampling noise that sounded like an army. It continued to get louder and louder as something was nearing. Chief motioned right; we sprinted off the beaten path hiding in the bushes. Hidden, we peaked out watching to see what the hell was making such a thunderous noise. To our dismay, over the hill came a frightful presence of the Four Horsemen galloping towards the road. I could only say to myself, 'what now?' The sight of Grim Reapers riding their daunting horses reminded me of The Book of Revelations in the Bible. In Revelations, it mentions God holding a scroll in his right hand that is sealed with seven seals. The Lamb and the Lion open the first four of seven seals, which summon God's murderous killing machines:

Then I saw when the Lamb broke one of the seven seals, and I heard one of the four living creatures saying as with a voice of thunder, "Come." I looked, and behold, a white horse, and he who sat on it had a bow; and a crown was given to him, and he went out conquering and to conquer.
— Revelation 6:1-2
The 1st Omen "Conquest"

When He broke the second seal, I heard the second living creature saying, "Come." And another, a red horse, went out; and to him who sat on it, it was granted to take peace from the earth, and that men would slay one another; and a great sword was given to him.
— Revelation 6:3-4
The 2nd Omen "War"

When He broke the third seal, I heard the third living creature saying, "Come." I looked, and behold, a black horse; and he who sat on it had a pair of scales in his hand. And I heard something like a voice in the center of the four living creatures saying, "A quart of wheat for a denarius, and three quarts of barley for a denarius; and do not damage the oil and the wine."
— Revelation 6:5-6
The 3rd Omen "Famine"

When the Lamb broke the fourth seal, I heard the voice of the fourth living creature saying, "Come." I looked, and behold, an ashen horse; and he who sat on it had the name Death; and Hades was following with him. Authority was given to them over a fourth of the earth, to kill with sword and with famine and with pestilence and by the wild beasts of the earth.
— Revelation 6:7-8
The 4th Omen "Death"

The horses stopped, the reaper on the pale horse circled around the other three, and then looked in our direction. Too bad I didn't have a radio because I swear I would have played "Don't Fear the Reaper" by Blue Oyster Cult. Everyone was lying perfectly still. I couldn't move; all I could do was stare at the reaper and his pale horse. You couldn't see his face from behind his cloak, all you could see was his beaming red eyes with no emotion. Within a few minutes they rode off in the direction of the Dark Forest. I spoke, "And Hell followed with them." Beast asked, "Who the hell was that?" I replied, "The Four Horsemen." Staring at Chief, I said, "If you still have a bone to pick with the man they call Death, you just got a firsthand look at your own nemesis." Nobody said a word. For a brief moment I thought my prayers were finally answered, my waiting was over as the divine Apocalypse was finally upon us. I couldn't wait for Judgment Day. However, as usual I was disappointed. The coward lie silent, the promises from a higher being that used mortal men to write the greatest story ever told, only left with words of time or value. Again the greatest miracle I ever witnessed was "nothing"; further proof of prayers falling on deaf ears. We left after the Grim Reapers did, only in the opposite direction. I think they were running away from Hell, while we were headed straight for it.

CHAPTER EIGHT: UNBELIEVABLE OBSTACLES

Journals by Preacher

I can honestly say our boot camp training paid off with physical fitness. We were jogging at a pretty good pace when Chief stopped, giving everyone a break. I began to notice the scenery had changed: trees with no leaves, flowers black, brown grass, and the backdrop of a red burning moon seen in the daylight. The clouds' dark moody behavior was becoming apparent. The winds of change seemed to be crying out an eerie tune to us. There was a distinct aura of winter time without the snow, everything around us appeared dead. Maverick said, "I can see my breath." I noticed it as we all talked, it was bizarre. Ghost pointed toward an old cooling tower when Animal said, "Hey, look over there." If there was ever a time to hear the song "Long Cool Women in a Black Dress" by the Hollies, this was that time. We neared the gigantic grass wormhole where seven sexy gothic girls stood.

The closer we got, the sexier they became. They looked like dominatrix. I mean their makeup and dark lipstick were perfect; each one had tight leather outfits with thigh-high spiked heel boots, perfect bodies, tattoos, large hoop earrings, lots of silver jewelry on their fingers and neck. Their nails and hair matched. My God they were sexy! Each girl had different color hair: black, red, pink, blue, yellow, white, and green. Looking closer at them I noticed one peculiar thing that stood out: their cross necklaces were reversed, which spooked me. The guys were surrounding the girls like horn dogs. I immediately got Ninja's attention about the crosses when he said, "God damn Preacher, you just had to find something wrong with them!" Chief heard the remarks so he called everyone over for a minute. The guys were bitching and grumbling a bit as we huddled up. Chief said, "Guys be careful, do not trust them." Zombie rolled his eyes while bitching to me and Chief, "Stop being a bunch of cock blocks! This is our chance to get some stray ass." When we turned around the girls were gone - they vanished into thin air just like the Tall Man and the demon girl. Ghost asked, "Where did they go?" Maverick said, "Nice going Preacher, are you happy now? Your crying scared them off." Zombie yelled, "This sucks! The chicks were hot for me." Shadow replied, "Zombie, the only thing that burns for you is your dick caught on your own pants zipper." Magic asked, "Where did they disappear to?" I answered, "I don't know where they are, though I can tell you where we're at." Animal asked, "Where?" I replied, "Guys, look around you."

Raven answered, "Land of the Dead." I said, "Correct." Ninja spoke, "Shit that sucks! Those chicks were hot as hell bro! We should come here more often." Shadow responded, "Nice choice of words dickhead, we might just be in hell, you moron." Chief yelled, "Knock it off! Now move out." I looked down the wormhole's bottomless pit when Chief said, "I certainly wouldn't want to fall down there."

Walking through the cooling tower the guys were still bitching about the Goth Chicks when a heavy fog formed around the area. Instant goose bumps tickled the skin. The fog was a sign of things to come. Shortly after, rain came pouring down followed by the sounds of crashing thunder. Searching for shelter Shadow spotted an old building; Chief told Ninja to go check it out. Ninja approached the building cautiously when Shadow rushed in front of him kicking the door open. Ninja yelled to Shadow, "My fucking hero!" The lightning was spectacular up in the sky as we raced to the building to get out of the rain. The building turned out to be a former funeral parlor. Ninja walked in the kitchen when the door quickly slammed shut; you could hear what sounded like a struggle and things were banging around. We hurried to the door, it was locked. We yelled out to Ninja. The door creaked open slowly when Ninja popped out laughing. Maverick yelled, "Ninja, you scared the shit out of us!" Shadow screamed, "I should kick your ass!" Ninja answered, "Make your best move, I promise it will be your last." Shadow sarcastically remarked, "In your dreams!" Tensions were mounting again between the two. It was getting on everyone's nerves. Ninja took a bow then walked up to Shadow grinning and asked, "Why don't we finish the game right here?" Shadow answered, "It will be your last nightmare. When I am done with you, you will be talking to the flies, dickhead!" Wolf yelled out, "Knock that shit off right now you two!" Chief said to the others, "Let's check this place out; we'll make camp here tonight." Within a couple of minutes everyone yelled "all clear" with the exception of Ghost and Magic. Ghost yelled out, "Come quick, check this out!" Everyone scampered to meet Ghost. Magic pointed down to a stair-less basement when Chief said, "Well there's no reason we need to go down there. Shut the hatch and lock it up." Zombie became nervous and yelled, "We can't stay here; this place is an old funeral parlor!" Ignoring Zombie, Chief said, "Let's eat, I need to get some sleep tonight." Zombie asked, "Where are we going to sleep? There are no beds, just coffins." Chief responded back, "We'll find a comfy coffin to sleep in because it beats the floor." Zombie whined, "You guys are all nuts!" Raven said, "Don't worry about it man, just pretend you're dead." Zombie walked away disgusted.

Later that night, Shadow woke up from a constant banging noise coming from the basement door. Shadow in turn woke up Animal, who then turned around and woke his brother Beast. Shadow said, "There is something in the basement, let's go check it out." The three went to the room then slowly stuck their heads by the locked door to listen. The door banged, it scared the shit out of them as they all fell backwards over one another. Beast got up mad, rushed to the door, unlocking and opening it. They all looked to see what was there, but they saw nothing. Animal asked, "Is anybody down there?" Beast said, "Let's go have a look." Beast jumped down first, Animal followed next, and then Shadow. It was really dark so Beast pulled out a lighter from his pocket, shining it around. Animal said, "I don't see much except dark open space, cobwebs, and a few gas cans." Beast spotted a door so he opened it. He looked inside. Surprised, he said, "Holy shit! Come check this shit out." Animal and Shadow ran to the door behind Beast to check out the unknown.

Shadow and Animal followed Beast into the dark room when an old radio in the far corner came on full of static before it played "Mr. Blackwell" by Kiss; it scared the crap out of everyone. Shadow yelled, "No fucking way!" Animal asked, "What are the chances of this song playing on the radio?" Shadow replied, "I don't think it's a coincidence." A familiar voice answered, "It's not a coincidence, rather fate." The voice scared the shit out of Animal who asked, "Who are you?" Looking around the dark room Beast noticed rows of medical tables with sheets covering up what appeared to be bodies. Animal nervously asked, "What the hell?" The familiar voice answered, "Yes, it is your hell. You see, this is what happens when you don't have faith." Shadow asked, "How could these be down here? There are no stairs to get them down here." The shadow figure moved around in the darkness laughing. Putting two and two together, Beast solved the mystery when he said, "I will be God damned, Blackwell." The voice remarked, "Yes, indeed! Oh boys, this is a real surprise treat today."

We walked deeper into the center of the room, Beast's suspicions were right: the wheeled tables were bodies. The corpses still had their shoes on with sheets draped over them. We all scanned around the room in distrust and pondering what was going on when one of the sheets closest to us slowly began sitting straight up, then more corpses followed doing the same thing. In a frantic voice, Animal asked, "What in the fuck is going on?" The figure moved from the corner walking towards the dim light of Beast's lighter. Father Blackwell emerged in a dark cloak answering, "These are God's soldiers who I created to do His work." Beast yelled, "You're crazy!" Some of the corpses slowly removed their sheets. The dead were rising; they looked pale with decaying skin, several even had blue faces with yellow eyes. I could see Father Blackwell's shadow moving back to the corner. The song "Mr. Blackwell" played over and over again. Animal yelled, "I don't know about you guys but this isn't the Kiss Army; I'm getting the fuck out of here!" He took off running towards the door when he crashed into a blue faced zombie. Animal punched him in the face knocking the zombie down; he looked down at his hand full of decaying skin and yellow goo. Scared out of his mind, Animal sprinted as fast as he could for the open stairwell. Shadow ran out of the room next, kicking the same zombie trying to get back up, as he kept running towards Animal. Animal held his hands together using them as a step stool while Shadow lifted his way up onto the ledge floor. Shadow then turned around dangling his hand out for Animal, pulling him up.

Meanwhile, Beast kicked one of the pale zombies in the chest as it crashed into several other zombies, knocking the radio to the floor as it continued playing music. Beast yelled, "Where are you Blackwell? You sick bastard!" Beast couldn't find Blackwell though he could hear his laughter. Another zombie grabbed Beast from behind; Beast head-butted the zombie with the back of his head, yellow goo splashed out all over Beast. He then picked the zombie up and threw him at the nearest zombies, then raced out of the door, turned around, slammed the door shut and locked it. Animal and Shadow were screaming, "Come on, run God damn it!" Beast jumped up to the open arms of Animal as Shadow was trying to help pull him up. While pulling Beast up, a straggling zombie grabbed a hold of Beast's waist, then the zombie's hands slipped trying to hold his leg. Panicking, Beast back-kicked the zombie in the head using his other leg, knocking the pesky zombie to the floor. Animal quickly lifted Beast to safety, slammed the main entrance door and locked it. You could hear commotion coming from down the stairs.

Furious, Chief opened the door and staring at Beast asked, "What in Christ is going on? I thought I told you guys to keep it locked!" Animal yelled back, "There are real zombies down in the basement! Father Blackwell is also here! He is involved in bringing the dead back to life. We have to get the hell out of here! No offense, Zombie." Zombie answered, "None taken." Chief asked, "What are you talking about? Why would Blackwell be here?" Beast answered, "Father Blackwell is Crowley! The dead are the monks I think." Smoke was coming from underneath the basement door, our vision blurred as everyone began coughing. We quickly grabbed our stuff; I ran outside first. It must have been about 5 a.m. Following behind me, Shadow yelled, "There's an army of zombies out here!" I said to Zombie while staring out into the graveyard, "Your family is waiting for you." Everyone chuckled for a brief moment. Magic asked, "How did the fire start?" Animal asked Beast, "Where is your lighter?" Beast reached inside his pocket, feeling no lighter, answered, "I don't have it, I must have dropped it; maybe one of the zombies started a fire by accident." Ghost shouted out, "A God damn zombie lit the house and himself on fire! Oh that's just perfect. We can't go back inside! Out here these bastards are multiplying like the plague!" The zombies were slowly moving toward the front of the parlor, they were hesitant; it seemed as if they wanted nothing to do with the fire. Medicine Man asked, "What are we going to do?" Magic said, "I've got an idea: I have several smoke bombs and a couple cans of Mist. That ought to give us a running chance." Chief said, "Light them up; let's run to higher ground." Before Magic had a chance to set his stuff off Shadow remembered about the gas cans, he suddenly yelled, "Run!" Without thinking we took off running, knocking several zombies to the ground when we heard an explosion go off. We were damn lucky to get out of there when we did. Another minute and we would've been marshmallows. Over the course of the early morning we eventually got to high ground way up in the trees.

Later on that afternoon I woke up with the sun at my back. I could hear the sweet sounds of chirping birds. Half groggy I looked down with no trace of zombies. Medicine Man yelled, "I can see Crowley's Tomb in the distance!" I turned to locate what appeared to be a black castle with a pyramid behind it from a distance. It was daunting to stare at. Magic was above us all singing "Hold Me Down" by Tommy Lee. I swear the guy was a walking jukebox, though I have to admit it helped relieve the stress. Magic was one of those who pushed himself to the edge with every step.

Our journey on one hand was so incredible, yet on the other hand farfetched. I was wondering if our imagination had played a trick on us or maybe I was dreaming. We had never seen such madness or violence. The things we were experiencing had become unexplainable. I wondered who would even believe us when we got home, that is, if we made it home. I felt as if we were in a nightmare running around in a nut house.

As we got down from the trees a strange red human-like being with wings flew between the trees before it landed in front of us. Raven looked at everyone, paused while pointing at the Angel, then asked, "Did that just really happen man?" The Red Angel peacefully asked,

"What do you seek from here?" Chief looked at me and said, "Help me out here, Preacher." All eyes were on the Red Angel as I asked him, "Who are you?" The Red Angel softly asked again, "What do you seek from here?" I wondered, 'Am I dreaming?' I figured honesty was the best policy so I answered, "We are on a quest to unlock the mystery of Crowley's Tomb." The Red Angel burst into laughter. Raven was not amused; neither were the rest of us. Raven stretched out his bow, setting his sights with dead aim on the Red Angel. I said, "Calm down, give me a minute" with my hand in the air. The Red Angel had wings, long black hair, and a long pointed tail, his face partially covered by a black goatee. I asked, "What is your purpose here?" The Red Angel responded, "I am an angel of God." Raven replied, "I don't think so. Angels don't have wings." With the blink of an eye I heard Raven's arrow deliver death, hitting the Red Angel in the chest. The Red Angel spattered into a giant puddle of blood. There was no body or bones, just a pool of blood on the ground along with Raven's bloody arrow. Its spirit screamed echoing all around us as if it was a warning bell for others, then it just stopped. It was louder than anything I had ever heard in my life. Wolf yelled, "We have to get out of here, now!" We heard a loud horn sound off in the distance. It sounded like an old Viking horn. So we ran through the woods trying to keep up with Wolf.

CHAPTER NINE: THE STORY IS TRUE!

Journals by Preacher

We followed Wolf to a wooded river bank just short of the bridge that led to the Unholy Land near what was thought to be Crowley's Tomb. Wolf stopped running while Chief barked orders, "I'm hungry, let's secure the area and get some much needed rest. At night fall we'll go to Crowley's Tomb." After securing the area, we ate dried jerky with cold beans. Medicine Man passed a cup of Indian potion for us to take a sip of. Medicine Man said, "This will make you relax; it will also give you a vision of your destiny while warding off evil in the spirit world. It will make you sleep; when you awake you will be energized by adrenaline. Do not fear, just embrace it." The song "Snow Blind" by Styx played in my head. I sniffed the cup, its odor was foul. It smelled like shit, tasted bitter, worse it dried my tongue out. Everyone in the tribe chattered when I noticed others began to slur their words. We all giggled nonstop. My head was spinning; squinting I could only see fragments of faces. All of a sudden things slowed down to a crawl; I felt no pain when I blacked out. Somehow subconsciously I experienced this out-of-body experience. I might have even crossed over to the next place; hell it might have been the spirit world, I really couldn't say for sure.

In my vision, I watched my new body leave the old one. I remember fighting the Devil himself while the Tall Man watched. I was stabbed several times as I fell to the ground. I tried waking my dead body only to see my reflection stare back at me with lifeless eyes. I witnessed a bright light approaching when I awoke inside a bubble that floated above me. I yelled but to no avail. I floated into space above the stars; during that time I watched a rerun of my life before things faded to eternal darkness. I woke up in a giant mausoleum. I saw Wizard standing over me but I couldn't hear him. My vision abruptly disappeared without a trace. I woke up in a panic, my heart racing. I felt sick so I leaned over puking. Afterwards I felt calm. Medicine Man was right, my adrenaline was rushing throughout my body. I felt my ears ringing, I couldn't hear anyone. I put my arms over my head as I felt a sense of confusion. I tripped over myself several times trying to get my balance. My legs were so wobbly. I watched everyone else barfing. It looked as if they were screaming at each other with intense confusion. Within a couple minutes my hearing came back; I could finally hear everyone talking clearly. I could feel my legs coming back from the numbness. Raven said, "Wow man, what a fucking rush. That was an intense high brother. It felt like a mixed injection of Demerol, a hit of pot, and speed all rolled in one. What the hell was that man?" Medicine Man replied, "Old plants." Raven asked, "Can I get more of that? What a wild, wild rush, man." Medicine Man smirked as he answered, "No, this was a one-time anecdote." I glanced over as the whole tribe finally came down from their highs.

Chief said, "Take a moment to compose yourselves, this is our moment of destiny and glory, cherish it because I promise, you won't forget it." We all stood in a circle taking in that moment looking around at each other. The night sky was filled with stars. In the moment it was like a brief meditation as we attempted to remove our anxiety. My gut feeling inside was this might be the last time we would all be together. Speaking to the tribe, Chief said, "Let's go give Crowley's Tomb the surprise of a lifetime. Stay close, now let's move out." We jogged down by the bridge paired up in threes as we crossed over the wooden bridge. We walked for awhile when we came upon the last bridge. I could see the old canoes. Chief said, "Over this bridge is the Unholy Land. If this turns out to be Crowley's Tomb, keep in mind we will be walking into the Ultimate Evil. If you scream, scream loud for a good death." Wolf said, "Preacher, why don't you give us a quick prayer." I replied, "There is no point in prayer here. It will only fall on deaf ears anyway. If you choose to pray to the Greek Gods, the Gods of Nature, or anyone else for that matter so be it. Pray within. My words of wisdom to you all: Pray for a quick death. Pray that you may inflict an eternity of pain and death on your enemies of evil. In the end I will meet you all in Elysium." Wolf replied, "That works just as good." Standing in front of the tribe, Chief stated, "Over the years we have heard all the rumors of the ultimate evil of Crowley's Tomb. We have watched the SG and the establishments sweep things under the rug while ignoring the problem. Society has refused to do anything about it, other than a pity party. The beauty in this pie is history is waiting for our names to make a difference, so let's not disappoint. Let's show the cowards in Heaven that we are up to the task of doing their job. Now follow me in your groups and let's take what is rightfully ours."

We followed Chief to the world of bad dreams jogging over the bridge. We passed incredible hand carved statues of evil demons and gargoyles. I said to myself, 'whoever did the landscaping put a nice touch placing two large Sphinx statues at the bridge front entrance down below Crowley's Tomb'. I had hate pumping in my heart, anger in my body, and fear rolling around in the mind like loose marbles. Running in the dark I could feel the killer within just waiting for the moment to justify it. We all made it to the outer fence. Chief climbed over the metal barbed wire fence as each tribe carefully followed one after the other. I could see the gloomy church in the near distance. Leading the way, Chief ran to the front of the crumbled old church building. Quickly we all followed in our tribe one at a time. Being that we had endured so much already, I was just happy we had made it in one piece to this point. We sat there for a minute looking around at the surroundings when Maverick said, "Can you hear that sound? My ears are ringing." We were all suffering from it. Magic pointed to the top of the church; freaked out he said, "Guys, in case you haven't noticed, Jesus Christ is upside down on a cross." I said to Magic, "Don't open your mind to it, don't let it in, stay focused." Zombie felt raindrops on his head so he looked up only to be met with blood drops falling down from the statue of Christ. Zombie panicked; Shadow covered his mouth to keep him quiet. Maverick said, "I've never seen that before. What the hell is going on?" I said to everyone, "Ignore it; block it out of your minds." Chief ordered, "Follow me." Abruptly we left the old sacrilegious church. Lagging behind, Medicine Man stood at the church staring until he noticed the Jesus statue open its eyes with blood dripping down. Scared, alone, and behind he ran like a bat out of hell trying to catch up to his tribe. There was no doubt in my mind this was Crowley's Tomb. We reached the pentacle of evil, this was the real deal. Running into the wind I could feel the presence of evil. My gut instinct was this place had no morality.

Following Chief to the backfields of the church there stood the sight of horror. I couldn't believe my eyes: thousands of headstones surrounded by reverse crucifixes that went all the way up the hill. Some of the guys stood there overwhelmed at the sight. Chief said, "Alright now, listen up, stay in your tribe, do not separate from it. I will go up first in a zigzag pattern using the gravestones as cover, each group do the same thing in a single file. I will see you at the top of the hill by the gate. There is plenty of cover by the bushes. If you get lost, look for the Fighting Angels statue near the top of the hill just to the right of the front gate. Good luck, I'll see you up top." Looking down at his hands Ghost said, "My hands are shaking; I keep waiting for Guns & Roses to yell, "Welcome to the Jungle." Chief quickly ran off in the distance. The first tribe gave Chief a minute head start then sprinted up the hill; the second tribe did the same, while the third tribe followed from the rear. The moonlight gave the graveyard a bright glow. I could hear the sound of wolves howling in the distance. It was so eerie running from one spot to another. I had this feeling we were being watched as we dodged from the gravestones. The hill itself was a challenge to climb.

While running up the hill, everyone's legs began to get fatigued; we were getting farther and farther separated from one another. My tribe was the caboose, unaware we were being trailed by monks who quietly followed behind us. Every time I looked back there was nothing there, the monks were hiding behind gravestones, mocking the tribe's zigzag pattern. The monks were gaining on the tribe and were now within striking range of Medicine Man. Medicine Man heard something behind him so he turned around. Out of the blue, before he had a chance to react, he was hit in the head by a wooden staff, knocked unconscious. I turned around only to be rushed by dark-cloaked monks who threw a net over me; that was the last thing I remembered. The monks separated into two groups: one group dragged me and Medicine Man away, while the other group continued their pursuit of the other tribe members. For all they knew, there were only two left still to capture. Our group was far behind the others.

Journals by Chief

Ghost turned around whispering, "Preacher!" Realizing part of the tribe missing, Ghost pulled out his sling shot then loaded it with marble size metal balls with sharp spikes; Magic had his spear-staff cocked. The monks were moving closer, but not within striking distance to grab the remaining tribe members. Ghost fired his slingshot at a nearby gravestone; that shot must have scared a couple of the monks because Ghost saw figures moving around hiding behind the stones. Then without notice the monks charged at Magic. Ghost again fired his slingshot hitting the first monk right in the face; he rolled backwards knocking down two more monks as they went tumbling down the hill. The monks made a mad rush for Magic only to run into a handful of smoke bomb. The bewildered monks looked around but Magic and Ghost disappeared without a trace. That little magic trick spooked the monks.

In the meantime, we waited by the statues when Ninja asked, "Where the hell are they?" Maverick answered, "Dragging their heels apparently." I replied, "Something's gotta be wrong, they're running almost thirty minutes late." The shocking answer came quicker than I expected as we watched the monks drag Medicine Man and Preacher towards the front gate. With great concern in his voice, Zombie asked, "Holy shit, what are we going to do now?" I answered, "Well, this complicates things a bit." Then out of nowhere Magic and Ghost plopped down, scaring the shit out of the tribe with their sudden appearance. Ghost, in a frantic voice started telling the tribe what happened. Ninja replied, "We know, we just witnessed the monks dragging them past the gate." Ghost asked, "What are we going to do?" Shadow answered, "I guess I have to save the day again." Ninja replied, "That would be a first." I whispered, "Follow me." We all ran near the entrance of the gate and peeked inside. I could see monks frantically running around all over the place; there must have been hundreds inside the gates. Zombie said, "Well it certainly doesn't look abandoned to me." I spotted several monks who gathered around Preacher and Medicine Man in a circle. I realized the significance as I said out loud, "I'll be God damned, it's really true. This place really is Crowley's Tomb." It didn't look very promising at this point since we never thought of how to handle a capture. Looking back that was an arrogant mistake. Quietly the tribe watched helplessly as Medicine Man and Preacher were being escorted by monks near the bell tower. The monks dragged them into a red church. The building had a massive reverse crucifix on the top. Shadow leaned in to take another peak when all of a sudden a loud bell went off. It scared the shit out of the tribe. It was extremely loud with the creepiest sound you would ever want to hear, which kept on and on. In frustration, Shadow turned to the tribe only to yell to no avail. Whatever he said fell on deaf ears. The tribe stood there trying to decipher what he was saying.

With the constant loud bell going off monks were running all over the open grounds in a panic like a Chinese fire drill. A large group of monks on command started racing towards the front gate. I yelled, "Fuck me! We gotta go!" Nobody heard me as we ran behind some bushes when suddenly the bell stopped. Loud ambient music began to play in the courtyard. I said, "We have to find better cover to buy a little more time." Regretfully I looked towards Ghost and Magic; they already knew what I was going to say. I said, "You guys are gonna have to walk towards the front gate and surrender. They had to know there were more in the group. It will buy us time serving as a distraction until we figure out how to get in the temple. I will take Beast, Shadow and Raven to Crowley's Tomb. Wolf will lead the rest of you guys to the red church; there the tribe will rescue you guys to save the fucking day.

When you guys get out of the building meet us at the rendezvous near the edge of the river. If we are not all there by sunlight make the journey back home as fast as you can and contact the police. I don't see any other way. I am truly sorry guys, it sucks to surrender, this is our only chance; you need to sacrifice for the tribe if the plan's going to work. We will get you all out of there, I promise. Go now, so we can get inside." Ghost and Magic never argued; they knew what needed to be done to save the others. The look in the eyes of the tribe hit home: that the story of Crowley's Tomb was true. Fear has a look that can't be denied or even masked. The fear wasn't of Crowley's place, but the fear of our friends capture not to mention what lied ahead. Mom once warned, "Be careful what you ask for because you might just get it." Our wish was right in front of us, just not exactly how we planned it. For better or worse we were all in and there was no turning back.

CHAPTER TEN: MEETING THE DEVIL

Journals by Preacher

I remember being dragged inside a dark hallway by what appeared to be monks in black cloaks. I had a terrible headache from being hit in the head. I was confused and dizzy. In that moment it seemed so surreal. It was a bad dream of village folklore that was now the reality of my worst nightmare. Inside the Church of Hell, Medicine Man and I were dragged down dark hallways with what appeared to be flashing lights. Suddenly we entered a dark room with candles then thrown to the ground. I heard some of the monks talking when one of the monks, staring at our vests, said, "Cemetery Boys, interesting." The other monks were busy tying us up by the wrists then hung our arms from a rope connected to the rafters; they pulled the rope to stretch us. Our ankles were also bounded together. A monk in a green robe spread chunks of broken glass on the floor. My body was hanging off the floor when suddenly they let go of the rope and my knees hit the floor full force. Glass pierced deep into my knees. We both screamed out in pain. They made sure as our arms hung in the air the weight of our bodies were on our knees. Pain shot up my body every time I attempted to move. They forced us to kneel on top of broken glass on a painted pentagram floor, seemingly enjoying watching us suffer. I felt the warm blood soaking my pants as I helplessly watched blood oozing down onto the floor. The pain was too much to bear; every movement opened another wound.

The room was dark, glowing with dim lighted black candles on pagan holders. I was no longer scared because all my thoughts were on the pain in my knees. I watched as they soaked a white wash cloth in a bowl then gagged our mouths with the soaked cloths. The taste was salty and very foul. I could feel the liquid dripping down my face. I turned towards Medicine Man and I could see the liquid appeared to be blood dripping from his face. The liquid must have been animal blood. Helpless, I couldn't get the taste out of my mouth. A couple of the black cloaked monks left the room. We were left guarded by monks - all in dark green cloaks - surrounded in a circle with red lit candles. The monks were chanting words backwards while others were hymning some creepy song. You know when you're in the presence of evil because evil uses everything in reverse. Most don't understand evil; evil does everything backwards. It always comes in the form of peace but that is never the case. I couldn't make any sense as to what they were saying. I knew we were in real trouble as my heart began to race. My imagination pictured the worst things possible but I knew I had to regain my wits if we were to survive this ordeal. The door opened behind us without warning, the room lit up for a brief second before it went back to darkness. Medicine Man stared at me with fear in his eyes. I'm sure I had the same stare back. It's so weird under the worst of situations how things could suddenly pop in your head; for me the song "Don't Get Fooled Again" by the Who popped into mine.

I could hear synchronized footsteps walking behind me. With pain shooting through my body I lifted my head up; walking toward us, the carrier of the light approached us. Standing before us three monks were wearing very different colored cloaks; it was obvious we were about to face the leading hierarchy. The monk on my left in a purple cloak walked up and took the gags out of our mouths, saying, "Preacher, what an interesting name." Obviously they read my name from the vest. I also figured my nickname disturbed their beliefs, possibly even offending them. I looked up and answered, "Yep, that's me." The monk on my right in a multi-colored black and red cloak walked up with his staff and poked me in the stomach full force; I tried to recover my breath as I coughed up my own blood. Medicine Man yelled, "Leave him alone you assholes!" The monk in multi-colors pulled out a long skeleton bone dagger, slashing Medicine Man across the face. Medicine Man screamed out in pain, "I am going to kill you!" The monk in the center wearing the red cloak walked up closer, glared at Medicine Man and said, "Save it son, you boys aren't that good. Cemetery Boys, how many more little filthy bastards are there roaming around?" Medicine Man yelled, "Fuck you man!" This time the monk in purple smacked Medicine Man in the face. Blood ran down from his nose. I quickly answered, "There are four of us. May I ask a question?" The confident monk in red replied, "You may indeed sir." I asked, "Who are you?" The monk answered, "I am Doctor Natas at your service. As you know, I live in peace as you can see by the surroundings. I also come in peace as you have experienced already." I interrupted, "Your definition is much different than my peace." He ignored me as he pointed to the monk in purple and said, "This is Magus Nosnam, and you have already gotten well acquainted with our High Priest Reltih. The nine special panel members around you are Elite Rellik Members." It didn't take a brain surgeon to figure out evil always hides in the shadows. I couldn't help but burst out in laughter in the face of sure death. Intrigued by my laughter, Doctor Natas asked, "Why don't you humor me as to what is so funny?" I answered, "We came to see the great forbidden Crowley's Tomb, yet what we have come to witness is a fraud of clowns named Doctor Satan, High Priest Hitler, Magus better known as Reverend Manson, your Elite Killer Members, and not to mention the infamous clowns dressed in black called Monks outside. Have I missed anything?" Satan, now a bit more irritated, said, "Oh I see, I forgot you Cemetery Boys believe in God, so let's see if your God actually answers your dear boys' prayers."

Hitler swung his staff in my direction as I watched helplessly. The staff hit me near the neck and shoulder area; I could feel my collarbone break. I screamed out in agony. Then with another quick swing of his staff he hit Medicine Man in the ribs, I knew by the sound and Medicine Man's reaction that several of his ribs were probably broken. Blood was also spewing out of his mouth. We were becoming a bloody mess. Satan then put a thorn crown over my head; he pushed down with great force as the thorns dug into my skin. I could feel the blood trickling down my face. I screamed out in pain, "Oh God!" Satan asked, "Where is your God? We are waiting for his appearance. I know my patience is wearing thin. How about yours? He does nothing as you scream out his name for help. Where is his mercy?" Now really pissed off despite unbearable pain, I answered, "My God and beliefs are not what you are referring to: of Christian faith I hope." Satan asked, "Do you believe in your God and savior Jesus Christ?" I responded back, "Christ is no God! I serve no being of self worship. I worship no one who has servants as slaves. I don't believe in any deceivers of good or evil whether called Satan or God. I worship nature and its beauty. My God is an ideology of peace; not a self worshipping ruler or of God's Christian mythology." Satan said, "Watch your tongue boy for I shall cut it off! So, you do know the stories in the good book." I replied, "If you really are Satan then by the story of the Bible itself, you already know that you are not a God, your fate is already sealed. That is why you are so angry. That is why you wish to take as many as you can down with you. You hate mankind because God created it and that made you jealous, your heart is filled with envy. You may have fooled the SG, the establishment, and even those in Hollywood who have taken part in your petty evil but I am not fooled. My eyes are wide open. Natas, Satan, or whoever you are, you're not a God!" Satan with a grin responded, "If you want to see a true God, hang in there, I'll be back soon enough." Medicine Man said, "Famous last words of the Bible." Humored, Satan laughed out loud with a sinister grin on his face along with Manson and Hitler. During our conversation I remember staring at the psycho right in the eyes: he had the deepest, blackest, most lifeless eyes I had ever seen. He had the disturbing look of the devil; there was no arguing that point. I got the feeling that the crazy bastard had no morality or compassion: he was born of evil, maybe the ultimate evil. This nut job had the audacity to call himself Satan and I think in his own head believed he was the Devil himself.

Suddenly the door slammed open, more monks dragged Ghost and Magic into the room; the monks threw them to the floor next to me. I watched my friends' eyes light up with fear. They were mortified at the bloody crime scene. The monks proceeded to rough them up with a few kicks and punches. Then the boys were strung up just like we were and made to kneel on glass. Magic screamed out in pain while Ghost didn't make a sound. Laughing, Manson looked down at Ghost and said, "Go ahead, cry out, it's gotta hurt." Ghost refused to give the pricks the satisfaction. Shaking his head in disgust, Satan said, "More vagrants I see. Well I'm glad you could come and join the party. Obviously it's not All Hallows' Eve yet but we will make your trick a real treat tonight. You have trespassed, broken our laws; you must all be punished. Before purification you will be given time to pray to your God and given a chance to reconsider serving a higher God as you all worship me. Later, we'll come back and see if the God you hail has answered your prayers, if not, you will answer mine! Gag them all!" He walked away laughing, everyone else followed him out of the room as the door shut from behind, we heard it being locked. We were left listening to some sort of demonic church music playing. It was loud enough to scare us half to death.

I wondered about the others and their well being. What started out with a room of two was now four, and counting. I hoped the others would turn back, only I knew all too well of Chief's heroics. Chief had too much integrity to turn back; this was the fight he was searching for his whole life. As scary as this place was, the monks had no idea of Chief's burning anger. He was like a man on fire. I loved Chief, though I always knew deep down he was a ticking time bomb just waiting to go off. This was the perfect battlefield for his rage. After seeing Satan's monks first hand, I knew we finally had an archenemy worth dying for. At this point my body was so numb from the pain I couldn't even feel it anymore.

Journals by Zombie

With the capture of the tribe, the monks' excitement began to calm down outside. Our prayers must have been answered because a mist had begun to float throughout the fortress. Each group weaved through the mist as they separated in different directions. For a night that started out with such smothering humidity, the cold winds of change fell upon us once more. Wolf led the way towards the red church. We had jumped several monks so we could wear their robes as a disguise. We marched straight to the red church, falling in line following a handful of monks to the steps. My legs were shaking with fear and self doubt with this ballsy plan. I had no choice, there was little alternative. Wolf led the way, continuing to follow the monks inside. There were bizarre pictures hanging on the walls of the seven sins. The monks walked near an area that had thorns growing around giant poles which reminded me of evil monuments. The walls were reddish-black, the artwork downright freaky to even glance at. A glow came from red or black candle lights. Continuing to walk through the church we passed several monks. I kept my head down while walking at a fast pace. I fell behind and barged into the front of a demon-like altar; there were also two doors in opposite directions. The monks went to the door on the left, so we quickly went towards the door on the right. Wolf slowly cracked the door open as we went through it. The hallway was long with doors on both sides. Dimmed white candles on the walls made it downright scary. The bad vibes began to give me a panic attack. Ninja whispered, "I feel like we're in a black and white movie." Animal said, "Guys, I can hear creepy music down the hall." We kept moving towards the sound of the music to investigate when I whispered, "Guys, I've got to take a piss." Animal whispered back, "Piss your pants!" I stopped long enough for me to piss on the wall. Wolf whispered in anger, "Are you trying to get us all killed or what?"

At the end of the hall we came upon yet another dark long hallway. In the center of the next hallway Wolf saw two monks guarding a door. As we approached, Maverick grabbed the neck of one of the monks, slamming his head into the wall which knocked him out cold. In a moment of rage Animal sucker-punched the other guard in the throat, which turned out to be fatal for the poor bastard. Ninja unlocked the door then stood there in shock; Maverick standing behind him said, "Ahh shit!" The boys were hanging from the rafters. Wolf and Animal quickly dragged the monks' bodies inside as everyone else ran to help the tribe. Medicine Man was a bloody mess. I pulled the gags out of their mouths. Medicine Man said, "Wow, am I glad to see you guys!" We quickly lifted each of them off the ground and untied the restraints. Excited to see the boys, Magic pleaded, "We gotta get out of here!" Wolf asked, "Can you all walk?" Preacher and Medicine Man were having a hard time standing, let alone walking. I helped pull large chunks of glass out of their knees. Medicine Man and Preacher answered, "No." Ghost and Magic answered, "Yes." Wolf said, "We don't have much time." Maverick and some of the boys decided to add a little shock value by tying the monks up and hanging them from the rafters. Wolf said to Ninja, "Lead us out of here; kill anything that moves in front of you. Medicine Man, stand between me and Zombie using us as crutches. Same goes for you Preacher, stand in between Ghost and Magic." Preacher said, "I think my collarbone is broke, be careful." Preacher was in so much pain Maverick said, "I'll carry him out of here." Wolf yelled to Animal, "Watch our backs from the rear! Now let's get the fuck out of here!" We traveled through the building cautiously, trembling in fear. I never saw a monk the entire time. Ninja opened the door as if he knew we were running out like lambs to the slaughter. Yet we were only greeted by the dark sky, the sound of silence, and the mist that surrounded the area. We used it as cover and vanished into the night.

CHAPTER ELEVEN: CROWLEY'S TOMB

Journals by Raven

Shadow, Beast and I weaved in and out of the mist following Chief. We ran through the satanic garden maze where we came upon the front of the temple. It was a strangely constructed building, black in color, shaped like a pyramid. On the front sloping wall it had a monumental silver pentagram on it. That sight alone had me ready to turn back and go home. There was incomprehensible writing and petroglyphs down the walls of the pyramid. It had a piercing white light shooting up in the air. It was an astonishing ancient building. I was intimidated by how large it was. We ran up the red stairs; frustration quickly sank in because we couldn't find a doorway or entrance. Beast asked, "Now what, there is no fucking door?" Chief answered, "Look around, there has to be a secret passage to get in." We all kept fiddling around with things when I turned a loose, small silver pentagram counter-clockwise, the wall door suddenly opened. We all ran inside; I was shocked at how clean it was. I expected it to be covered with dust; on the contrary, it was magnificent inside. I thought the walls had the distinct flair of what Elysium might have looked like. Whoever created this place must have had an endless budget. The floors where we stood were made of white marble; it had a Roman decorative style. It was uncanny how it combined ancient times with modern times. The temple had giant open rooms which led us to hallways that resembled mausoleums. Chief led the way as we passed eloquent carved symbols and drawings on the walls. I said, "Man, I wish Preacher was here to decipher this shit." I was alarmed at how big the maze inside was. Many of the walls were bright white, while others were mixed colors. The whiteness didn't seem to fit for all the creepy darkness that surrounded this place on the outside. There was almost a small sense of peace that came over us for a brief minute. We kept passing objects embedded in the floor. Altars, statues, art, and caskets kept reminding me of how spooky this place was.

Walking down the hall I kept thinking we were inside a giant mausoleum. Some of the walls changed shapes with endless writing on them. Pictures changed images right in front of you. That scared me when I asked, "What if they are watching us?" Chief answered, "Possible, but I doubt it." Beast opened up one of the small square vault doors on the wall when Shadow grabbed Beast's shoulder, scaring the daylights out of him. Chief whispered to Beast, "What the hell are you doing?" Beast peaked inside, glaring at some old skeleton remains. I glanced at the sight of the dead then walked away. Chief, frustrated at Beast, whispered, "Get out of there, we've gotta go!" Beast heisted the necklace from the dead then shut the crypt. He slipped the medallion in his pocket without anyone else noticing. Chief scolded Beast, "Don't touch anything, don't look at anything, and whatever you do don't open anything else! Please keep your eyes on the prize. Do you understand?" Beast muttered something when Chief again asked, "Do you understand?" Disappointed with Chief's question, Beast answered, "Yeah I understand. My question is why? There might be something else I might find." I rolled my eyes because I knew Chief was beginning to get mad. Beast had a terrible habit of wandering around at the worst times. Chief whispered louder, "Why, what? We don't have time for your wandering around bullshit right now. Seriously, we don't have time for babysitting! I sometimes think you need medication." Shadow said, "Come on, we've got to keep moving." Beast yelled back, "You guys are fucking turds!" Suddenly eerie sounds were ringing in our ears that made demonic sounds. It stung my ears like a bee sting. I was complaining when Shadow yelled, "Shut up Raven! I think I heard what sounded like a door close." So we ran towards that area when we turned the corner. Chief out front said, "Hold on."

There were hundreds of square crypts imbedded into the walls surrounded with red roses; the floor was immaculate. We then heard footsteps in front of us. Before we could react, a large man calmly stood in front of us dressed in a black cloak with the hood off. He had a bad case of leprosy all over his face. He stood there smiling with heinous, rotten crooked teeth. I swear the teeth were so brown I wondered if he knew what a toothbrush looked like. I could only imagine his breath as a weapon of death. He had the crazy white eyes of a madman. The old geezer hesitated, lifting his head up smelling the air like a dog. The odor must not have been to his liking because his demeanor changed into a wild, crazed lunatic. He pulled out a rather large shiny butcher knife with a shit-eating grin. Chief said, "Come on, you ugly mother fucker, I'm gonna shove that knife up your ass and gut you like a pig!" Without notice both rushed towards each other as Chief leg-swept the madman, who fell flat on his face. I said, "Oh shit man!" Chief stabbed the madman in the right hamstring; he never made a sound. He turned on his side, kicking Chief in the mouth. Chief certainly felt it as he fell against the wall. The madman jumped up only to be met with a punch to the face from Beast; he wasn't fazed. He sliced Beast across the forearm when I shot the madman in the face with an arrow. He fell flat on his back, appearing dead. Celebrating I yelled, "I killed him!" Suddenly he slowly sat straight up and got up like nothing happened, then rushed right at me only this time he was met with an arrow to the chest. I yelled, "Let's get out of here!" We were discombobulated when we ran the wrong way. I meant to turn around so we could get out of there, but I was scared and without thinking we all headed in the opposite direction. I was leading the pack; I had no idea where I was running, I only focused on running away from the madman. Racing down the hall we stumbled upon a gigantic open circular entrance. There were nine torches and nine red doors that I could see. Shadow right away noticed a large pentagram on the floor. The sight was so disturbing it sent chills down my spine. Each doorway had some sort of bizarre half-man/half-animal skeleton statue posted outside the door. It reminded me of posted guards or something. We had no clue of their symbolic meaning. Shadow asked, "What is that thumping noise I hear?" I answered, "That is my own beating heart I think." Beast said, "Take it easy bro."

Chief looked around the open room trying to make sense of it all. Pointing to the corner, Shadow said, "There's another door." I didn't see anything when I asked, "Where?" We quietly walked over to investigate the wall; you could barely hear the sound of wind. Chief said, "There has to be another secret door. Check around." I again found the hidden pentagram near the wall next to a lighted candle. I turned it counter-clockwise, the door began to open. As it opened a bright light came beaming through from the moonlight. There was this beautiful red and white marble floor leading to a path outside. At quick glance it resembled blood. We followed the bloody path which led us right to the replication of Stone Hedge. I marveled at its beauty. The stones were extremely large in size, black in color, seeming out of place in the center of the backyard walls. Walking through the backyard area I could feel a supernatural force of energy around me. The scent from Beast's wound dripping blood seemed to only attract the energy force's appetite. The gardens were well lit by torches. It was a site to behold. There was no one here, which seemed very odd. The satanic altar had a disturbing presence.

I said, "Not to be negative but this feels like a trap, man." Beast answered, "I don't think so. It feels like we're walking through Heaven's gate. There is a real sense of peace here." Shadow said, "Your nuts Beast!" Evil is a master of disguise that always represents itself in the opposite image. I always knew silence came before the storm; it was the same terrifying parallel of having dinner with my family waiting for the violent arguments to occur. This night had that same feel to it. We walked through a dark stone tunnel when in front of us stood six mausoleums. There were five on the outside with one in the middle. The one in the middle was surrounded with tons of black crows, perfectly cut grass and strange monuments that appeared as monsters. As we moved closer, we noticed that the monuments were sculpted demigods. We continued on the marble path; it lead straight to the mausoleum in the center. I said, "This has got to be Crowley's Tomb, man." Beast asked, "How do you know?" Chief pointed to an inscription on the top front wall. It read "CROWLEY'S TOMB". Chief smiled from ear to ear then said, "Son of a bitch, I knew it." Everyone else was so excited of the findings; I did not share their same enthusiasm. There was no door, just a buzzing noise coming from within it. Shadow said, "It sounds a lot like the electric power lines in the cemetery." Shadow hit the nail right on the head because it did sound a lot like an electrical power plant. Beast pointed to one of the mausoleums in panic, yelling, "I saw something move over there!" Chief turned around quickly scanning the area and said, "I don't see anything. Relax! Let's enjoy Crowley's riches."

I leaned on a hand sized gold pentagram next to a peephole. I peaked inside the peephole, the next thing I knew I was thrown six feet in the air backwards. Beast and Shadow came to make sure I was okay. Chief put his hand on the pentagram while squinting inside the peepholes; he saw a blue neon light, then suddenly a reflection of a face stared back at him. He also flew backwards, only he had the gold pentagram in his hand. It appeared as if an invisible force had tossed us around like rag dolls to the ground. Chief jumped up immediately warning, "We've got to get the fuck out of here right now!" Seeing the fear in Chief's eyes, the tribe began to panic, asking, "What did you see? What did you guys see?" Chief answered, "It's the fucking Tall Man! He really is Crowley! Now run!" We hauled our asses out of there. Beast turned around for a brief moment noticing several monks were coming after us and yelled, "The monks are coming!" I yelled to Beast, "Come on!" We ran all the way to the back side of the temple. This time the door automatically opened with the madman standing at the entrance. I ran between his legs while Chief kicked the madman in the knee, shattering his kneecap. Beast kicked him in the balls while Shadow plowed him over. We dashed off down the halls. I felt the skin crawling on my back; it felt like there were a hundred monks chasing us. I had enormous tingling sensations all over my body. I turned around yelling at Beast, "Get down!" Beast dove down, sliding across the floor. Me and Shadow unloaded arrows at the monks. I was dropping them like flies. Chief grabbed Beast, I yelled, "Let's go man!" Shadow caught up when we finally made it to the front temple.

Chief yelled to Beast, "Find the pentagram to open the door!" Monks were running from down the hall towards us. I hit the first three monks with arrows. Shadow continued his assault as well. Beast finally got the front door to open when we retreated outside. All you could see outside was a black sky while the mist roamed the open field. We ran as fast as we could into the mist, disappearing like magicians. Without hesitation we scaled the front fence; I could hear yelling behind us. Shadow looked back to a familiar sight: as headlights turned on, he yelled, "The hearse is coming!" The familiar sound of the engine's roar along with classic rock music blaring "Black Betty" by Ram Jam kind of gave it away that the Tall Man was coming. We took off running down the hill when I tripped, colliding into Shadow. We tumbled all the way down the hill. I could hear someone yelling at Beast in the background, which was no surprise.

We ran towards the back of the old church where we were met by several monks holding wooden staffs. There was nowhere to run so we quickly spread out when this pale monk asked, "Are you going somewhere?" Chief answered, "Yeah, right through you." They obviously didn't like the answer so they charged at us. I certainly leveled the playing field when I shot the first two monks closest to me in the face; then the third monk whacked me in the shoulder with his staff, knocking me to the ground. Chief fended off two monks using his twin Kama's. Shadow instantly killed a monk by shooting an arrow into his stomach. Beast body-slammed another monk who tried rushing in too quick, knocking him unconscious. The monk attacking me pulled out a knife when another of Shadow's arrows punctured his lung, ending his fate. Chief blocked the staff of the charging monk as Beast tackled the monk from behind. Without hesitation, Chief threw one of his Kama's, striking the monk in the face killing him instantly. Meanwhile, the remaining monk got loose after hitting Beast several times in the face then quickly began to run away. Shadow aimed carefully but missed. Beast yelled, "He's getting away!" I calmly set my sight in the distance as I stretched my bow, responding, "No he's not." In the black night the arrow traveled some distance, hitting the escaping monk right in the back. He screamed for a brief moment before silence came upon us. Chief said, "That was a great shot!"

Unfortunately silence didn't last long. We could hear the hearse's brakes come to a screeching halt in front of the crumbled church, a Jefferson Airplane song called "White Rabbit" jammed through the car speakers. Sarcastically, Beast asked, "Doesn't this psycho ever give it a rest?" You could hear Crowley continually revving up the engine. Shadow answered, "Evil has no end." Chief picked up a long staff and said, "I am tired of being harassed by this crazy old fuck. It's time to bring the fight to him." We also grabbed staffs and headed down towards the front of the church to faceoff with Crowley. I watched Chief charge the hearse, heaving a staff at the window when the hearse backed up at the last minute; the staff missed the target. I shot an arrow at the window of the car; surprisingly it didn't make a scratch. The hearse swerved at Chief, fortunately Crowley missed. We took off running again when in the distance we could see the first bridge, as did Crowley who raced towards us. Chief yelled, "Come on! We've got to make a run for it!" We sprinted for the bridge but we were no match for the hearse. There was no time; we were not going to make it across the bridge in time when I yelled, "Jump!" So, Beast and I jumped off one side while Chief and Shadow dove off the other.

We hit the water making a thunderous splash. We swam under the bridge; I could hear the hearse come to a screeching halt. You could hear the tires spinning as he backed up onto the bridge. He sat there quietly for several minutes before he cranked the song, "Edmund Fitzgerald" by Gordon Lightfoot. Hearing that song in the water gave me chills down my spine. When the song was over Crowley yelled, "You little bastards have nothing to worry about; I will bring Hell to you!" I whispered, "This decrepit crazy old fart obviously doesn't understand we are already in Hell man." Evil continued to lurk in the shadows as we floated in the cold water when the hearse finally left. Luckily we didn't have far to go. I only hoped the others made it back. I knew from this moment on the fight with evil would have no bounds in an everlasting war that would have no end. I realized eternity was the definition of irony.

CHAPTER TWELVE: THE PARTY

Journals by Preacher

Waiting for Chief and the rest of his tribe had my stomach in knots. They should've been back by now. Nobody said anything out loud because we didn't want to jinx anything. Yep, we were all a superstitious bunch. Fear can be a very tough thing to fight off. I couldn't help imagining the worst. I kept wondering if they would ever make it back. The one thing I can tell you about Chief: he has nerves of steel; being scared is not an option in his book. He is a tough bastard. Chief is like a pit bull; he will not back down from anyone or anything. I think he had a death wish for immortality. Chief had more street smarts than book intelligence. He had good common sense when overzealous ambition didn't get in the way. Chief was built like a Greek God with short hair; you could easily mistake him for a drill sergeant, not to mention being the only person I know that wanted to kill Death. I was starting to question the decision within myself, was Crowley's Tomb really worth the risk? I underestimated the wickedness of Crowley's place. The monks were a bunch of psychopaths.

I distracted myself by reminiscing about the night we had the party before leaving for Crowley's Tomb. During the day we were setting up for the party. Chief sent Maverick, Ghost, Magic and Raven to go round up the party supplies, which meant booze, drugs and girls. Shadow was busy blazing burgers, hotdogs and chicken on the grill. Wizard prepared for us a large container of antipasto salad along with his famous spaghetti and meatballs; he also made a ton of Italian cannolis. Music kicked off that day with "Gypsy Road" by Cinderella, followed by The Sweet's "The Ballroom Blitz". A few hours passed when Magic walked in the backyard carrying a cooler full of soda while Maverick shouldered a keg of beer. We were high-fiving each other knowing we were going to have real beer that night. Chief asked, "How did you get the beer without being carded?" Maverick answered with a smile, "The Wizard." Surprised, Chief said, "I'll be damned, the old man came through." Ninja asked, "Where are the girls?" Beast interrupted, "Yeah, how many are coming over tonight?" Magic answered, "Why do you care? You'll have a beer in one hand and your dick in the other." Some of the guys belted out in laughter. Animal asked, "Magic, really, how many girls?" Magic answered, "Believe me there will be so much pussy you'll think you won the lottery." Chief said, "Guys, I told you to invite some girls, not the whole fucking pussy wagon over.

Where are Ghost and Raven?" Maverick answered, "Chief, relax, the guys will be here shortly. Let's have a good time." Chief replied, "That's what worries me about you horny toads." Maverick asked, "Who is playing that shitty music? Are you guys serious - Twisted Sister?" Chief said, "Hey man, watch it! At least they play rock 'n roll, not that untalented bubble gum pop music you hear on the radio lately." Shadow replied, "I agree with you Chief, I hate that rap shit! Pop, rap, and disco simply suck!"

Magic unplugged Twisted Sisters "I Wanna Rock" by mistake. He then yelled in the microphone, "What do you want to do with your life?" Everyone replied back, "I wanna rock!" So Magic blasted the stereo singing along with the Bullet Boys song "Hang on St. Christopher." Medicine Man began jamming his guitar as Animal started passing beers around. Hot looking girls found their way to the backyard as the party began to heat up. "Strange Brew" by Cream played when Raven made his grand entrance, strolling in smoking a bong with gorgeous women by his side. Ghost had a bottle of tequila in his hand; now the party was in full swing. Beast and Animal did a great job building a stage so we could take turns jamming. Looking around there were women in every direction. I have to admit, Raven knew how to recruit only the hottest women. I preferred women with black hair. Women with red, brown or blonde hair worked just as good, I guess. Chief gathered everyone at the party in a circle, walked in the middle of it and toasted, "To Crowley's Tomb." Raven and Ghost yelled out, "Salute!" Everyone took a swig of alcohol and the party officially kicked off.

Ghost walked away for a bathroom break when Chief warned us all about Ghost, "Once Ghost gets on stage he will play all night, so anyone wanting to play the drums better get on stage now." Medicine Man was already on stage playing a guitar riff from Howlin' Wolf called "Little Red Rooster." The girls were going crazy. Wolf had already disappeared into Chief's basement with a long legged sweetie with black hair. Beast and Animal were taking turns with Ghost in the barber chair. They would sit back in the chair, leaning their head back, while the other would fill their mouth with booze; then the chair would lean forward and the next man up would repeat the process. Shadow collected money from the girls then gave out plastic cups for the draft beer while also assisting with the beer bongs. He was the smart one as he was having a good time drinking and flirting. We rotated playing throughout the night, but when it was all said and done Ghost was stealing the show on the drums. Complaining to Chief, Zombie said, "I want to play the drums now." Chief replied, "I told you dipshits to get on the drums because once Ghost is on stage nobody can make him stop drinking or playing. I'll be damned if I'm gonna interrupt him now." I think Zombie went to every member in the tribe to complain about it, yet nobody paid him any mind.

In the end Magic was belting out tune after tune on the microphone while Ghost handled the drums, Medicine Man was wailing on the lead guitar, Raven played rhythm guitar, and Maverick was on the bass. Raven stood on stage lighting up a joint, everyone went wild. Raven, who never really sings much, grabbed the microphone and began singing "Free Bird" by Lynyrd Skynyrd. All the girls stood there with their lighters in the air as they sang along. The guys were really putting on a show. The girls would call out a song and the boys played it regardless of their own musical taste. They played "A Horse With No Name" by America, "Summer Breeze" by Seals & Croft, "Radar Love" by Golden Earring, and one of my favorites "The Guitar Man" by Bread. The joy of the music gave me the shivers, while also bringing me to another place in time in my life. The power of music transforms you to another place and time is why we all loved it so much. Chief walked on stage, speaking into the microphone, "Let me take you back in time with these gems." Chief played "The Joker" by The Steve Miller Band. The girls went nuts as they sang along. You would have thought the Beatles were on stage. Chief followed it up with "Chevy Van" by Sammy John and "Wildfire" by Michael Murphy when Chief, in the middle of the song, changed it up by playing "Sun Down" by Gordon Lightfoot. Everyone began clapping. It was a cool experience and a night I didn't want to end. Chief bowed to the crowd then announced, "Last song of the night for me, so let me share one of my favorites with you. Follow along guys." So Chief played his favorite song "Cat's in the Cradle" by Cat Stevens. The crowd went berserk. Chief walked off the stage when someone yelled, "Encore!" Chief smiled then turned around as Raven handed him his electric guitar. They huddled up when the boys played "Fooled Around and Fell in Love" by Elvin Bishop. Medicine Man nailed the guitar solo. I had goose bumps all over me, this time for all the right reasons. Chief walked off stage to the applause of the crowd. A girl in the crowd yelled, "Play Shannon!" Chief yelled back, "I can't sing that high." She was referring to the song "Shannon" by Henry Gross. Magic yelled, "I can!" The band played on as Magic sang, "Can't You See" by The Marshall Tucker Band. We were having fun playing on stage, the girls were happy, food was disappearing; hell, even I found the time to make out with the shortest girl at the party. You couldn't ask for a better time. We didn't have a worry in the world that night. Magic yelled, "Preacher, get up here and play a song!" I walked on the stage grabbing Chief's acoustic guitar; it was obvious the boys wanted a booze break. As I sat down someone yelled a request. I responded in the microphone, "I don't do requests." The audience immediately quieted. I began strumming the guitar when I sang the song "Intro" by Aaron Lewis. When I was finished, the audience seemed stunned by the powerful lyrics, gave me a loud applause, then I walked directly to the barber chair for refreshments.

Chief walked in the house having to drain the main vain; unfortunately the bathroom door was locked. He could hear water splashing around. Knocking on the door, Chief asked, "Hey, who's in there?" Someone knocked back from the other side of the door mocking Chief. Chief said, "Hey, open the door." The door opened, Zombie walked out with a sense of accomplishment, asking Chief, "How do you spell relief? Psssssss!" Chief walked in the bathroom; getting a strong whiff of Zombie's leftover trophies he yelled, "Jesus H. Christ, Zombie, this place smells like a God damn zoo! Fuck me man, what the hell did you eat? Damn it to hell, it smells like rotten eggs in here!" Zombie was giggling as he headed down the hallway. Plugging his nose, Chief sat on the toilet only to drop a small deuce of rabbit turds himself by doubling down draining the main vein. Peacefully reading a rock magazine, Chief reached back, pushed the handle on the toilet, flushing while still enjoying his magazine when suddenly he felt water touching his ass as the toilet was now overflowing. Mad as hell, he watched the water overflowing towards the bathroom door. Chief yelled, "Oh God, please no" while scrambling to find the plunger. He couldn't find it anywhere; helplessly he watched the river of rabbit turds flowing underneath the door. As his panic and embarrassment subsided, a cooler head prevailed; Chief turned off the water supply behind the toilet. Sometimes under these circumstances we just don't think well. He looked under the counter, scrambled to grab the plunger, only to find the plunger was wet and broken in half. Chief yelled, "God damn it Zombie, I am going to kill you!" Chief could hear the guys laughing and girls screaming as if Jaws was chasing them down the hallway. In disgust, Chief mumbled, "Just fucking great" as he used every towel he could find to clean the bathroom floor. Chief was really pissed off when there was a knock at the door; he screamed out, "Can't you see that the fucking bathroom is closed here?"

A frantic knock continued as Chief yelled, "Now I am really pissed! Who is it?" The knocking continued as Chief opened the door, only to see two hot girls walking away repulsed at him. Chief turned to look down the hall as he yelled, "Shit!" He turned around to get more towels only to see Delilah staring at him. Now more mortified and embarrassed than before, Chief put his head down in shame. Delilah said, "I don't want to know, but let me help you darling." Chief angrily mumbled, "I am going to kill that little shit Zombie." Smirking, Delilah asked, "Maybe we should clean this shit up first, don't you think?" Chief replied, "That little shit dropped the bomb on me!" Delilah answered, "Yes he did." Love really is grand. Chief no doubt was the unquestioned leader of the tribe; behind the scenes I think Delilah was the leader of his heart.

Ninja made out with a little honey when he was rudely interrupted by a bunch of strangers. Someone tapped him on the shoulder asking, "Hey flash, where do we get beer cups?" Ninja, noticing that the strangers who came to crash the party were the jocks from school, responded, "Sorry guys, this is a private party so you're going to have to leave." One of the jocks said, "How can this be a party if we weren't invited?" Ninja, quickly losing his patience, answered, "That's why it's called a private party you dip shit." The biggest jock of the bunch yelled, "Ninja, don't be a dick! Where are the beer cups, dude?" Ninja replied, "Look man, we don't want any trouble." The jocks started pushing Ninja around. Again he tried to stay calm, using patience and practicing peace so things wouldn't get out of hand, but the jocks wouldn't stop pushing; it was obvious they were looking for a fight. I think Ninja was worried that trouble would only bring wrath from the Wizard. The jocks surrounded Ninja. In the meantime, not realizing what was happening, the boys were having fun playing Muddy Waters "Reefer & Champagne". Raven was ripping it up on the harmonica.

Several girls noticed that things were escalating and getting out of hand for Ninja. One girl yelled at the jocks, "Why don't you leave him alone you assholes!" As more began to push Ninja a jock asked, "What are you prepared to do, woozy boy?" The girls, not knowing what to do in the commotion, ran towards the stage screaming hysterically; the music stopped instantly. The boys jumped off the stage running towards the jocks. Backed into a corner, Ninja had finally retaliated with a few kicks that knocked out four of the trouble-making jocks when he was jumped and taken to the ground. All hell broke loose as it became a free-for-all. Beast grabbed and lifted a jock over his head, then threw the poor bastard into the fire pit. The jock was screaming, rolling around the ground trying to put the fire out. At the same time, Animal threw another jock on top of the BBQ grill. I think that was the loudest scream I ever heard; the jock popped up and down on the grill like a hot potato. I've never seen someone move so fast; it was actually pretty funny.

Meanwhile, Maverick leaped into a pile of jocks. Unaware of the situation, Chief walked outside watching me and the rest of the boys brawling, he yelled, "What the fuck is going on?" Now everyone was involved in the brawl, except for Zombie, who began jamming on a guitar singing "Free for All" by Ted Nugent. Zombie decided to play something more in tune with the situation, finding humor by playing a Johnny Cash song called "A Boy Named Sue". As the free for all continued to escalate, the music was motivating the boys; the tide had changed as the jocks were getting their asses handed to them now. Zombie kept playing while mocking the fight by singing "Kung Fu Fighting" by Carl Douglas. When it was all said and done the fighting stopped, both sides took a beating; in the end I think the jocks got the worst of it. Zombie was singing "Headknocker" by Foreigner when suddenly it got very quiet; everyone noticed Wizard was standing in the backyard. All you could hear were whispers. The jocks helped one another off the ground then took off running out of the backyard. Chief, wiping off his bloody lip said, "Shit, now we're toast." Wizard glanced around at Chief's backyard, which was trashed, and said, "Good job, at least you kicked their asses. Never let anyone cause trouble in our neighborhood. Have this place picked up by morning. Chief's aunt will be home in two days." Wizard motioned at Zombie to get down from the stage to come see him immediately. Medicine Man said, "This can't be good." Wizard, staring down Zombie, said in front of everyone, "So you like plugging up toilets for everyone else to clean? Well, my toilet needs a good cleaning." Everyone at the party was laughing while watching Wizard pull Zombie by the ear, dragging him away from the party.

The girls began singing "We are the Champions" by Queen as the boys joined in. Ghost yelled out, "Let's party on my friends." The boys started jamming as Ghost sang "Born To Be Wild" by Steppenwolf when Delilah made a request for a song. Magic said, "Delilah honey, you know we will play anything you wish." Delilah requested "All Right Now" by Free. The boys played on through the night until no one was left standing. I will never forget waking up to the song "Alabama Song (Whiskey Bar)" by The Doors. With a massive hangover, that song kept lingering in my head. Chief's house was trashed; the backyard looked like a junkyard. Stumbling down the hall I could hear noise coming from the closet so I opened the door, lo and behold there was our little friend Zombie getting a hand job while wearing pantyhose over his head by (let's be kind) a thick dragon queen. I asked, "Hey clogger, haven't you had enough? The party's over. Come on, we have a lot of cleaning to do so take the panty hose off your head, you freak." Zombie yelled, "I'm not finished!" Hearing the conversation in the hallway, Chief yelled, "I don't give a fuck! It's time for you to clean, shitty!" It took us half the day to get the place back in shape. Chief made Zombie clean the bathroom twice while replacing his plunger with a new one. Before we left the house I remember Chief handed Zombie a bag when Zombie asked, "What is it?" Chief answered back, "A gift of memories you'll never forget." Smiling, Zombie replied in excitement, "Chief, you shouldn't have." Grinning back at Zombie, Chief answered, "I spared no expense." Zombie opened the bag, his face turned red while everyone watched in anticipation; he then reached in the bag pulling out the old broken plunger and Chief's Aunt's old pantyhose. The guys were rolling on the floor in tears laughing. Shadow yelled out, "Don't forget to wash your hands!" Zombie's face was priceless. He yelled back in embarrassment, "You assholes!"

I remember glancing over at Ninja who had a welt over his eye from last night's brawl. It was a quick reminder of what a bad ass Ninja really was. He didn't take shit from anybody outside of maybe Shadow. He had fooled many with his small, skinny frame, quiet nature, and soft spoken mannerisms. His parents were hard working people who worked seven days a week; they were workaholics. Ninja was very close to his father, not so much with his mom. I think she drifted away when Ninja's brother died of cancer. Ninja relied on meditation a lot, it helped keep him centered, well balanced. He was a master at martial arts but his first love was sword fighting. If you put any form of blade in this guy's hand he was deadly. I think the only real problem he had was dealing with

Shadow's disdain for him. It would have been interesting to find out who really was the best sword fighter between Ninja and Shadow. It would have been an epic battle for sure.

Just as my mind wandered off even more, I heard Chief and the rest of the boys come running past the bridge. For a brief second the song "Snowbound" By Genesis popped into my head. Happy to see his brother, Animal said, "Thank Christ, you guys made it back." Ninja asked, "What took you guys so long?" Shadow yelled out, "While you fools have been living on easy street we have been fighting an entire army of monks!" Zombie yelled, "That's bullshit bro! We had to take on the Devil's army!" Magic and Ghost rolled their eyes knowing Zombie was the ultimate drama queen. Shadow stood there staring at Zombie knowing he had just opened a Pandora's Box to the over-hyped drama replying, "Never mind. I don't want to hear anymore exaggerations."

As the two continued on arguing, Chief surveyed the other tribe then asked Wolf, "What's the damage?" Wolf answered, "Preacher and Medicine Man are in bad shape; I'm not sure if they are going to be able to travel the distance needed. Ghost and Magic are a little banged up." Calling out names, Chief said, "Ghost, Magic, Preacher, Medicine Man, Animal and Beast, get in the canoes, go take the river home." Animal began to argue when Chief looked at him shaking his head commanding, "Do as I say, this isn't up for discussion. We've got to get out of here." So the remaining tribe members helped us into the canoes then sent us on our way. Magic hummed while playing air guitar to "Smoke on the Water" by Deep Purple for the guys; maybe it was a little bit inappropriate timing, though I admit it was a pretty cool send off for our journey home. Looking at the rest of the group, Chief said, "We need to get back to the Dark Forest as quick as we can. Your endurance will be tested to get back home, so keep up." Zombie said, "Lucky us racing against the Devil in his own playground, how convenient for him." Chief took off into the woods with the others behind him with Zombie whining the entire way.

Back at Crowley's Tomb, inside his evil lure some of the elite monks notified Manson that the Cemetery Boys had escaped. Manson shook his head while walking away. Manson went to the Room of Chant, interrupting Hitler and Satan's meditation session. Manson said, "The Cemetery Boys escaped." Hitler responded, "They are good, I will give them that." Concerned, Manson replied, "No one has ever escaped before." Not surprised, Satan answered, "They have taken the bait, now let the real games begin." Hitler asked, "Do you want us to go hunt them down in the cemetery?" Satan reached in his pocket, grabbed a red crystal ball then placed it in his outstretched hand. In it you could see Chief running through the woods. Satan replied, "They have to survive the cemetery to get home. If they make it home, we shall make a house call and go visit them. I need a road trip. The Cemetery Boys will come back, I assure you. The trap has been set." Satan began laughing when Manson said, "That's a great idea, dark one." Satan questioned in a harsh voice, "Is it?" In an angry voice, Hitler replied, "Let's drink their blood and burn them at the stake." Smiling, Satan said, "Patience, all in good time rotten ones, the tide is about to change. The catching of one's soul is the best part of the hunt. Devouring a man's heart is pure pleasure which I take great pride in. Where there is no suffering, there is no pleasure. I live for chaos and drama; where would the world be without it? Breaking a person down, taking everything he has or will ever have gives me enormous satisfaction." Satan walked away massaging his neatly trimmed goatee with a sinister look on his face. Laughter echoed throughout the hallways.

Dejilaw

CHAPTER THIRTEEN: THE STRUGGLE HOME

Journals by Raven

Dashing through the woods Chief stopped on a dime, raising his right arm up the air. We needed to rest; everyone was exhausted. Chief said, "Let's take a 5 minute break. Keep your eyes open." We rested on a couple of tree stumps; I glanced over at the tribe - everyone soaked in sweat. Zombie asked Chief, "What have we gotten ourselves into? This place is loaded with evil." Wolf interrupted, "Zombie, take it easy bro. Take a chill pill." Zombie yelled, "What do you mean take it easy? Nobody rests in peace here! There are satanic monks chasing us!" Chief answered, "The world has been in darkness since time began. War is upon us." Zombie yelled back, "War? You might think we are safe but you're wrong, dead wrong! All you have done is taken us straight to hell!" Wolf said, "Step back Zombie, we all voted on coming here, so there is no point crying about it now. You're right; we all crossed the boundaries by our own choice, that's life." Zombie answered back, "You assholes lost your own souls by choice, not me. This place is gonna take us right down to hell. And you know what the worst thing is? We can't do a fiddlers fucking thing about it!" Chief calmly responded, "You're right, some of us will rise, some will fall, but none will be forgotten." Zombie lunged towards Chief as Wolf held him back, Zombie yelled, "Fuck you Chief!"

The tribe was getting restless arguing with each other when Shadow yelled, "Shut up!" Wolf focused his sights towards the woods. He had the nose of a bloodhound. "Shit, we got company" Wolf said in disappointment. Ninja replied, "It's the Shape Changers." Maverick asked, "Well, who the fuck are the shape changers?" Ninja answered, "Society's unwanted vagrants who became the biggest gang in the City. They are best known as 'Berserkers' and they no longer take shit from anybody." Shadow said, "We've been spotted." Maverick responded, "Fuck them, I'm tired of all this running bullshit." Alarmed, Wolf instructed, "Get out your weapons, be ready to fight." Ninja warned, "These bastards are merciless." Chief replied, "Well, we better put the merciless bastards to the test." Maverick said, "It's time to stand our ground and show the Berserkers who the real king of the jungle is." There was no chance of running, it was too late. Shadow quipped, "Fuck these lame gorillas! I'll give them a war they'll never forget!" Ninja warned, "They won't quit, forget or negotiate. The Berserkers fight to the death." Shadow responded, "So do I." The Berserkers were drawing closer to us when we drew our weapons. These were some big and nasty looking mother fuckers. Each Shape Changer wore animal heads masking their face; their bodies looked like sculpted giants from the biblical days. It was becoming evident they had an advantage; they were bigger and there were more of them. Wolf counted 10 Berserkers as they began to walk towards us. Zombie's eyes got bigger as they moved closer. He said, "Damn they are big." Wolf agreed, "Yeah, that's for sure." Snickering, Maverick replied, "So are we." That was easy to say coming from Maverick who was as big as a fucking tree.

The tribe spread out when Shadow yelled out, "Let's play!" By the Berserkers' reaction I don't think they appreciated the comment. Obviously they were up to the challenge to pick a fight. "Oh shit!" Wolf replied. Shadow just rubbed them the wrong way. In that moment I knew there wouldn't be any negotiations, just a brutal confrontation. The Berserkers were charging in the near distance right at us. Astonishingly enough, Maverick was humming the song "Take Hold of the Flame" by Queensryche. I had been quiet until now, but thought I needed to do something so I said, "Let's even the playing field a little bit, man." All you could see was an arrow hit one of the Berserker's right in the throat as he collapsed backwards. With the enemy nearing, Shadow fired a crossbow blasting one right in the eye, which subtracted another one. Ninja simultaneously fired his yumi bow, assassinating a third Berserker right in the heart. Laughing, Shadow yelled out, "I guess that levels the playing field!"

The Berserkers, not finding the humor, kept charging when the fight broke out. The one-on-one fights were fierce. Maverick took on the first Berserker that was wearing a deer head charging with an axe, Maverick had a Japanese staff. The Berserker swung his mighty axe from the left, Maverick suddenly ducked under it then quickly flicking his staff with great speed launched a knife out of the opening, stabbing the Berserker in the neck. Needless to say he dropped like a stone. Chief twirled his dual Kama's at the Berserker with a pig head when the Berserker swung his chained mallet, just missing Chief as he ducked down and crouched. Chief undercut the Berserker at the ankle, slicing his left ankle to the bone. The war pig fell to the ground. He tried getting up when Chief swung his other arm with the Kama, this time hitting the pig in the head; the Berserker was dead on contact.

Ironically, Wolf was launched at by a Berserker with a wolves head. Wolf ducked under the attacker, flipping the Berserker on his back. The shape changer rolled over in anger then quickly nailed Wolf with a knife in the left shoulder. The Berserker charged after Wolf again. With the knife lodged in Wolf's left shoulder he drew out his own knife, stabbing the Berserker's left lung; he then twirled around 360 degrees pulling the knife out of his shoulder and piercing the Berserker's jugular vein. Blood gushed from the Berserker and he immediately dropped like a falling star.

Ninja clashed in a sword fight with a Berserker wearing a bear head. The Berserker swung his sword several times at Ninja who blocked each attempt with his katana sword; the Berserker was powerful but slow. Ninja had lightning fast speed but the Berserker's power was keeping him at bay; you could hear the swords colliding over and over again. With all his might the Berserker again met with Ninja's sword, only this time Ninja's sword blade broke in half and the enemy's sword brazed his shoulder opening a wound. Without a sword, the Berserker quickly went in for the kill swinging his sword wildly at Ninja. His reckless anger was met with one of Ninja's throwing stars that struck the Berserker in the neck. The undisciplined shape changer dropped his sword, immediately falling to his knees. Ninja showed no mercy as he kicked the star further into the Berserker's neck and he went crashing to the ground.

Another angry Berserker was within arm's length when Shadow calmly smiled, then blew out a poison dart from his blow gun. The dart seemed to have no immediate impact as the Berserker kept charging even though the dart stuck to his forehead. He relentlessly kept poking at Shadow with a spear then finally drew first blood scratching Shadow's arm, blood trickling down. Now more confident, the Berserker lunged at Shadow; again the spear tip hit the ground. Extremely pissed off, Shadow attacked the spear, cracking it in half with a side kick then instantly threw the spear tip at the Berserker, hitting him in the chest. With a running start Shadow jumped into the Berserker with a flying kick. Falling backwards, the Berserker landed in quicksand, ending his fate.

Meanwhile, Zombie was unloading both of his pellet guns into the largest hulking Berserker; pellets pierced all over his body yet the Berserker seemed immune to them when abruptly the Berserker kicked Zombie in the chest. The force of the blow sent him tumbling to the ground. The screaming Berserker lifted the axe high over his head to finish Zombie off; Zombie swiftly unloaded the rest of his pellets, hitting the Berserker in both eyes. Suddenly from the agony and loss of sight he dropped the axe, holding both hands to his face in extreme pain. Zombie hastily grabbed the axe and with all his might severed the Berserker's neck, watching the head go rolling off into the grass while his body stood for a few seconds before crashing forward to the ground.

The final remaining Berserker rushed at me heaving his spear only to miss as he got closer. I pulled out my nunchakus; swinging rapidly I launched an attack smacking the Berserker several times in the head. The Berserker was dazed and confused when I kicked him in the left knee; I could hear a loud snap as he fell to the ground reeling in pain. To his credit, like wounded prey he tried to get up; I immediately wrapped the nunchakus around his neck and yanked his body over mine; his neck broke like a cheap toy. The sting of battle was over. I remember looking at each other while being surrounded by dead bodies. Maverick asked Ninja, "I thought you said these guys were tough?" Ninja answered, "We got lucky today. Never underestimate your opponent." Shadow, smiling confidently replied, "Shit! We're just that good, dick. It would take an army to kill me." The tribe, amused at Shadow's arrogance, chuckled for a few minutes. Chief asked, "Is everyone okay?" Wolf answered, "I am going to need a few minutes to patch my wounds." Shadow said, "I second that." The rest of us were either stitching up one another or gathering whatever weapons and supplies we could scavenge from the Berserkers. I was out of arrows so I needed to flag down the only one I had.

Shadow was a tough customer. It's questionable which one was better at martial arts combat between Shadow and Ninja. I only know Shadow loved fighting. He was untouchable with a sword in his hand. If he had to take on a room of a hundred warriors he would die trying with a smile on his face. Shadow enjoyed toying with someone as he broke them down in battle. He came from a big family and never got much attention; he was like the forgotten son. His parents were tireless workers who were never home. His father was a locksmith; Shadow learned from the family business how to be a master at it for all the wrong reasons. Shadow was a loner by nature. I guess you could say he was eccentric. He was the true rebel without a cause, no doubt about it. He had that James Dean thing about him. Cool as a cat with a very rough edge. He had a knack for getting under your skin when he wanted to. I guess you could say, much like Zombie, he enjoyed stirring the pot: the only difference being that Ninja was always his favorite soup, per se. No one ever knew what his beef with Ninja was; he wouldn't tell anyone when they asked. He was stubborn like the Wizard. I think Shadow was threatened by Ninja's equal fighting skills.

I myself believe it had to be envy; man, were they ever polar opposites in style in every form of life, including fighting.

We were all tired as the first sign of morning light shined upon us; we had little choice but to keep moving. Chief kept pushing us past our physical limitations. To our surprise the day was uneventful for the first time on the journey. It was nice not dealing with any threat or drama. Just like before, hours seemed like days. Zombie joked, "I hope we see those Goth chicks again." A few giggles came out when Wolf said, "You have a one tract mind Zombie." Zombie responded, "Did you guys all turn into faggots?" Wolf rolled his eyes when Zombie said, "Well maybe I'll have to give Wanda a call when I get back." The tribe busted out laughing knowing what a horny toad Zombie was. Chief was in front of us then suddenly stopped. Wolf asked, "What's wrong now?" Chief pointed at some familiar trees that once again had vultures flying around it. I saw mausoleums in the distance. As we walked closer to the trees the stench was unbearable. I looked into the tree, noticing the body was majorly decayed and the turkey vultures were in business again. My worst suspicions came true: it was the same girl we wrapped up in a blanket and buried. In a disturbed voice, Maverick yelled, "Those mother fuckers! Who in their right fucking mind would hang that poor girl back up?" Chief demanded, "Ninja, cut her down now!" Shadow said, "Unbelievable, they took the blanket and tokens." Chief answered, "It doesn't matter, this time we are going to bury her away from here so she can rest in the next place." The stench was inconceivable; I had a hard time fighting back from vomiting a second time. Chief found a peaceful place near a large rock where there were no trees. We took turns digging a deeper hole while Ninja covered what was left of her eye sockets with tokens. Maverick, not known for his religious beliefs, said a quick prayer out of respect for the dead girl. We then laid her to rest.

Chief was fuming; you could see the rage burning in his eyes. All it took was an event like this to set him off. Chief never hid his emotions; his temper could intimidate even the toughest of people. He was a tyrant when his anger blew. We kept moving till we reached a safe place to rest. The guys were physically exhausted, I was mentally drained. Making it back home was becoming an unforetold grind. Chief said, "We have a few more hours, let's take a long break." Eventually we all got a chance to rest. The nap helped me get some much needed energy back. Marching on we made it to the tip of the Dark Forest. A strong wind blew into the dark shade as if the trees knew we were traveling through the Dark Forest again; the wind whispered secrets conspiring about our fates. The wind's strong howling echoed throughout the forest. My skin began to crawl. I just wanted to get home but the wind had other ideas. We fought against the wind, darkness and the noisy tree branches. Finally Wolf located the first tree marking. I was relieved knowing we were finally entering Camp Zip. I couldn't wait to get off my feet and close my eye lids. Chief said, "Let's get something to eat, re-secure the camp, and rotate guard duty. At first light let's hightail it home. I'll take first watch."

Journals by Preacher

Paddling through the misty fog I couldn't see a thing. I kept wondering how the other tribe was doing. I couldn't fight back the thoughts of the monks chasing the tribe. They had a long journey in front of them to Camp Zip. The possibilities of them making it home seemed like a stretch considering what they were up against. The guilt was killing me. We took turns patching each other's wounds under tough circumstances. After experiencing capture at Crowley's Tomb I was becoming aware of what Wizard was trying to tell us. Animal asked me, "What happened in there Preacher? Who are these people?" I answered, "You don't want to know. This place really is the ultimate evil. The crazy bastards are involved in some sort of Devil worship. The leader actually believes he's Satan, what a joke." Beast asked, "Do you think it's possible he really is the Devil?" I answered, "Not a chance. These jerk-offs are radical believers with warped minds." In a tangent, Medicine Man said, "This is the beginning of the final conflict I'm afraid. If they want us, trust me the devil and his monks will get us. We just disturbed the hornet's nest; Satan and his mental midgets are never going to stop till they hunt us down and kill us." Animal responded, "That's bullshit! We're home free, pal." Even in pain, Medicine Man still found the humor in Animal's comments, laughing in his face. I answered, "We've made it when we finally get home." Beast said, "Hey man, don't sweat the small stuff. The Village will probably have a parade waiting for us back home." Medicine Man laughing again said, "Shit, you're dreaming. If any of you have any sense left, you better pray begging for mercy because hell is coming." Magic said, "Take it easy man, now that you have us all spooked; you know as well as I do we just need to get down below and stay there for a while till things cool off." Medicine Man responded sarcastically, "Oh don't worry, you'll get down below alright, Animal. Matter of fact, Satan plans to put us all down below, that's a fact." Beast yelled, "That's a fact my ass pal! I am tired of listening to your gibberish." Annoyed, Medicine Man replied, "Hell is gonna come calling, you can bet on it. When the time is right Satan will be back, and if he catches any of us I promise, you'll wish you were dead. You all better hope you catch your last breath because in the spirit world it will start all over again. Evil has no end, don't you get it? This maniac is the ultimate evil. I looked into the eyes of darkness; Satan left the reservation long ago. He is on planet fucking Pluto!" Things were turning ugly so I interrupted Medicine Man before things got worse and asked, "Maybe we should just focus on getting home, don't you think?"

In my own mind I still couldn't believe we escaped harm's way at Crowley's Tomb. If we made it back, we could be the first ever to escape and live to tell the story. I kept thinking to myself how we were going to be heroes in the minds of the village people. The real question was, would anybody believe us? As I continued talking to myself I was tiring, fighting to keep my eyes open. Eventually my mind got tired of rambling, so I focused on the voices of Magic and Ghost singing the song "Dance With Me" by Orleans; shortly after that I fell into a deep sleep. I subconsciously felt like I was floating on air. Was I dreaming or just in a dream state? The answer came quickly. Bang! I woke up startled out of my mind only to look up in disbelief. An early morning fog had surrounded us. I could see something move in and out of the fog but wasn't sure what it was. With a troubled look on his face, Magic asked, "Is that really a ship I'm seeing?" Medicine Man answered, "No, I think we are in the spirit world." Ghost yelled, "Well that means we're already dead!" Another loud bang went off as a big splash of water came near the canoe. Soaked, Ghost yelled, "I don't think we're in the spirit world for fuck sake! Those cannon balls are real!" I said, "It's all in our mind; just ignore it." Again another bang went off with more water being splashed up at us. Panicking, Animal answered in a sarcastic voice, "I don't think that's going to work either." I could hear singing coming from the fog. Bang! Another explosion went off near the side of the canoe. Alarmed, Beast asked, "What are we going to do?" I said to Animal, "Take one of the paddles using your vest and wave it around in a gesture of surrender." Animal yelled, "Are you nuts?" Bang, another shot just missed one of the canoes. Animal waved the vest back and forth in panic. The fog was clearing when a pirate ship moved next to our canoe; a laddered rope thrown over on the side of the ship. We heard a voice that yelled, "Come aboard!" You could hear music coming from on top of the ship. Beast asked, "Do you hear that?" Animal laughed answering, "Yeah, It's 'Slow Ride' by Foghat."

One at a time we climbed aboard even though I struggled badly with a broken collarbone, but I eventually made it on deck. I was stunned to see an old scraggly grey bearded Captain accompanied by grungy drunken pirates. To myself I said, 'this can't be.' Animal asked, "Am I dreaming? Can someone please pinch me?" We watched pirates dancing to classic rock music. I didn't know whether to laugh or start crying. The music stopped, the mood rapidly changed as the Captain said, "Welcome aboard the Queen Dipper, I am Captain Yid, this is my first mate Horntoad and my famous crew better known as the Rumrunners of the sea." Ghost wasn't impressed or paying attention to the Captain when Yid pointed towards Ghost, yelling, "You there, what is your name and rank?" Ghost replied, "Sorry, Captain Shit. I don't have a rank, my name is Ghost." In bad taste, we laughed out loud. Irked, Captain Yid barked, "What did you call me?" Ghost, who misunderstood the Captain's name answered, "Captain Shit." Captain Yid was not amused as his mood changed for the worse; he ordered Horntoad and the Rumrunner pirates to immediately tie us up. That drastically changed our mood as well. Beast leaned over towards Ghost whispering, "Nice going jerk-weed!"

I happened to look closer at the ship's mast, noticing what appeared to be a head attached to it. That certainly got my attention rather quickly. I nudged the others to look up. Concerned faces came upon us all except Ghost, who just seemed unfazed. The Captain then asked in a grumpy old voice, "Are any of you of Spanish descent?" I could hear Beast gulp as he stared at the head above us. The Captain went on mumbling, "I hate the Spanish! So if you are, I am going to cut your heart out and eat for a snack." We all answered emphatically, "No! No! No! Not us!" We now had a real problem on our hands because Beast was of Mexican-Caucasian descent even though he really didn't look Spanish. The Captain was very disturbed by our antics as he asked another question, "Where is the treasure?" Worried and in utter confusion, Animal responded, "We don't know what you're talking about." Now very annoyed Captain Yid answered, "So, you don't know where the treasure is eh? Well, we shall see about that." He grabbed an old bottle, handed it to the first mate Horntoad, who took a sip then forced us to take a long swig. The burn that went down my throat had me gagging when I vomited all over the first mate from that nasty poison. He was not amused. I asked myself, 'how could anyone not regurgitate that shit?' The pirates meanwhile burst out in laughter. The distained bottle was passed around only to witness Ghost drink the entire bottle as if it was water. The pirate's laughter turned to silence. Ghost asked the Captain nonchalantly, "Hey Captain Shit, does the Queen Shitter have a toilet I can use? Oh, one more thing, can I get another bottle?" I put my head down and said to Ghost, "Oh boy, you've done it now." The Captain yelled, "You are getting on my last nerve you little filth! Lock them down in the basement dungeon! I can't afford the liquor the way that heathen drinks!"

The stinky drunken Rumrunners forced us down into the cellar basement of the ship while the pissed off first mate pushed us inside, locked the door, and left in a hissy. Medicine Man said, "I can't believe we have been captured again." Frustrated, Animal asked, "Who are these crazy rumrunners? What are we going to do now?" Bewildered, Beast answered, "I don't know, you might want to come take a look at this shit." We all saw two skeleton remains in chains. One of the skeletons had an old Napoleon hat on while the other had a bandana over his head sitting against the wall in chains. Ghost was a mess, stumbling around drunk, singing, "Rye Whiskey" by Tex Ritter. Magic yelled, "Can't you guys see these people are crazy?" Ghost blurted out, "Can't you see I don't give a shit?" Panic set in for the rest of us. We each sat down with our hands tied behind our backs. After a few minutes we heard laughter coming from inside the room. We looked back and forth at each other, none of us were laughing. We all turned our heads at the same time toward the two skeletons sitting up staring at us in laughter. Startled, we all jumped up scared. The nearest skeleton with the Napoleon hat screamed, "You're all going to die here!" The other creepy skeleton laughed at us in a spooky tone. Ghost and Magic ran to the door kicking on it. Ghost was staggering around yelling at the top of his lungs, "Hey! Get me out of here!" So much for his I don't give a shit attitude. In a louder panic Magic yelled, "Hurry, get us the fuck out of here!"

With perfect timing the prison door opened; the pirates grabbed Magic and Ghost. A few minutes later they came back then grabbed Animal and Beast. Within a couple minutes Medicine Man and I were taken to the top of the deck. I asked Captain Yid, "Where are our friends?" Several pirates pushed us toward the plank. Medicine Man was the first to walk the plank standing at the edge. Horntoad, wielding a long bent sword, was behind him. Captain asked, "Where is the treasure?" Before the Captain could get an answer from him, Medicine Man turned his head, smiled at the Captain, then without notice jumped overboard. The Captain said to me, "I hope you're not as stupid as your friend." Horntoad pushed me to walk the plank, standing at the edge. I bowed my head down in shame; my heart was full of sorrow with the loss of my friends, not to mention witnessing the death of my best friend. The thought of jumping in shark infested waters didn't thrill me.

I hesitated in taking that last step to the unknown when a song from the pirate ship played "In The End" by Lincoln Park. Captain Yid once again like a robot asked, "Where is the treasure?" I turned fully around with my back at the sea and answered, "Captain Shit, may you live forever." Horntoad charged at me with his swashbuckling sword when I looked directly at him and said, "Fuck you shit bag!" I then stepped back, falling into the jaws of the eternal black sea as my feet hit the cold water first. I could feel my body sinking deeper into the abyss when on my last grasp of breath my eyes opened to a glowing white statue of Christ. For some reason, in that moment of fate, I prayed to one of the beings I was so pissed off at throughout my childhood for the last time as my lungs filled with water and my body sank to the bottom of the ocean floor. I rested there. It seemed my body died but my mind had not. I thought in those fading moments 'this was not my vision when I drank Medicine Man's potion. How could I die such a forgettable death? My destiny was not fulfilled, life sucks!'

Journals by Raven

Back at Camp Zip it was pitched dark out; we were all in separate tree platforms while rotating guard duty. Our tree lines go in a circle so we can zip line to each other. We also have two zip lines to escape. The zip line was much higher than the normal tree lines at Five Points. If you fell from one of the zip lines at Camp Zip, you have pretty much zipped yourself to the afterlife. If the fall didn't kill you, the booby traps certainly would. The ground area had been booby trapped all around our perimeter by Wolf. The closer on the ground one came to the camp, the worse the trap. Tonight the wolves were busy howling out while noises from other creatures responded in their own cries of fate. Just by the noises alone you could feel this night was going to be troublesome. The tree branches made sounds as if monkeys were playing on them. I could feel the sweat dripping from my body. It was a very humid night. Tree leaves and branches made noise in every direction. I spotted a light in the far distance that was heading our way. I made a strange whistle to alarm everyone that danger was present. Chief whistled back to let everyone know to stand ready. We were all watching intently as the light was coming closer; if I had to guess, I would say maybe a hundred yards away and closing fast. I happened to look down, there were skeletons everywhere. I wasn't sure if the skeleton gang was here out of revenge or just passing through. In the silence I could hear my heart beating faster and faster. I tried taking deep breaths to calm my nerves but the skeleton gang was roaming all around us down below.

All of a sudden you heard a snap; someone screamed in obvious pain. A second snap was heard and that same eerie scream of pain cried out, only this time it was directly below me. Wolf had set three metal jaw traps near the hidden tree ladders. When closed, the metal jaws would cause extreme damage and pain. The jaws of the traps showed no mercy, just the endless taste of destruction, pain and possible death. It would take several people to remove the jaws from the victim's leg. I heard more screams as the skeletons walked into the snare traps as well. Those ankle snares tore straight through the bone. I kept hearing the traps going off with more screams of pain coming closer. Some skeletons even fell into hidden pits of spikes which we had all pissed on. The more screams I heard, the more skeletons that multiplied around us. We had to be out-numbered 15-to-1 in strength. Fear was among us!

At the same time the light was getting even closer. I could now hear some form of drum beat harmonized with a chanting ground force of marching. As the screams became louder, the skeletons were roaming in every direction like ants. The marching became faster; I could tell it was getting closer. The chanting got louder and louder. We all stayed very still. The marching changed to running, the chanting turned into screaming until it was underneath us. Hell broke loose. I could hear the cries of battle coming from down below. I heard the song "Symphony of Destruction" by Megadeth rattling around in my brain. Murder was in the air. Shape Changers surrounded the perimeter thirsty for death; tonight they weren't taking any prisoners. Berserkers were killing anything that moved. You could only hear swipes from their steel weapons hitting flesh making gruesome sounds of terror; the unforgivable screams were haunting. It was pure mayhem underneath us. The forgotten souls of the cemetery cheered for the death of the slaughtered.

Some of the skeletons were now on their way up, climbing the trees desperately to escape harm's way. I was thinking to myself, 'as good as we are, if they find us, we will be nothing more than buzzard meat just like the skeletons'. There had to be twenty or more skeletons climbing the trees; maybe fifty dead on the ground. Some of the skeletons noticed the platforms as they were making a desperate attempt up to avoid sure death. I certainly wasn't scared of some idiotic weird gang that dressed up in skeleton tights as the Third Reich acting like thugs; I was becoming more scared about an entire platoon of menacing pissed off Berserkers who were on a murdering rampage. Chief gave the order so we immediately zip lined out of there with pandemonium and death occurring beneath us. The Berserkers were too busy butchering the skeleton gang for them to actually notice us fleeing.

We cut the zip lines behind us. One by one we reached the final escape platform; last across was Chief who was singing "Bad Moon Rising" by Credence Clearwater Revival. Everyone got a kick out of that. It was Chief's way of dealing with the fear of heights I guess. There was a huge sense of relief. We once again found some way to cheat death. I think Death himself must have been frustrated at the fact we were able to elude his calling. It certainly didn't bother me of his inabilities to kill us. We high-fived each other, but our celebration was short-lived. We knew we had to get home. The cemetery was hungry tonight; we had no plans of being the barbeque.

We continued running through the cemetery that night when we finally reached the original base camp at Five Points. Maverick pointed to the tree house; as we all looked up, the tree house had been destroyed. It was a sad sight because we invested a lot of time into that tree house. Maverick said, "Looks like the cops burned our home to the ground." Chief replied, "It doesn't matter, we can build another one. We are close to home, take a ten minute break then get ready to move out." We were all tired, but relieved that the Village was within our grasp. I was playing melodic music on my harmonica. As we moved out I could see the early morning fog rising from the ground. It was a creepy site, but then again it always was.

We continued to run through our old stomping ground when we ran into Pusher and his gang of thugs. Pusher was a drug dealer who did all his business in the cemetery. Actually that was pretty smart on Pusher's part, tough to get caught, plenty of buyers and lots of escape routes to get away. Pusher's brutal thugs were very dangerous, not to mention being one of our arch rivals in the cemetery. We had ongoing feuds with his crew; including a history of turf issues. In their mind they believed we should pay a tax to travel through while we believed in free travel. They hated us because we always found a way to elude them. Well, that was about to change.

Out of nowhere three black Cadillacs pulled in front of us as we all stood in a straight line to see what was going on. Pusher got out of his car. You could hear the song "Voodoo Child" by Jimi Hendrix coming from one of the Cadillacs. Pusher walked up to Chief, greeting him face to face said, "We have a problem again I see. This time you and your fucking outcasts are not going to avoid me." I started playing my harmonica, which obviously bothered Pusher. Chief answered, "We have never avoided you or anyone else. We are just trying to get home. I see you have a new hook for your hand." It hit me like lightning when Chief said that. I realized Pusher killed those kids in the station wagon. He was sporting a gold hook for a hand. Pusher got within nose hairs of Chief's face and replied, "You run through my turf, disturbing my business, running around like a bunch of homeless fucking jerk-offs and you have the audacity to say you are not interrupting my business? You all must be insane. I personally don't give a shit! I figure you owe us for back taxes." Chief asked, "How do you figure that?" Pusher answered, "Let's call it an even hundred a person." Chief said, "You're dreaming; we've never seen a hundred dollars let alone seven hundred bucks." Pusher yelled, "I don't give a shit cornbread!" Agitated, Chief interrupted Pusher and said, "Pusher, you have us outnumbered, out-gunned, and I promise you, while we might all die here today, you will see your end as well." Pusher looked in Chief's eyes as he contemplated, you could tell Pusher was scared as he hesitated. Pusher knew he was in the danger zone. He was too close and he knew it. He laughed as he back pedaled a bit. As he stared at us all, he said, "Whoever is the toughest in your gang take a step forward." We all looked at each other; after a brief discussion we all took a step forward. Pusher said, "You assholes really are a bunch of fucking cowboys. I am going to give you a choice, you can all die right here together or let your toughest fighter fight one of mine." Chief, putting his hands through his hair, was tired, cranky, and trying to be patient not to bark at Pusher, calmly asked, "Is this really necessary?" Pusher answered, "If you want to go home, that's entirely up to you." Chief answered, "Okay, bring your best man on. If I win, you will let us go home, right?" Laughing, Pusher answered, "Chief, your only way home is in a body bag." In laughter, his thugs mocked us with bigoted remarks in the background. Chief made a face rolling his eyes, then looked dead into Pusher's eyes responding, "Don't bet on it."

Maverick turned to Chief, begging with common sense, "All egos aside, you know I am the one for this." Chief knew as tough as he was, Maverick was the best boxer and street fighter of the bunch. Chief looked at Maverick, answering, "Kick this monkey's ass and let's go home." All smiles, Maverick said, "This won't take long." I continued to bother Pusher by playing my harmonica replicating the famous dramatic song "Duello Finale" by Ennio Morricone to perfection. The more Pusher told me to stop playing the harmonica the more I kept replaying the same song over and over again. Pusher then called out to one of his thugs with a confident grin on his face. With bravado a giant of a man came forward, and I mean giant. Zombie said, "Oh shit!" Pusher replied, "That's right."

Ninja said, "Shit! It's the Junkyard Dog." Everyone knew of the Junkyard Dog, he was legendary around the Village. Rumors swirled around about what a badass this guy was. As we all cleared out of the way, both walked up to each other, it was like watching an old western gun fight. Junkyard Dog was as big as a house, while Maverick was cool as a cat. My heart was pounding with anticipation. Maverick was strong as an ox with lightning fast hands. Many saw Maverick as a big dumb kid. Assumptions can be fatal because I knew firsthand what a very nasty fighter he could be. We had faith in Maverick, but fighting the Junkyard Dog was different. They say he beat and killed five guys at once including breaking someone's back. His reputation was well known. It didn't seem like a good idea, unfortunately there was no choice in the matter. Junkyard Dog stared in Maverick's eyes making faces while showing off his gold teeth, asking, "Are you ready to die, boy?" Maverick kindly smiled back then responded, "I promise to give you a painless death." Junkyard Dog laughed then lunged toward Maverick. In the blink of an eye Maverick swung with a thunderous uppercut, you could hear the punch on impact have grave effects on Junkyard Dog's life. Lying at Maverick's feet, Junkyard Dog was lifeless on the ground. I don't think anybody could believe it ended so quickly with just one punch. As we roared in victory, shocked and in disbelief, Pusher yelled, "Get the fuck out of here before I kill you all!" Pusher was a bad man, but at least he was true to his word by letting us go home. Maverick's punch scared Pusher; you could see the fear in his eyes. Wolf said, "I have seen many things, but I have never seen that before. I guess he's now the Graveyard Dog. Let's go home." Some of the guys chuckled. I continued to play that eerie song on my harmonica as we walked home. I'm pretty sure Pusher will never get that song out of his head.

Maverick was a survivor in life. He helped take care of his father at home till he passed last summer. His mom worked nights, slept most of the day. His closest family was his best friend… me. When I looked at Maverick I always thought of John Wayne. He just had that type of presence about himself. Maverick wasn't the brightest of the bunch but he certainly was the most honorable. He was a big boy so most people never wanted to mess with him. At school he always took on the bullies who picked on the weak and because of it, he was a usual suspect in the detention center at school. He never gave a fuck if it meant helping others. If Maverick ever had a weakness it was with the girls. He chased them constantly, like I did; between the two of us we banged the girls like bowling pins.

Journals by Preacher

Upon awakening, our canoes were drifting. I jumped up in excitement screaming, "Holy shit! Holy shit! We're alive!" I heard this old classic song go off in my head called "Dear Mr. Fantasy" by Traffic. I must have been in a deep sleep to find this song in the archives of my mind. Who knows, maybe Wizard telepathically saved us. The guys were celebrating in excitement when I noticed we had drifted to Riverside Cemetery. Animal asked, "What happened to us Preacher? I remember being on a pirate ship, dumped in the water to drown, left for dead, and now here we are somehow back in canoes. What the fuck is going on here?" Medicine Man answered, "We must have been in the spirit world." Beast replied, "I hope you're not going to start that shit again, are you? Fuck the spirit world!" I answered, "Actually Medicine Man is somewhat correct. I think as we all fell asleep we somehow astro-traveled back in time. It's possible we drifted into some type of wormhole that drifted us in the spirit world. The Wizard was right; it is possible to go back and forth in other worlds traveling in time." Arguing the point, Beast said, "That's really fucking thin Preacher and you know it!" I responded with a smirk, "I think we just experienced time travel boys." Magic pointed towards the outer banks at an ice cream truck. As our canoes passed by we noticed several people dressed in clown suits staring at us. One of the clowns, wearing green, had a giant reverse cross painted on his face; he pointed his fingers as if he had a gun in his hands acting as if he was shooting us. Ghost asked, "What the fuck is that all about?" Beast yelled out to the clown, "Fuck you creep!" The clown yelled back, "I'll see ya soon!" Beast responded back, "I don't think so, fuck face!" Ghost yelled at Beast, "What the hell is the matter with you? Sit your ass down and shut up!" Animal said to his brother, "Hey chill out bro, that psycho could have been a killer, plus I think we have enough enemies as it is. Use your head!" Beast mocked, "Shit, those wimps couldn't hurt a fly." Medicine Man said, "Keep talking, shit brain." I could hear in the faded distance the ice cream truck's loud music jamming the song, "Ice Cream Man" by Van Halen. Magic said, "Let's just get home."

We canoed through the flooded mausoleums till we hit land during the daylight. I think we all felt the effects of numbness in our bodies. We looked like a motley crew. The pain I felt in my shoulder still hurt like a bitch. We leaned on each other as we began limping our way home. Medicine Man was one tough hombre; managing to limp around with broken ribs. He grinned and beared it pretty well. Without incident, we made it to the open gates of the cemetery. Ghost yelled, "We made it."

I was relieved; I just couldn't believe we actually made it. Animal said, "Let's go to Bishops to see if Chief and the rest of the boys made it." Medicine Man said, "I doubt it." So we walked right out of the open gates making our way to Bishops when I could hear the jukebox jamming "Living After Midnight" by Judas Priest. We walked through the doors to the sweet sounds of the jukebox playing "Boys Are Back In Town" by Thin Lizzy when Zombie yelled, "They made it!" Shadow asked us, "What took you guys so long? You guys should have made it way before us." All of us celebrated by hugging one another. I sat down while Chief ordered a round of near beers with some hot chili from Delilah who was serving that day. Wow, was she a sight for sore eyes and giddy to see us all as well. She was busy doting on Chief when she played a song for the guys on the jukebox called, "Seagull" by Bad Company.

CHAPTER FOURTEEN: NIGHTMARES

Journals by Preacher

Since being home I began experiencing really bad dreams. The dreadful visions were always the same about the monks chasing us, when it wasn't that, it was the Tall Man. Almost a month went by as we licked our wounds trying to recover from Crowley's Tomb. I had gotten word that Wizard was anxiously awaiting our arrival; of course I was less than thrilled. Summer break was coming to an end, as was healing time. I could hear the song "Ah! Leah" by Donnie Iris on the radio at the house playing in the background as we all discussed our nightmare problems. Apparently everyone was having the same nightmares. We all knew a major lecture from Wizard was coming. As we all walked up the block, true to form Wizard was waiting for us smoking his pipe and sipping on his alcoholic beverage. Wizard had a thirst for whiskey on ice. As we walked up the stairs to the porch, Wizard was calmly sitting down while in a gentle voice asked, "Are you boys hungry?" As if he was really going to give us a choice in the matter. If you happen to say no he would just give you a double portion and stare you down till you licked the plate clean. He was a pain in the ass that way. Wizard had us come inside as we devoured his amazing Lasagna.

The talk was light at dinner but I knew it wouldn't be long before Wizard would start his probing. Later that evening we all went out to sit on the porch and relax. Wizard took a long gulp of his whiskey then asked, "So tell me, what happened boys?" We took turns telling Wizard what happened. I felt as if Wizard was putting us in a trance. Wizard seemed like he didn't believe us until Beast handed the head honcho a medallion. Wizard got up suddenly as we followed him back inside. He pulled out a giant magnifying glass from his desk to examine the medallion closer. He kept flipping it back and forth. Chief said to Beast with steam coming out of his ears, "I thought I told you to leave that shit alone." Beast replied, "What did I do? It was a gift." Zombie gave Beast a dirty look asking, "A gift my ass, why can't you ever leave shit alone?" Wizard said, "This can't be." Chief asked, "What is it?" Wizard answered, "There has never been any living proof left behind that druid monks ever existed." Excited, Beast asked, "Is it worth anything?" Wizard answered, "Oh yes, it's worth a fortune." Celebrating we all high fived one another. Chief quickly opened his bag, setting the gold pentagram on the table, impatiently asking, "What might this be worth? Do you believe us now?" Wizard sat up in his chair with a startled look on his face and asked, "Do you boys have any idea what you have done?" We all looked at each other confused.

Wizard yelled, "I told you before not to go there but you boys refused to listen and went anyway! You have brought evil here! You need to bring that stuff back immediately!" Beast responded, "Are you crazy? We aren't going back there to risk our necks again!" Wizard answered back, "They will come here hunting every last one of you down." I got into the argument and said, "They aren't going to expose themselves for Christ sake, they live in the cemetery." Wizard was so furious at us I could see the redness in his face as he answered, "They are already here. Dream much, boys?" Chief responded, "That's bullshit Wizard! I agree they are whacked out no doubt, but no way do they have the balls to enter into the Village."

Down deep we all knew what Wizard was talking about because we were all having the same nightmares. With fear in his eyes Wizard asked, "Who do you think owns the cemetery? They are already here, you not only disturbed the hornet's nest you have stolen from them." Just like I thought, we were now in full swing as everyone got into the argument about how we were going to deal with this when Zombie yelled out, "There is no way I am going back to that fucking place! I say let's sell the medallion and pentagram; let whoever buys it worry about it." Staring down Wizard, Chief said, "You told us we wouldn't make it back, yet we did. We exposed Crowley and his jerk-off monks for who they are. You're just pissed off because the best man lost. Their fable is full of shit! And you don't like it! Of course they're pissed off because we exposed them!" Wizard asked, "Exposed what? Who are they?" Chief stumbled his words in anger answered, "The occult! They are psychotic, crazy, demented, devil worshippers who are a phony fucking fraud!" Angry, Wizard replied, "You boys have no clue what you have done. These people are evil. You will leave that pentagram and medallion here until we figure out what to do with it. I need some time to think. I want you boys to promise me not to go back to the cemetery until we figure this out." We all looked at each other, gathering in a huddle to decide on the matter. Chief finally said, "We will leave this with you for now, but we will bring it to a trader to find out what it's worth later." Wizard said, "Come back the first weekend of school and I will tell you what you boys need to do." Chief was reluctant but we all agreed. Wizard, as always still wanting to get the last jab in, said, "You boys are just clueless, you better get your heads screwed on and get a fucking clue. I am so pissed off and disappointed right now I can't even think. You fucked up my mojo, now leave me alone."

It was getting late; we were all tired of arguing with the Wizard anyway, so we all began walking each other home like we always do when Zombie yelled out, "Did you see that?" Chief asked, "See what?" Zombie pointed toward the bushes behind us and said, "There is someone following us." We all stopped, looked back, saw nothing. Chief said to Zombie, "Stop being paranoid. No one is that stupid." Zombie persisted, "I am telling you I saw someone." Chief grabbed Zombie and looked behind the bushes, nothing was there. Chief replied, "Are you satisfied?"

We continued to walk; this time it was Wolf who stopped, pointed towards the bushes in front of us, warning, "There's someone in the bushes." Wolf saw what appeared to be a figure standing in the bushes and then the phantom vanished. Wolf took off running toward the bushes, again nobody was there. As we all caught up to Wolf, Chief asked, "What the hell is wrong?" Wolf answered, "Zombie is right, someone's following us." In disbelief Chief said, "Guys come on, there is nobody here. There is no fucking Boogieman! God damn it! We are all just tired." Angered, Zombie yelled back at Chief, "Are you fucking blind man! Something is wrong. He was there one minute and gone the next. Whatever it is disappeared like Houdini." Raven asked, "Did you ever consider maybe he is the fucking Boogieman?" Chief asked, "Okay, what did the Boogieman look like?" Wolf answered, "Whoever it was dressed in black with a white charade mask." Frustrated, Chief replied, "Guys, there are thirteen of us, nobody is that stupid to do that in our own neighborhood." Wolf asked, "What if there is more than one?" Chief wiping the sweat from his face, answered, "Okay, guys come on! Listen to yourselves. Now we have the Boogieman loose in the neighborhood while Houdini's doing a magic act. Let's just go home and get some fucking sleep!" You could hear some of the guys complaining about Chief not believing them on the walk home. Zombie was the most disgruntled by Chief's reaction.

As we began to drop each other off one at a time, I said good night to Chief and went inside. I watched Chief walk away without a worry in the world. Chief only had another block to walk anyway. As Chief walked toward the house he saw for himself someone standing in the bushes next to his house. They both stood there staring at one another when suddenly Chief yelled at the figure running through the bushes. The Boogieman ran towards the alley as dogs barked in the background; Chief with reckless abandon chased after the creepy phantom. The Boogieman jumped a fence, infringing onto someone else's back yard; there was a small dim light on and laundry hanging everywhere on clotheslines. Chief saw the figure go between the sheets hanging from the linen lines. Chief removed the sheets one at a time when someone came out yelling from the back door. Chief stood still as the neighbor walked down the stairs and asked, "What are you doing out this late? Why are you taking my sheets down?" Chief pulled the last sheet down but no one was there; he looked around but the Boogieman was gone. Chief apologized to his neighbor, handed her the sheets and simply walked away. He walked back to his house a little rattled.

I tossed and turned in the sheets that night as thoughts continued to roll around in my head. I found my thoughts to be overpowering me night after night, but this night was different. It felt like someone was talking to me subconsciously with no voice, just in thought. It was scary, even my own room was creeping me out. Just like the guys, I was having trouble sleeping. And when I did sleep it was constant nightmares. I came to the conclusion we all might be suffering from post traumatic stress syndrome. My visions and thoughts kept being triggered by something. I kept wondering to myself if I had gone mad. I was reading a book in the spare bedroom when I finally fell back asleep. Later that night I awoke and slowly opened my eyes; I noticed someone staring at me in the window. I was frozen stiff, I couldn't move. I don't think he could see that my eyes were open but I laid in shock; the figure had a dark cloak on with a white charade mask. It had a Mardi Gras look to it. Paralyzed, I stared right at the Boogieman. I was terrified. It was so scary the eyes behind the mask were pitch black and emotionless. There was more passion in the eyes of a shark. The Boogieman had a blank stare. It reminded me of Blackwell actually. I couldn't believe of all people, I froze up. The Boogieman stood there moving his head side to side watching me while I was vulnerable. Suddenly he began rattling the window trying to open it.

At that very moment my body finally freed itself from shock. I jumped up and ran to the window, the shadow figure was gone. I opened the window; Chief was standing in front of it. I fell back almost pissing myself. As I got back up gathering my composure I asked Chief, "What the hell are you doing out there? Someone was staring in at me." Chief said, "Close the window, I'll check it out." I left the room, opened the back door for Chief; we could see fear in each other's eyes like never before. Chief said, "I saw someone by my house and chased him through the neighborhood, he then in vanished like Houdini. Later I couldn't sleep, I heard noises from my basement window, yet nobody was there. Zombie and Wolf were right, someone was following us." I asked, "Do you think it was the Boogieman? What about the monks from Crowley's place?" Chief answered, "Preacher, there is no such thing as the fucking Boogieman and I highly doubt it's the monks. I don't know who the fuck it could be. I can promise you this: I am going to find out who it is. When I do, I am going to send whoever it is straight to hell - that's a fact."

I was shaken up and scared; I tried gathering my thoughts to recollect what happened. I said to Chief, "As I woke up someone was staring at me." Chief said, "Well, what did he look like?" I answered as my voice began to crack, "He was in a black cloak, with a white charade mask, and had lifeless black eyes. Whoever or whatever it is, it was pure evil." Chief asked, "Honestly, do you think it's the monks?" I answered back, "I don't know. Just spend the night here; we can meet up with the guys in the morning on the way to school." Chief agreed. For the first time in my life, I saw Chief was frightened, while I was beyond scared – no, terrified to death, freaked out. I just couldn't help wondering about the rest of the tribe. We went upstairs to my room where "Children of the Sun" by Billie Thorpe played on the radio while I talked to Chief; that was the last thing I remembered.

CHAPTER FIFTEEN: VISITORS

Journals by Preacher

Sitting in class listening to some boring lecture about the reiterated stories of past history over and over again was not my idea of fun. I found it offensive that at every level in school we continued to talk about the same things in history. It was a joke. School was beginning to bore me to death. Nothing was being taught about the future or how to deal with everyday life. School was becoming a brainwashing grind of unreality. Worse was listening to lectures on politics. The funny thing about political science is it's taught from the teacher's own political views, which I always found quite disturbing. I mean, why not teach from a factual basis? Whether on the left or right side of politics I would have preferred just the facts, versus the media spin zone. I was becoming a big boy who preferred free will to formulate my own opinions instead of the opinions of others. As each year passed you could see in plain sight the SG as well as the churches' plans of attempting every means necessary to get their message across through continued control, manipulation, guilt, and brainwashing. I noticed that when a leader spoke, that leader died when opposing the opinions of the SG. It seemed like the political agenda being shoved down our throats was never going to end. The media was brainwashing people to be superficial in judging others by what they looked like instead of who they were as a person. The worst part about it: it was working. Kids in school were acting that way. It was like the great divide even from an economic standpoint. The world was under attack without an enemy in sight. Most never realized we were under attack.

Medicine Man was listening to "Copperhead Road" by Steve Earle on his walkman unnoticed. While jamming to his music, he happened to look out the window when suddenly he jumped up out of his seat. He put his head against the window to get a better look outside. I also ran from my seat to go see what the fuss was. We stood in shock as the monks, in plain daylight, were staring right back at us. Medicine Man yelled, "Oh my God! Shit! They are fucking here!" Ghost along with several students rushed to look out the window but just like that, the monks disappeared. Ghost said, "I don't see anything." The teacher yelled at everyone to get back in their seats. All of the students went back to their seats except Ghost and Medicine Man. Ghost asked, "Who's here?" Medicine Man answered, "It's the monks." Ghost answered, "That's impossible." The teacher was talking to both of them as I tried to whisper to the guys to sit down; regrettably they were both in another world talking back and forth between each other and paid no attention.

The teacher was extremely pissed so she decided to send all three of us down to the Principal's office. As we walked out of the Principal's office we ran into Chief who heard about the ruckus in class and asked, "What the hell happened upstairs in history class?" Ghost answered, "We got detention after school today for an outburst in class." Chief asked, "No, what happened in class?" Medicine Man answered, "Chief, the monks are here." Chief asked, "Are you sure?" Medicine Man, who was frightened, answered, "Manson and Hitler were staring at me in the classroom window. Once they noticed I saw them, they just vanished into thin air." Chief said, "Shit! Wizard warned us of this. Let's all meet at my house tonight; we need to have a meeting. I got to get to class, have fun in detention." Ghost answered, "Fuck you!" The bell rang for the next class.

Zombie and I were in our assigned group researching for an English project in the library. We went in opposite ends searching through different book titles on the shelves. The library is a great reminder of the cemetery. It is such a quiet place that it can be a little scary sometimes just by its silence. Zombie walked from aisle to aisle when he felt a presence watching over him. Old reliable began panicking, looking around in both directions, before deciding to pull out a thick book off the shelf. When he did, he got the surprise of a lifetime. Zombie noticed there was someone staring back at him on the other side of the bookshelf with a mask on. Zombie screamed out so loud that everyone turned in his direction. I thought he was being stabbed to death with a butcher knife. Without thinking twice he turned around and collided right into the bookshelf with great force, which tipped the bookshelf, it went crashing into another one, which crashed into another one; the shelves continued crashing into one another like dominos. Zombie stood there watching helplessly saying, "Shit!" Kids were astonished at the damage Zombie caused, all the while laughing hysterically in the library. Teachers from other classes came running down the hall to see what happened. The librarian stood speechless and stunned. Needless to say, Zombie found himself at the Principal's office. His luck was still running hot; he ended up with detention for the whole school year. I can tell you, he was one unhappy camper. He wasn't worried about detention because it was a regular occurrence for us to spend time there. Typically we were the usual suspects in detention, just another home away from home. I personally enjoyed it because we had more time together to goof off. Zombie's only concern was being on trial with the Wizard. Zombie feared the Wizard's wrath and absolutely hated the guy's heckling. Zombie knew he was never going to be able to live this event down. I myself would've loved to hear the conversation with Zombie and the Principal. I am sure the Fisher King himself had more stories of bullshit than a Fisherman. I later heard it was a classic animated conversation between the two. As for me, I had to finish the English project on my own, which sucked.

Later on the final bell rang as school got out, but our sentence began; we had to meet each other for detention. Ghost whispered to Zombie, "I heard you crashed the entire library." We were all giggling when the teacher, staring at Ghost, asked, "Do you want detention the rest of the year?" All of us answered, "No ma'am." I really wanted to tell that militant bitch to go piss off. The only thing that stopped me was Wizard. He would have our ass for something disrespectful like that. The teacher warned, "If I were you I would behave and get your homework done." The teacher got up, leaving the room for a few minutes. Ghost leaned over his chair whispering to Zombie, "What the hell happened in the library?" Zombie answered, "I was looking at some books trying to find the 'Animal Farm' when I found my favorite book the 'Odyssey' so I pulled it off the shelf; immediately I noticed that someone was staring back at me." Ghost being a smart ass asked, "No shit, what did he look like?" Zombie answered, "He had a white charade mask on; it scared the shit out of me. I honestly can tell you I almost shit my pants twice! I didn't mean to run into the fucking bookshelves. I believe that is the same person who followed us home the other night. He might actually be the Boogieman." Medicine Man asked, "Well where did the Boogieman go? Christ, you destroyed the entire library." Zombie answered in an irate voice, "God damn it! Those black eyes scared the shit out of me. Whoever it was just disappeared. I am telling you the Boogieman is here!" Ghost, immediately disputing Zombie's claims, responded back, "You're trying to tell us the Boogieman walked out of the library full of people without ever being noticed and now is running around loose in our school, no fucking way! Come on slick, do you really expect us to buy your bullshit?" Medicine Man yelled, "I am telling you guys it's the fucking monks, man!"

The teacher suddenly strutted back in the detention center; of course, we acted as if we were studying our homework. Ghost raised his hand and asked, "Could I go to the bathroom?" Medicine Man asked to go as well. The teacher answered in a stern voice, "I am not going to let you both go terrorizing the halls together. God only knows what havoc and destruction you might create. You can go one at a time, but I don't want any foolishness, you hear?" So Ghost went first. As Ghost walked down the hall he noticed how empty and quiet the halls were. As he continued down the hall he heard a door shut near the bathroom. As he entered the bathroom, he got that eerie feeling that he wasn't alone. He walked by pushing each stall door open but saw nothing. So he went into the last stall on the left, closed the door and locked it. As he was sitting on the pot he heard the bathroom door open, then quickly slam shut. The lights went off. Ghost yelled, "Hey man, turn the lights on." The lights went back on. Laughing, Ghost said, "Alright guys, stop fucking around." The lights went back off. The room was silent; Ghost could hear a slow drip from the sink. Ghost asked, "Is there anybody here? Come on guys, can you please turn the lights on?" The lights went back on. Ghost finished his business and flushed the toilet. The lights went back off. Ghost slowly leaned under the stall door; he was greeted with a person in a white charade mask staring at him. Ghost jumped back, crashing into the toilet scared to death. Someone was banging on the other side of the door trying to open the stall door; luckily the lock prevented it from opening. The lights went on again. This time Ghost unlocked the door, quickly opened it, but there was no one in front of it. He slowly walked out of the stall, looked around and found that nobody was in the bathroom. He made a conscious decision that washing his hands was not very important at the moment. He dashed for the door, opened it, and crashed into the school maintenance man. The maintenance man yelled, "Slow down kid!" Ghost got up quickly, running down the hall to the detention center frantically opening the door. He was greeted by a very annoyed teacher. He tried to explain to the teacher what happened; she on the other hand was not interested in hearing his antics, yelling, "Sit down! I will not have this foolishness going on any longer!" Other kids who were also serving detention busted out in laughter.

Medicine Man started walking out of the room as Ghost yelled, "Don't go to the bathroom!" The teacher stood up and yelled, "Ghost, you just added another week of detention!" Ghost yelled back, "That's bullshit." The teacher replied, "Maybe another week will quiet you down." Ghost pounded his fist on top of the desk in anger. She looked right back saying in a calm voice, "That just cost you another. Would you like to add another week?" Ghost's face was burning red; he shut up and put his head on the desk in total frustration.

Medicine Man walked to his locker, opened his bag and grabbed his holster which had two tomahawks like a gunslinger. He walked to the bathroom, slowly opening the door. He too looked in at each stall, again there was no one there. Medicine Man went to the other side where there were standup latrines and took a piss. He looked down while washing his hands in the sink; as he looked up he was startled to see recognizable faces reflecting in the mirror; he immediately turned around and was met by five monks. In a familiar voice, one of the monks asked, "Are you still going to kill me?" Medicine Man looked at Hitler and said, "You know you're a tough guy when the odds are in your favor at five to one." Hitler responded, "I am going to enjoy killing you. There is no such thing as a fair fight my friend." Suddenly Medicine Man drew out his tomahawks, slashing one of the oncoming monks in the head. He then swung his other tomahawk, slashing another one of the monk's right in the neck. A third monk lunged forward; through Medicine Man's rage he drilled his tomahawk right into the monk's chest. His adrenaline was in high gear as he fought for his life. As he swung at Hitler, Hitler ducked then stuck his bone dagger into Medicine Man's left lung. Staring in Hitler's eyes, Medicine Man fell to the ground while the other monk punched and kicked him repeatedly. Hitler put a choker around Medicine Man's neck and squeezed whatever life was left out of him.

Meanwhile the teacher made faces and shook her head staring at her watch. You could tell she was becoming impatient with Medicine Man's disappearance. Her patience was nearing an end; she grew irritated with us in detention. She was a bitch the whole time. I was getting alarmed myself because Medicine Man had been gone for awhile. We shook our heads in agreement with each other when I said, "Screw it, let's go find him." The three of us got up, heading for the door. The teacher stood up brewing with anger yelling, "Where are you going?" Ghost replied, "Lady, I don't give a damn about your detention! We need to go look for our friend." We ran down the hall to the bathroom as she followed us; there was no sight of Medicine Man. We looked down the hall, the bathrooms, upstairs, outside, and even the cafeteria; there was no sight of him anywhere. Zombie asked, "Preacher, do you think he ditched detention?" I answered, "I doubt it." Zombie asked, "Do you think it's possible he just went home?" Ghost answered, "Not likely. Something is very wrong. Come on, let's go to his house and see if he ditched."

We sprinted all the way to Medicine Man's house. His parents told us he hadn't come home yet. We then ran as fast as we could to Chief's house. When we got there we were frantic trying to tell Chief about Medicine Man's disappearance. Ghost also told Chief about his little bathroom incident. Chief said, "Let's gather a search party and find him." We searched everywhere only to come up empty. I went to bed late that night, it seemed like tomorrow would never get here. I can't ever remember a day that I wanted to go to school so bad. I kept trying to think to myself where Medicine Man could've disappeared to. I wondered if he was hiding from someone or if something happened to him. You envision the worst when it comes to someone you love. My gut feeling was it had something to do with the monks. Maybe the Boogieman got him. He mentioned the hierarchy, could they really be here? Hell, I didn't know anymore - it was like a momentary lapse of reason. I turned the radio on attempting to meditate to rock music. "The Confessor" by Joe Walsh played on the radio so I leaned back on my bed relaxing; eventually the music eroded my worries as I fell asleep.

In the middle of the night, I woke up to the song "You Shook Me" by Led Zeppelin when I heard something hit the window. I sat up in bed when something else hit the window. I got up thinking it might be Medicine Man. As I walked towards the window I witnessed a small pebble hit again. I peeked out the window watching the lawn catch fire, shaped in a pentagram with a large upside down cross in the middle of it. I could feel the fear running down my spine briefly before I became pissed off. I realized at that moment the dogs of war were sending us a message which happened to be on my front lawn. I'd had enough of this shit. My best friend was missing and I was determined to get to the bottom of this, so I rushed to put some clothes on, ran down the stairs, shoving the front door open. When I looked out at the lawn there was no fire. I looked around but nothing was burning. Outside, the neighborhood was silent. I checked around only to see my lawn was perfect. I was beginning to think I was going crazy. I went back inside, left my clothes on and crashed back in bed. I focused on listening to the radio which was now playing "Dazed and Confused" by Led Zeppelin. I guess it must have been classic album night.

Two minutes couldn't have gone by when once again a pebble of some kind hit the window. Now I was really pissed off. I jumped up, ran to the window to peek out; to my horror there was the Tall Man standing on the front lawn holding something in his hands. It appeared to be a necklace. I also noticed his hands had six fingers on each hand. He had a coy smirk on his face. My heart felt as if it was going to jump outside my body. There appeared to be a blue neon light surrounding him, almost as if it were a spotlight. Black crows circled above him while one perched on his shoulder. The old rocker was terrifying to look at. Nobody likes admitting being scared, well I was. The Tall Man had such a menacing presence about him, I think it was the grimacing faces he made that spooked me most. Of all people he picked my house, my shitty luck. I wonder if the music drew him to me. The old man obviously enjoyed rock music. The Tall Man was like a well dressed Frankenstein all in black. His long hair, top hat, and giant height seemed so out of place for an old fucker. This dude was not normal or right in the head. I have never seen someone so pale before. My fear was beginning to boil into hatred and anger as he danced around the pentagram staring at me, all the time waving the necklace.

I was tired of this fucking shit, so I ran down the stairs, grabbing my father's old .38 hand gun from his desk drawer in the study. I ran outside to the front porch; again, the Tall Man wasn't there. I glanced around yet I saw nothing; all you could hear were crickets. Was I going mad, I wondered? As I headed back in the house, I suddenly turned around without notice again, but nothing was in the front lawn. I kept the gun as I walked up the stairs. I was tired, pissed off, and frustrated. The stress was taking a toll on me. I put the gun in my nightstand drawer. I crashed on my bed lying on my stomach. As I laid my head on the pillow I put my hands under the pillow. I felt something under it. I pulled it out and in absolute horror I was staring at Medicine Man's necklace. I pulled the gun from the dresser drawer. I pointed it all over the room. I was downright petrified. I felt so violated. I proceeded to go throughout the whole house with the exception of my mom's room. I found nothing. I was so confused. I kept asking myself over and over, "How could Medicine Man's necklace get in my room?" I put the necklace on a desktop bronze lady justice statue. I went back to bed with my clothes on with gun in hand. As I fought to go to sleep, my eyes finally closed, my mind shut off, and I relented going to sleep to the song "How Many More Times" by Led Zeppelin.

CHAPTER SIXTEEN: THE DISCOVERY

Journals by Preacher

The alarm clock went off in the morning; I awoke startled pointing the gun straight ahead but no one was there. I was really tired from lack of sleep. The radio was still playing Led Zeppelin tunes as I laid in bed listening to "Stairway To Heaven"; I was overcome by sadness. My gut feeling was Medicine Man was dead. I just thought this song was a bad omen. I am a believer you have to read the signs and this sign was not a good one. I took a hot shower. The bathroom was steamed up afterwards as I brushed my teeth in the sink. I wiped the mirror so I could floss when out jumped the face of the Tall Man wearing Medicine Man's necklace. I fell backwards into the towel rack. I went to open the bathroom door but it wouldn't open. I tried opening the door again, this time it opened so I ran out of there. I went to my bedroom, checked the bronze statue; the necklace was gone. The radio played "Valley of the Kings" by Blue Murder as I got dressed. I fell back onto my bed trying to race getting my clothes on. I grabbed my stuff, went down the stairs, and put the gun back in my father's old study.

As I ran out the door I was greeted by the tribe members. I said to the guys, "Are you ready to be petrified?" Zombie immediately asked, "What happened?" I told the guys about my run in with Tall Man. Zombie asked, "Preacher, who is the Tall Man?" Chief answered, "The Tall Man is Crowley." Zombie asked, "What does he want?" I answered, "He is possessed by the Devil. With this maniac, there is no place to run, there is no place to hide, and begging for your soul to keep will only prolong death. From what I can tell there is nothing we can do to stop him. How you stop a killing machine like him, I have no idea." Wolf said, "Fear has been reborn in the Village, evil has returned for the reckoning. Crowley and his druid monks have come to deliver hell at our front door." Maverick remarked, "Ah fuck him!" Ghost asked, "What about the Boogieman?" Chief asked, "What about him?" Ghost asked, "Well who is he? Is he with the monks?" Wolf answered, "Whoever that creepy bastard is, he has come to release evil here." Raven asked, "Hey man, how do we kill the supernatural?" I answered, "I don't know yet, I can only tell you Crowley came home." Chief said, "The only facts we know is God created the sick fucks and Satan delivered them."

I asked, "Has anyone heard from Medicine Man yet?" Wolf answered, "I've already been to Medicine Man's house; he's still missing. His parents contacted the police yesterday but they have to wait 24 hours to file a missing persons report." Animal interrupted, "That is so fucked up." Wolf stated, "His parents are worried sick over this. Preacher, after school you should go talk with his parents. Need I remind you we also have another problem to deal with?" Stressed out, Zombie asked, "What? Don't you think our plates are pretty full with worry already?" Wolf answered, "With everything that's going on, we have overlooked Blackwell." Chief responded, "Shit, we have been so busy I forgot all about Blackwell. After school let's go check out the church." I said, "Guys, my gut feeling is something bad happened." Some of the boys disagreed with me, so I was hoping for the best. Entering the school we were all late for class.

In math class I could see Zombie, sitting in the back of the room, ogling one of the girls. The teacher called on Zombie to come up to the blackboard to illustrate solving the math equation. Zombie answered, "That's okay, I'll take the zero." The classroom was in an uproar filled with laughter. Zombie was always a hotdog; showing off to the world how good he was in math was always a proud moment for him. I was puzzled. The teacher again told Zombie to get up and solve the equation, again Zombie said, "No, I'll take the zero." The teacher threatened Zombie with going to the Principal's office. Zombie couldn't afford any more trouble, so he reluctantly got up from his desk, slowly walked to the blackboard holding his book in front of him, which again was unusual. The teacher said, "Well put the book down; let's get to work." All of a sudden a girl started laughing pointing to Zombie's private parts while the classroom erupted hysterically in laughter. I couldn't believe my eyes: Zombie had a giant hard-on. It figures, only Zombie. In less than a minute, he had knocked out the math equation to perfection. The teacher, fighting back from laughing herself, asked sarcastically, "Would you like to take a few minutes to air it out?" The class again erupted with laughter.

Without warning I heard a scream from down the hall; a girl ran inside and said, "They found Medicine Man." We bolted from class and followed everyone else to the gym auditorium. As we opened the gym doors, we bumped into the other tribe members who stood in shock looking up to see Medicine Man's body hanging from the gym rafters. I fell to my knees crying. It was devastating to see my best friend that way. I looked around, speechless and dizzy. I felt as if someone ripped my heart out. I felt so lightheaded trying to keep my balance as I walked underneath my hanging friend. My mind kept replaying memories in high speed and I couldn't shut it off. Many students were yelling, crying, and screaming. Chief demanded, "Somebody get him down from there!" I have no idea how anyone could have hung him up there. We had no way of getting him down. I could tell he had been through hell. I noticed he was wearing his necklace when I blacked out.

When I awoke the Fire Department had gotten Medicine Man's body down from the rafters. There were cops everywhere. I knew we were all going to be visited and questioned by the police; worse was knowing they weren't going to believe us. Rumors were flying around the school about what happened to him. It was tough listening to the rumors circulate. There was no detention that day and we all needed to visit the Wizard immediately. More conflict was on the horizon when media reporter Marilyn Jenner broke the bad news that the Mayor's daughter had gone missing. This was the second girl reported missing in less than a week. The neighborhood was in panic mode; that's when finger pointing exploded throughout the village.

Wizard was saddened by the news of Medicine Man and the Mayor's daughter. He looked at all of us while feeling our pain as well as his own. Wizard grabbed Chief and said, "I can see the rage burning inside you." Chief yelled, "I am going to kill them all!" Wizard replied, "You have already done enough! I warned you all but you didn't listen to my warning. Evil is upon us! It's time to survive! Your suffering and anger won't change the world. Revenge won't bring Medicine Man back." Chief looked at Wizard with tears falling down his cheek, took a deep breath then exhaled, "I'm not looking to change the world; I am going to burn it down." Chief opened the front door then simply walked away. I told everyone let him go. Delilah will rehabilitate him.

My best friend had been killed and my emotions were all over the place. The air was hard to breathe watching Chief feel responsible. It was killing me inside. I said to Wizard, "We have another problem." Wizard asked, "And what is that? You boys have several problems now, I assure you." I answered, "Blackwell is a psychopath." Wizard said, "Preacher, you got to let this silly feud with Blackwell go. It serves no purpose. It will not bring your father back. Your father strayed from his faith." I answered back in anger, "This has nothing to do with my father! I knew who my father was. My father had a disease. Blackwell has a couple screws loose in his head. He is bringing zombies to life from the dead. Have you seen Father Blackwell since we left?" Wizard responded, "No. I heard he went on vacation. I look forward to talking with Father when he gets back." Beast said, "Well I don't think he will be making it back anytime soon. That is, unless you plan on visiting him in the resurrection and I don't foresee that happening." Wizard asked, "What are you talking about?" Beast answered, "There was a problem in the cemetery at some old funeral parlor where zombies lit up the parlor; Blackwell died in the basement fire. Hell, the whole parlor exploded." Wizard replied, "What have you boys done? Why didn't you help him? Crowley himself used to partake in this type of behavior before he disappeared. Now you're telling me not only is Blackwell involved with Crowley's Tomb, now he's dead. Why didn't you tell me of this before?" Zombie yelled, "We have been preoccupied by the Boogie Man, the Tall Man, and those crazy monks for Christ sake, Wizard!" Wizard yelled back, "I warned you all of this! Evil is among us now! The Village's suffering will be legendary and so will yours. We're all going straight to hell for this! Crowley will send us all there in body bags, you can bet on that!" In a confident tone of revenge I answered, "Hell is gonna have to wait a little longer until I kill that bastard. I plan to send him to his original maker." Wizard replied, "Preacher, Hell is the only place you will meet him." Shadow answered, "We'll be waiting for him Wizard." I said, "Every dipshit has a weakness. We just have to find his." Wizard responded, "What weakness? The only thing you boys will find is death. You kids don't understand they fight from a different plane and realm. You're fighting an ancient battle that you can't possibly win! It was not your battle to fight; that destiny was ordained by God and his army of the apocalypse. This has become a fucking mess!"

Changing the subject my voice cracked as I said to Wizard, "We need to borrow your van." Wizard asked, "Why?" I answered, "You don't want to know." Wizard threw me the keys and said, "Preacher, whatever you boys do, be careful." We all piled up in the old van, drove down the street, picking up Chief along the way. We drove to Animal's house, grabbed some tools, plywood, and loaded a bunch of 2x4's in the back of the van. We squeezed into the van when Chief said, "Let's go to the morgue." We drove off headed towards that creepy place.

It was after midnight, rain was pouring in sorrow outside as we drove by countless street lights. We were listening to "Shout at the Devil" by Motley Crue on the radio. As we pulled in the dark parking lot I turned off the lights, parking the van near a large dumpster. I left the keys in the ignition then said, "Whoever gets out first, be ready to pick us up."

We got out of the van; the thunder was crashing while the lightning streaked across the sky. I noticed the sky was blacker than the ace of spades. There were only a handful of cars in the parking lot. We crept to the front door, the doors were locked. The morgue was closed to the public at that hour. As I looked in the front door there was someone asleep at the front desk.

We followed Ninja who lead us around to the back of the building. We saw two people on a smoke break outside. Ninja sprinted to get closer to the door without being seen. As the workers turned their back to walk inside, Ninja rushed for the door. Just as it went to close, Ninja latched onto the door. He waved to us and we all raced to the door. We slowly made our way in following Ninja down a long hallway. It was quiet as we continued downstairs until we found the autopsy room. The hallway lights made a creepy buzzing sound. Ninja slightly cracked the door open, peeking inside he saw three people around the table performing an autopsy. We followed him down another long hallway where we came across an intersection of hallways. One sign pointed upstairs to the front. So we split up into three groups of four investigating the other hallways. Chief, Animal, Beast and Magic took the emergency stairs down to avoid being caught in the elevator. Wolf, Shadow, Raven and Zombie took the hallway going left, while Ninja, Maverick, Ghost and I went to the hallway on the right.

Traveling down the emergency stairs Chief came to a door. Beast became impatient and opened it while Chief shook his head in frustration. Chief whispered to Beast, "By all means, take the lead, dickhead!" The hallway was dark; only lit up by exit signs. Beast headed away from the exit signs. The silence of the hall was creepy. After passing several rooms Beast came across big stainless steel doors. Magic said, "I don't think this is a good idea. Why would they put Medicine Man down here?" Chief said, "They have to store him somewhere." Magic answered back, "Yeah, my guess would be the viewing room and this certainly isn't going to be that room." Without thinking as usual, Beast opened the stainless steel doors; they could feel the cold smother them. Beast walked inside while Chief turned on the light next to the wall. It was colder than a windy winter's night during Christmas. There were bodies everywhere the guys looked. Beast said, "It's like dawn of the dead down here. It's a good thing Blackwell can't get his hands on them." The unknown bodies were on shelves just like you would put food on a rack. Animal asked, "What the hell is this?" Chief answered, "It's a big fridge to store bodies I guess. I don't think this is protocol to store dead people. These poor bastards! Start searching for Medicine Man." Animal said, "Man it stinks in here." Magic replied, "Whoever smelt it dealt it." Bodies were piled on pallets; bodies stacked one on top of the other. There were racks throughout the storage area. It was one big meat locker. Beast asked, "How many bodies do you think there are?" Animal answered, "Too many." Magic found a clipboard hanging on the wall with individual lists protected in plastic. Magic quickly scrolled down pages of names with no luck; Medicine Man's name was not on the list. Magic said, "There are over three hundred bodies down here, Medicine Man's not one of them." Chief said, "If they ever did an inspection of this shit hole, this place would be shut down. Let's get the fuck out of here and wait for the others outside." Magic replied, "Now that's the best news I've heard all night."

Ninja meanwhile darted down the hall as we followed behind him. We came upon a door that had a lock on it. Maverick pulled out bolt cutters then cut the lock. We quickly entered the room. It was freezing in there. Ghost hit the light switch; I couldn't believe my eyes. There was an enormous amount of steel doors stacked high on each wall. It looked as though the entire walls were made of large file cabinets, except the drawers contained bodies instead of documents. Mortified, Ghost asked, "Jesus! What do we do now?" I answered, "Start looking through the storage doors for Medicine Man." Ninja responded, "That might take all night." I gave him a dirty look pointing to the storage doors. We were rapidly opening and closing, unzipping and zipping, as fast as we could. The faces were the hardest to look at. I could hear grumbling when Ninja yelled, "Oh Shit! I found him." We all rushed over to see our friend; we were disheartened by what we saw. Ninja said, "God damn! They did a number on him." Ghost asked, "I wonder how many of those bastards he took with him?" Maverick answered, "Obviously not enough." I said, "Zip him up. Let's take him home." So I lead us out of the room while the others formed a line lifting him up to rest on their shoulders and carried him out.

Wolf was leading his pack down the hall when he heard loud conversations coming from one of the doors. Wolf whispered, "Hurry up", then bent under the break room lounge door as the rest followed. Zombie heard the song "Creep" by Radiohead on the lounge radio. The smell of popcorn made everyone hungry. Wolf passed a few offices when he found the embalming room. Beginning to panic, Zombie asked, "Are you nuts? I am not going in there! You guys are out of your sick demented minds. Why are we even considering going in there? This sucks! I don't know why I keep letting you talk me into this creepy shit." Raven grabbed Zombie whispering, "Stop fucking whining man! It's driving me crazy! While you're at it, stop waving that stick around, you almost hit me." Wolf made a signal to quiet down. So we quietly walked in the room; there were several tables with big overhead lights and weird medical tools on the tables. Also sitting on the stainless tables were several different types of machines for God only knows what purposes. We noticed two tables that actually had bodies on them. We looked at the bodies in disgust. Zombie covered his mouth then began to vomit all over the tile floor. Shaking his head, Wolf yelled, "For Christ sake Zombie! Let's get the hell out of here!" We raced out of there, but unfortunately there were still a couple more rooms to explore. Wolf whispered, "Let's split up, me and Raven will check the laboratory room. I don't want whiny to puke all over the floors again. Whiny, go with Shadow and check the room with double doors at the end of the hall."

Raven carefully opened the laboratory door as they entered. The lab room shelves had dim lights containing tons of jars with really creepy-looking remains inside. They walked to the end of the room which had a connecting door. The door had a round glass window on it. Raven said, "Be my guest man, the last time I looked inside something I almost pissed myself." Wolf leaned his head onto the glass but couldn't see anything; it was too dark. Wolf slowly turned the knob as they entered the room. Raven said, "My God, it's cold in here." Wolf was feeling around the wall for the light switch when we heard a click, the lights went on. To Raven's dismay, he saw two rows of stainless steel tables with sheets covering dead bodies, only the feet were uncovered with tags on their toes. Wolf said, "You take the row on the left and I'll take the other one." Raven answered, "Shit! This really sucks bro." One at a time they uncovered each sheet in horror. They made it to the last two bodies but none were Medicine Man. Relieved, Raven said, "Let's get out of here man, this place gives me the willies."

Meanwhile Shadow and Zombie made it to the end of the hall. The sign on the door was marked *Viewing Room*. Shadow said, "Bingo." Zombie tried pulling the double doors open but the doors were locked. Shadow said, "I can fix that." Shadow stuck something in the key lock and after a few minutes was able to unlock one of the doors. Just as Shadow opened the door, for a brief second he was met with a neon blue glow. Suddenly the Tall Man appeared in the room. Laughing, the Tall Man said, "I've been waiting for you." Shadow answered back, "I haven't." The Tall Man lunged, attempting to grab Shadow but missed. Zombie screamed out, "Oh no! Shut the fucking door!" Opening the door must have tripped off a sensor or something because the alarm went off. Shadow slammed the door shut while Zombie quickly stuck his wooden stick between the door handles as they took off running down the hall. The alarm was disturbingly loud; the hallway lights were flashing. Raven and Wolf were just ahead running for their lives. Wolf passed the break room when someone opened the door and yelled out, "Stop!" Raven collided with the lady, knocking her to the floor. Zombie ran past the employee while Shadow leaped over the lady who was attempting to get up. The tribe kept running through the morgue when Shadow yelled to the others, "Hurry up, security is behind us!" The tribe ran past Raven who had stopped while winding his manriki chain as fast as he could, then launched the chain at the closest security guard. The chain stuck then wrapped around the guard's ankles; he quickly fell to the ground as the other guards were tripping over his body. Raven reached in his pouch, dropping several small caltrops on the floor then took off running to catch up with the others. As the security guards chased them down the hall, one of the guards landed on the caltrops, He slid then lost his balance, falling to the ground only to land on more of the caltrops that pierced and dug into his skin all over his body. Raven laughed while he ran out the door when he heard the guards screaming in pain from the caltrops. He had a smirk on his face as he met the others. Raven quickly jumped in the back of the van. The van radio blasted Aerosmith's "Train Kept A Rollin". Chief hit the pedal to the metal and we all got the fuck out of there.

We drove to the cemetery, cut the gate lock, and drove through an isolated back road till we came upon the power lines. It had stopped raining as we drove down a muddy road until we found a safe opening and pulled over. We all took turns unloading the wood in the back. Animal and Beast made a platform that stood off the ground. We lifted Medicines Man's body onto it. We played Medicine Man's favorite album, Pink Floyd's "Dark Side of the Moon" as a tribute to our fallen friend. Wolf put two tokens over his eyes then we all said our last goodbyes to our friend. I was inconsolable; my best friend's death shook me to the core. Chief lit the platform on fire as we gave our brother an honorable Indian burial at his parent's request. I did what I thought was right, but there was no way in hell I was going to hand over my best friend's body to Crowley or anyone else for that matter.

We stayed most of the night taking turns telling old stories about our lost brother. Medicine Man had long silky black hair. On special occasions he would braid his hair. He was one tough warrior. He was always mild mannered, liked talking in riddles, aspired to go to medical school, had very hard working parents and was an only child. He never backed down from anyone or took any shit. He was so musically talented. He loved playing his guitar and rocking out to Pink Floyd. Medicine Man always talked about the spirit world, which drove Animal and Beast crazy. Medicine Man enjoyed getting high with Raven often. He was a true warrior. That's what I remember most about him. Chief was hit hard from Medicine Man's death. I think he felt guilty and responsible, but that was why he was named Chief in the first place. He might have had a tough exterior to most, but we all knew his interior character was a heart of gold. Medicine Man wasn't the only one who would have followed Chief off a bridge, we all would. He was our pied piper. Just before early morning light we left Medicine Man and drove the van back to Wizard's. I left the keys under the mat. We only had a few hours to sneak back home, get a few hours of sleep, and then get ready for school. Saying goodbye to my friend will be the only thing I will remember about this night. I only hope the gate keeper finds Medicine Man's soul a nice resting spot on the other side.

CHAPTER SEVENTEEN: THE INTERROGATION

Journals by Preacher

Things were starting to calm down a little, but unfortunately for us we were in for a rude awakening when we got to school. It seemed our luck was still running south. Meanwhile, Wizard noticed a few media trucks parked on the front curb, while he was still reeling from the death of Medicine Man. It was as if he was mourning the loss of a son. He went to investigate the truck parked in the street when he was surprised by that bitch reporter Marilyn Jenner and others. She put a microphone in his face then asked, "Do the Cemetery Boys worship the Devil?" Not amused, Wizard replied, "Are you kidding me?" Jenner asked, "So does that mean they are involved in a satanic occult?" Irked, Wizard answered, "No they are not. These are good kids. Where do you get off making such assumptions or accusations?" Jenner asked, "Did the Cemetery Boys have anything to do with the disappearance of Lisa Miller or Taylor Wilson?" Wizard, about to erupt answered, "Absolutely not! Did you?" The bitch was just throwing out questions and pissing on our name. She kept pushing when she asked, "Did they kill a student at school?" Wizard shouted, "Lady, that student was the boys' best friend! It would be wise to back off. I don't think you know what you're dealing with here." Ignoring him, she asked, "What is your involvement with the Cemetery Boys?" Wizard had enough and yelled, "Who gave you the right to play judge, jury, and executioner? The media has ruined mankind with irresponsible, shallow and judgmental behavior! You love to destroy people because of your own insecurities! You people would do anything for the almighty buck! You're a fucking disgrace! Why not stick to positive stories instead of slandering the world. Why must you butcher the common man and woman with unrealistic expectations, you fucking cunt? All you do is murder the world. I assure you the kids have no illegal or criminal involvement! This sharpshooting incident of yours is over!!" Wizard walked into his house slamming the door shut.

We walked into our separate classes only to be informed to go down to the conference room by the Principal's office. As we all walked unsuspectingly into the room, there were two older gentlemen waiting for us. One of the guys said, "Good morning gentlemen. My name is Detective Parks and this is my partner Detective Bloom." Raven asked, "Detective of what?" We broke out in laughter. Both immediately flashed their badges. Detective Bloom said, "That's really funny son."

Raven angrily replied, "I'm not your fucking son, man!" Bloom in a stern voice responded back, "You minnows all better take a seat. We can do this the easy way or the hard way. It's your choice, but you better figure it out quick and cooperate! Things could get very unpleasant in the very near future for you boys." None of us flinched with any emotion. The funny thing about police is they lie and play mind-fuck games to trap you. We weren't having any of their BS.

Bloom said, "When I yell out your name say 'here'. George St. Louie!" I said, "Here." Bonzo McAfee! Ghost answered, "Present." Casey Lesnar! Maverick said, "Yep!" Layne Hendrix! Zombie answered, "In the flesh." Moto Musashi! Ninja answered, "Present." Conrad Achilles! Wolf answered, "Here." Rocky Luciano! Magic answered, "The one and only." Ramone Fuentes! Beast answered, "Si." Moses King! Animal shouted, "Yes indeed!" John Morrison! Chief answered, "Here for the moment." Zachary Wallace, Raven sighed, "Yeah man." And Mercury Panzani! Mercury Panzani! Mercury Panzani! Shadow sarcastically asked, "For the love of Christ man, who else would it be sir?" Bloom yelled, "Hey Jesus, did you forget your fucking name? Keep an eye on Jesus for me!" Shadow responded, "Never call me that for I am not so willing to let the enemy nail me to a cross without a fight sir!" Detective Parks said, "Seems like you boys have had quite an adventurous summer. We have two missing students: one which you know is the Mayor's daughter, not to mention a murdered student and a missing body. Witnesses at the morgue said some teenagers broke into the viewing room, and to top it off assaulted three staff members. You tadpoles wouldn't know anything about that, would you?" Bloom was carefully observing everyone's reaction. Parks said, "So nobody knows what happened to the body of Geronimo Achak?" I answered, "His name is Medicine Man sir! He was my best friend, now he has crossed over to the next place as a menacing spirit of death known as the grey rider. He will come back for his own revenge that I assure you." Parks said, "That's a very amusing and touching story but I don't believe a word of that shit! Maybe you can tell us about what happened to Gina Taylor and Bill Stanzi. You little toads spend an awful lot of time in the cemetery, so let's have it."

Parks walked around, stopped, stood still in front of Raven. He looked directly in Raven's eyes and asked, "What can you tell me about this?" Raven answered, "Medicine Man was our friend, more like a brother, man." Chief said, "We are looking into it ourselves as well; not sure about the rest of the accusations, Detective." Raven asked sarcastically, "Don't you officers have a job to do? The bad guys are out there, not in here man." Detective Parks warned, "Don't man me boy! I would watch that tone and clean up that attitude if I were you son." Raven answered, "I already told you once, I am not your fucking son, man. You are not me. You will never be me, man. I think I speak for all of us here. You can do what you want to us, but we didn't kill our friend. We have no idea about the others, dude!" Chief stood up, leaned very close to Detective Park's face, and said, "I pray you don't catch them before we do; I want their suffering to be epic! They will not escape my wrath!"

Bloom interrupted, "Who are *they*?" The room became silent. All eyes were on Detective Bloom. Chief answered, "Detectives, if you are going to charge us, then charge us, if not, leave us the fuck alone." Bloom and Parks looked at each other. Bloom turned to me and asked, "Why didn't you stay when you were told to stay at school the other day for questioning?" I answered, "Detectives, we answered all questions needed. That was my best friend, I'll be damned if I am going to spend all day answering the same questions we already answered." Bloom asked, "I suppose you don't know about the whereabouts of Lisa Miller or Taylor Wilson either, do you?" Shadow answered, "No we don't! Have you checked Crowley's Tomb? Maybe you should ask Crowley himself." Bloom answered, "That is very funny kid considering there is no such thing as Crowley's Tomb. That place doesn't exist. It's just an old wise tale so everyone can commit crimes then play the blame game on poor old Crowley's Tomb." Parks said, "You know, a strange thing happened several weeks ago in the cemetery, maybe you boys heard about it. A few police officers were assaulted in a tree house. You wouldn't happen to know anything about that, would you?" The room was silent, nobody said a word. Parks said with a smile, "It's too bad about that piece of shit tree house in the cemetery at Five Points. I heard it was a bad fire that burnt that piece of shit straight to the ground. Nothing but ashes, oh hell, I wouldn't know who did it of course. I guess you wouldn't know about that either though would you?" Nobody made a peep. Bloom decided to put his two cents in as he said, "Funny thing about playing with fire is you usually get burnt, badly! The funnier thing Minions, there will be blood spilled, mainly your own, if you don't tell us what you know. My gut feeling is we will be in touch very soon so don't go anywhere. Whatever is out there is evil, it has a taste for killing, and it won't stop until everything is dead. If you don't start talking, you might not get another chance. Whoever you boys pissed off they have come a calling." Parks said, "I'll give you tonight to think about it; if I don't hear from you tomorrow I'll be making house calls. One way or the other I promise you're going to talk to me." Bloom said, "I wouldn't leave the house if I were you, it is a very unsafe place right now for you boys. The killer is stalking the neighborhood, you never know if you'll be next. Have a good day gentlemen."

As the detectives turned their backs, Chief stood up, put his index finger by his mouth and gave us the sign to be quiet. The detectives left the room. Chief, still keeping his finger near his mouth, walked down the hall as we followed. Shadow whispered under his breath, "You have a safe weekend as well, onion breath." We all followed Chief outside as we sat in the grass. Chief said, "Dumb and dumber don't have anything but suspicion and assumptions. These clowns have no leads whatsoever, they're just fishing. They probably think we are going to ditch school so they can follow us. Let's go back to class and let those turds fry all day in the car playing detectives. After school, go home; let's meet up at Bishops, say 8:00 pm. From there we can go visit the Wizard." Zombie sarcastically blurted out, "Oh, I am sure he already knows about the detectives coming here. They think we had something to do with those girls. What if they suspect we had something to do with the station wagon murder? What if they suspect we killed that girl hanging in the tree? Use your heads; they gotta know it was us that assaulted the cops in the cemetery. Wizard is going to have our fucking asses!" Chief replied, "Don't worry, I will handle the Wizard."

Sitting in an unmarked car parked outside, Bloom said to Parks, "These little shits know a lot more than what they're telling." Parks answered, "I know, that's why we are going to leave them alone. It's time to be patient, sit back, and observe while this whole thing unfolds." Bloom said, "Whoever killed those kids isn't finished." Parks looked out the car window, turned to Bloom and responded, "Those kids are going to expose the killer to us. I just hope we stop him before the killer kills again." Bloom asked, "If they know who it is, why don't they just tell us?" Parks answered back, "My first thought would be revenge. I'm not sure yet, maybe they don't know, but we will find out soon enough. I have a hunch this is much bigger than we realize. These kids are defiant. In this neighborhood we're not going to be able to break them down. They might be worse than criminals; their loyalty to one another is a bond that won't allow them to rat on each other. Also, look at the way they dress, the way they act, and where they hang out." Bloom agreed then said, "They are morbid little bastards, I'll give them that." Parks remarked, "So much for the glory of the cemetery."

Journals by Raven

We walked home together with the exception of a few who had detention. I was mentally exhausted from all this, man. When I got home I sat on my bed and turned my small radio on, Pantera's "Walk" was jamming. I turned the volume up. I was blowing off steam imitating the lead singer from Pantera, dancing around my room as if I was the singer at a concert. I was stripping as I threw my clothes all over the room. I jumped in bed wanting the music to put me to sleep for awhile so I could relax. Just as I dozed off, I heard a voice interrupt the song through the radio talking directly at me, "We're watching you." I jumped up, looked inside my closet then outside my bedroom window but there was no one there. I leaned over, staring in the mirror when the voice from the radio said, "We're waiting for you." I yelled out, "Waiting for what?" The voice on the radio answered, "To kill you." In anger I picked up the radio and threw it against the wall. It broke into several pieces. The voice still coming from the broken speaker said, "See you soon." Laughter came from it next. I opened my window then threw the broken radio out the fucking window. I covered my ears falling to my knees. I had a migraine headache that was pounding like a drum. My stomach was in a sickened knot. I was stressed out, a bit scared while talking to myself. All these events seemed like a bad dream. I got up from my knees, composed myself, got dressed, and ran out of the house. I continued running till I reached Chief's house.

I told Chief about the paranormal activity. Chief said, "Let's go meet the others at Bishops." As we walked through the neighborhood the other tribe members joined us. Preacher opened the door as we all walked in hearing Nickelback's "Side of a Bullet" playing on the jukebox. We sat in the last couple of booths in the back. The diner was packed. I waved at Mel while he waved back. Ghost said, "Mel has to be happy tonight, this place is jumping." We all agreed. Shadow mentioned, "An unmarked car followed us." Chief, looking out the window said, "I wouldn't worry about those assholes."

Glancing at Chief, Delilah asked, "What can I get you guys tonight?" It was no secret Delilah had eyes for Chief. Chief gazing in her eyes with a grin answered, "Give all the boys chili and a near beer on me tonight." She smiled at Chief, gave him a wink, replying, "Last of the big spenders" then walked away. Maverick asked, "Chief why don't you ask Delilah out?" Chief smiled, hesitated then answered, "I never go out with women with symbolic names." Some of the guys laughed.

Confused, Maverick asked, "Why?" Preacher answered for Chief, "Chief is worried he will lose his powers if he gets involved with Delilah." Ninja asked, "What's so bad about Delilah?" Everyone listened closely as Preacher said, "Samson loved Delilah but she betrayed Samson for money. Haven't you guys ever seen the famous painting of Delilah cutting Samson's hair while he was sleeping?" Maverick remarked, "Well, it's a little late for that. Chief doesn't have much hair anymore by his own free will." I chimed in, "Man, all women betray for one reason or another." Chief answered, "Usually for money or the lust of someone else." Preacher again shared his opinion, "Through the history of time it's been proven that the grass isn't greener on the other side, they merely trade it for weeds." Chief replied, "I have a bigger calling, destiny awaits my name to be remembered forever. I'm not going to make the same mistakes Adam made." Maverick asked, "Who is Adam?" Preacher answered, "Chief's talking about Adam and Eve. Eve could've had anything she wanted but as all women do, she desired what she couldn't have. She didn't have the willpower to say no to Satan's temptations, she had no appreciation for life, she was selfish. She not only convinced herself but also Adam to eat from the tree of life, she selfishly felt she deserved it. Instant gratification has us still fucked even to this day. So much for Jesus paying for our sins, he cruised up to Heaven while we were left to suffer endlessly as Satan pisses all over us on a daily basis. Chief believes we are all paying for Eve's sin. That's how his warped mind works." Zombie yelled out, "Well hell, I prefer a symbolic woman just like Wanda." Everyone laughed as Zombie patted Preacher on the shoulder. Delilah with the help of Mel brought us our near beers and chili. Preacher said, "It feels like the last supper." Ghost stood up, held up a can of near beer and toasted, "If it is our last supper, not a better supper than Bishops. May we one day be remembered as the legendary Cemetery Boys who became immortal men." Everyone held up their beers and said, "I'll drink to that, cheers!" The juke box played "Draggin the Line" by Tommy James.

Journals by Preacher

Later that night as we approached the Wizard's house we noticed he wasn't outside on his front porch. Wolf said, "That's odd, the old man is always on his porch drinking and smoking." I jogged to the front porch, noticed the front door was open while the screen door was still closed. So we decided to wait for him while sitting on the front steps. Ten minutes had gone by, nobody came to the door. Chief said, "I'll go get the old man." I said, "I'll go with you." As I got to the top of the porch I noticed the door handle had dry blood on it. I knocked, nobody answered. Chief called out to the Wizard a couple times yet there was no response. I said, "Let's go in." As we opened the screen door we called Wizard's name but again there was no response. We went room to room; nobody was home. We searched the kitchen, down the stairs to the backyard and in the basement. Wizard's old van was still there. I said, "Something is definitely wrong Chief." Chief said, "Wizard hasn't left his house since his wife died." I asked, "Do you think the crazy bastards from Crowley's Tomb came looking for the items we took?" Chief answered, "I don't know, you better call the guys in. We need to start searching for that fucking pentagram and medallion." The guys searched Wizard's house thoroughly, unfortunately no pentagram or medallion was found. Wizard had vanished without a trace.

We waited several hours for Wizard with no luck; he never came back to the house. I asked, "I know this might be a stretch, but do you think that pentagram had special powers that led the monks to Wizard?" Wolf answered, "I doubt it." Raven asked, "They could have killed us all if they wanted to, why didn't they? Those bastards have been toying with us, man." Magic asked, "Why would they do that?" Raven answered, "I believe they could've caught us before we made it out of the cemetery if they really wanted to, man. I think the monks did it for the love of the game. This is a game to them, they enjoy the hunt; just like the adrenaline rush we get running around in the cemetery or Crowley's Tomb." Maverick yelled, "Well let the fucking games begin!" Ninja said, "I agree with Raven. These assholes killed Medicine Man to get us to go back to their neck of the woods. It didn't work. We didn't hurry right back there for revenge. So my guess is the pentagram and medallion led them to Wizard somehow. More than likely they are holding him hostage knowing we will go right back to those bastards. I also believe the Tall Man really is Crowley; somehow he has powers to affect our subconscious mind through thoughts and dreams. I think Preacher was right, he might be a demon." Chief replied, "I think you guys are right. It was my idea, my vote, and my decision to go to Crowley's Tomb. It was my poor judgment that brought not only the pentagram here but the death of our friend." Wolf said, "That's bullshit! We all wanted to go, even those that may have voted no originally still wanted to go, and we all did it of our own free will. Wizard has been a father figure to us all. I think we all owe it to Wizard to go rescue and save his life from those misfits." Chief answered back, "There won't be any vote on this. Anyone who doesn't want to come with, I truly understand, you will not be looked down upon in any form of judgment. For those that are going, pack heavy with weapons and light on food. We need every weapon we can get our hands on. If they want us to bring the fight to them, we will do just that, let's give them a war they can't believe. I think it's time for Crowley's monks to bleed. I am going to kill every one of his henchmen including Crowley himself. I am leaving tomorrow at noon. Anyone who wants to join me, I'll be at Bishops. I suggest you all go home and decide what's best for you." Chief turned on the radio, sat out on the Wizard's porch drinking whiskey and listening to "Mama Told Me Not To Come" by Three Dog Night.

CHAPTER EIGHTEEN: THE GREAT DIVIDE

Journals by Chief

Early morning I walked alone through the neighborhood reminiscing of the past. I kept hearing the song "Moving in Stereo" by the Cars in the back of my mind. My heart felt like someone was wringing the life out of it. I walked by Wizard's with the eerie reminder why I had to go back to Crowley's Tomb. He was like a father to me. I had no idea if Wizard was dead or alive. In the back of my mind a tug of war was going on. My guilt was eating me alive like cancer. Wizard was well respected; he loved the Village. I loved Wizard; I know he loved me too. I owed him everything. If he could be saved, I was going to save him against all odds somehow. I wasn't sure if the guys were coming or not. Maybe it was suicide, what choice did I really have? As I walked along the outside of the cemetery gates the song "Lunatic Fringe" by Red Rider came to mind.

Hope in my book is a failed word. Whatever came from hope? Hope never brought God before me, hope never brought Medicine Man back to life, hoping the world would change never brought out the good in people; hope is the beautiful letdown. Hope is like blood in the water and Satan could smell it miles away. Hope in God's eyes meant human suffering as he witnessed with a smile. Apparently he was still bitter about his son's sacrifice on the cross because I never witnessed his forgiveness myself; though I did read about his wrath for revenge and murder in the Bible. I guess there is no forgiving and there certainly is no forgetting. It only fueled my anger that was growing inside me like a disease. The message was simple for me: kill or be killed. I wasn't giving my revenge to God, that's for sure. My revenge would be of my own hand and it would be legendary. Unlike the goals of my fellow tribe members, not only did I want to be remembered, I wanted to kill Satan, his Demons, and the person they called Death. I wanted to kill the hypocrite himself known as God for his irresponsibility of creating such evilness not to mention his jealous Angels. I had every intention of killing the monks as well. My rage was so bad I wanted to kill anything at this point. God created the world including Satan; I wanted him to take responsibility just as he wanted us to pay for our sins. I had no intention of going to a Heaven that was predicated to bowing down to such a self-worshiping prick. I wasn't going to be anyone's servant or slave. As I walked to Bishops clearing my head I concluded my mission in life was of vengeance. My wrath for revenge would go beyond Heaven or Hell. My fury was prepared for eternity in Hell.

I walked in Bishops after wandering around for hours. I immediately greeted Delilah with a big smile as I winked at her. The jukebox played "More than A Feeling" by Boston. As I sat at the counter Delilah playfully asked me, "What can I get you today?" I just ordered a hot chocolate while I glanced out the window. Delilah brought me the hot chocolate topped with extra whipped cream and a cherry on top when she said, "I heard Wizard's missing." I answered "Yeah." She replied, "Don't leave." I asked her, "What makes you say that?" Delilah put her head down; fighting back tears she answered, "I see it in your eyes. The backpack gives it away as well." Delilah had a worried look in her eyes as she stared into my eyes. One by one all the guys walked through the front entrance as the song "Rooster" by Alice in Chains played on the jukebox. Preacher smiled and gave me a bear-hug while asking, "You didn't think we'd let you go alone did you?" The guys took turns embracing me. I was overwhelmed with emotions. Wolf asked, "Are you ready?" I answered, "Let's go finish the game." We all said our goodbyes to Delilah and Mel.

The guys walked out the door when I turned to Delilah and slowly walked up to her by the jukebox. I gave her a long, deep, slow, wet kiss then looked in her eyes with a smile and said, "I have been meaning to play a couple songs for you." I reached in my pocket, putting a quarter in the jukebox. I selected two songs: the first was "Loving You Sunday Morning" by the Scorpions. The second one was "In Loving Memory" by Alter Bridge. I said to Delilah, "I dedicate these two songs to you. I love you and always will. This is not goodbye, for we will meet in eternity where I will wait for you." Tears flowed like a river down Delilah's face. We embraced each other as I wiped the tears from her eyes when she cracked a smile and hugged me as tight as she could. Delilah said, "I have loved you from the first time I set eyes on you. I loved you then and I love you now. I want you to know I will love no other." I leaned over giving her my last kiss of sorrow then I simply walked out. I always hated goodbye so I chose not to say anything at all. As we walked across the street near the gates, I broke my own rule as I looked back one last time. With the door opened Mel had his arm around Delilah when she smiled then yelled, "I dedicate this song to you!" I could hear the song "I Remember You" by Skid Row as Delilah and Mel waved. We waved back then walked through the open gates. Preacher said to the others, "I am happy to see Chief finally show his feelings for Delilah." I knew I had to focus on what was ahead but it was hard not to think about Delilah. Delilah was amazing. She had a beautiful personality, big red luscious lips, and beautiful dark brown eyes. She was always kind, compassionate, and giving to a fault. There was no mistaking how we loved each other. She was my only purity in life. I had held back all this time, when I finally relented to her. It was the first and last time, but a memory that will last forever. If anyone could have witnessed that kiss they would have understood. The tribe witnessed it from outside of the window. She was far more pure than an angel could ever be. She had to come from a place much farther than Elysium. Delilah was so pure that Heaven was not worthy enough for her.

It was a shitty day out as I refocused on the task at hand. The sky was overcast, windy, and a bad scent in the air of trouble was falling upon us. Shadow noticed an unmarked car turning into the cemetery yelling, "That's the car that has been following us!" I took off running as the tribe scrambled behind me. I stopped for a minute trying to figure out what to do when I saw what appeared to be Medicine Man on a horse. He waved to a path then simply disappeared. It freaked me out but I knew it had to be a sign so I ran to the path where he stood. It was near the creek where no car could get through. I glanced around trying to find Medicine Man when Maverick said, "I think it's Parks and Bloom." I replied, "Where we're going they will never be able to keep up." To their credit they had ditched their car attempting to follow us on foot. Maverick asked, "What's the plan, Chief?" I said, "I don't have a plan but we might be able to use them as an asset." With a plan brewing in his head, Wolf said, "Listen, I have an idea, let's split up. Preacher can take the boys going through Grove Cemetery then take a shortcut to Riverside Cemetery traveling to Crowley's Tomb by canoe. The rest of us will travel upward through Resurrection Cemetery leaving clues behind so the cops can keep up. We can bop through Gateway Cemetery where we'll eventually meet up under the old wooden bridge by Crowley's." In total disagreement, Zombie yelled, "Are you nuts? That's suicide in every direction for all of us! Going through the wastelands to play with the devil is a bad fucking idea! That plan of yours is fucked!" Wolf shouted, "Do you have a better idea?" I got between the two and said, "Wolf is right, there is no reason for us all to go by foot. We don't have a lot of time for debate." So we divided the tribes. Tribe one walked toward Wasteland Cemetery on foot consisting of me, Wolf, Maverick, Raven, Beast, and his brother Animal. Tribe two led by Preacher consisted of Ninja, Shadow,

Magic, Zombie, and Ghost. Preacher gave a quick speech to everyone before we separated, "A famous person once said, 'If we meet again we will rejoice and embrace, if not, this parting was well made.'" We then parted company in opposite directions. A few minutes later Bloom came to a pathway that split in two opposite directions. One was by the creek that lead west, the other dirt pathway went south. Bloom asked, "What do you think?" Parks answered, "They have no choice but to go south. West leads to the water. I don't think they came here for a swim." Parks and Bloom did not come alone, they had two other off-duty detectives along for the investigation. Parks said, "Let's go south; we need to see what these morbid little shits are up to."

Journals by Preacher

We had taken our shoes off in the creek so the cops couldn't follow our trail. I loathed walking through Grove Cemetery. As we headed down a dirt path near the cemetery, the landscape changed. The gravestones got bigger. Cats were all over the place. I hated the sounds they made. Leaves began to fall off the trees. Ninja asked, "Did they ever catch that sick person here who was digging up corpses?" I answered, "They arrested Gunnar Hornsbee, but later had to let him go because he had a bullshit alibi." Zombie, Mr. Eagle Eyes himself, pointed to an old, gated run-down house. I walked toward it to go check it out. The yard had a foul odor surrounded by roaming chickens. I opened the gate trying to avoid feces on the ground. The front screen door was cracked open so I knocked. With no answer Shadow said, "Let's go in." Ghost said, "I don't think that's a good idea bro." Zombie yelled, "I think it's a really fucked up idea!" I walked in and almost barfed. You could see old raw meat on the table while flies buzzed around everywhere. The place had garbage all over the place. Chicken feathers were on the ground. Suddenly a baby pig ran across the living room screeching. It about scared me to death. Stuffed creatures were mounted all over the walls. Magic said, "Looks like someone still lives here. Whoever it is must be a fanatic hunter." Shadow replied, "Well if someone still lives here they live like pigs." Whining, Zombie answered, "It is obvious pigs live here. Let's get out of here, this place is demented."

I asked, "Did you guys hear that? I swear I heard something running around in the other room." Shadow answered, "Let's go check it out." Zombie replied, "I think we should get out of here. We don't need any more trouble damn it!" Ignoring Zombie, we continued our search through each room when I noticed in the kitchen there were different types of cutting tools near the sink. The counters were full of trash. Dust must have been piled up an inch thick. Magic joked, "This place looks like it hasn't been cleaned in a decade." Ghost opened one of the kitchen cabinets then reached for a weird jar. He looked at the jar in disgust, saying, "Guys you better come check this out." We all stared at the jar, it was full of teeth. I said, "Put that down; let's get out of here." Spooked, we all rushed out the back door. Shadow noticed a large wooden shed further back in the yard. I followed Shadow out of curiosity towards the shed. Shadow opened the shed door like it was his place when he was greeted without warning to the most heinous smell. I couldn't help from dry heaving. The shed was extremely dark inside. Magic felt something bump into him. I turned on a small flashlight and pointed it towards Magic who stood in absolute horror. In an alarmed voice, Magic said, "Oh, shit!" Inside the wood shed was a disturbing sight. We all witnessed a body hanging upside down by its ankles, gutted like a wild animal; it was a naked female body hung from a rope. Her head had been decapitated. Ghost shouted, "We have to report this to the police now God damn it!" Ninja picked up a brown paper sack then peeked inside the bag. It looked like hair. Without thinking he picked the hair out of the bag. It was more than just hair; it was a leather skinned mask with real hair sewn to it. Ghost, recognizing the familiar face, screamed out, "Oh my God, that's Lisa Miller's face!" Zombie demanded, "Let's get the fuck out of here! What if this psycho is here watching us?" We looked at one another then suddenly raced outside of the shed.

We stopped outside to take in a few breaths of fresh air. Hysterical, Zombie yelled, "We've got to report this to the police!" Ghost said, "I agree, there is a psycho on the loose." Meanwhile Magic began singing, "Got You Where I Want You" by the Flys. Zombie lunged at Magic in anger as we had to intervene so a fight didn't break out. Zombie yelled, "You sick fuck! That's not funny! One of our classmates has been butchered like a wild animal and you're mocking the situation with a song! What the fuck is the matter with you?" Magic yelled back, "What the hell is wrong with you man?" Zombie yelled, "You fucking animal!" The arguing stopped when I noticed the kitchen curtains moved. I yelled, "Someone is behind the kitchen curtains!" We came together quickly as we made a dash towards the creek. I could feel the hair on my skin sticking straight out. We were scared out of our fucking minds. We ran through the graveyard; I finally stopped long enough to catch my breath. Ninja leaned over a gravestone only to fall inside a hole. Ninja yelled, "Guys, you better come and take a look at this shit." Shadow asked, "Now what?" Ninja pointed to the gravesite. Ghost asked, "What the hell is going on here?" Magic answered, "It's a little early for Halloween." Zombie yelled, "That's not funny!" I said, "This is one sick individual." Three gravesites had been dug up. Shadow asked, "How do we know it's just one person involved in the digging?" Zombie answered in a panicked voice, "We don't." Magic asked, "Where are we?" I answered, "I think we're about an hour away from the canoes at Riverside. Let's go!"

We continued running until I spotted the mausoleums, that's when I knew we were at Riverside Cemetery. Shadow glanced in the distance asking, "Do you hear that noise?" Ninja said, "It sounds like a tree trimmer or chainsaw. Groundskeepers must be doing work in the area." We reached the unmarked mausoleum where we hid the old canoes. Riverside is a pain in the ass because of the way it floods. Ninja, Zombie and I set the first canoe in the water. Zombie handed the paddles to Ninja as we got in the canoe, waiting for the others. Magic went to take a leak near the bushes. Magic was singing "Uncle Tom's Cabin" by Warrant while taking a leak when he noticed a young boy streak past him. Startled, Magic pissed on his own leg. He yelled, "Shit! Hey kid! Are you lost?" Unfortunately, at the same time the high-pitched grinding noise was nearing him behind the bushes. Grumbling to himself he asked, "Do you think they could have found another bush to trim other than the one I am using?" As Magic turned his back away from the bush, zipping up his pants, he could see everyone in canoes talking to the young kid. Magic laughed out in aggravation between the kid, the noise interrupting his private moment, and of course pissing on his own pants leg.

The buzzing noise was now directly behind him. Clueless, Magic was smiling when we all screamed frantically, "Behind you!" Magic quickly turned around as his jaw dropped; he was met by an ugly deformed beast. Caught totally off-guard, he screamed, "You crazy, ugly bitch!" Her face was deformed; she was tall and grossly overweight, running towards Magic holding a chainsaw. She swung the chainsaw at Magic who ducked out of the way. Magic stumbled as he back pedaled, tripped on a small stump and fell backwards. The bitch again lunged with the chainsaw; the blade sliced Magic's left leg. Blood splattered in the air as she relentlessly lunged at Magic several more times. Zombie reacted without hesitation. He filled that deformed butcher bitch full of bullet holes from his full-size 9mm Beretta handgun from the canoe.

She immediately fell on her back as the chainsaw flung in the air before it dropped, landing on her own leg. The chainsaw sliced right through her leg like hot butter. Terrified, Magic hobbled to the canoe as Shadow tried to help him in the canoe. Within seconds a boned arrow went through the back of Magic's neck. His body fell forward, crashing into the canoe. Terrified, I pulled the kid into the canoe as we paddled to get away.

Zombie fired a couple more shots into the bushes. Looking back, Ghost yelled, "They're behind us!" Ninja paddling asked, "Who?" Ghost yelled, "A family full of butchers!" The butchers screamed at us while making some sort of gestures. Zombie fired several more shots; I think he might have even hit another one, I couldn't say for sure because we were rattled trying to get away. They disappeared with the sound of gunshots. Out of pure desperation we paddled between mausoleums. Shadow almost got bit by a lunging snake dangling in a tree. Stunned, Ghost yelled at me, "They killed Magic!" I yelled back, "Stay down!" We escaped the deformed butchers, but with all the excitement we were lost trying to make it through the flooded mausoleums. Freaked out, Zombie asked, "What are we going to do?" I answered, "Just keep your paddle busy." During all of the commotion the young kid never made a sound.

MAGIC

CHAPTER NINETEEN: UNINVITED

Journals by Chief

It was getting dark out yet we kept leaving little clues behind for the detectives. Resurrection Cemetery was a place we avoided because it was so alien to us. We were not very familiar with it, other than rumors we heard. That cemetery just seemed as if it came from a foreign land. Its landscapes were very unique; I felt as if I were overseas. The change of sceneries felt so unrelated from one to the next. Eventually we walked into a heavily wooded area. The headstones were bent over and nearly right on top of one another. I had to climb over most of them. The grass looked as if the groundskeepers forgot about it. The journey towards the Devil's den was painful for me. I realized it gave me too much time to think. It wasn't the cemetery that scared me; ultimately it was the insanity of the darkness. It was my own demons that brought me to despair. It wasn't the dark of night that bothered me; it was the darkness within that I hated. My own guilt was slowly killing me. My sickness was forcing me to explore a side of me I never knew existed. I tried hard to lead the tribe but at times my demons would come to rule the roost. I never had much, nor did I really want anything. I just wanted to be remembered. My heaven was peace within myself but I could never find it no matter where I searched. All the money in the world couldn't give me peace. All the power in the world couldn't give me peace either. In my insanity I kept seeing visions of Medicine Man. My delusions were the least of my problems. The darkness of my depression was so bad at times that my only survival was through rage and anger. I hated the outside world for it filled my disease twice as fast, but the calm moments of the cemetery's jungle only brought a choking darkness. I needed the sting of battle to keep my wits as I walked a tightrope on the outer edges of madness.

The day had been uneventful until we got to a hill. The hill had a cement staircase going up it with two large open mausoleums on both sides. There was a small gate at the front. Wolf said, "Hold up." Raven pointed to the top of the hill. We all looked up at the sight of lighted torches with someone standing at the top of the stairs staring down at us. The person was dressed in black with a backpack, while also wearing a pig mask of some sort. Heavily armed, he carried a giant axe along with a cross bow. Without warning he vanished. Raven asked, "Did you see that?" Animal asked, "Holy shit, who is that? Where did he go?" Wolf answered, "I have no idea, only one way to find out." I could feel that tingling sensation going down my spine again. The adrenaline rush made us pure junkies. We rushed up the hill; as I made it to the top Animal was the last to make it up the stairs. I looked in awe at a sign that read "City of the Dead." The city had an old European flair. There was a street that had dingy brick buildings in very close quarters mixed in with large rundown mausoleums on both sides. Animal gazed back down at the cemetery where he could see four people in the far distance. Animal said, "We've got company." I said, "It's Parks and Bloom. Looks as if they brought more help, let's keep moving." Wolf replied, "The more the merrier."

I walked down the center of the narrow brick road. Lamps were posted sporadically down the street that gave the road an eerie glow. I could see our shadows at every turn. The brick road was too small to get a car through. I kept waiting for the headless horseman to come galloping down the street. It was actually a very cool yet creepy place in its own way. I think it just depended on how you interpreted it. Animal said, "I keep waiting for Jack the Ripper to come bouncing out with London policemen chasing after him." Maverick replied, "I was thinking the same thing." The cemetery city was filled with exotic European statues. I read a few of the building walls; they were very poetic. This ancient city was so misplaced with its artistic flair. You could hear coyotes howling in the distance which gave it an edge. Wolf said, "I feel like we're in a time warp." Raven lit up a joint as we came upon a bend in the road. There stood a large extravagant architectural building. It was bigger than all the rest, very unique from the other buildings.

Beast asked, "I'm tired, can we rest?" I said, "Yeah, take ten." Animal asked, "Where do you think that weirdo vanished off to?" Wolf said, "I don't know, he's not our problem." Animal was attempting to read a sign. We all stared at it when Wolf commented, "It's in French." Animal asked, "So what the hell does it say?" Wolf answered, "The Medieval City; it mentions something about lights of the past and great age. I know some French but by no means am I an expert." Beast said, "Maybe you should have paid more attention in class." Wolf replied, "You asked me, remember? I'm gonna check the building out." So we all followed him up the stairs. The door was locked so Wolf kicked it open. We walked inside the building, it was pitch dark inside. Wolf and Raven turned their small flashlights on. Wolf flashed his light on one of the walls at a picture, underneath it read Chateau du Louvre. As we followed the light beams I could tell the building had been abandoned for a long time. It looked as if it was an old hotel. Down the hallway led to an old pub which had a few broken bar stools with rats wandering on top of the bar. Dust and spider webs filled the joint. Animal happened to peak out the front window towards the street when he was met with a surprise, yelling, "There's someone standing in the middle of the street!" Animal leaned his face against the window to get a better view. Before we could get a look out the window, there was a loud bang with the sound of glass shattering. Animal was driven back by a powerful force as the back of his head hit the floor. We were startled as our reflexes caused us all to drop to the floor. Beast yelled, "Oh God, no!" He crawled on the floor to his brother. I looked over toward Animal; his face had been blown off. Wolf and Raven ran to the door, barricading it with an old bookshelf. Suddenly an arrow went flying through the window hitting the back wall. Picking Beast up from the floor, Maverick screamed, "Come on, we have to go!" We ran down the hall to the back door when a big bang hit the door, it banged again, and with the third bang you could see the edge of an axe blade. Raven yelled, "Shit, let's get out of here." We followed Wolf back to the front. Maverick removed the barricade from the door as we ran out of the hotel.

ANIMAL

I made it down the stairs, surprised by Parks, Bloom and the other officers staring us down with shotguns. Bloom yelled, "Freeze, hold it right there! Put your hands in the air!" We froze by the street. Beast yelled at the cops, "There is someone trying to kill us you idiots! He killed my brother!" Parks asked, "Who killed your brother?" Maverick screamed at Parks, "There is a raving lunatic in there!" Bloom said to us, "You boys are all crazy. We should have arrested all of you at the school and got you off the streets." I said in defiance, "You stupid bastards if you don't believe us, go inside, take a look for yourselves." Parks ordered detective Johnson to go take a peek inside. It was dead silent. I watched Johnson go inside; suddenly I heard a loud scream, then silence. Parks yelled out Johnson's name, there was no response. Detective Turks ran to the door with Bloom right behind him, their guns ready. Turks walked in first only to be met with an arrow to his chest. He fell back onto Bloom who pushed his body aside as he fired his shotgun twice in the dark room. Parks barked out, "Get down and stay down!" Parks ran inside the door. I quickly yelled, "Run!" We all took off running down the street.

Parks met up with Bloom. Bloom said, "The kids are right, there is a crazed lunatic in here." Parks looked down at Animal's motionless dead body. As he looked up, Johnson's body was nailed to the wall with an arrow through his mouth. Parks said, "That son of a bitch! Did you get a look at him?" Bloom answered, "No, it was too dark." Parks said, "Obviously he is armed and dangerous." They ran down the hall to the back, the door was hacked open. Parks moved swiftly outside when the song "Blackout In The Red Room" by Love/Hate pierced the ears of Bloom and Parks. Bloom yelled, "It's coming from upstairs!" The music stopped. Bloom walked up the stairs; the stairs creaked with every footstep. It was dark as Bloom turned his flashlight on. Bloom and Parks reached upstairs to witness multiple hallways. Doors were on both sides all the way down the halls. Parks said, "Shit! Let's stick together, we'll check room by room." Bloom asked, "Why don't we split up?" Parks answered, "No way, we don't need to put ourselves in a cross-fire situation." Parks went to the first door, it was locked. Bloom kicked the door open; a dead body lay on the bed decaying with a gravestone on top of the bed. The room was filled with white candles. Bloom yelled, "This is one sick fuck!" Parks led the way to the next room where he witnessed a young girl hanging from a rope, the chair underneath her tipped over. The body was fresh. The long awaited answer was over as Bloom said, "Fuck, that's the Mayor's daughter!" Parks yelled, "Jesus Christ, this place is a house of horrors. We've got to nail that son of a bitch! "

Suddenly music played at the other end of the hallway. The song was "In-a-Gadda-Da-Vida" by Iron Butterfly. The detectives simultaneously turned around, pointed their shotguns, and quickly ran out towards the hallway. Bloom said, "That music scared the shit out of me. Let's go check it out." Bloom quickly led the way to the end of the hall. The music stopped. Each one stood on the opposite side of the door. Parks nodded to Bloom. With Bloom's adrenaline pumping he kicked the door in; in the heat of the moment he rushed in not paying attention to the floor, only to immediately scream in pain. He had stepped into a room that was loaded with long nails sticking out of the floor. The nails went straight through the bottom of his shoes and deep into his feet. Bloom immediately fell forward as the nails pierced through his entire body. Parks stopped at the doorway. The door behind Parks quietly opened and he could hear the wood floor creak. Parks quickly turned around to the blade of an axe coming at him when he blocked the axe with the shotgun. The lunatic tugged on the axe, which freed the shotgun away from Parks as it hit the floor. Parks lunged at the lunatic as they crashed into the hallway wall. The lunatic was too strong as he hit Parks with the butt of the axe, knocking him down. Bloom painfully attempted to get up from all the nails in the room. The lunatic threw the axe at Bloom, hitting him in the chest. His momentum sent him falling backwards back onto a bed of nails. The lunatic pulled out a butcher knife to finish Parks off when Parks, still on the floor, pulled out a 357 Magnum from his holster, firing three shots in rapid succession that lifted the lunatic off his feet as his body hit the end of the hallway wall. Parks got to his feet and walked over to what was left of the lunatic splattered all over the wall. He removed the pig mask, shook his head in disbelief, stating, "Jesus Christ! It's Gunnar Hornsbee. You sick son of a bitch!" He stared inside the room at Bloom's dead body from the hallway then walked down the stairs wiping the blood away from his broken nose. Using his police radio, he notified the station reporting the incident.

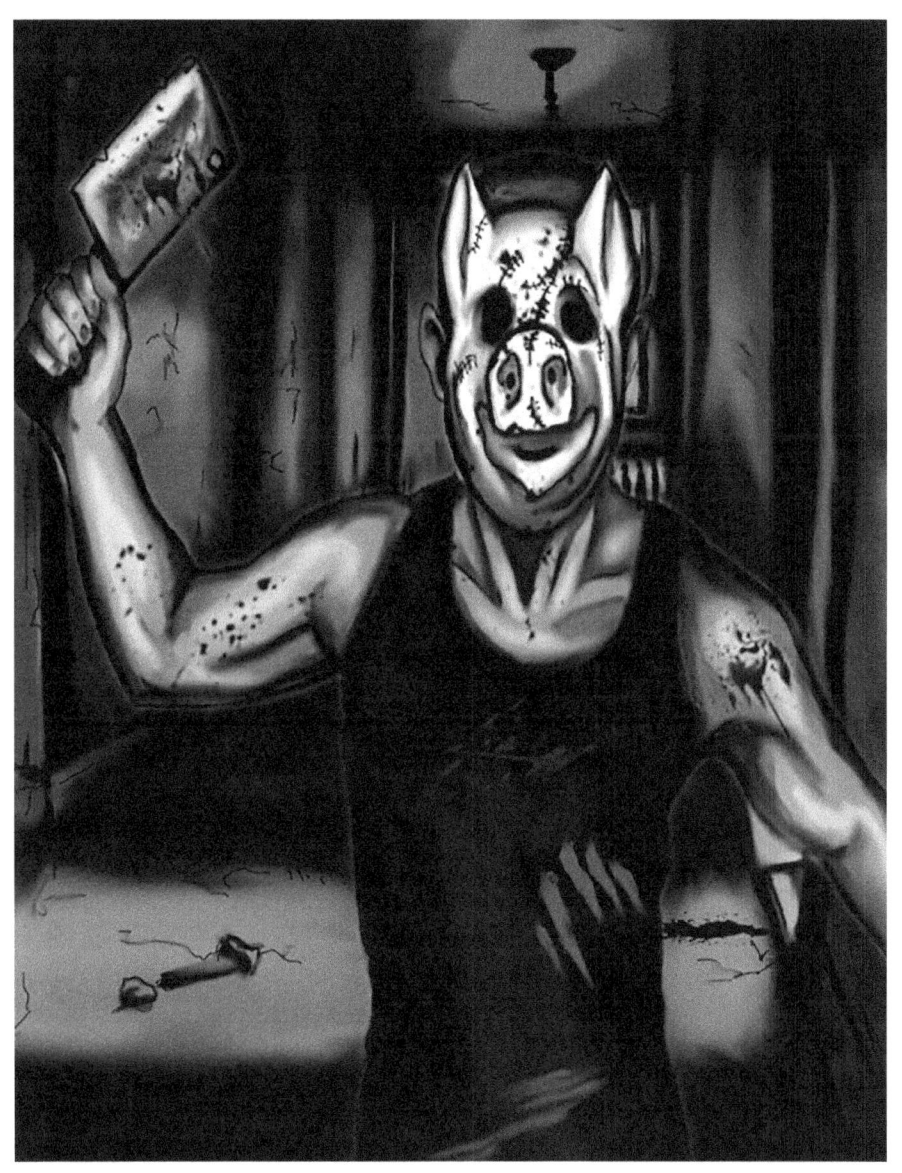

CHAPTER TWENTY: THE STAND

Journals by Preacher

We kept paddling through the mausoleums to elude those crazy deformed butchers. Looking down at my dead friend in the canoe made me realize just how mortal we all were. The farther we traveled the darker the journey had become. I couldn't help but feel like someone was watching us at every turn. A sixth sense told me evil lurked over our shoulder. We were surrounded by half sunken mausoleums and statues. The water was as murky as a swamp. The fall winds were upon us and the cold water splashed my skin as a reminder to stay alert. I think we all had questions for the young kid but this wasn't the time or place. We were too focused on the deformed butchers. Ghost asked, "Do you think we lost those crazy mutants?" Suddenly the sound of a motorized boat answered his own question. Ninja looked back only to see a john boat filled with terrifying butchers coming toward us. I turned around; the deformed butchers became excited pointing at us screaming. Apparently we were on their dinner menu. Ghost yelled out, "Jesus Christ! Are they that hungry for blood?" Ninja answered, "Yep! They're gaining on us; we have to dump the canoes. We can lose them by foot." We made it ashore, hastily leaving the canoes behind. I heard the boat racing closer. Shadow carried Magic's dead body over his shoulder. I said, "We have to dump Magic's body or they will catch us." Shadow refused to listen as we kept running.

We came upon an entrance of a giant cathedral. The cemetery had no name. The architecture was beautiful. The front gates were removed; I guess this particular cemetery was always open for business. The butchers were gaining on us screaming for the taste of a kill. I yelled, "Keep up kid!" Shadow stopped and said, "We need to make a stand, I am tired of running from these freaks." I said, "Our choices are to continue running or make a stand and fight." Ninja yelled, "Let's finish these assholes!" Shadow, grinning at Ninja said, "Well, we finally agree on something." Shadow set Magic's body near some bushes then said to Ghost, "Stay behind and protect the kid with your life." We quickly made our way back to confront the butchers. I could see them entering the cemetery before they dispersed amongst themselves. I wasn't sure, but there appeared to be four of them. Ninja said, "Let's go hunting, boys." We also spread out from one another. It was like playing chess in the cemetery. The graveyard between us was the battlefield. Ninja ran full speed from mausoleum to mausoleum. He had his bow ready.

He noticed movement in front of him behind a tree. He aimed carefully towards the tree and waited patiently. The butcher came out from the tree when Ninja stretched his bow further, then let it rip. The butcher never knew what hit him. Ninja nailed the butcher with a kill shot to the heart. Zombie walked in panic when he heard that familiar chainsaw. Suddenly a female butcher ran out between the mausoleums hunting Zombie. Zombie said, "You got to be fucking kidding me bringing a chainsaw to a gunfight." Zombie fired off a shot hitting the butcher in the chest; without flinching she kept on coming. Zombie fired a second shot this time hitting her in the left shoulder; she stopped only for a brief moment but kept charging with the chainsaw in one hand. Zombie screamed out, "Come on you stupid bitch!" He fired again, the fatal shot hitting her in the forehead as she fell on top of an unmarked gravestone. Zombie yelled, "Fuck you, your family, and your name-brand chainsaws!"

Shadow crept around a military statue which had four old cavalry soldiers wrapped around it. Out of nowhere a large tall deformed butcher jumped out in front of Shadow holding an old farmers tool scythe as a weapon. The blade looked like something you would see Death hold. Shadow yelled, "Come on, you ugly old bastard!" The butcher swung at Shadow, Shadow tried moving out of the way but the blade was long and caught his left arm, slicing it open; blood squirted on the white monument behind one of the old cavalry soldiers. Shadow yelled, "Come on you ugly halfwit! I'm going to enjoy killing you!" Holding his medieval sword in a plow stance, Shadow struck the deformed butcher like lightning in the left shoulder, without hesitation thrusting his sword into the butcher's abdomen. Shadow thrived on sword fighting. The ugly butcher dropped his scythe then slowly fell to his knees. With all his might, Shadow swung the sword and beheaded the butcher. Shadow said, "You got off lucky, freak."

I roamed the grounds hunting but I couldn't find anyone so I ran back towards Ghost. Before I reached him, I happened to gaze up in a tree when I spotted a butcher loading its bow while staring at Ghost. I suddenly pulled out my knife and threw it at the butcher. The knife pierced the butcher in the jaw simultaneously as she shot her bow. The butcher fell crashing down from the tree. The arrow flew by Ghost's head, narrowly missing him. Ghost pushed the kid to the ground and whispered, "Stay down kid!" Ghost hid behind a tree next to the kid. I was enraged about Magic's death when I walked up to the deformed butcher. I was shocked to realize it was a female. She swung at me when I kicked her in the chest. She fell back to the ground and rolled over attempting to crawl away. I grabbed the angry bitch by the hair then yanked her neck back when I pulled my knife out of her jaw. She squirmed around as I slit her throat in rage. I had not one ounce of pity for a cannibal murderer. Her crazy, insane family killed my friend. Today I found out what it was like to become God.

As we all gathered next to each other I walked towards Ghost, who jumped up and yelled, "A fucking arrow almost ended my life man!" Zombie of all people yelled back, "Stop bitching!" A few of the guys got a bang out of that, including the kid. Ninja pointed toward Ghost, screaming "Look out!" Ghost turned around, pushing the kid aside as the deformed butcher said, "Let's embrace." Before anyone could react the butcher quickly pierced an animal bone spear through Ghost's stomach. Blood shot out of Ghost's mouth as he screamed in pain. In anger, Ghost pulled the spear through him so he could get closer to the deformed butcher; he pulled his knife out then stabbed the butcher in her neck as he fell to the ground. The kid stood in shock as we raced to Ghost but it was too late, he was fatally wounded. In Ghost's last breath he said, "I saw this in a dream." He died abruptly with his eyes open in front of us. I stood there crying. My voice cracked as I said, "I only saw four of them. I swear I only saw four of them." Shadow answered, "It's not your fault Preacher." Ninja warned, "Keep your eyes open, there might be more of them. We need to get out of here!" Shadow said to me, "I need you to stitch my wound." Though I was rattled, I shook my head yes. Zombie consoled me but my guilt from that moment on never left me. I made a mistake; that mistake cost the life of a friend. Shadow grabbed the kid and said, "It's all right kid, you'll be safe with me." Ninja said, "I saw a mausoleum that had a knight in front of it. It would be a good place for Magic and Ghost to be put to rest." The boys waited for me to clean Shadow's wound as I stitched his left arm. It was a nasty cut worthy of about 20 stitches or so. I said, "You'll live." Shadow replied, "For now."

We carried Ghost's and Magic's dead bodies to the mausoleum. I watched a falling star fall from the sky. It was a sign that the boys moved on to the next place. I put tokens over their eyes, wrapped them in blankets, then removed the mausoleum door and put their bodies inside. We collected enough branches to start a fire. Out of hypocrisy I said a short prayer. The fire burned rapidly when Zombie half-shut the door as we said our last goodbyes. I said to everyone, "The boatman will take them to the gatekeeper for their final resting place." Shadow mentioned, "We need to find a safe place to camp."

Zombie asked, "What's safe anymore?" I answered, "Let's get back to the canoes; we can find a secure place somewhere other than here." We cautiously walked back to the canoes, setting them in the water and began to paddle away. Ninja asked, "Where do you think their boat is?" Shadow glanced back at Ninja and replied, "Who gives a shit." Ninja answered back, "Hey mutt face, there could be more of them out here waiting to jap us." I yelled, "Knock it off! Let's just get back on course so we can meet the others." The peace between those two was short lived; apparently the feud was back on.

I pondered about Magic and Ghost as we paddled. Magic's death happened so fast but Ghost's death was miserable to witness. Watching helplessly at his last breath was painful. I will never forget his lifeless stare down; Ghost died with his eyes open. That was traumatic for me to experience. That last moment of Ghost leaving us was a haunting image I couldn't get out of my head. I kept hearing that terrible sound as Magic's body crashed in the canoe. I just kept hearing my ears ring to the sounds of the chainsaw while picturing in my head the face of that ugly female butcher. The vision of Ghost's anger as he kept sliding the spear through himself while killing that butcher kept playing over and over again in my head. I couldn't get it to stop. That was the most heroic thing I had ever seen.

Ghost was playful and well liked by everyone. He came from a broken home, his father raised him but he wasn't home much. Ghost was an iconic drummer, probably would have been a rock star one day. Ghost was a teddy bear who always lived his life in the moment. Ghost's downfall was his demons to alcohol from the bottle, much like my father. At times Ghost had a split personality. He was like Jekyll & Hyde. When Ghost got drunk you didn't want to be in the same room with him; he could be a nasty individual. I have to admit he never drank while adventuring off in the cemetery but away from it, the stories were legendary. When Ghost was sober he was kind, friendly, and very happy about life. The only things important to Ghost were playing drums, listening to music, drinking alcohol, and the Cemetery Boys. He would have given the shirt off his back to a stranger. He was a party animal that hung out mostly with Raven when not with the group. He loathed authority and was very defiant to it. I worried about telling the tribe of his loss because I knew it would mortally wound Raven. It was painful enough losing Magic, now losing Ghost, I dreaded what the tribe was going to say. The odds were already stacked against us, so losing two made the journey all that more impossible. I kept wondering how we would make it against the elements of the paranormal, nature, the enemy, and possible ourselves. I kept hearing Wizard's words of warning to us rattling around like marbles in my head.

I was second guessing everything we did up to this point. I wished we had all gone on foot together. I think Wolf was wrong in splitting the tribe up. I was beginning to realize Chief's wars were based on hate. We could win a thousand battles but there was no doubt in my mind we were now fighting a war against ourselves. They say 'know your enemy' which we didn't. Worse, how could we win the war when we didn't even know who we were? If we didn't conquer that battle soon it was obvious we were all going to perish quickly. It didn't matter anymore how many goons of evil we killed because we were becoming them. Unknowingly, to this point Satan was winning the war of attrition. Our tribe was imploding at the seams; we couldn't see it because of our blinding anger and rage. I also wished I knew nothing of the Bible or its destructive nature. Religion was a toxic chemical that fueled a breakdown in us all. I believe the SG set it up that way since the beginning of time. In the end nothing really matters, we all die regardless if we are the conqueror or the conquered. We all die that's fact: it's just a matter of when, where, and how. If you're lucky it's a quick and honorable death. I knew our demise was inevitable; I just needed to make it long enough to kill Satan and his clan. I had a debt of revenge to carry out for my friends and I would see that through no matter what. I couldn't help but wonder whether we would be infamous or martyrs some day.

CHAPTER TWENTY ONE: CHILD'S PLAY

Journals by Chief

We ran through the twists and turns of the "City of the Dead." I really don't understand why they named it twice. I guess it was a reference from the past to the present. I think we ran five miles through this forgotten ancient place. I stopped running as we came upon a stoned bridge. We all looked down from the bridge when Wolf said, "I had no idea the river ran through here. This must be where the city ends." As I gathered my thoughts, my heart went out to Beast who just lost his brother. Animal was a great loss for us all. Animal was physically the strongest among us. He was an avid weightlifter and probably the best wrestler of the bunch. His grappling skills were second to none. Animal had great carpentry skills; his knack for attention to details was extraordinary. I think he would have gone on in life to be one of the best carpenters of his time. I will miss his opinionated thoughts and ideas; one thing about Animal he wasted no time sharing them. Animal and Beast were foster brothers, they were polar opposites from each other but in the end they stuck together when it counted. They didn't normally hang together unless they were with the guys. Animal sported very short hair; he was a much tougher and rougher image of his foster brother. Animal was a great athlete. He always did what he was told versus Beast who was more disobedient. I loved their parents; they were so normal and down to earth. Animal and Beast's foster father was a very strict disciplinarian who traveled a lot, he was always working on big projects with his carpentry business in the city so he would be gone for weeks at a time. Their mom was a softy who spoiled not only them rotten but us as well. I couldn't imagine the heartbreak for them. This was a tough loss for everyone. I was concerned what affect it was going to have on Beast. I took a coin from my pocket, made a wish that we would get revenge, and then tossed it in the water.

We crossed to the other side of the bridge to a wooden walkway. On both sides of us sticking out of the ground were thousands of wooden crosses of all colors. I couldn't leave the pathway because the thorn bushes were mixed in with all the crosses. There was only one way to travel on the path and that was west. That's how I knew we were on the right path towards the Gateway Cemetery. I knew at some point we would have to cut across the Gates of Hell. We continued to follow the wooden pathway up a hill. As I got to the top of the hill there was a very old two-story house with only one problem: there was no way to get into it. There was no entrance except on the second floor that I could see. Raven asked, "Man, what kind of house has a front door on the second floor leading out with nothing underneath it?" Maverick answered, "I don't know but we better find a place to sleep soon. I'm tired." Wolf said, "Yeah I am getting hungry as well." Suddenly a light turned on upstairs; I could see people wearing what appeared to be pumpkins over their heads as they opened the window. From the house I could hear "Aqualung" playing by Jethro Tull. We didn't stay to find out what they were yelling out the window because we were hauling ass down the other side of the hill like bats out of hell.

When I got down the hill Maverick asked, "Why are we running?" Beast answered, "Hey, toad breath, we have had enough excitement for one day. My brother is dead because of it." I yelled, "Knock it off you two!" Wolf pointed and said, "Check it out." We all turned around to the sight of a lit-up rose garden. What was more interesting was an old, elongated brick building beyond it. As we ran through the rose garden, Raven said, "Hey man, I have heard of this place, we're in the Asylum Gardens. Just past this place should be a rundown hospital that closed years ago." Maverick remarked, "Shelter at last." We made it out of the gardens; in front of us was an extensive red brick building with a cement sidewalk leading to the entrance's brick arches above us. A sign read "Morningside Hospital." Excited, I said, "Home sweet home for the night boys." Shell shocked from his brother's incident, Beast replied, "Chief, I am not sure this is a good idea." I answered, "Look we've got to sleep somewhere. Don't worry we'll check the building out together." Beast yelled, "Hey Chief, what if someone is in there? Maybe we better sleep out here tonight." Maverick asked, "Are you nuts? There might be beds in there. Fuck these mosquitoes out here bro!" Wolf said, "We're not any safer sleeping outdoors." Maverick pushed the rundown door open. It was eerily dark inside. We all took our pocket flashlights out while Maverick and Wolf lead the way through the front entrance. We went through half the building before Wolf found some useable hospital beds upstairs. We bunked in three adjacent rooms. I slept in my own room, while Wolf and Raven bunked together, which left Beast and Maverick to take the last room on the left. Wolf had no patience in dealing or rooming with Beast who always had a hard time sitting still.

Later in the night, Beast was bored and decided to roam the hallways downstairs. I believe Beast, who was always hyper, suffered from attention deficit disorder. He also had a penchant for getting into things. I guess his curiosity was just too much to overcome. Beast had found an office downstairs and in typical fashion ravished through file cabinets when he came across a book that turned out to be a documented journal. Beast sat in a dusty old wooden office chair; finally relaxed he began reading the journal. Beast read several pages when he happened to glance over his shoulder and witnessed a young girl standing in the doorway. Beast jumped up out of his chair startled. The girl calmly said, "Don't be scared." Beast asked, "Who are you?" She took a hold of Beast's hand and said, "Let me show you around." Beast grabbed the journal then quickly put it in his pouch. They walked hand in hand down to the basement where Beast saw hundreds of kids running around the halls. Beast asked, "Is this a dream?" The girl answered, "No silly." Beast asked, "What is your name?" She answered, "Lola." Beast said, "What a pretty name." The kids ran around tugging on Beast singing with an echo "This Old Man", it sounded as if they were singing in distortion. Beast asked, "Where did all these kids come from?" Lola answered, "They live here silly." Walking together Lola stopped short of a dark hallway then warned Beast, "Don't go down there." Beast asked, "Why?" Lola answered, "That's where they lock up the crazy people, silly." Beast let go of the girl's hand while he strutted down the forsaken hall.

Beast glanced inside the first room when his vision seemed as though he was looking through an 8mm camera. He watched a priest shaving young kids' heads bald while being strapped to a chair. Creepy nuns proceeded to pull the screaming kids' teeth out. He turned to look in the next room where doctors wearing all red were operating on people who were half machines. They screamed out as if they were being tortured. One of the doctors resembling Blackwell smiled at Beast. Beast quickly turned his attention to another room that had blood running down the walls. Midgets in black latex were dismembering bodies. None of this made sense to Beast. Frightened, he couldn't help but to continue meddling through the unknown out of habit I guess. The deeper down the hall he walked the darker the visions. The next room was even more disturbing. The room, made of glass, was filled with crying kids who all had open wounds on their bodies. They were playing with broken toys as the open hatch above dumped a combination of maggots, worms, fire ants, snakes, scorpions, and hairy spiders down on them. The kids cried and struggled as they were suffocated by creepy crawlers. Room by room it became more horrific. Crazy people were yelling, screaming, and even crying. Beast watched a young boy at the end of the hall with a shit eating grin on his face in front of the elevator. He was dressed in a black suit, white shirt and wore a Mormon hat. He had a very sinister appearance. The suffering people chanted the name "Cain" several times when the elevator dinged. The chants turned to screams when blood splashed out of the elevator like a tidal wave. Beast couldn't take any more as he held his hands to each side of his ears and yelled, "Shut up! Shut Up! Stop it! Stop it!" His eyes were closed as if he was having a panic attack. When he opened his eyes the rooms were empty, the screams stopped, and the river of blood vanished. In confusion he walked back to where he first met the kids. The kids all disappeared without a trace. The basement was silent when he could hear the voices of kids giggling in the distance.

Beast finally had enough horror for the night so he took off running through the halls and up the stairs. He ran into my room trying to wake me up. He shook me until I woke up; startled I asked, "What is it?" Beast tried to tell me about Lola and the kids down in the basement. I wasn't really in the mood for the haunted past. I was exhausted. I warned Beast, "I told you to get some sleep; you've had a rough night. I think you're having delusions." Beast answered, "Chief, I swear I'm not." He started reading the journal to me, which talked about people from the village a long time ago who were sent here from the courts. Many of them were sent here because kids with mental issues were considered criminal. Among those arrested and escorted out of their towns by the early SG because of so-called "crimes of madness" included everything from schizophrenia, depression, behavioral issues, tuberculosis, epilepsy, down syndrome, syphilis, alcoholism, and even those thought to be homosexuals. They were never visited by their families or heard from again. Fearful, Beast said to me, "Chief, we are sleeping in a rundown government mental hospital. For Christ sake! We are camping in an asylum!" Tired, irritated, and impatient I yelled, "Beast you got to get it together man, go to sleep! We have a long day ahead of us with only a couple more hours to sleep." Beast walked out feeling dejected.

Maverick was sound asleep snoring. Beast plopped on the bed, covered his head with a blanket watching rats run around on the floor when he heard the door knob turning; he watched the door slowly open as it screeched. He peaked through the blanket when an old man wearing a top hat holding a lantern poked his head in the doorway and said, "Relax. Is everything alright?" Beast was relieved because he felt a very calming presence from the old man. Befuddled, Beast asked, "Who are you?" The old man answered, "I am the Night Man." Beast asked, "What do you do?" The Night Man answered, "I look after things." Feeling a sense of trust talking to the Night Man, Beast said, "We're leaving in the morning for Crowley's Tomb." The Night Man scoffed, "Son, you can check out anytime you want, but you can never leave this place!" Beast felt confused by the Night Man's comments. He glanced over to Maverick who was snoring away when the door closed and the room became dark again. Beast jumped up trying to wake Maverick but he just pushed Beast away.

Beast ran back into my room shaking me to wake up again. Rolling my eyes I looked at Beast and said, "Now what?" Beast tried telling me now about the Night Man as I grew impatient. Shaking my head, I said to Beast, "Get a grip man. I don't want to hear about child's play or the Night Man. I have heard enough of this shit to last a lifetime. Now please let me sleep bro." I was tired; I wasn't interested in any more of Beast's drama or delusions. I was becoming angry to say the least with all his drama. Beast yelled, "There is a kid dressed like a Mormon downstairs named Cain, I think he is the Devil's son. I saw Blackwell dressed as a doctor!" At the end of my wits I finally yelled at Beast, "Go to bed for fuck sake! You seem to be the only one having these delusions. Come on man, get it together, Blackwell is dead. I don't want to hear anymore about this shit. This is child's play; now get in your fucking bunk." Beast again stomped out of the room slamming the door. Frustrated, Beast gazed down the hall only to see hundreds of kids coming up the stairs. He screamed hysterically while running down the hall.

Startled, everyone got up from bed to check out what all the commotion was about. I myself was furious at Beast, so I opened the door and screamed down the hallway, "Beast, I swear to God I am going to put you to sleep myself!" As everyone met in the hall, Maverick yelled, "Holy mother of God!" Wolf replied, "Wrong guess." Raven shouted, "Those are the Devil's kids! We've got to get the hell out of here man!" We all bolted back to our rooms slamming the doors shut then escaped by jumping out the windows. I said, "Thank God it was only the second floor." Beast glanced at everyone then looked directly at me and asked, "Do you believe me now?" Wolf yelled, "Follow me!" We went on a mad dash through a flat grass field from the side of the building. Maverick looked back and saw thousands of kids chasing us from behind in the field. Maverick screamed, "There are thousands of filthy kids behind us!" We raced through a forest in the early morning until we saw gates leading to another cemetery just ahead. I ran to the gate only to look back as the kids vanished without a trace. Out of breath I said, "I think we're safe." Beast sarcastically replied, "Oh, I am sure we are perfectly safe now." Wolf said, "This must be the side entrance to the Gateway Cemetery." Continuing with his sarcasm, Beast said, "Well I feel so much safer going into the Gates of Hell." I grabbed Beast in frustration and said, "Come on." So we climbed over the fence in search of a place to get a few more hours of shut eye.

CHAPTER TWENTY TWO:
THE IRONY OF GIVING

Journals by Preacher

As we paddled away from the scene of a grisly crime, I wondered how many people those deformed butchers killed. I could certainly understand why they wanted to wear masks. Shadow noticed our canoes were leaking in water. It began to rain which made matters worse when Zombie yelled in disappointment, "Shit! We have to go back to land." I was reflecting back to the moment we ran ashore and stranded our canoes trying to escape the butchers. As I watched water leak into the boat I pondered where the butcher's boat was. I asked myself, *'when would these deformed butchers have time to poke holes in our canoes?'* Obviously the butchers punctured a few holes in the canoes; maybe there were more running around the graveyard. Nobody noticed the holes because we were in such a hurry to escape the butcher shop. I quickly paddled back to shore where we came upon some rocks and climbed out. In anger, Zombie yelled, "This fucking sucks!" Ninja said, "Stop your bitching." Zombie answered back, "Up yours, creep!" Shadow said to Ninja, "Why don't you leave him alone before I punch you in the face." Ninja replied, "Shadow, I'll drop you like a stone." I got between them both to calm the situation down. We were already facing a crisis; the tension between those two seemed ready to blow at any moment. Shadow asked me, "Do you know where we are?" I answered, "Not exactly." Ninja said, "I hope the tribe waits for us. We are running way behind." Shadow sarcastically remarked, "What else would they do?" Ninja replied, "Whatever."

Shadow asked, "Hey kid, what's your name?" The kid answered, "Gabriel." I said with a smile, "The messenger from God, well I sure hope so because it would be a first." Zombie replied, "Maybe it's a sign, Preacher." I responded, "Don't bet on it." Zombie asked, "How old are you Gabriel?" Gabriel answered, "Ten." Shadow asked, "Gabriel, where did you come from?" Gabriel answered, "The village, where else." I asked out of curiosity, "Where are your parents?" Gabriel answered, "I have no idea. I was raised in the church orphanage." I continued my questions as we walked, "What were you doing roaming around in the cemetery?" Gabriel explained, "I ran away. I grew tired of the abuse from Father Blackwell so I came to live here. I was doing fine on my own until I ran into those monster people." Shadow said, "I can relate kid, stick with us Gabriel, we'll take care of ya. You're one of us now, you can be our mascot." Gabriel asked, "Really?" Shadow answered, "Sure kid." I wondered to myself if this was the kid Beast saw that day at the church. Either way it was the past, there was no reason to bring it up. Gabriel had been through enough. The kid should have been named "Job" for withstanding all of Father Blackwell's abusive bullshit. I couldn't imagine dealing with that freak on a daily basis.

It was amazing witnessing all the mausoleums that had become waterfront property. Gazing out at the reflection of the moonlight was breathtaking. We pointed our flashlights towards the water; I could see some of the tops of the mausoleums sticking out after being submerged from the floods. There were a few statues that appeared to be walking on water. It looked really cool. Ninja spotted someone on top of one of the mausoleums as we were passing by. Grass had grown on top of it. A homeless man asked, "Hey, could you boys spare any change?" I reached in my pouch and flipped the man a silver dollar coin. Shadow asked, "I thought that was your lucky coin?" I responded, "Where we're going luck has nothing to do with it. Anyway, he needs a little more luck than I do." Ninja said, "Sometimes, Preacher, I can't figure you out. Your mood can change at the drop of a dime." I answered back, "Don't get me confused with my father." Excited, Shadow said, "I know where we are." Ninja asked, "Where?" Shadow answered, "We're near the Doe Cemetery. This is where the unknown, unclaimed, and the poor are buried. It leads into the woods then comes out near the southwest tip of the Plantation Maze I believe." I said, "Well let's shake a leg; we need to find a place to set up camp. I'm tired." We jogged through the cemetery. It was amazing to see so many unmarked graves. Zombie asked, "What are all the cement squares over there for?" Shadow answered, "Those are all the graves where they buried people standing up to save room." I said, "Jesus, they can't even rest in peace. That sucks!"

We came across a resting spot with a few beaten down benches and an old wood picnic table. On one side of the cemetery there were hundreds of small American flags sticking out of the ground while on the other side there were thousands of Confederate flags. I remarked while shaking my head, "What a place you pick." Shadow answered, "The ghosts of the unknown soldiers can't hurt you." Ninja said, "Keep talking dipshit." Ninja built a nice campfire. We ate some snacks, roasted some marshmallows as we sat by the fire reminiscing about Magic and Ghost. Zombie asked, "I wonder how the boys are doing?" I answered, "Well I hope a lot better than we are. They are going to be in for a shock when I tell them about Magic and Ghost." Shadow asked, "Do you think Wizard is still alive?" I answered back, "Anything is possible I guess. I really don't know. I can tell you, I hope I get a chance to kick the shit out of the monks who tortured us. I owe it to Medicine Man." Zombie said, "I'll bet Wizard is giving them a ton of shit. Hell, they would have to cut out his heart to calm him down." Ninja said, "Let's worry about that stuff in the morning. We need to get some sleep." Eventually we all zonked out.

In the middle of the night Ninja woke up to go to the bathroom. He took a short walk by some trees. A white fog was lifting across the water pushing it through the trees. While peeing on a small bush Ninja could see movement from behind a couple trees up ahead. Staring at the tree he noticed two heads peeking from each side of the tree. Ninja watched only to see more people stepping away from the trees. They all had one thing in common: each one had some form of white sack over their heads holding lighted torches. Ninja said, "Screw this." He turned around and high-tailed it back to camp. Concerned, Ninja yelled at us by the campfire, "Get up! Get the fuck up!" We all jumped up, Shadow asked, "What's wrong now?" Ninja answered, "There's a fucking lynch mob coming." Shadow sardonically said, "Ninja, this better not be another one of your stupid pranks. I have had enough of your bullshit on this trip." Zombie looked over Ninja's shoulder and said, "He's not lying." We all looked over his shoulder. I could see within fifteen to twenty yards behind us there were more people than I wanted to count with white sacks over their heads. Zombie asked, "What the hell is this? Who are they?" They had the path blocked. Shadow looked down at Gabriel and said, "Don't worry kid, I'll protect you. Give me your hand; we're out of here." I yelled, "Run!" We followed Shadow and the kid through the Confederate cemetery. I glanced back to see the lighted torches gaining on us from behind. Shadow yelled, "Come on, run damn it!"

We made it to a patch of forest where we continued running feverishly through it. Tree branches were slapping us in the face. I remember Zombie ran straight through a spider web screaming when we made it to the outer path of the riverbank. Even in the eyes of death we couldn't help but laugh at Zombie. He yelled like a girl. I turned around; the lynch mob was nearing the end of the woods. We had no choice but to keep running. You could hear them yelling at us when Shadow yelled back, "Go to hell!" A shot rang out ricocheting off a sign, just missing Shadows head. We just kept on running. We ran back into the woods trying to lose these idiots. I stopped for a minute; I could see torches coming our way. Ninja said, "We need to hide." Zombie asked, "Where?" Ninja, looking up answered, "High in the trees." Ninja, Gabriel and Shadow climbed one tree while Zombie and I climbed another. We climbed almost to the top. We were well camouflaged with the branches, leaves and moss. The light was coming closer as my heart pumped harder with each footstep. The lynch mob was right underneath us. I was so nervous that I became lightheaded. The lynch mob looked around but continued further into the woods. We waited and watched until I could no longer see their lighted torches. We immediately climbed down and ran towards the outer riverbank.

I cautiously ran down the path when Shadow pointed to an old Masonic Temple up the trail. We reached the temple running up the front cement stairs. Ninja tried opening the door, but it was locked. He banged on the door several times to no avail. Shadow said, "Shithead move out of the way, I can open it." Sure enough he put something in the lock, like magic Shadow opened the door. There was a light switch by the door so Shadow checked to see if the lights would come on: to our surprise they did. I locked the door when Zombie asked, "Shouldn't we continue to run?" Shadow replied, "Why, so we can be in the open to be assassinated?" I said, "Shadow is right. Let's check this place out; we'll booby trap the piss out of it. We should be able to create a defensive stronghold till the morning."

The Masonic Temple was huge. We walked down a black and white checkered tile floor. As we came to a door Shadow opened it with Gabriel following behind. There was purple carpet throughout the room with an altar in the center. We continued down the hall to another door; Shadow opened the door to a full kitchen. Without a word we all rushed at the same time to see if there was any food in the fridge. Zombie opened the door where we found some apples, oranges, a carton of cranberry juice, and a bag of carrots. Gabriel found a bag of chocolate candy bars in the cabinet. We quickly munched on the food before we checked the rest of the place out. I found a few offices, a bathroom and a big auditorium that had a stage with purple curtains. There were rows of purple chairs that lead all around the stage. Zombie asked, "How are we going to defend this place? It's too big." Ninja answered, "We have to try." Shadow found a maintenance room with carpentry tools, wood, nails, hacksaw, wire, duct tape, old chemical spray cans, some half filled paint buckets, along with a shovel, a pick, an axe, and some rope. Shadow said, "Stick with me and I will show you how to make this stuff useful for our defense."

Holding the hacksaw Ninja said, "I'll be right back, we need some tree branches." I said, "I'll cover you."

The temple was made out of block, most of the windows were high and near the ceiling, the doors were made of heavy wood. The weakness was the front lower side window near the river bend. So we began quickly setting up booby traps wherever we thought might fend off intruders. As we were making the traps Zombie asked, "Hey, what if someone who is innocent comes back here?" Shadow answered, "Nobody's innocent at this time of night and if they do, it sucks to be them. Sooner or later, Zombie, we all have to die." Zombie replied, "Damn, that's cold bro." Shadow said, "No, not really. Do you know most people live their lives with no honor? It's the same way they perish. People are assholes. They have no compassion for animals or others. The world is full of selfish, shallow jerk-offs that die dishonorably. I don't care when, where, or how I die, just as long as it is honorable. I can tell you one thing: I have lived honorably and I will die honorably." Zombie said, "Damn, that's some deep shit bro." Shadow smiled as he put a trap together, "The world is full of bad people; you better remember that if you're going to survive. We keep getting more people who come to our country constantly trying to change it. They want it to be something it's not. They come here not shedding an ounce of blood for it. This is the land of the free and home of the brave. My oldest brother died defending it while another brother came home to protesters spitting on him. You know the worst thing about it?" Zombie asked, "What?" Shadow answered, "He didn't even have a choice; he was drafted and he went. He did what was asked. Funny thing about killing: the governments say who, where, and when it's okay to butcher people. It's like they give you a line pass and say okay now you can kill; then you come home to someone robbing you, threatening you, or cheating on you then all of a sudden they take the license back and say you can't kill. You are suddenly supposed to just turn it off even if it means defending yourself, family, and your rights. What a crock of shit. My second oldest brother came home to ignorant, judgmental people, who never spilled their own family's blood for freedom. They just used someone else's. The media portrayed him as a bad person. You know, the worst thing about it was the government that drafted him never cared about him when he came back from their bullshit war. My brother didn't die in combat; he died from a broken heart in his own country. The only thing he ever talked about was the band of brothers he was with and the comradery they shared. Those were his best moments in life. The irony of it, give a person a tin badge and authority; somehow they will have the taste to kill even if it's their own. Give a government the power and it will find a reason for war. Give the media fuel and they will use it to burn one another to the ground. But those same bastards won't fight themselves in a war or let their families die for their country. People protest for equal rights, what is that? Have they paid their taxes, have they sacrificed their family for the betterment of the country?" Zombie answered, "Hell no!"

Shadow ranted, "Find me an illegal alien, government, or rich family member who hasn't raped, stolen, or pillaged from this country, then cried wolf when they were given what the normal person can't even get who paid into it in the first place and I will retract my statement. The system is fucked! The SG is full of shit! I keep watching the media talk about racism. It's funny; every race in some fashion is racist against another. There's the all-Spanish networks and the all-black channels, those seem pretty racist to me. God forbid if it was announced there would be an all-white network; it would cause a fucking riot! Now, that my friend is inequality. Find me a Caucasian person working in a government job these days and I might piss myself. You can't even understand what anyone is saying anymore; English has become the forgotten language. Yet, I would be called a racist if anyone heard me say that, just for speaking the truth!"

"Corporations outsource jobs screwing our village just so a few executives can suck up all the profits like thieves in the night. At the same time the real contributors are treated as slaves. You need to be an interpreter to get through all the red tape nowadays. The SG is killing our village for control and profit. This was not the vision my brothers had nor do I. My brothers died for a country that has been invaded with other cultures and double standards. I'm choking on the hypocrisy of it all. It's almost hard to breathe. We ourselves have proven as a brotherhood in the Cemetery Boys that we could all equally exist. You know why that is?" Zombie shook his head no. Shadow answered, "Because we're not trying to take something from one another. We actually love our fellow man. It's not about ethnic supremacy; it's about respect for one another. That is the country my brothers died for. Once the SG took over things changed. It became about control and the almighty dollar, regardless of who they have to butcher for it. The SG has become the silent assassins. Not until the day when society loves each other again can we truly heal, getting back what was lost: God, country, family, freedom, and a dream to live as men, not slaves. I believe this vision has been lost forever." Zombie replied, "You don't really believe that do you?" Shadow answered, "We lost a long time ago, I'm afraid. When they created TV and learned how to manipulate it they stole the values right under our feet. When you see a breaking story what do you see?" Zombie answered, "Something important." Shadow replied, "See that's exactly my point. That's what they want you to see. The real story is the one they don't want you to see or hear. That is the most dangerous time for us all. It is the great illusion and the SG has become masters at it. It's what you don't hear that is troubling, man. When we stop letting a secret society run our country and we all live by the same principles in life, only then can we reunite as a country. Without this there will never be peace in the world. There is too much money in war to stop. Until then cheating, divorce, stealing, killing, raping, greed, etc… will only continue. Stop the church's manipulation, the government's control, the people's selfishness across the globe and only then can we live in an equally free society." Zombie said, "You know, I never saw this side of you before. Maybe you should be a speaker and let the truth be told. Anyway, we better get back to business. Finding the maintenance room was a gold mine, wasn't it?" Shadow answered, "Yes it was. We better get these traps set. Hey Zombie." Zombie asked, "What?" Shadow answered, "Thanks man. It felt good to finally get that shit off my chest." Zombie stared at Shadow with a smile replying, "I am honored brother. Cemetery Boys forever, right?" Shadow said, "Fucking right, Cemetery Boys forever."

Gabriel wandered down the hall when Zombie heard a noise near the back, so he peeked down the opposite hall to take a look. Without warning a rock came crashing through, breaking the side window near the front. It scared Zombie half to death. Zombie collected himself, pulled out his Beretta handgun, quickly loading it with an extended magazine which had twenty eight bullets. It was the last of his ammunition. He cautiously made it to the window, slowly peeked out the curtains and was mortified. The lynch mob stood in the street holding torches with bags over their heads with dark markings of reverse crucifixes over the eyes: what a scary site to behold. Zombie yelled to the others, "Holy shit! There must be at least twenty of them out there! The bastards are multiplying!" Gabriel ran off to find Shadow.

Another rock came crashing through the window; Zombie randomly fired several shots at the mob outside in a panic. When it was all said and done three lay dead on the ground, while the others disappeared. The tribe came running to the front. Ninja asked, "What the hell are you doing?" Zombie answered, "They broke the window; the ass heads attempted to get in. What the hell else was I suppose to do?" Ninja gave Zombie a dirty look. Zombie yelled, "I wasn't going to hold their fucking hand to invite them in numb nuts! We're good but this is getting ridiculous!" I could hear a banging from the back door so Ninja and I ran to the back when banging came from the front door. Zombie looked out the window; one mobster stood near the window. Zombie jumped back against the wall frightened, when he composed himself he pointed the gun out the window, no one was there. Shadow stood in the front hallway near the door with his crossbow. Zombie yelled to Shadow, "Go hide Gabriel. I'll guard the window." Shadow took Gabriel to the entrance and said, "Go hide in the auditorium under the stage. Don't come out till I get you. Now go!" Gabriel hugged Shadow then took off running down towards the stage.

The back door was being pounded on until the end of a sledge hammer started making it through the door. Ninja yelled to me and Shadow, "They're going to break the door down! Run to the church auditorium." All the lights went out from inside the temple. Realizing being alone wasn't so fun, Zombie said, "Shit, this sucks." Suddenly the front of the wooden door was being cut through with an axe. Zombie yelled, "Fuck this!" He ran to the back behind Ninja, who had his bow ready waiting for the door to be broken open. The pounding continued on both doors till the back door finally broke open. A mobster holding a sledgehammer in the doorway was met with an arrow to the stomach. Another mobster started running in the back entrance; Zombie pulled the trigger twice, hitting the screaming bag head in the face with both shots. Ninja said, "I've been meaning to tell you, thank God you brought that cannon with you. I don't think your pellet gun would've had that same outcome."

In the meantime a bag head was climbing through the window when he gripped the inner window ledge only to scream out from razor blades taped around the inner ledge. His hand was a bloody mess yet he still managed to make it through the window. The bag head noticed that the front door had been destroyed by the axe in the center of the door. He watched a hand reach inside unlocking the door. The remainder of the door opened as the lynch mob began to rush in. The bag head noticed the trap, he screamed trying to warn the others but it was too late. Opening the door set off the booby trap roped to the wooden platform above, which came crashing straight down with spikes on it. The spikes punctured straight through four of the lynch mobs' bodies. Blood drenched the walls while a pool of blood flowed down the floor like a river.

The savages hunted room to room, I could hear them ranting down the halls like crazed animals. A member of the lynch mob angrily shook his injured hand up in the air to remove the blood flowing from his hand. He opened the door to check the bathroom only to land on the prongs of a rake lying on the floor. The handle, fastened with a sharp stick, bounced up and punctured him in the neck. The unfortunate bag head pulled out the stick, holding his neck as blood gushed all over the floor. He fell to the tile floor trying to gasp his last breath. Another bag head pulled the kitchen door open only to be met with a pick stuck in his chest from the booby trapped door. A rather heavyset bag head rushed in the office only to fall from tripwire. He landed on large homemade wooden caltrops that looked like enlarged sharpened jumping jacks. We had marinated the sticks in piss so certainly not the best way to go.

I could see Ninja and Zombie entering the auditorium as we were hiding behind the upper rows of chairs. I tried to see where they went but their shadows disappeared in the dark. I could hear screams coming from the hall. We crawled behind rows of chairs when suddenly the auditorium doors opened. Commotion echoed throughout the place. I could see the savages searching every row on the other side holding torches. I was only left to wonder where Ninja and Zombie hid. Then I heard someone yell, "There they are!" I didn't know at first if they spotted Ninja and Zombie or us. Shadow said, "Shit, they spotted us." Shadow fired his bow, hitting the first bag head coming toward us in the neck. The arrow went through him like sliced butter. A sack head fired back with a handgun hitting Shadow in the left shoulder, knocking him back as he dropped the bow on the floor. I grabbed the cross bow while pulling Shadow to his feet. More shots were fired which hit the chairs next to us. We continued running down the stairs as shots rang out, bullets ricocheting off the wall. A bag head came out of nowhere as Shadow kicked him in the face, sending him tumbling down the stairs. We jumped on the stage to hide behind the curtain when I shot the last arrow, hitting another bag head in the groin. On stage we were met with four more bag heads armed with clubs. Shadow pulled out his sword, quickly slicing two before anyone could even react. I pulled out a flammable liquid spray can. Gunshots were fired into the curtain hitting Shadow in the leg as he dropped to the stage floor reeling in pain. The two bag heads rushed in on me when I simultaneously sprayed and lit the chemical setting the bag heads on fire. Several shots were fired from under the stage. Zombie killed four more mobsters when Ninja fired his bow, killing the last stray lynch member running down the stairs.

The lights came back on while the curtains automatically opened. Ninja asked, "Are you guys okay?" I answered, "No, Shadow is in bad shape." Zombie asked, "Who turned on the lights?" Ninja asked, "Who opened the curtains?" In pain Shadow screamed out, "Someone is still roaming around." I yelled out to the auditorium in anger, "What do you want?" An echo answered in the distance, "You!" Shadow tried to make it to his feet. Ninja and Zombie went to hunt the voice in the auditorium. I helped Shadow to his feet when unnoticed, someone was creeping toward me and Shadow from behind. I was so pissed off I yelled out toward the auditorium, "Why?" Gabriel came out from under the stage yelling, "Look out!" Shadow turned around first. Within a split second Shadow jumped in front of me as the bag head stabbed Shadow in the abdomen. The bag head answered, "Because you were there." Shadow, grimacing in pain yelled, "Fuck you!" The bag head continued to insert the knife deeper into Shadow's abdomen when he finally collapsed to the stage floor. Ninja and Zombie rushed toward the stage yelling. I pulled out my knife demanding Zombie, Ninja, and Gabriel to stand pat. The bag head quickly sliced me in the left forearm. I grunted in pain and yelled, "Fuck it!" I threw my knife at the bag head; the knife struck him in the chest. He fell to his knees. I pulled the knife out and slit his throat. You could hear him gasping for air when I heard a thud hit the floor. I leaned over and took the bag off the dead body's head. Stunned at his face, I asked, "What the fuck is this?" Ninja and Gabriel ran to the stage, only to see the bag head was a familiar face. Ninja said, "That's the homeless bum you gave the silver dollar to." Zombie said, "That's totally fucked! You help a swine; this is what you get in return." Shadow whispered, "Fuck that turd!" I reached in the dead man's pocket pulling out my lucky silver dollar and said, "I guess it didn't bring him any luck." Ninja checked on Shadow and screamed out in anger, "Noooo!" Ninja was holding Shadow crying along with Gabriel. Zombie said, "He's dead." Tears flowed down all of our cheeks. Shadow saved my life; in an instant he was gone. I felt sick to my stomach. I sat in a nearby chair shocked. Shadow died valiantly while my guilt was drowning me. Shadow was one tough son of a bitch. He was a security blanket for all of us, he feared nothing. Three of my friends were now dead and we hadn't even made it to Crowley's Tomb to save the Wizard. I had failed up to this point but knew we had to push on. I hugged Gabriel, he said, "If something ever happens I will find you." I said to everyone, "We have to take care of Shadow's body first, grab anything we can use from these lame fucks, then let's get the hell out of this shithole." I don't know how many we killed, after this there wasn't enough to satisfy my anger. The odds continued to stack against us, I wasn't sure if we would even make it to Crowley's Tomb at this point. Heading back home towards the butchers didn't seem appealing. There was no going back, we were all-in; we had reached the point of no return.

SHADOW

CHAPTER TWENTY THREE:
CLOWNING AROUND

Journals by Chief

I woke up feeling like we fell on black days. Somehow we managed to fall asleep near a large gravestone that read, "Rest in Peace Dead Poet." Pretty fucked up if you ask me. Beast was reading that creepy journal from the asylum while Maverick was still sleeping. Raven meanwhile was flying high as a kite smoking a joint. Wolf was in the woods taking a movement. I was in an annoyed mood because I couldn't find my peanuts in my backpack. I asked, "Has anyone seen my bag of peanuts?" Beast apologized, "Sorry Chief, I had a few this morning, here are the rest." I commented, "Why didn't you ask?" Beast replied, "I didn't want to wake you." I sarcastically laughed and said, "You didn't want to wake me, if I recall you didn't have a problem waking me up every five minutes with your creepy ghost stories last night." Beast replied, "That was different." Beast became fidgety when I asked, "What are you doing now?" Beast answered, "Reading Morningside's journal." Raven rolled his eyes as I said to Beast, "Do us a favor, don't read anymore, please!" Maverick woke up in laughter saying, "That was a crazy night, man." Maverick walked up to Raven and took a couple hits of the sweet leaf. Back from the woods, Wolf said, "Let's get ready to move out, we have a long day ahead of us."

It was a cold and cloudy day out when we came to an intersection in the path. I told the guys, "I don't know which one to take." Wolf answered, "When in doubt take the one in the middle." Maverick and Raven laughed at anything being said. Feeling buzzed at this point, who could blame them. I suddenly saw Medicine Man on a horse galloping down the middle path. Wolf asked, "Chief you alright?" I answered, "I saw Medicine Man riding down the path." Beast replied, "Damn Chief, you are tired." I said, "I wonder why that is." Beast snickered as we walked down the dirt trail. Eventually we ran into a small swinging bridge. A sign posted read "The Rainbow Bridge." I knew exactly what that meant. There are many who believe when their pets die they will one day be reunited with their furry friends. It is said your pet will hear your footsteps, meeting you at the Rainbow Bridge. We walked across the bridge to a white picket fence. There were two large stray dogs lying near the entrance. One was a Germen Sheppard; the other was a Doberman Pincher. The entrance gate read, "Cozy Hills Pet Cemetery." Beast said, "We're in a pet cemetery." I replied,

"You just figured that out." Raven threw a few jerky scraps to the dogs. The gates weren't locked so Wolf pushed the gate open. The dogs followed Raven. I stopped long enough to stare at the dogs and said to Raven, "You fed them, now they're going to follow us." Raven remarked, "So what." I said, "I am not even going to argue, hell they might as well come with, everyone else is." I spit a peanut shell towards the dogs then walked away. The dogs growled at me; Raven immediately gave them affection. Raven continued to feed his new pals more jerky. Maverick asked, "What are their names?" Raved answered, "The Sheppard's Cheech and the Doberman is Chong." Maverick said, "That's fitting coming from you." The day was so peaceful through the Pet Cemetery. There were fresh flowers everywhere with long stretches of flat grass. Hills and valleys abounded as if we walked into heaven. I would have never guessed this would be part of Gateway Cemetery.

We walked most of the day uneventful when someone walked towards us. Maverick asked, "Is that Bonzo the Clown?" I have to admit, it did look like the clown from Bonzo's Circus. Bewildered, Beast asked, "I have a question. Why is someone walking through a cemetery in a clown outfit?" Maverick answered, "I don't know; maybe he is going to work." Raven butted in, "That's pretty fucking thin don't you think? There is no circus in town." Raven was right, but at the same time we wore makeup on our faces quite a bit. Everyone has their reasons; honestly I didn't want to know either. I just wanted to meet the others. The way we had chosen was totally out of the way in order to get to Crowley's. The risk was becoming more dangerous with every step. The clown walked right by us with a creepy smile on his face staring at all of us singing "Californication" by the Red Hot Chili Peppers. The dogs growled, obviously they didn't like the clown's vibes either. He clowned around as he danced by us; I was not amused. The creep was tall, dressed in a blue clown suit with big red shoes. His red hair stood straight up like Bonzo's. His makeup was creepy; the big bold red lipstick around his lips didn't look normal. He kept honking some annoying bike horn. It was the first time I was spooked by a clown. Wolf said, "God, I have always found clowns to be creepy." Raven said, "Yeah, I agree with you bro." I looked back, he was standing still staring at us when he let five red balloons go in the air then he waved. I said, "Fuck this nonsense." I took off running to catch up with the rest of the tribe. Beast asked, "What the hell is his problem?" I answered "Who gives a fuck? Whatever his malfunction, it's his problem." Beast yelled back at the clown, "Fuck you!" Wolf yelled at Beast, "What the hell is wrong with you? Don't you think we have enough problems?"

We all turned back to see the clown give us the finger then run off in the distance. In frustration Wolf said, "Great, just what we need more problems. He'll probably come back with reinforcements."

We made it to a paved road where I saw another clown holding his thumb up as if he was hitchhiking. He was dressed in all green with long green hair. He reminded me of a fucking martian. The creep turned around staring at us. He had green stars over his eyes but what I remember most was a reverse cross on his forehead. Raven said, "That clown looks fucking crazy man." The clown had a wicked smile on his face. Maverick said, "Ah fuck him! He is just clowning around with ya." Before we could cross the road we heard music coming from a beat-up old white ice cream truck. The song was "The Beautiful People" by Marilyn Manson. The ice cream truck drove past us slowly. The driver was dressed as a jester. The ice cream truck stopped as the clown in green shaped his fingers to that of a gun, pointed his finger directly at me, then acted as if he fired at all of us one at a time. The ice cream truck was playing the earsplitting song "Killing In The Name" by Rage Against The Machine. Wolf asked, "Did you see the gesture that fucking clown made at us?" I answered, "Stay cool, fuck that toad! We have bigger fish to fry than that fool." Beast said, "Hey, I have seen these guys before, they are fucking assholes!"

We walked across the street to an enclosed walkway that reached another cemetery. I walked through the corridor which had lit candles of all colors inside. I was reaching a point in my mind where all I wanted was a state of nirvana. Voices crying out from nowhere screamed, "Help me!" "Want to play?" "You're next!" We took off running like greyhounds. Ultimately we reached the end of the hall where there was a glass door, so Wolf opened it and we all hurried to the other side to get back outside, only there was one problem: we were stuck in an open room with no doors or windows. The door quickly shut behind us. Suddenly things went dark. Raven tried to reopen the door from behind yelling, "It won't open." We turned our pocket flashlights on to observe what was going on around us. I realized we were in a peculiar trapped room. Beast asked, "What the fuck is going on? I'm getting freaked out!" Beast was claustrophobic. The room felt like it was spinning while getting smaller. Circus music began playing in the background. I was actually laughing while others were afraid. Beast screamed in fear begging, "Please stop! Please!" The room lit up in all different colors while spinning. It was like watching fireworks on the Fourth of July. The dogs were getting sick. The lights came back on when the movement stopped; the room then began to get bigger. Dizzy, I saw a door, but every time we walked towards it, it got farther away as we stumbled around. Raven said, "Hold on a minute man, don't move." We all stopped, even the dogs. Then a weird thing happened: the door was right in front of us. Raven opened the door, Cheech and Chong followed him as we followed behind the dogs. As luck would have it, we could see each other but were now all in different places in some sort of see-through glass maze. I could see the person in front of me but I couldn't follow him because I would run into a glass wall. Somehow Raven, Maverick and the dogs disappeared into thin air. Freaking out, Beast yelled, "Somehow they figured out how to get out of here. I need to get the hell out of here now!" We on the other hand had the misfortune of bumping into endless invisible glass walls for hours. It was like trying to figure out a Rubik's cube with a bad hangover.

A few hours later we finally figured out how to get the hell out of one room only to end up in another bizarre room with deafening music playing "Unholy" by Kiss, all while staring at ourselves in these odd shaped mirrors. I was frustrated listening to Beast cry; not to mention looking in the mirror at my own reflection, I looked really fat. Wolf looked at himself in another mirror only to see nothing in the reflection. Wolf asked, "Why the hell can't I see myself in the mirror?" Beast looked at himself in another mirror only to see Bonzo the Clown staring back at him. Beast jumped backwards screaming. I yelled, "What the hell is wrong now?" Beast whined, "I saw Bonzo's reflection in the mirror." I walked over only to see my own normal reflection. I grabbed Beast and said, "Come here, I don't need this shit today, I'm tired. You're putting me in a very bad fucking mood again!" I shoved Beast in front of the mirror. Beast stared in the mirror only to see me and him in the mirror. Beast frantically said, "Chief, I swear to God I saw that clown in the mirror." I asked, "Can you stop this shit long enough for us to get the fuck out of here? The only clown I see is you!" Beast yelled out, "I am telling you Chief, that crazy fucker is going to get me." In an annoyed voice I replied, "The only thing you have to fear is my boot in your ass. Now pull it together!"

We only had one problem: we couldn't figure out how to get the hell out of the house of mirrors. It felt like a loony bin. The mirrors kept changing while our bodies appeared disfigured as we weaved through the mirror maze. I was intrigued at how our images could change from one mirror to the other. In one particular mirror I saw only my head. I said, "How could this be possible? These are some tricky ass mirrors."

Wolf peeked in the mirror at himself only to see himself upside down. Laughing, Wolf said, "I never saw myself this way before." I was also laughing when I said, "It's your reality pal." Meanwhile, Beast glanced in the mirror only to see Bonzo peeking back at him again. Startled, he flew back against the wall behind him, peeked his head in the mirror once more, this time kneeling down. He saw Bonzo's reflection kneeling down back at him. Beast said, Fuck me!" I yelled at Beast, "We are not coming over there so you can fuck with us again!" Beast walked directly up to the mirror only to see Bonzo's reflection walk closer to the mirror. Beast touched his own face; he saw Bonzo's reflection touch his face. Beast smiled and then Bonzo smiled back showing his teeth which appeared like long fangs. Beast froze then screamed as Bonzo's eyes stared back at him with pure evil. Suddenly Bonzo grabbed Beast's hair pulling him through the mirror, then quickly hacked him with a machete several times. Beast screamed in agony. Wolf and I ran to the mirror, there was no reflection, no broken glass, just Beast lying on the other side of the mirror in a puddle of blood. Wolf rushed through the mirror to help Beast. Wolf lifted his head up as Beast said in a fading voice, "Bonzo." Beast's head rolled over as if someone just euthanized him. In an angry voice I screamed, "I'm going to kill you, Bonzo!" Wolf said, "We can't take Beast's body with us with this crazed clown on the hunt." I put two tokens over Beast's eyes for the boatman. Then we left his body behind. It was a sickening decision; we just didn't have a choice. Beast had always been a drama queen. I felt responsible because I didn't believe him.

Wolf and I wasted a lot of time trying to hunt the clown down, but somehow he left without a trace. In time Wolf stumbled onto a door that pushed open and we finally made it outside. The smell of fresh air was fleeting. Regrettably there was no sign of Raven, Maverick or the dogs. What I did spot was an old abandoned Western ghost town up ahead past the graveyard. I could hear music playing in the distance. Wolf said, "I know that song." An eagle screeched across the night sky. I asked, "What's the name of the song?" Wolf answered, "Kings and Queens" by 30 Seconds To Mars. I said, "This ass clown has got to be around here somewhere." Wolf answered, "He could be anywhere, Chief." I replied, "I can feel him. He's here." Wolf said, "Let's go hunt the bastard down." We walked side by side down the street like gunfighters in the old west. Wolf pulled out two big hunting knives from his holster. He twirled the knives in each hand as if they were western pistols. I swung both of my Kama's around. I said, "We're not taking any prisoners tonight, my friend." With a grin, Wolf said "I can hear the song 'Dead or Alive' by Bon Jovi playing in my head." I said, "I'll tell you mine later. Now let's go kill this fucking clown."

We went in the first few buildings but came up empty. We heard a familiar song being played down the street called "Kiss the Clown" by Enuff Z'Nuff, so we went to investigate the music. As we walked to the building I could hear people laughing inside; the place sounded like it was jumping. Wolf said, "Sounds like a party." I replied, "Well, we better go crash it." We walked up the stairs to the saloon doors. I was getting ready to walk in when Wolf asked, "Hey, what song was playing in your head?" I answered, "Wanted Man by Ratt." Wolf said, "That's a great fucking choice man." I pushed the saloon doors open with Wolf trailing behind me. There was a clown bartender, two clowns sitting at the bar having a drink, and four clowns playing cards at a table. I walked to the bar while Wolf walked by the four clowns sitting at the table. The bartender said, "I need to see some ID's." I said, "We don't have any fucking ID's. Where is Bonzo the clown?" The bartender answered, "At the circus." The clowns laughed in the background. I squinted at the clowns sitting on the bar stools and said, "I don't find it funny you laughing at me because I missed Bonzo's Circus." The clowns stopped the laughter. It got so quiet you could've heard a pin drop. I smiled when the clowns broke out in laughter again. In seconds flat I swung my Kama striking the first clown in the head then twisting around I smashed the second clown in the chest with both Kama's. Before the clown bartender could react I had both Kama's at each side of his neck like scissors then removed his head. I grabbed a bottle of whiskey from the bar and poured myself a drink.

At the same time a clown tried getting up from the table when Wolf stabbed him in the groin with one knife then slit his throat with the other. Wolf stabbed the next clown in the neck then quickly threw his other knife across the table at the third clown. The knife struck the clown in the chest as the chair fell backwards crashing to the floor. The last clown went to stab Wolf in the back when in the nick of time I threw my Kama into the last clown's back as he tumbled to the floor. I laughed then said, "I actually changed my song to 'Lay It Down' by Ratt at the last second." Wolf laughed as he poured himself a shot of whiskey. I said "No worries, I had your back." We went through most of the abandoned houses with just one more to go, which was the last house on the left. Wolf walked to the door and without warning kicked it open. That's as far as we needed to go, in front of the stairs was Bonzo the Clown hanging from the hallway stair rail. I said, "Holy shit! Looks like Bonzo bit off more than he could chew." Wolf replied,

"Looks like he ran into Maverick. Wow, the dogs really helped do a number on him. Well, either way he had it coming." I sighed, took a long swig of whiskey from the bottle and said, "I'm afraid we've all got it coming sooner or later, Wolf. We better go find the others."

Beast

CHAPTER TWENTY FOUR: DINNER'S SERVED

Journals by Preacher

We took care of Shadow's body, pillaged everything that we could from the lynch mob worth taking and got the hell out of that Masonic temple. We made it to the Plantation Cemetery's labyrinth area where we got some sleep. The labyrinth is where the elite rich and ultra famous are buried. It's known all over the world as the most peaceful and tranquil resting place. Word on the street had it this was the road less traveled for spirits seeking Heaven. It was a maze like no other: it had marble walls with odd openings, an infinite number of paths to travel. The walls were of all colors, heights, and shapes. It was really like walking in the afterlife. Mausoleums and grave plots were scattered throughout the maze. It had every kind of statue you could imagine. We knew it as a place of safety but it also had its own dangers. The biggest challenge ahead of us was getting to the other side which would be a daunting task. We had never been through here before, so my worries were many, safety wasn't really one of them. We slept in peace for the first time.

I began to dream when I saw Medicine Man on the "Horse of Revenge". I followed him into the night. No words were spoken as we came to a cliff. I gazed out to a full moon when Medicine Man whispered, putting me in a revealing meditative trance. I heard Magic's voice singing "Baba O'Riley" by the Who when I began seeing visions of people I didn't know then shortly after I saw bright calculations, numbers, and letters in the sky. I had no idea what it meant or what this had to do with me. It was a very surreal metric experience. After sleeping longer than I should have I awoke only to discover Gabriel was missing. We were all perplexed. Zombie said, "Maybe he ran away to be alone." I answered, "I can only hope but I don't know. Where we're going maybe it's for the best." We searched everywhere before finally giving up. We decided as a whole to move on and hoped for the best for Gabriel. While splitting a small bag of licorice I said, "Follow me." Ninja asked, "How do you know where to go?" I said, "I just know."

As we moved though the labyrinth, I stopped at what appeared to be the middle of a never-ending road. I saw a beautiful marble octagon building with no windows or doors. The marble had all the colors of a rainbow. I marveled at the sanctuary in awe. Zombie said, "If I am to die, I sure hope they bring me to this place to rest." I stared at the boys then replied, "Be careful what you wish for, you might just get it. Not to worry, nothing lasts forever; sooner or later we'll all get down below in a pine box." Next to the building was the bluest pond I ever saw. We looked at each other when we all began to strip, racing for the water. God did it feel good. It was cold as ice but very refreshing. I felt like I was being baptized as I went under the water. I could hear the song "Simple Man" by Lynyrd Skynyrd. I guess it was all part of the equation, hell I don't know. Some things are not meant to be understood. We eventually dried off then bopped and weaved our way through the labyrinth. Ninja said, "God Damn, we made it! I can't believe it. What would've taken us an eternity, Preacher, you managed to lead us out of in under five hours." I responded, "You can thank Medicine Man." The guys stood there stumped. I just smiled in a brief moment of happiness.

As we stood at the opening of the labyrinth Zombie bent over in frustration yelling, "Fuck, another maze!" I read the sign: Tudor Castle. It was shut down many years ago. I remember reading about it in the local paper. It used to be a booming town and eventually it shut down, turning into a ghost town. It was later turned into a National Park by the government, which never did open. It's not even used as a cemetery anymore. It is rumored to be a place of mysterious toxic waste spills, satanic sacrifices, and where families dropped off their elders who they could no longer take care of. Certainly not on your travel agenda, that's for sure. We had to be crazy to go through there. We only had two choices: go back or continue on. The hedges around us were tall, maybe over twelve feet. We had no choice but to enter cautiously. As I walked inside the Castle Maze the hedges made it a pretty shady place to walk around. The landscape eventually changed into a cornfield maze. I put my hood over my head as the cold wind howled. Hundreds of black crows flew over us. I could feel that eerie feeling coming on. Every once in a while we would come across old scarecrows. A couple times we came to dead ends. I began to meditate so that I might find a way out. I opened my eyes to see my old friend Ghost walking ahead of us toward a bridge, then he vanished. We ran across some creaky old bridge that put us in the direct path of thousands of hanging dolls in the woods. I stopped long enough to witness spiders coming out of their hollow, rotten, plastic bodies with large cobwebs surrounding the tree branches. Zombie asked, "What the hell?" Ninja answered, "We might just be there."

Most of the dolls had pentagrams on their foreheads which was not the best sign for us. I hated looking into the dolls' eyes. They had the face of evil through a mindless stare. As we got over the shock value of the creepy dolls hanging all over the place we continued moving through the forest. Zombie asked, "Do you hear that?" Ninja answered, "Yeah, it sounds like people crying." There was a major divide in the path. I pointed to smoke up ahead. We chose the path that had smoke in the air. I followed the smoke until the path led us to a fire pit, a few huts, and a log cabin. The air had a putrid smell to it.

We walked up to the cabin, where I met an old lady sitting in a creaking rocking chair holding a small baby wrapped in a blanket. The lady was humming, "Give Me That Old Time Religion." I asked, "Are you okay?" The old lady looked up at us and answered, "Of course, safer than you I suppose." We introduced ourselves when she said, "I am Mary. My family always called me Bloody Mary." Joking, Zombie said, "Yes I will have one." Ninja nudged Zombie. Bloody Mary replied, "Why don't you boys come inside; I will make you something to eat for your journey." We were hesitant, hungry and tired as we went inside, then Mary locked the door behind us and put the baby in a crib. Mary said, "You can never be too safe nowadays." She smiled showing her teeth, which were all rotten. I smiled back then looked at the others as we tried not to laugh. We sat at the table when Mary said, "I hope you kids are hungry because I have a lot of stew." Ninja asked, "What's the baby's name?" Mary answered, "Lucifer." I replied, "Wow, what a name. Do you have any other kids?" Mary answered, "I had two sons that were taken from me at birth." I apologized, "I am sorry to hear that." Ninja asked, "Is Lucifer your grandson?" Mary answered, "No. Lucifer is my own flesh and blood." We looked at each other kind of confused. I asked, "What were your son's names?" Mary answered, "Gabriel and Cain." Ninja began coughing when Mary gave him some water. I was shocked. I wondered if we had met her son. In a panic Zombie got up from the table, walked next to Mary in the kitchen and peeked out the back window. Zombie yelled, "Jesus!" Bloody Mary replied, "You won't find him here. What's wrong dear?" Zombie answered, "I saw a man running into the woods in a straight jacket." I stared down Zombie with a dirty look as to say "shut up".

Bloody Mary looked out the window as did Zombie, Mary said, "That's my husband Ivan. You might have seen that lunatic Herod who escaped from a mental hospital." Zombie sarcastically responded, "Herod, is that the infamous Jew who broke in the village hospital butchering children? My God he should have been executed. How did he get here?" Bloody Mary answered, "I don't know of these stories you tell." Zombie replied, "What a couple of notorious names to live

with. I guess it could have been worse being named Ivan the Terrible."
Bloody Mary laughed as she asked Zombie, "How did you know his name?" Zombie mumbled to himself, as he looked frantically at us then quickly back out the window. I barked an obscenity at Zombie while giving him a dirty look in embarrassment. There was a man grilling out in the back wearing a Mormon hat and suit. Zombie said, "Well this is a first. I have never seen anyone grilling in a suit before." Bloody Mary walked away to stir the pot. Zombie kept a close eye on Ivan. Zombie spotted Ivan placing human hands and feet on the grill. Shocked, Zombie walked backwards yelling, "Oh my God!" Mary bumped into me and said, "I will be right back." Bloody Mary walked out the back door; you could hear it being locked from the outside. The cabin only had one window and that was the small kitchen window. The cabin was open like a studio apartment.

Ninja yelled at Zombie, "What the fuck is wrong with you man? Are you trying to insult this poor old lady or what?" Zombie walked over and opened the hot lid with a rag and yelled, "Jesus Christ! We got to get out of here right now you guys!" I asked, "What is wrong with you dude?" Zombie ran frantically to the front door trying to open it but it was locked. Now whining hysterically, Zombie cried, "I saw Ivan put human remains on the BBQ!" Ninja responded back, "That's bullshit Zombie!" Zombie yelled, "Go check the fucking stew out for yourselves, see what you're being served for dinner." I got up to look inside the pot; to our horror, multiple fingers and toes were floating in the stew. Ninja yelled, "Oh my God!" Looking around in a panic I shouted, "Shit you're right! We've got to get out of here, Mary and Ivan are cannibals!" Zombie yelled back, "Of course their fucking cannibals you idiots!" Zombie checked the baby in the crib then suddenly jumped back, screaming, "Jesus, it's a plastic doll for Christ sake! I am getting the fuck out of here now!" Zombie ran to the back door only to be greeted by Ivan and Bloody Mary. Ivan said in a deep voice, "Don't worry, dinner is ready. Go sit back down." Ivan was holding a plate full of meat in one hand and a handgun in the other. Zombie responded, "We were just getting ready to sit down because Preacher and Ninja are so damn hungry." Ivan laughed hysterically while pointing at Zombie remarking, "You are a very funny guy" in a broken Russian accent.

Bloody Mary was setting the table; unfortunately I was sitting across from Ivan, while Ninja was sitting across from Zombie. Blood Mary sat in between Zombie and her husband. Mary began serving stew to Zombie who said, "Mary, I will just take the vegetables because I am a vegetarian, but not to worry, Preacher and Ninja will likely have extra helpings of meat." Zombie, trying to hold back from laughter, had a coy smile on his face. Ninja gave Zombie a smug look then said to Mary "Just a little; I am not that hungry, but Preacher really does prefer extra meat over vegetables." Befuddled, I stared at Ninja with a stunned look on my face. Mary took her time picking out just the human fingers and toes as she set them on my plate. I looked at Mary and said, "I can't imagine all the trouble you had to go through to get all this delicious meat but with that said, I must tell you the truth: Zombie here really is a closet meat-eater." I smiled at Zombie, exchanging my plate for his. Now pale, Zombie had a face of death.

Mary said, "I love a man who eats meat." Ivan yelled, "Enough exchanging plates already! Mary come sit down so we can say grace." Ivan eyed the three of us when he zeroed in on me then suggested, "Why don't you say grace." Everyone bowed their head; Zombie kept peeking at me with a smile while Ivan stared at me. I prayed, "Umm. Dear Heavenly Father, thank you for this lively surprising feast, may my friends really enjoy eating their meat." Zombie interrupted as he coughed in laughter. Ivan pounded on the table, paused then yelled, "Continue!" Ivan closely watched Zombie. Zombie fought off hard attempting not to laugh. I continued the prayer, "Lord I have always kept my promise to you to never eat meat but bless those who indulge in such lively appetites. May you watch for Ivan and Mary soon; Amen." Ivan shook his head said, "Well that's an interesting prayer, now let's eat." Mary immediately put a thumb in her mouth like it was a chicken bone. Ivan grabbed a big toe eating it whole as he watched our reactions. Mary put her other hand under the table groping Zombie's man parts. Zombie bounced up coughing. Ivan yelled, "Sit down and eat your meat!" I noticed Bloody Mary rubbing Zombie's knob under the table so I gave Zombie a funny look then glanced directly across the table at Ivan.

Bloody Mary had to be in her mid 70's while Ivan might have been in his early 40's. Ninja asked, "So Ivan, how long have you been married to this cougar?" Ivan answered, "twenty-five years." The room reached dead silence. With his face blush red from Grandma Mary fondling him under the table, Zombie squirmed all over the chair. Grumpy, Ivan asked Zombie, "Maybe it's time you eat, hmm?" Ivan pointed the gun at Zombie waiting for him to taste the meat. Zombie put the finger in his mouth trying to chew on the rubbery meat when he began to gag. Ivan said, "The meat is a little spicy." Zombie couldn't swallow the meat. I could see he was about to heave. Ivan yelled, "Well, how does it taste? Well? Well, out with it son!" Zombie puked all over Ivan's plate and lap. Ninja yelled at Mary, "You are one sick bitch!" Ivan pointed his gun at Ninja and asked "What did you say?" I had no choice so I fired two shots from under the table as Ivan's head fell into his plate of food. Mary lunged over the table with a steak knife at Ninja. Ninja grabbed the gun from Ivan's hand; without hesitation he shot Mary in the head. She collapsed to her death right on the table. That was the true meaning of dinner served.

I said with sarcasm, "Well I think we can skip supper." We quickly rummaged through the cabin, finding a few clips for Ivan's handgun. It was a CZ-75 9mm semi automatic. Ninja now owned his first gun. I had a Glock 40 caliber handgun from the lynch mob. We might not have had the best weapons but we were gathering more modern weapons throughout our journey. Ninja said to Zombie, "I guess you don't need Wanda anymore because you got Grandma." I laughed when Zombie yelled back, "Screw you guys; she tried to rape me!" Busting Zombie's chops I asked, "Aren't you capable of landing someone your own age instead of an old hag? And to think you could've handled Wanda, what a pity." Ninja added, "That cougar obviously wasn't right in the head." After composing himself, Zombie said, "You're certainly right about that whack job." I yelled, "Come on guys, we better get a move on it!" We zinged on down the path only to hear crying of some sort, it was getting louder. Out of nowhere we witnessed old people coming out of the woods running back towards the cabin. Zombie asked, "Do you think those old demented people are cannibals too?" I answered, "I don't know, I certainly don't want to find out." We looked back to see Herod running toward us in a straight jacket with the cannibals chasing him. Zombie said, "Herod, what comes around, goes around my friend." Zombie shot Herod in the leg. The lunatic fell down; all you could see were old people on top of him like starved wolves. We had seen enough so we bolted like true heroes.

The sun was fading in the distance and we were on borrowed time. I was growing tired of the puzzled mazes. We walked for hours in the blackness only to see the stars out in force. I bet there were over a thousand beaming stars in the night sky. I heard an owl hooting in front of us. Excited, Zombie yelled, "Check it out!" We flashed our lights forward; there stood a gigantic shiny silver castle that glowed. Ninja said, "I'll be damned, you did it again." We raced toward the castle when without warning the drawbridge came crashing down. Bright lights shined upon us. I said, "Unless I am seeing things a knight is coming out to greet us." The knight's armor was shiny silver with a lighted glow around him. God, he looked ancient but magnificent, and not from this realm. We met him at the edge of the drawbridge. He pointed his sword, challenging us not to come across. I said, "We wish not to harm you; we come in peace." The knight answered, "There are only two ways to come across: one by your death or that of my own. I must warn you I have never lost in combat. Go back to where you came from and your lives will be spared." I asked, "Let me understand this, you want us to duel with you in order to get to the other side, is that right? What is your name?" The knight answered, "I am the ancient one who knows nothing of time." Zombie asked, "Do I need to shoot this prick?" The knight answered, "You can't kill me other than by sword. It has been written in honor and time. If you try you will only murder your own souls with dishonor." I looked back at the guys and asked, "Where is Shadow when you need him? This was his destiny, not mine." Ninja replied, "No, this is my destiny. I am the best of us at sword fighting." I responded, "I can't let you do this. There must be another way." Ninja answered, "Preacher, you and I know what I speak is the truth. We can't turn back. Now let me do what must be done. Everything has its end."

Ninja put all his stuff down then slowly drew out his sword. Zombie and I could only watch. Ninja bowed to the knight in a gesture of respect. The ancient knight said to Ninja, "It is my honor to kill you. I will send your soul home so it may be free at last." Ninja replied, "Let it be written, let it be done." Ninja bowed to the knight once more then out of the blue the clash of swords began. Sparks came from the steel of their blades. Ninja moved gracefully while the ancient knight moved effortlessly and with tremendous balance. On a counter-move, the knight swiftly sliced Ninja on his right side of his ribs to draw first blood. Ninja stayed focused again he went on the attack. The knight blocked everything Ninja had to offer. Ninja rushed in again and again with aggressive swordsmanship but the knight's defenses were superb.

Ninja began to grow reckless as he attacked wildly, charging in only to once again have the ancient knight use a counter attack, this time slicing Ninja in the left calf. Ninja was tiring while the ancient knight was still going strong. With great concentration, Ninja focused on his breathing, closed his eyes for a brief second when a vision of Shadow came to him showing Ninja the knight's weakness. Ninja hesitated as he awaited the knight's attack. Ninja had been the aggressor so far while the knight counter attacked. Shadow's secret was to reverse the roles. The knight became impatient. As the knight became unbalanced with a full attack, he also got sloppy. It was at this moment that Ninja seized his opportunity and in spectacular fashion stuck his sword into the ancient knight's neck. The ancient one had finally seen time come to his rescue. The knight's honorable fate had finally ended to the other side of the realm. Ninja bowed then said, "I am sorry for your death ancient one. You are a valiant warrior." A loud voice from above commanded, "Come across."

We walked across as the drawbridge began closing. I looked around but there was little to see. As one drawbridge closed the other side opened. We ran out of the other drawbridge. I glanced back at the castle where we all saw a big bright bubble in the sky with the knight's body floating as if it was going to Elysium. I said to Ninja, "Let me look at your wounds." To our surprise, Ninja's wounds were healed as if he had none. Zombie yelled, "I can't believe it!" I replied, "It was the knight's honor that healed Ninja's wounds." A beautiful sword appeared embedded in the grass next to Ninja. It was a gift from the honorable knight. Ninja grabbed the sword; he could feel an amazing power from its handle. He gave me the sword that belonged to his father and said, "This will serve you well one day." I said to Ninja, "Thank you. I am honored to have it." Feeling left out Zombie asked, "Hey, what about me?" Ninja looked at Zombie and said, "You suck at sword fighting; best you stick with guns." I laughed as Ninja handed Zombie Ivan's handgun. I commented, "Ninja, you suck at shooting anyway." Excited, Zombie said, "Thanks, now let's get the hell out of here."

CHAPTER TWENTY FIVE: DECEIVED

Journals by Raven

The next morning I woke up to the sounds of Cheech and Chong barking. Maverick opened his eyes to see Wolf standing in front of him. Wolf said sarcastically, "You guys sure know how to pick a place to camp at." I asked, "Where's Beast at, man?" Chief answered, "The clowns killed him." Maverick cried, "Damn, I can't believe it. We killed that crazy clown Bonzo." Wolf replied, "Yeah we know. We found his body hanging in the stairwell." I asked, "Where are we man?" Wolf answered, "You dip shits have been sleeping in the Suicide Forest. Thanks to your mutts, I was able to track you guys down." Maverick asked, "What's the story behind the Suicide Forest?" Wolf answered, "This is the place where they dance with the Devil. The demon spirits of the forest are conjured up by the practice of Voodoo they say. Many confused souls come here to meet their end. Hope is lost only to be consumed by an eternity of darkness. This is where a great many black folks are buried as well. The suicide forest is no joke. Hell is an eternal punishment." Chief added, "So what Wolf is trying to say is we need all our wits today, so no indulging with the sweet leaf. Be ready to move out in ten minutes."

It wasn't long before we got the opportunity to experience the mystic dead zone. I heard music in the distance. I said, "Hey man that sounds like 'Casey Jones' by the Grateful Dead." The music got louder when I saw a young kid lying against a tree. He was wearing a tie-dye Grateful Dead t-shirt, jeans, and a black bandana on his head. A radio next to him played "Truckin" also by the Grateful Dead while there was a needle sticking out of his arm. Chief said, "Poor bastard." I said, "Well at least he got a great buzz listening to awesome music before he checked out." I rummaged through the kid's pocket and found a bag of pot. I said to the dead kid, "You won't need this anymore." Chief asked, "Do you always need that shit?" I answered, "My reality man, only way to stay high on life. Anyway, everyone on earth has a vice. Some just hide it better than others." Chief answered, "I guess you're right."

It couldn't have been more than twenty feet before we came upon a girl lying in a dead flowerbed. As morbid as it may sound the vision looked like a famous painting. Wolf noticed she had slit her wrists. Wolf checked her pulse then said, "Her body is still warm. She recently checked out. What a fucking waste." We continued through the forest finding several more bodies along the way. Broken people committing suicide to die alone was a very depressing sight. Wolf kept following the path as reggae music got louder. Pausing, Maverick said, "I haven't heard that song in a while." He was referring to the song "Waiting In Vain" by Bob Marley. I replied, "I don't think this is such a bad place to die man. If I could overdose with drugs while music flowed through my veins this wouldn't be the worst resting place for eternity." Maverick said, "You are morbid, brother." I smiled, laughing at Maverick. I was trying hard to fight off the temptation of my own demons. My body urged for some drugs. I tried hiding the fact I was a junkie. The demons in my head wouldn't leave me alone.

We followed the reggae music until Wolf found a dirt road leading out of the woods. We came to a small village with straw huts on both sides of the road. Passing by I saw people selling animal remains along with bartering human bones, including skulls. One thing was for certain: we stuck out like a sore thumb. I never knew there was a ghetto area in the cemetery. All the huts seemed to have one thing in common: they all were selling and bartering Voodoo. Chief said, "I see our luck is still running." The people were fucking creepy man. Some spooky villager attempted to sell me chicken claws and a human skull. He yelled, "Ten dollars, you buy, you buy, cheap, cheap!" I think they were surprised to see white boys traveling through. I believe they were either scared of us because they thought we were crazy spirits or shocked that we had the balls to walk through their turf to begin with. Either way they never gave us any trouble other than trying to peddle us their witchcraft. I was getting annoyed with how pushy they were.

There was a strange church at the end of the street. I could hear choir music along with yelling and screaming coming from that direction. As we got to the front Maverick said, "Wow, look at this place." From the ground up the church was made of human bones. We walked inside to see what was happening. I saw some people singing while a priest (or Voodoo witch doctor) was performing some peculiar ritual on a naked woman kneeling on the floor. The witch doctor was holding up a beheaded chicken dancing around the woman as blood was being poured over her. Cheech and Chong were beginning to growl so Chief told me, "Get the dogs out of here." Maverick said, "This is the craziest thing I have ever seen." Chief replied, "I don't want to interrupt their witchcraft so let's get out of here." The rest of the guys walked through the church of bones when they ran into another witch doctor. He was a big man wearing a boned mask and jacket. He held a chicken leg in one hand and a catholic cross in the other. He had bone jewelry all over his body. Shocking would be an understatement. The witch doctor asked, "Can I help you?" Wolf answered, "We were just passing through. We didn't mean to interrupt the chicken cock-a-doodle-doo party." The witch doctor replied, "If I were you white bread I would get the fuck out of here." Wolf answered, "You don't have to tell us twice, we are leaving without issue." Maverick said, "Thank God I hate chickens." The boys met me around back as the dogs pissed on about every spot marking their territory. Chief said, "Let's get out of this bizarre ghetto." Maverick replied, "I'll bet this place isn't even on a map."

We walked through the woods when I noticed an open field of rusted anchors of all sizes and shapes by the thousands. Maverick asked, "Why are there anchors all around with no water?" Wolf answered, "I don't know, maybe we're not far from the ocean." It wasn't long before we were in the midst of a thick fog. We came upon the front gates, shaped like spiders. Chief said, "Shit, we're at the Cursed Village as he pushed the gates open. We had to be insane to go through this place. At one point or another we all experienced the sighting of haunted apparitions that would appear then disappear. I hated dealing with the supernatural man. Finally Chief stopped for a break. We sat on the steps of some old creepy house. I nibbled on the last of my food as the guys pitched in to feed the dogs. Wolf commented, "From here on out it looks like we'll be hunting for our food." Maverick said, "These cemeteries are like hell in a bucket." Wolf replied, "Your thoughts are really strange sometimes."

I wondered if the others had made it to the shores of Crowley's place. I hoped they were having an easier time than we were. I couldn't wait to hang with my friend Ghost again. I could hear the sound of screeching horses galloping on the dirt road when out of nowhere we spotted maybe twenty monks on horseback. Nobody had to say a word as we ran for our lives back into the woods. Luckily for us we finally caught a break later in the day, stumbling upon an ancient church. I read the sign, "Church of the Dead." Chief said, "Jesus, just when you thought hypocrisy had no bounds." I walked inside the church only to be greeted with a glass cabinet full of mummies dressed in unthinkable costumes. The one that hit me the most was a mummy dressed as a Nazi officer of the Third Reich. Chills went down my spine. The floor tiles surrounded a massive black cross emblem on the floor. You talk about deranged art and architecture, this place had it all. I wondered to myself how they could call this place a church. It was sacrilegious, man.

The ceilings were vaulted with paintings drawn of angels and demons fighting one another; it didn't look like the angels were winning, by the way.

I heard footsteps behind us as we all turned around; there was an old couple walking toward us. The old man asked, "Are you here for the reckoning?" This old fucker was terrifying to look at. Chief answered, "No we are not." The old man said, "I am giving a sermon in an hour; you all should really come." We looked at each other scratching our heads when Chief asked, "Who are you? What kind of church is this?" The old man answered, "I am sorry for not introducing myself young man. My name is Samael Bathory and this is my wife Illuminati. We own the church. You have nothing to worry about, we preach the true religion. We are the bringers of the light." Exhaling I said, "Man, some church Reverend." Wolf said, "Let me guess, if we put money in the offerings we can come see your show." Illuminati said, "You all need saving and salvation." Chief asked, "Saving from what?" Samael answered, "From yourselves of course. You need to join the Church of the Dead so that you can become the anointed ones. You must be part of the one hundred and forty-four thousand chosen ones." The old couple looked as if they were a thousand years old. Their body odor was disgusting. Chief said, "Thanks for the offer Reverend but we are going to have to pass." The Reverend answered back, "Well if you change your mind service is in an hour." The old couple walked slowly past us as Illuminati petted Chong; Chong let out a loud squeal before they went out the door. My poor dog was shaking; he felt an evil presence. So I took both dogs on a walk. The guys meanwhile walked around the creepy church. At one point they noticed a black room with a stage and carved animal chairs made of wood. Wolf finally said, "We are burning daylight, let's get out of here." The boys were taking a break near the front entrance of the church while I walked the dogs. I began daydreaming while having a conversation with myself. My thoughts were wrestling with the voices in my head. I tried to make sense of the world we lived in.

It's amazing to see all the shit that goes on in the cemetery. Most people are mistaken thinking that dead people rest here when in fact the cemetery is the liveliest place to be. The graveyard's never dull; it only makes the heart beat faster living on the edge. It turns out that the Underworld is the same as it is on the outside only more exciting. This is a gateway to abandoned buildings, neighborhoods, churches, funeral parlors, asylums, towns, castles, and even pubs. It's an ancient world in here. The people roaming around are from all walks of life and time. In the cemetery all things are possible. The unexplained is reality here, paranormal is not uncommon. The logical person might argue this point until he spends a couple days and nights here. I promise a person's opinion will change quickly.

If you read the Bible or tried asking a priest questions that he doesn't know or he can't explain, the priest will always use the excuse, "you must have faith". It is no different in the cemetery. My answer is no different than any priest would give, so I'll just use their answer as well when it comes to the cemetery, "Have faith baby." It's at least a better answer than what our governments give us with lies and corruption. Are the people we deem crazy really insane? We throw them away like they weren't even human then justify it with drugs, then locking the door and throwing away the key. To me it is just a modern way of pimping. You want to see a doctor, they give you medication to help but it's really a hidden agenda to pimp you out for money for the next prescription. The only difference between a doctor and a drug pusher on the street is that the government justifies it with laws, regulations, and red tape. Legalization is justified by what some say is law. The governments continue to take our freedoms, all the while giving the illusion of freedom. Governments across the globe are the biggest drug pushers of all. Talk about calling the kettle black. Families dropped their clinically sick and older family members off as if they were getting rid of an unwanted dog by stranding them here in the cemetery. This is the government's and medical establishment's best answer, for better or worse. God forbid the drug actually works...you are a slave to modern legal drug pushers whose only purpose is to make a profit. I prefer my own free will by growing my own drugs. Make no mistake: I realized the cemetery was a dangerous free for all, much like the Wild West. This place is a parallel to civilization where only the strong survive. Paper money will always drive human greed but in here it is the journey, kill or be killed, nothing more to it. Survival of the fittest is such a fucking contradiction between civilization and the cemetery. The truth of the matter is it's no different on the outside, just another door or world to explore with the same ugly instincts in here.

Heaven and hell in my view are the same. Humans didn't build the world or the galaxy. We certainly didn't make ourselves nor did we ask to be created. Who is at fault is up for debate. Man is flawed badly but so is his maker. Maybe God and Satan are guilty of the same thing Adam and Eve were. I think they all ate from the tree of life; that's why things are so fucked up. Humans are guilty of their greed but so are the almighty ones. God and Satan fight for their own self-worshiping power struggles. Hell, I actually think those two could be brothers fighting over the same thing while unfortunately mankind is stuck in the middle of it. It certainly makes me wonder if we are just pawns from an ancient chess set. You can't make the world then say you're not going to take blame for it; sounds like passing the buck to me. More wars and bloodshed have been fought over religion than any other reason. Whether you believe in good or evil, governments or religions, they all have one thing in common: the ultimate goal to conquer and conform others by any means *necessary. I just know there have been way too many people who lost their lives and freedom because of it. There is no such thing as freedom: that's just an illusion. I used to think religion and the Bible's main message was compassion for one another. Now you get a sermon asking for money so he can make his show even bigger. Every religion preaches they are the true religion. I think religions hold just as much corrupt power as governments with their justifications for their actions: child abuse, drugs, lust, murder, greed and the struggle for power. That's what those two represent these days and their biggest weapon is preaching fear for their own agendas. Whoever controls the media controls the propaganda and whoever controls the military also controls the power. What they fail to understand or grasp is what we know as Karma. It comes to each of us, this much I know. The only Revelation I have seen is what goes on in the world and in the cemetery. One is no better than the other, it's just the cemetery's rite of passage to shuttle those to other worlds. Every person picks a side in their lifetime. The same wars of greed continue like Groundhog Day over and over again. History just keeps repeating itself; the only things that change are the endless names and faces. Responsibility in the universe has never existed. Like anything else shit rolls down hill.*

My question is, "How do you trust a faceless man or entity who preaches to the world for eternity yet does not show himself?" We all have recreational vices. God's vice is to sit in judgment of his own creation playing the blame game. I can never trust someone who says, "Do as I say, not as I do." Murder is murder. I see it in the world, in the cemetery; I certainly have read it throughout the history of the Bible. Even his holiness has killed. Even in eternity, laws have political bearings. We have now become the reflection of our makers and adversaries. I've grown tired with the lies that I can now see with wisdom because my eyes are wide open. My consciousness is burning with rage and anger within my own soul. They say if you really want to find the guilty in the world, you only have to look as far as those who make the laws; they are the same ones breaking the laws. Lawmakers are the guilty ones using such trickery as deceit and manipulation of others through fear and force. Sadly, the leader who does speak out in opposition is the leader who dies from it. Just look at our past and there lies the rotten truth. One might see the Cemetery Boys as crusaders, but that would be a wrong conclusion. The rich and powerful have always walked over the poor and always will. Those who are offended by this know my words are the truth. I say, too bad, you made your bed, now lie in it with Karma next to you. My criticism of mankind, God, and Satan is: genocide can never be the solution. All three are guilty with no defense for their actions.

My thoughts turned to Chief; he races to death so he can embrace it. His rage is not only with mankind or Satan. He wants the ultimate embrace with the one who made the laws but couldn't follow his own laws. Chief's vision is to strike down with his sword in one blow that of angels, demons, Satan, Jesus, and God. He believes this will be the only way to purify the world again. As deranged as it may sound, no one has changed it for the better as of yet. I do know many have suffered for it. If you followed the lawmakers' answer to things, they just remove the leaders who have the courage to speak the truth. Bold maybe, but when you can't practice what you preach, Chief only believes in punishment, just like his maker. "Vengeance is mine" said the Lord, but it never came. It seemed to be nothing more than a threat to his brothers Satan and older sibling known as Death. Confusion must have set in because his brothers were the only ones who followed through. Chief's father used to say, "Keep your friends close but your enemies closer; thirst to embrace the enemy with death when opportunity knocks." The world, the Bible, and the cemetery were warping our minds, not to mention Satan himself. Hell, maybe we all needed to go see a shrink so we could work out what was fiction from reality. I certainly didn't know anymore. I could only watch it slip away on a daily basis.

As I drifted back to reality, I heard the others talking. I was waiting by the stairs when I saw the Gothic Girls outside smoking near the church. Their French smoking was very sexy, the way they exhaled the smoke slowly from their mouth. Maverick said, "What a blessing; these girls are hot." They all looked at us, checking us up and down. The girl with black hair gave Maverick a wink as she walked inside the church. Ecstatic, Maverick yelled, "It's time to get some stray-ass boys!" Chief looked at Maverick and said, "We don't have time for that right now." Maverick replied, "Go ahead, I'll catch up with you later." Chief said, "Don't be a fool man. Let's go." Maverick yelled, "That's bullshit Chief! Let's get a little trim then we can be on our way." Chief warned, "Hey man, I am not going to tell you again. Forget these spellbinders." You could see that Maverick was getting defensive, asking, "Or what? What are you going to do?" Chief got in Maverick's face then said, "It's your funeral man." Chief walked away. This was the first time I ever saw Maverick disagree with Chief. Wolf followed Chief up the hill. I said to Maverick, "Come on man, we can do this another time." Maverick replied, "Hey, we are all going to die; stay with me, let's at least get some trim like old times." I answered, "Not this time bro. Wizard is counting on us." I walked away hoping my friend would follow. Maverick yelled out, "You're being a bunch of pussies!"

I turned back watching Maverick walk back into the church. He walked around searching for the Gothic Girls when he spotted three of them sitting in the front row by the stage. He suddenly felt a tap on the shoulder. A girl with black hair smiled at Maverick asking, "Are you looking for me?" Maverick answered back, "As a matter of fact I am. Where are the rest of the girls?" She asked, "Wow you are hungry, am I not enough for you?" She grabbed Maverick's hand and said, "Come on, I will introduce you to the girls, you can have your pick." Maverick smiled while checking out the girls, "Shit you ladies are smoking hot!" The girls started giggling. Maverick introduced himself when the girl with black hair said, "Maverick, what an interesting name. My name is Violent X, the girl with white hair is Moonlight, blue hair is Stormy, and our beautiful redhead is Raven. Here come the other girls now. The girl with pink hair is Rayne, yellow is Autumn and last with green hair is Anastasia." Maverick remarked, "Wow, my own harem." Violent X stared Maverick down asking, "So, who is your pick?" Maverick, grinning ear to ear answered, "All of you." Violent X looking up at the other girls, said in a deviant voice, "He wants us all, girls. What a great choice." Moonlight asked Maverick, "Do you think you can handle all this candy?" Maverick answered, "I don't know but I would love to find out." Anastasia licked her lips with her long tongue while staring at Maverick.

The girls locked the door, moved several chairs out of the way, set a dark blanket on the floor. Maverick began to kiss his harem of Gothic Girls one at a time. Music from Linkin Park's "Crawling" played on the intercom. Several girls formed a circle, moving as one counter-clockwise. Maverick's lust for passion made him vulnerable. Moonlight and Violent X were aggressive, both kissing him on each side of his neck. Passion was taking over as he became relaxed. Maverick felt a pierce in his neck then an immediate burning sensation. He pushed the girls away when he realized they were vampires. All the girls began surging in on Maverick. Blood dripped down his neck. He witnessed Violent X's mouth trickling his blood down her cheeks. His temper took over as the girls were attacking him, but he couldn't do anything about it. The bites made him feel faint and dizzy. His strength disappeared; he fell to the floor, the vampire girls showed him no mercy. Within minutes Maverick was fighting for his life. He was becoming lifeless, his body severely drained of blood. The black stage curtains opened with Reverend Samael and his wife Illuminati waiting for the girls to drag his body to the stage. A guillotine awaited Maverick.

In the meantime I walked through the cemetery when I said, "Hey man, we better go back for him." Wolf agreed; Chief hesitated as he gazed out towards the hill when he saw visions of Medicine Man standing at the church door. Chief yelled, "Come on, we gotta go back now!" We raced to the church. The girls set Maverick in the guillotine; six of the girls plus the Reverend's wife formed a circle around it. Reverend led the girls in singing some twisted church hymn. Violent X pulled Maverick's neck back whispering, "Not to worry, it will all be over soon lover. You will be with us forever as we drink the remaining blood from your body. Don't worry babe, I'll eat your flesh later for dinner." Maverick whispered back, "Fuck you bitch!" Violent X laughed as the Reverend looked down at Maverick and said, "Your suffering will not go in vain son." Maverick softly said, "I'm not your fucking son." Just like that the Reverend let go of the rope, Maverick could only helplessly watch the blade come down on his neck as Violent X smiled at him.

We broke the fucking door down, rushed inside the room, but it was too late. "Heart Shaped Box" by Nirvana played on the intercom. On stage the vampire girls with the Reverend and his sick wife were eating Maverick as if they never ate a meal before. They looked up when the door broke open. Wolf yelled out, "You sick bitches!" I shot my bow hitting Reverend right in the heart. Chief rushed to the stage like a madman swinging his Kama's with full force. Wolf used his giant knives slaying everything that moved. One by one we killed the Gothic vampire girls like wild savages. I shot the old bitch Illuminati in the forehead as she screamed. The attack happened so fast we lost ourselves in the killing spree. In the end, the room looked like a slaughterhouse. The crime scene was a nightmare. Our actions were worse than anything I could have ever imagined. Chief was covered in blood, his rage out of control. The only one left was a dying Violent X. Wolf held her down in the guillotine as Chief took his turn pulling the rope up only to let it go. Just like that Violent X was beheaded like John the Baptist. Chief began hammering his Kama's into her body. Blood splattered everywhere as Chief yelled. Wolf had to scream at Chief to stop. Finally Chief's rage had seized. There was very little left of Maverick or Violent X.

I yelled, "Let's get washed up, we've done enough here man!" My heart was broken with Maverick's death. I felt responsible. Chief mentally broke today. He scared me. In reality we all had lost it when we didn't heed Wizard's warning long ago. As I walked out of the church I could hear "People are Strange" by the Doors on the intercom. It was a perfect song to a day of insanity. Maverick and I were huge Doors fans so it was surreal. I was so lightheaded I couldn't think rationally anymore. We were losing our way on the journey. Something was taking control over us. We were changing with every step. We were losing control, becoming no different than those of evil. Wizard was right: we invited evil into our souls and now we were playing in the devil's playground. I think it was the first time I realized our thirst for revenge was a war we couldn't win. All our chips were in at the center of the table, there was no chance of asking the dealer to re-deal us a better hand. We had to save Wizard at all costs even if it meant death or the loss of our souls. We had nowhere to run except straight to Hell. It was our actions that sealed Wizard's fate.

I was coming to terms with the insanity of the world and my own reality. So my conclusion of the good, the bad and the ugly was: they were just like me. Insane, psychopath, sociopath, murderer, was this who we had become? Was this the real me? My head had more questions than answers. Things were becoming foggy while irrational thoughts and behaviors were becoming instinctive. Chief always strived to be happy yet he was never satisfied. He always wanted to push the limits of the unknown no matter what the cost. If there was ever a Holy Grail we needed it now more than ever. Not even living in the moment could we find it, it seemed as if hope was lost. Maybe Wizard was right all along; our best defense was our own mind. Unfortunately mine felt warped. I was feeling faint while voices talked to me and alarm clocks went off in my head. The lunatic inside me wouldn't leave me alone. I swear to God the lunatic was not me. I could hear the song "Brain Damage" by Pink Floyd rattling upstairs in my inner darkness. I began singing the song. The boys laughed wondering where that came from within me. Dreams, nightmares and thoughts were surfing around in my mind as if I were in a straight jacket trying to keep the loonies away during a bad acid trip.

Later in the evening we slept in an open field. My dream kept playing in my head like a rerun. It was Jesus and Satan grappling. Their war was about forgiving yet neither had the courage to forgive one another. I no longer wanted an easy life; I wanted the strength to endure its hell. Somehow we must not have listened to the conductor. We were on the fast track on the wrong train. I just remember when he yelled in my nightmare, "All aboard the crazy train of life." The train had left the station with all passengers aboard including Misfits, Angels, Demons, Jesus, Satan and God. We were on a collision course with Heaven, Hell, Crowley's Tomb and Death all at one time. I think we were about to unlock the mysteries and secrets of our friend they call Death. We were no longer walking towards it, we were galloping to it.

MAVERICK

CHAPTER TWENTY SIX: EPIPHANY

Journals by Zombie

I heard screams as I woke up on the beach. It was extremely foggy that morning. Preacher ran out of the fog screaming with a crab clung to his nose. Ninja separated the crab by breaking the body from the claw. Preacher screamed in pain as the claw still hung from his nose. Preacher said, "Son of a bitch does that hurt." We laughed deliriously as blood dripped from Preacher's nose. I asked Preacher, "Are we condemned or what?" Preacher answered, "The only condemned man is a dead man." The fog was parting when Ninja said, "I don't believe my eyes." I asked, "What is it?" Ninja pointed behind us and said, "It's the Secret Temple. I can't believe it actually exists." I reluctantly asked, "What is so special about this place?" Ninja answered, "It is rumored to be a junction point between Earth and the Underworld where rampaging demons snatch unaware souls." I yelled out, "Well fuck that place! I am not going there." Preacher interrupted, "Relax Zombie, it's just a fable." I said, "I see it with my own eyes. How can it be a fable? Has this journey been just a fucking myth? What is wrong with you both?" Preacher answered, "Only one way to find out if the story is true." Ninja jumped up in excitement high fiving Preacher. I was very upset with this idea. Ninja asked me, "Do we really have a choice here?" I was really pissed off at them as I answered, "Yes, let's go back and find another way." Preacher ranted, "Are you out of your mind? We are lost, we have no food, and we are running behind schedule! Did you forget we have to meet the others?" In total frustration I yelled back, "Ok, fuck it! You want to go get us killed fighting demon warriors, fine let's do it. My blood is on your hands my friends." Ninja responded, "Now that's the spirit. I promise you I won't let anything happen to you. I would jump in front of harm's way for you guys." I mumbled, "Well, famous last words buddy. I hope you remember that later." Preacher said, "No worries, last one there eats dog dodo."

I reached the bottom of the mountain jungle last but I certainly wasn't eating dog dodo. I admit it was beautiful. Back at the beach I could partially see the city but from here it was well hidden. We began the long awaited walk up the mountain stairs. Little did I know the wrapping stairs would take us over two hours before we would reach the mountain top. There was no city to be found. Ninja pointed to another mountain. I was getting less thrilled as there were rocks between the two mountains. It would only take one slip to your own death. Ninja said, "This is the Immortal Bridge." I asked, "Are you nuts? That's suicide to walk across!" Ninja said, "Oh we haven't got to that bridge yet." I answered back, "Oh that's just perfect." We carefully walked across the bridge when we came upon what Ninja called the Emperors Peak. I said, "Boy oh boy this just keeps on getting better." Preacher said, "Why don't you stop your bitching, enjoy the moment." I replied, "At least you got the moment part right." We walked up another mountain staircase before burning another hour of daylight when we finally reached the top. I noticed an ancient stone bridge with a bunch of cats standing on top of the old side rails. For no apparent reason the cats jumped to their deaths. More copycats ran to the rail then jumped off. We ran to look over the edge to see what happened. Preacher said, "Oh my God! Did you see those cats commit suicide?" I answered, "No cat is going to rightfully jump off a bridge. They could have jumped down and ran away. I am telling you guys this is just a glance of what is to come. Let's get out of here now!" Another cat landed on Ninja's back only to jump to its death. I yelled, "What the fuck is going on?" We ran toward a pack of cats that hurried by us only to repeat the process of the other ill-fated cats.

Finally we made it to the front gate where a sign had foreign writing on it. I asked, "What in the hell does it say?" Ninja answered, "The Seventeen Serpents of the Forbidden City." I asked, "Well doesn't that mean we are not to go in there?" The walls around it were gigantic and incredible in length. The gates were huge; out of the blue the gates slowly opened. Without thinking about it we walked through the doors. Suddenly the gate behind us slammed shut. There was no one in plain sight. The architecture was breathtaking, I admit I was excited, yet scared at the same time. Ninja from time to time used to talk about a place that had many names. The one that stuck out in my mind was called, "The Forbidden City of the Gods." The size of this great city alone, not to mention being abandoned, was overwhelming. Preacher asked Ninja, "Where do we go from here?" Ninja said, "My Father always told stories of the tyrant who believed he was the son of heaven, king of the air, and was chosen to rule the earth. We have to find the center. The self-anointed one believed the construction of the city should be aligned with the kings of the south and the kings of the north. The empire structure would align with the stars in order to serve the deities. The center of the great city was called the "Sacred Tabernacle". It is rumored over twelve thousand rooms existed throughout the Secret Temple. I only remember bits and pieces of the story my Father once told me about this place. I never thought this gem actually existed. He said the night sky above the empire took the shape of a cross. I wonder how this place was not discovered. We should be honored to find it." I replied, "I will be honored just to get the fuck out of here." Preacher said, "You are really something man. You have to learn to appreciate what we have found here because no one else has, ever. We have stumbled onto history bro." I responded, "I don't want to be part of history, especially here. This place gives me the creeps. Let's just find our way out of here." Preacher asked, "Do you think there is treasure here?" Ninja answered, "Oh yes, if you're into necrophilia. The treasure was that of virgin women at the Imperial Harem who, after the Tyrant died, were hung so they could serve him in the afterlife." Preacher scoffed, "Lucky him, shit for us." I asked, "Is this a place for the Gods or for the Devil?" Ninja answered, "There was a great war in Heaven before the days of Noah. Later they built a place of peace only to have the prince of darkness come and betray the world." I said, "You mean Lucifer. My father never used names, so I don't know who he was referring to. I always thought he was making up tales of the Emperor."

Walking from one monument to another I was awestruck. I asked Preacher, "How is the entire universe put together?" Preacher stopped. Stumped, he replied, "I have to think about that, let me get back to you on that one." As we turned the corner I walked in the room first only to be met by a room full of dead people who were hung from ropes. I yelled, "Jesus Christ!" Preacher replied, "I don't think we are going to be able to conjure him here." There were women, servants, and what Ninja called eunuchs hanging from several rooms. Terrified I asked, "What is a eunuch?" Ninja answered, "A man with his balls removed." I yelled, "Fuck me! To think my balls sag from time to time. Let's get out of here! I appreciate my balls thank you very much." Ninja ordered, "Just close your eyes, the spirits of the dead are playing mind games." I closed my eyes only to slowly open them to a eunuch staring at me with his tongue sticking out. I screamed. "It's not working!" Preacher yelled back, "Focus harder!" The boys opened their eyes and the room was empty. With my eyes tightly shut I was still panicking when I cried out, "I don't want to lose my balls." Ninja patted me on the back replying, "That's not going to happen; it's just a bad dream. Open your eyes." I opened my eyes and remarked, "I'll say." Continuing on we went through many rooms only to be played with by demons; we were witnesses to traumatic and gruesome tortures from the past, but we just kept pushing through.

We had finally reached the center of the palace. Believe it or not I marveled at its beauty. I never expected that coming from here.

Someone had a true vision when building this palace. As we looked back to take in this cosmic view from the terrace we saw an unexpected visitor. It was the Tall Man leaning against his black hearse. He was acting out movements as a conductor from an orchestra. The song "O Fortuna" by Carl Orff raged from the speakers. It was the spookiest thing I ever saw. The Tall Man had to be about 8'6" in height. Validating my fears, I yelled, "Oh shit, it is the Tall Man!" Preacher asked, "How could a hearse possibly get up here? That's impossible!" Ninja shouted, "It's all in our minds; he doesn't really exist!" We closed our eyes, it had worked before. I opened my eyes and yelled, "He's rapidly walking toward the stairs smiling!" The Tall Man had long strides along with animated facial expressions. He had such an intimidating presence. He thrived on shock value I think. Every time we ran into this maniac he always seemed to move in slow motion with strobe light after-effects. I screamed, "Let's get the hell out of here!" We rushed down the outer halls when I looked back and said, "He is coming after us." While running, Ninja asked, "Doesn't this asshole ever get tired?" We ran through an open room, down another stairwell; there were open buildings, hallways, and stairs at every turn. At an intersection coming toward us was Death on a pale horse with his henchmen riding with a vengeance. We looked right. Climbing up the stairs, giants with rather large and long heads were coming at us. I saw a beautiful woman walk into a building on the left so we followed her.

We ran into the doorway following the woman where we witnessed mystical beasts in the center of the room. The woman vanished. The statues appeared as protectors from ancient times. Preacher asked Ninja, "What do they represent?" Ninja answered, "I think they symbolize good luck and fortune. Remember I am Japanese, not Chinese." I stuck my head out the doorway; the Tall Man, Death, Giants, and a slew of monks were coming around the corner. I shouted, "They are all coming around the bend!" Preacher asked, "What do we do?" Many beautiful apparition women floated around the room above. Ninja had a vision of our friend Ghost pushing the statues then he simply disappeared. Ninja demanded, "Come help me push these statues!" The statues moved as Ninja yelled, "Follow me!" We followed Ninja down a dark stairwell as the statues moved back closing the entrance behind. At that point I didn't care where it led to, it certainly beat the alternative. Our small flashlights were not much use. We made it to the bottom of the stairs to the dark, dirty underground. I flashed my light in front of us, where four skeleton remains stood like statues wearing dusty brown cloaks. The room had thousands of human skulls stacked on top of one other in different artistic patterns. You could see tons of spiders and even some snakes slithering around. There were several directions to choose from. I asked, "Where do we go now?" Ninja flashed his light at one of the skeletons holding a sign. Ninja struggled to read the translation, "We used to be you, it won't be long before you will become us, or something like that." I yelled, "This place is an underground genocide!" Ninja saw an apparition of our friend Ghost who appeared to walk down a jagged hallway. Ninja whispered, "Come on, follow the south gate of this abomination." As we moved south the walls were covered with bones and skulls. The farther we walked the creepier it got. You would have thought we were possibly in Auschwitz. Halls were filled with skeletons. Mummies were hanging all over the walls like shelf toys. Ninja stumbled on a big wooden cross on the floor where a skeleton's remains were nailed to it. It was cold and damp so I put my cloak hood up when suddenly I heard the sounds of rats making that screeching noise. It sounded as if they were fighting with each other. Who knows, maybe they thought we would be their next meal.

I asked sarcastically, "Well, where is all the good luck and gold at?" Ninja answered, "We are alive, that's enough gold for me." We walked down a tunnel when something slammed me into the wall from behind, knocking me unconscious as I fell to the dirt floor. Ninja and Preacher turned around to two uncanny demon creatures. Preacher screamed out, "Run!" It was a normal reaction as they both ran down the hall while forgetting about me. As Preacher ran down the dark hall an iron gate dropped behind him. Ninja could no longer follow Preacher. Preacher turned around as Ninja tried shaking the gate open. Ninja yelled, "I can't open it!" Preacher yelled, "Oh shit! Run!" Ninja ran down another dark tunnel as two tall creatures with large heads chased him. Frantic, Preacher yelled, "Zombie! Zombie! Where are you?" Preacher ran off.

I awoke with a massive headache only to witness Shadow, Ghost, and Magic fight an epic battle with the demons. The fight was furious when out of nowhere a bright light entered the room like fireworks; that was the last thing I remember before blacking out. When I awoke again I had rats all over me as I got up screaming. I rushed to pull the rats off me. I had several bite marks from those little bastards. There were no signs of Preacher or Ninja. I wasn't sure what path they took so I followed the shoe prints till suddenly my battery died. I was so mad that I threw it down the dark hall. I heard a splash as if it went into water. I learned quickly what it was like to be a blind person. I tried walking straight when I heard in the distance behind me a noise that I couldn't make out. It was loud, kind of sounded like either a lion or a gorilla. I ran toward the water where it reached knee deep. I felt the walls when luckily I latched onto a stick of some sort. I used it as a guide to feel in front of me. The water was fucking cold when I heard the frightening sound another time or two. I turned around to a gargled roar getting closer. At that very moment something latched onto the stick; with great force I immediately let go of the stick and ran for my life. I had no idea what direction I was running. I could only hear the echoes of my own screams and splashing water. I saw a flashing light ahead when I heard Ninja's voice yell my name. He flashed the light in my eyes while lifting me up a small muddy slope. Ninja flashed his light behind me yelling, "Run!" Large creatures with glowing eyes were on the prowl. Whatever it was made the sound of a gator or something. Trying to avoid the monster we ran side by side down some dark tunnel when out of nowhere we fell into a hole. We landed on a pile of rubies and pearls. Large skeleton remains surrounded the cavern pit holding torches. Ninja yelled, "Come on! I can see the stairwell. Let's get out of the Devil's Chambers!"

Journals by Preacher

I continued running down the underground hellhole, my flashlight dimming. I began to walk as I witnessed long glass crates stacked on top of one another. There were ancient remains inside. The skulls were long with big eyebrows and eye sockets. Some still even had hair on the skull. By their appearance it was obvious they weren't from this galaxy. The giant ones with hair on their head reminded me of vampires. I couldn't get over how big their heads and bodies were. I noticed they all had six fingers on each hand just like the Tall Man. The same could be said for their toes. I was scared. My battery died as I wandered in the pitch black tunnel. I think I walked into a few spider webs along the way, not much I could do but wipe them off. I just had to hope I didn't get bit by anything. With a bit of dumb luck I stumbled onto a low lit stairwell that led down to another level. I peeked my head into a doorway where I saw a monk in a brown robe with his back turned. He was pouring blood onto this covenant that appeared as two arch angels. I could hear faint whispers that said, "Hold the hand; hold the nail." The surrounding deity statues all seemed to have one thing in common and that was the serpent. Above the wall there was an inscription that read "Babel". In my mind Babel meant confusion. An etched pyramid was on another wall with what looked like the head of a penis. I'm sure it was an eye or something but that's what it reminded me of. The gold deity statues around the room looked like guards. I must have been in the lower level of the center temple. I watched monks walk across the room when what appeared to be a high priest whisper shit in tongues. It was becoming evident that the ability to summon demons was not only possible but real. The monk turned around when I quickly hid in a hall corner. I watched him and his cronies walk out of the room. One of the monks hesitated then followed the others up the stairs. The last monk had a red mask on that covered his entire face. I felt as if I was gonna have a heart attack. I walked near the room, snatched a torch off the wall then took off running down another hall.

I discovered another lighted room where there were tons of rows of books. It was the biggest library I had ever seen. So I pulled several books off the shelf, took a seat on the floor in a corner and skimmed through several books in the ancient library. I know I should have been looking to find a way out of there but the books were fascinating. I found myself unable to put them down. As I read the books I had an epiphany, I began to weep for I had read the truth. I realized what was in the crates were giants from biblical times. They were the fallen ones; the fallen angels before the great flood of Noah. I don't know how many were kicked out of heaven but one of the books mentioned over two hundred corpses of demons were here. The book said that was only one-third of the fallen ones kicked out of heaven. The rest of the demons were scattered throughout the world waiting for the final battle with God. The most terrifying thing I read was that throughout history and into the future the fallen ones were breeding with mankind by force. We were now among the hybrid children. These fallen angels who call themselves sons of God became giants on earth that over time evolved into demons.

The carnage in heaven and on earth was unspeakable acts of cruelty by the demons. I'm not sure of their many shapes and forms. In reading the books of the underworld I was having a hard time comprehending or differentiating the shadow people, shadow creatures, from the watchers. Maybe they were the same, I don't really know. I concluded they were all demons. I spoke several languages but Hebrew was not one of them. Many of the books were complicated and varied in languages. Hunting for books I could find in languages I knew took some time. At this point I no longer cared for my safety or that of the others. I was searching for the truth of God and Satan. The more I read the more I could see the parallel of earth and Hell. I was thinking they were one in the same. I thought of the seven sins along with the parallel of hate, anger, and bondage. The more I read about Hell the more I realized we were already in it. Satan himself masquerades as an "Angel of Light", the false prophet. The library was full of false idols with the sun or moon above them. I realized Satan ruled the sky below the moon. "The Skies of Hell" is where Satan played the bizarre game of deception, yet he dwelled in darkness. He denounced mankind. In Heaven he guided his secret society right out the door with that theory. That sick fuck portrayed himself as the Father while the angels were the sons of disobedience. He rejoiced in everyone's pain, poverty and hardship. The more I read the angrier I got.

I always wondered how Raven knew that red angel was a false prophet. It hit me like a ton of bricks. Angels don't have wings. I have never read or seen one shred of proof of this. This again was just another vital deception. The angels never had our best interest, they were jealous of mankind. The fallen ones not only hated us, they wished they could be us. Their insecurities even with a higher power were actually below us apparently. Satan softly whispered lies to the angels, "Ye shall become God." I began reading the final conflict with the battlefield being drawn between Israel and Babylon. I was reading a paragraph from another scroll that read, "What has been done will be undone; yet only through his name shall they be saved." I don't know who said it but I certainly know who promised it. Basically you needed to pick what side you were on. Just as I got into the meat and potatoes of another book I heard a noise. I hid behind a bookshelf only to see Ninja and Zombie. In that moment I got on my knees, prayed, and asked God for forgiveness as the boys approached me.

CHAPTER TWENTY SEVEN: THE PROPHECY

Journals by Preacher

What an incredible odyssey this had become. We managed to make it out from the underground tomb of the Secret City. We all lacked sleep, were dehydrated and starving. My body felt weak just walking to the other side of the mountain. At the edge we all stood gazing out at the ocean. The only thing between Crowley's place and us was a gigantic black reverse crucifix floating on a platform. We made the long journey down the mountain. It seemed like an eternity walking down the south end stairway. Reaching the edge of the shore Ninja said, "Preacher, I don't know how we managed to escape from there. I have no idea what type of monsters we ran into back there. I never thought I would be so anxious or relieved at the site of Crowley's hell hole." I replied, "The secret library revealed a prophecy to me. There is no question the universe is finite. Our bodies are nothing more than a vehicle to travel through time. Who we really are is linked in the blood, not the brain, not the heart, or even the soul. It's the blood that links us all together. That is the key to mankind. Reality is an empty space and I can tell you most things aren't random. After what I learned back there, reality is no more than an Illusion." Zombie asked, "Preacher, you okay? Your hair is turning gray bro. I don't understand what you're talking about." I turned to Zombie and said, "You asked me before how the entire universe was held together, well I have an answer for you. The holy grail of the universe is time, space, and matter. That is a scientific fact which is well documented, but the real answer you seek is 'unconditional love'. In my opinion mankind and angels don't deserve it either. We were born to be free. The world we live in was not the vision God had. A real kicker is the angels are not our friends. The Bible is a time capsule, the grand finale is at the end, and I am afraid the end is nearing. I am too deep in this thing to turn back now. We are all condemned like the rest of the world. We are just like the sons of disobedience." Ninja asked, "So, what can we do about it?" Smiling, I answered, "Even God has rebels. It's time to unleash the remaining seals on Crowley's Tomb; then we can all take the medicine that we got coming to us." Zombie asked, "Do we really have it coming to us?" I answered, "Unfortunately we all got it coming, Zombie. At this point I say kill them all and let God sort it out." Zombie laughed as Ninja said, "Damn, Preacher, you're one radical son of a bitch." I replied, "Death is our home now."

Zombie glanced back up the hill only to see the Tall Man waving. Zombie yelled, "We've got company again!" I yelled, "We're gonna have to make a swim for it!" Zombie said, "You've got to be kidding me!" Ninja yelled, "Let's go!" Ninja jumped in the water first, I dove in next. Zombie yelled, "I'm not doing it!" With monks coming down the stairs Zombie just needed a little more motivation. He yelled while jumping in the water, "I hate you assholes for this!" The water was crystal clear. As I opened my eyes underwater I could see old tires below with schools of fish. Tiring quickly, we reached the platform. I looked back only to see the shoreline full of monks. Ninja said, "It seems as if they purposely pushed us this way. Why didn't they kill us off back there?" Zombie answered, "I don't know but I'm not staying to find out." He immediately dove back into the water swimming towards Crowley's Tomb. I said, "For a guy who didn't want to get in the water he sure is in a hurry." Ninja and I followed suit diving head first into the water. Swimming across the abyss towards Crowley's I could see an underwater cemetery. I witnessed hundreds of statues that stared towards the surface. I saw a gated statue guarded by a lion and a serpent. There was even a statue that had a dog waiting for his master at the front steps of an underwater mausoleum. The ocean floor reminded me of an ancient battlefield. Out of breath, Zombie asked, "Have you guys ever heard of sharks, gators, or sea monsters?" I asked, "Zombie, really?" Ninja answered, "There are no fucking gators in here. Stop with your creative worrying for fuck sake!" Zombie was wearing on Ninja; I think he missed the bantered rivalry more with Shadow. I was exhausted from swimming; the only thing that saved me from drowning was our conversation crossing the abyss. As we reached the shores I realized this was not Crowley's Tomb. Zombie was pissed while even the mild mannered Ninja had become frustrated. I said, "I don't understand, I saw Crowley's place." Ninja said, "Come on, we need to find shelter. Let's go check the castle out." We walked up the hill tired and pissed off. We were wrong as we approached stairs leading to what looked to be a large mausoleum. In frustration, Ninja asked, "Preacher, what the hell are we going to do? We're wet, lost and starving. We are fucked bro! I have no idea where we are." I answered, "We only have one choice, keep pushing forward." Nothing could prepare us for what was next as we walked through the mausoleum tunnels. The site of ten-story dilapidated wood buildings with adult sized dolls hung on them was very intimidating. Ninja said, "I thought Crowley's was creepy but this place has bad intentions." Zombie yelled, "You assholes are crazy! We can't go in there." The buildings surrounded the area. There were no roads, only a wooden staircase that led up hill. Ninja said, "I have a bad feeling about this place." I replied, "We have no alternatives." Zombie yelled, "Yes we do, let's turn back! I don't even have a weapon anymore. We have lost just about everything we had in the water." I yelled back, "No way! I am not going back across that Waterway of Hell! I don't have the energy left." Between us we had wet clothes, two swords, a knife, a medical kit, and miscellaneous stuff in my satchel. I gave Zombie my knife. My jacket felt like fifty pounds on me. Zombie said, "Gee thanks a lot. What the hell am I going to do with this?" I answered, "Hunt." There was no choice in the matter. So we carried on up the wooden stairs.

The stairs curved from one building to the next outside. We came to a dead end surrounded by buildings where we had no choice but to walk through one. We came upon the demented site of crowded, dry blooded, adult sized mannequins hanging from the ceiling with their cat-like eyes open above staring at us. As I moved past the dolls they swung, knocking one doll into the other as we made it out of the enormous hanging doll room. I hated the squeaking chain noises from above. Between the chained doll noises and that of the floors that creaked below us, I will never forget that creepy image or its sounds. Ninja asked, "What the hell is this all about?" Shivering, Zombie answered, "I told you we are going the wrong way. We are in the dens of hell." As we moved through the swinging dolls I knocked into a heavyset doll at the end near a doorway. Just before I opened the door we heard a thump hit the floor; as we all turned around there was a baby mannequin on the floor under the heavyset female. We began to hear a baby crying when Zombie took off running out the door. It didn't take us long to follow suit. As we left I could hear the cries only get louder. Hearing the echoes of a baby crying might have been the most terrifying thing I had ever heard.

As we made it outside Zombie stopped in his tracks staring at something. When I caught up I witnessed a church near a creek in the distance. A reverse crucifix was burning on the front of the building. We had our weapons drawn only to be met by people dressed from head to toe in cloak outfits that reminded me of the Klu Klux Klan. The hoods were frightening to look at. This was our worst nightmare. On one side of the road was an army of these monks dressed in purple robes while on the opposite side was an army dressed in orange robes. They all stood still and stared at us through their creepy hoods holding torches. About to jump out of his skin, Zombie asked, "What the hell are we gonna do?" I answered, "Well, there is no running from hundreds of them. Follow me." We walked down the road as they stood still staring at us. As we walked, Ninja said, "If I am to die here I am going to take as many as I can with me. This is one of those times I truly miss Shadow's bravado." I walked to the front of the church where monks awaited in white cloaks with others in the background in red cloaks. I felt as if I was nearing the electric chair for execution. My fucking heart was beating so fast I thought I might have a major heart attack.

One of the monks removed his white hood and said, "Welcome, we have been waiting for you." I asked, "Waiting for what?" He replied, "For your arrival. Your journey has been preordained to fail. I am here to prep and guide you to your end." I asked, "End of what?" He answered, "I think you know." I said, "I don't think we do. What are we a fucking meal? Who are you? What is this place?" He answered, "I am the keeper of shadows and dust but if you must know my name it's Cyrus. You are standing on the lost souls of purgatory. It is here you will be prepped for your purification." I asked, "Purification for what?" Emotionless, Cyrus answered, "Satan was at your beginning; he will also be at your end." Zombie yelled, "Are we dead or something?" Cyrus answered, "Death is a mere way of traveling to your destination of the great Kingdom of Hell. In the meantime your stay in purgatory will be just as good." Cyrus was an old man. He was well shaved with a bald head. He had scars all over his face. He had white eyes and appeared blind. We stood silent when Cyrus said to me, "I see you have small scars on your forehead. You are the chosen one." I asked "Chosen for what?" Cyrus answered, "To suffer, what else? You will all suffer but it is the blood of the chosen one to suffer the most through draining of the blood." I yelled, "I don't think so!" Before I could swing my sword Cyrus knocked me unconscious with a kick to the head, while Zombie and Ninja were under an avalanche by Cyrus's army.

I woke up in a dark room surrounded by candles. The room had a terrible odor to it. I was splashing around in warm water, or so I thought. I splashed water on my face then felt the top of my hair only to realize my long hair had been shaved off. I got out of the tub, stepping onto a pentagram surrounded by candles. The walls had pictures of glowing pyramids, skeleton heads of goats, and demigods kneeling before Satan. I walked toward a mirror which I had to look at twice. I couldn't believe my eyes. My head was shaven while I was covered in blood. Freaking out, I examined my body, I had no injuries. As I turned back to the tub I noticed hanging on the wall was a cow's head. The tub was filled with blood from a fucking cow. I vomited in the sink. I turned the nozzle, nothing came out of it. I attempted to open the door, it was locked. There were no windows. I was so mad I punched the mirror, watching it shatter. At that moment the door opened; I was met by two crazy fucks sporting red hoods when I grabbed a couple pieces of glass, stabbing one in the eye while quickly jabbing the other in the neck. I quickly changed into their clothes, putting on the red hood. Unfortunately with my luck both were barefoot. So I ran down the hall where I heard yelling. I grabbed an old hatchet hanging on the wall as a display. I opened the door to three monks with sticks in their hands taking turns flogging Ninja's abdomen. Man, he had been severely beaten. His abdomen had large welts all over. I went through those three like melted butter. It happened so quick in my moment of rage. Ninja's head had been shaved along with deep cuts to his cheeks and forehead. I asked Ninja, "Where is Zombie?" In pain, Ninja answered, "They hung him outside for being defiant." I asked, "Is he dead?" Ninja answered, "I have no idea." I helped Ninja put on a cloak and hood as we took off down the hall. Moving down the stairs we passed a couple of monks when we located the back door. We slipped outside where I could see five rather large reverse crosses with Zombie on one of them further down the field. Burning crosses surrounded the larger ones. Six monks guarded the area. I could see two of the monks coming toward us as we approached the circle. It was hot as hell entering it. I cracked the first monk in the head while immediately slicing the other monk in the neck. The other four came running toward us when Ninja kicked one in the head; knocking him out cold. As one charged at me I kneeled while hacking at his knee. Another charged at me when I threw the hatchet hitting him in the chest. Ninja punched the monk several times before he knew what happened to him. The wounded monk tried crawling away when I kicked him over onto his back then stepped on his neck, caving in his voice box.

Luckily Zombie was bound by rope, not nails, so I cut him down as Ninja helped lessen the fall. He had taken a pretty good beating while also dealing with burn marks around his body from the fire. I said, "Well the burns should help clean out the rat bites." Zombie answered, "I hurt all over. The burn marks are nothing compared to the feeling of my lungs being strangled. Thanks for saving my life. I owe you one. I'm just glad they didn't get the chance to shave my head or take my clothes. I wouldn't want to wear those monkey suits. Jesus, do you guys look pathetic." Ninja replied, "Let's get the hell out of Purgatory." We took off through the woods. It sucked not having shoes because the sand spurs and sticks were merciless. I prayed to God the whole time to help us find our way out. Lo and behold somehow we managed to find the shoreline. I was never so happy to see the water and the night sky. For once in my life not only were my prayers answered once, but twice. We found an old canoe with paddles near a hut made of bones. It looked as if a mad witch doctor made it. I admit it was cleverly done but fucking weird. It had to be a gift from God. I thought to myself, 'how convenient'. Lady luck finally was on our side for a change. Ninja found an old fishing stick, a tackle box, and some raw guts on the hut table. We jumped in the canoe and paddled off into darkness. For once I didn't give a shit where we were headed as long as it was away from here. We were alive and that's all that mattered at that point.

CHAPTER TWENTY EIGHT: CONFRONTATION

Journals by Chief

The journey had become a haze of confusion for me. Our return to Crowley's Tomb was a trail of misery. Our quest was no longer fun with the loss of my friends. I was feeling the desperation for revenge. The thirst of the kill was eating me up inside like cancer. I never felt so deteriorated inside my soul. I wanted to bleed the freaks at Crowley's Tomb. I took Maverick's death hard, blaming myself. The helpless pain I felt was like nails through my hands. I realized as we walked through the Devil's playground he was winning while we were reacting, always on the defense. I wanted to strike on the offensive for a change. I wanted to rid myself of guilt. The cross I had to bear for us all was heavy. Blood was on our hands now and there was no washing it away. It was an eternal tattoo with no way of removal.

After passing incessant sad rusted out cars, planes, and anchors that had seen their fates come to an end, we came across another cemetery entrance. Raven said, "I am glad to be out of the junkyard man. This place is a shithole." Wolf answered, "Everything has its end my friend." The sudden weather change of cold air, gloomy skies, and fallen leaves put everyone in a bad mood. I said, "Another day in fucking paradise." Cheech and Chong barked at the gates before we entered the Deadwood Cemetery. There was a stained-glass replica of the "Last Supper" as we entered. Wolf remarked, "That's creepy." Deadwood Cemetery was over-populated with gravestones. Raven said, "I don't think they could send one more corpse to this descent of hell." We walked up a hill where we came upon a 200-foot long panorama of the Crucifixion of Christ. I said, "Damn, you just can't get away from this shit, not even at a cemetery, without religious persecution or political corruption. The scene of murder for the dead or those who come to visit it is sickening. When does the agenda end?" Wolf replied, "It doesn't."

Gazing down the hill Wolf pointed toward a familiar vehicle stating, "Check it out, the clown's ice cream truck is here." I answered, "They're up to something. Come on, let's go check it out." Raven got his bow ready just in case. We reached the vehicle where there was no sign of the clowns anywhere. Raven opened the unlocked door on the passenger side. He checked inside the glove box where he found a Smith & Wesson .44 Magnum Western Revolver. He yelled out, "Bingo! Zombie is going to love this baby, man." Meanwhile Wolf tried opening the back door but it was locked. Wolf yelled, "Damn it! Raven check for a button for the back door." Raven was busy checking under the seats when he found a brown bag. He looked inside the bag only to discover mushrooms wrapped in tin foil. He immediately put those in his jacket without word. Raven also found a button and pressed it. He asked, "Did it unlock?" Wolf tried opening the door, this time it opened. Wolf stood in silence shocked at the discovery. The site of assault weapons and gym bags awaited us. I opened the bags to find ammunition, grenades, handguns, combat knives along with dynamite. We had just struck pay dirt. With a concerned look on his face Wolf turned to me and asked, "What are these fucking clowns up to? They have an arsenal in here." I replied, "Not anymore they don't. We just hit the lotto brother." Raven came around to the back of the truck yelling, "Holy shit, man!" Wolf said, "Exactly." I said, "Well maybe it is true that every squirrel finds an acorn once in a while." Wolf laughed as he handed the weapons over. I said, "Grab as many guns as you can carry, we'll each carry two bags."

We slung several weapons over our shoulders when Raven said, "Shit! Maybe our luck isn't changing man." I looked up to see three clowns and a jester approaching the truck from a distance. I demanded, "Hurry up! Grab the fucking bags; let's get the hell out of here!" We ran from behind the truck so they couldn't see us. We hid behind some gravestones while watching the clowns near the truck. I could see the clowns talking to one another when Cheech and Chong ran off towards the clowns. Raven yelled, "Oh my God! Shit!" I grabbed Raven from not running after them while Wolf loaded a sniper rifle. The dogs charged after the clowns. The clowns took off running. Chong attacked the trailing clown from behind. Cheech joined the ruckus; it didn't take long before Chong had a hold of the clown's neck. The dogs did a number on the clown, killing him quickly. I suddenly heard a gunshot that startled me. The next thing I saw was a clown fall to the ground. Wolf shot the clown in the head. I yelled, "Why in hell did you do that?" Wolf answered, "He was going to shoot the dogs." I asked, "How did you know that?" Wolf responded, "I didn't. He was just in the wrong place at the wrong time." I replied, "That is just fucking great." Raven whistled out to the dogs and they raced back to him. I said, "You need to put those dogs on a fucking leash. Let's get the fuck out here!" We ran down the hill to hide. I could hear the ice cream truck roaring down the road as the radio blared "Never Enough" by the L.A. Guns. Wolf said, "Come on, we've got to go." In anger, Raven said, "I don't think we have seen the last of those creepy fucks, man." I said, "They're gun runners. You can add another enemy to the growing list. They will be after us now. We need to stay ahead of those crazy freaks." We rushed through the Deadwood Cemetery. Jogging with all this heavy stuff became strenuous and awkward. I knew we had to find shelter. The bitter cold winds were becoming intolerable. As fatigue set in we moved at a snail's pace. Finally we reached a brick path where crowded mausoleums on both sides set. Wolf said, "We have no food or water. I'll go hunt for food, Chief find a way to pry the door open to the Queen Mausoleum for shelter, Raven collect some branches and leaves." Raven asked, "Why the Queen Mausoleum?" Wolf gave Raven a dirty look answering, "Because it's the biggest, retard."

Later that evening, we were sitting near the fire trying to stay warm while eating rabbit. The dogs certainly were not complaining about the scraps. One thing for sure, Cheech and Chong took a great liking to Raven, as they all snuggled together. Wolf asked, "What do you think the clowns are gonna do?" I answered, "Probably going to send a fucking hit squad after us. Who knows, with any luck maybe Bloom and Parks will arrest or kill those sick freaks first." Raven, normally the night owl, had fallen asleep with the dogs when Wolf asked me, "What do you think happened to Bloom and Parks? I mean, what if the lunatic killed them?" I answered, "I don't know, I guess it's possible, Bloom and Parks are two mean pissed off detectives with shotguns. How else could it end?" Wolf asked, "Do you think they are still following us?" I answered, "I really don't know. Let's hope that's the case. My hope was they would radio in the cavalry at Crowley's Tomb. I wanted to even the odds." Wolf replied, "Well our odds are getting worse. I just hope we can find the others soon." I responded, "You're wrong, with the arsenal we have now, we might have turned the tide. Better get some sleep; we need to skin out early tomorrow."

When the morning came I felt so much better. I could feel my energy return along with my confidence for my drug of choice which was "revenge". Raven and the dogs lead the way down the red brick path. Wolf looked at me and said, "Those three are inseparable." Staring out toward Raven and the dogs I answered, "You're right about that, unfortunately it's a broken heart waiting to happen." I pointed to a grave that had an army tank on it. We walked for several hours before we came upon a red wall with a building that was built like a fortress. The top of the building and outside the walls looked like the Russian Kremlin. It was bravura to see. As we ran to the iron gates Raven was stunned. I pushed the gates open only to be greeted with the aftermath carnage of war. I noticed the ice cream truck had bullet holes throughout it. Raven asked, "What happened here?" Wolf answered, "It appears a civil war broke out between Pusher's thugs and the clowns. It doesn't look like either side won." Raven replied, "It looks like a massacre, man." I said, "There is no site of Pusher; let's go check inside."

The front door was open as we moved inside. Blood and bodies were all over the floor. The inside of the building had a look of luxury. I yelled out several times, "Hello! Is anyone here?" There was no reply. We went through every room on the bottom floor of the palace. We found a stocked kitchen and wine cellar in the basement. As we made it to the second floor it was plush with several bedrooms. As we reached the third floor it told a very different story. All over the third floor there were dead bodies throughout the hallways. I looked up at the ceiling where angels and demons were painted fighting each other between white clouds. Real symbolic shit only Preacher would've been able to decipher. As we reached the top level Cheech and Chong were barking. I couldn't believe my eyes; I felt like I was in a horror movie. It looked like a slaughter house that went severely wrong. Fresh blood was all over the walls and on the floor. There must have been over 40 bodies between the two parties. Most were mutilated and decapitated. There were pentagrams all down another hallway. Satanic symbols and writings in blood were on the walls that made no sense. I was pale as a ghost, confused and distraught. Raven asked, "Do you think the monks did this bro?" Wolf answered, "Maybe, whatever evil monster did this is truly fucked in the head." I replied, "In my opinion a deal went very wrong but this place has the smell of betrayal all over it. I can't say I would be surprised if the monks weren't involved. The clowns and Pusher's thugs were butchered like wild animals. I'd like to know where Pusher is. Hell, I don't know anymore. Let's lock this place down and stay here tonight." Wolf said, "I am going to booby trap the doors and windows on the first floor." I said to Raven, "Why don't you see what you can whip us up to eat while I clean this place up a bit."

CHAPTER TWENTY NINE:
THE MUSHROOM TRIP

Journals by Raven

I went downstairs to the kitchen with the dogs tagging along; I found canned stew in the pantry, hot dogs and potato salad in the fridge. I also found a loaf of French bread in the freezer so I set it out to defrost. I tuned the radio on to the rock station which played "Mary Jane" by Tom Petty. Searching through the cabinets I found a can opener along with some pots and pans. While heating the stew and boiling the hot dogs I fired up a joint, puffing away while playing with the dogs. "Blackberry" by the Black Crowes playing on the radio put me in the mood to sing. I found time to lip sync, imitating the singer with an unopened can while dancing around room to room. I was inhaling deep trying to get high as a kite when I stumbled on the wine cellar. I stood there for a brief moment smiling because I knew I hit the mother lode. Looking back at Cheech and Chong I said, "We're going to party tonight." The dogs sat up waving their front paws in the air. I asked my babies, "You want a treat?" The dogs barked as to answer yes. The wine cellar was stocked to the hilt. I selected a couple of California merlots. I divided the hot dogs up for the dogs then set the table. The stew was ready for the guys to eat along with the bread. The dogs were very happy as they devoured the hot dogs in no time. I yelled out, "Dinner is served."

The guys ran down the stairs ready to eat. As the guys put stew on their plates with some bread I opened the bottles of wine and said, "A feast fit for kings." We were chowing down the food faster than the dogs. I have to admit, for canned beef stew it was really good. Just being lucky enough to put food in our bellies was satisfying enough for me. I asked, "How are the traps coming?" Chief answered, "We just have to wire the stairs before bed." Wolf said, "I wonder how Preacher and the guys are doing." Chief answered, "Probably waiting impatiently as they listen to Zombie whine." We were laughing when Chief looked at us and said, "Make sure your weapons are loaded. If we get visitors tonight they are in for the surprise of a lifetime." I said, "I certainly hope they wait for us man." Chief replied, "I know Preacher well enough, they will wait for us even if hell freezes over. We should be able to make it to Crowley's late in the afternoon with any luck." Wolf said to me, "You clean while we finish the traps then let's go to bed so we can get an early start." Man, I hated waking up early in the morning.

I couldn't help myself to finally get the chance to indulge in taking some mushrooms. I really needed to escape from the loss of my friends. My release was to party and travel in my own mind. The radio played "Pretty Penny" by Hell or Highwater. Motivated, I cleaned the kitchen in less than twenty minutes while enjoying the mushrooms and wine. My body quickly felt tingles all over so it was time to get upstairs and get ready for takeoff. I yelled "goodnight" running up the stairs with Cheech and Chong. The dogs went under the bed while I climbed into bed ready for liftoff. I put headphones on that I found upstairs and listened to Audioslave's "Show Me How To Live". I was feeling euphoric, the music was tuned in, it felt rich man. I began experiencing shiny bright lights as if God had joined the party. The colors were vibrant, man. I was feeling so happy. I could see visions of lights meshing together. It felt as if I was in another galaxy. I couldn't stop giggling. Wherever I was, my trip was beyond the outside world. My conscious was taking me to a far deeper place. I would have sworn that Pink Floyd was in the room. The light show was incredible. Oh man, the sound was so crisp it was as if they were floating with me in the air while playing. It was my best trip yet. Whoever those clowns were, man they got the best drugs. If you've ever seen a kaleidoscope, you know the patterns and colors are simply amazing. I was seeing stars, unknown planets, bright shapes, colors from strange galaxies. Man, I wish all the guys could've experienced the mushroom trip because it would've lightened the mood.

We all went to bed early that night. The traps were set. Anyone trying to get in here was in for a very rude awakening; the traps were set for the ending of life. We all slept in separate bedrooms on the second floor. I could hear Wolf singing "Lola" by the Kinks in the room next to me. At one point I even heard Chief singing "I Just Want You" by Ozzy Osbourne. I knew he was thinking about Delilah; I think we all missed her. Chief suddenly changed tunes and began singing "Mr. Crowley" also by Ozzy Osbourne. That reminded me of his obsession with Crowley's Tomb. Later into the night, while talking to the dogs, I was feeling the effects of the mushroom trip taking a bad turn. The problem with a bad mushroom trip is that you can't get out of it because your subconscious won't allow you. I began to see and hear things. My visions were becoming sinister. I could hear the song "Cocaine" By Eric Clapton drowning my brain waves. I was getting paranoid; I couldn't escape my mushroom journey. The visions were of deformed monsters, the colors were dark, no longer shiny or bright. I was trapped in my own subconscious travels. I could hear noises coming from the hallway. Cheech and Chong were sound asleep snoring under the bed.

I ran across the hall naked which seemed like light years away. I barged into Chief's room. Stumbling to the floor, I yelled, "They're all around us man!" Half groggy, Chief pondered the situation while getting dressed as he stared at me. I was in a panic, which is not normal for me, so Chief seemed concerned. Now in a panic himself, Chief asked, "Who's around us? Where are they?" Bent over in the corner I answered, "The shadow creatures have horns on their heads man. They have us surrounded! Did you just see that man?" Chief turned to where I pointed responding in an agitated voice, "See what? That is fucking impossible! The traps would have gone off." Chief grabbed a gun and opened the door only to have Wolf pop in front of the door. They startled each other. Chief yelled out, "Jesus, you scared the shit out of me!" Wolf asked, "What is going on?" Chief answered, "Raven said there are monsters all around us." Disgusted, Wolf stared at me then back at Chief. After looking around, Wolf yelled, "There is nothing out here!" Both Wolf and Chief gave me dirty looks as I peeked out of Chief's blanket. My words slurred, I yelled, "We got to get out of here, man!" Wolf yelled back, "Jesus Christ, you're fucking stoned! You put us all at risk!" Beyond angry with me, Chief yelled, "Go to bed before I murder you first." Stoned, I yelled back, "Man, there are fucking monsters in my room." Chief responded, "I don't give a God damn what's in there! You could've gotten us all killed. Now go to fucking sleep." Wolf asked, "What the hell did you take?" I answered, "Just a few mushrooms, man." In disgust, Chief yelled, "Jesus H Christ! Where did you get those from?" I answered, "From the clowns, man." Now irate, Chief yelled, "Clowns! Are you out of your mind? Give me the rest!" I answered, "I swear man I don't have any more." Chief replied, "Thank Christ! I hate to do this to you, but we have to lock you in your room. You're a liability if something happens." I screamed, "Oh come on man! Don't leave me in here all alone!" Chief responded back, "This is for your own good. You dug your own grave." Wolf rigged the door then locked me in. Chief said, "Can you believe this fucking guy?" Wolf replied, "I will see you in the morning." In the background I could hear "Werewolves of London" on the radio by Warren Zevon. I yelled while pounding on the door, "They are all over the place man! Let me out of here!" Irritated, Chief answered back, "I don't give a shit! You can tell me all about it in the morning. Good night!" Both laughing, Chief and Wolf went back to bed. I put my face against the door calling out the guys' names several times; they just ignored me, man.

I laid back in bed hiding under the covers frantically looking around the room. Just like the guys, even Cheech and Chong were ignoring me. I eventually fell asleep to bad dreams, unluckily for me the nightmares were not finished. I dreamed of being chased by something. I was running in a field of bones, the color of the sky was burning red; pale-faced creatures came out from the ground. The dogs and I were fighting for our lives. Suddenly I woke up in a cold sweat. My high was gone, now replaced by nausea. I ran to the window, opened it, swiftly stuck my head out and puked. I could hear the splash hitting the ground. My stomach now bubbling, I urgently needed to go to the bathroom but the door was locked. I tried to pace for a few minutes then began to pound my fist on the door as I yelled, "Guys, I need to use the bathroom!" I yelled again "Guys, come on man! I need to go to the fucking bathroom!" Chief yelled out in laughter, "The shark does not pay attention to the opinion of the seal my friend!" Whatever the hell that meant I knew it was about to come out. It was either shit or get off the pot. In a desperate measure, I decided to stick my ass out the window, letting the diarrhea fly. Ironically the radio played "In the Summertime" by Mungo Jerry. Shit went everywhere: on the ground, on the window, dripping down the wall. I now realized I had no toilet paper. I looked around trying to find something I could substitute for toilet paper so I used my silk pillow case, then threw it out the window. Feeling relieved and back on earth from my mushroom trip, the night finally ended as I fell asleep to Don McLean's "American Pie". The dogs howled from the stench, scratching on the door to get out to no avail.

CHAPTER THIRTY: THE COST TO EMBRACE

Journals by Raven

Wolf took the first shower in the morning followed by Chief. Wolf went to go make breakfast while Chief checked on me; he opened the door only to be greeted by a smell that was so putrid it left him bent over and dry heaving. While his face turned red, he screamed, "Jesus Christ, who died in here? It smells worse than death! What climbed inside of you and died? You better go see a veterinarian!" I ran down the hall to the bathroom. Chief yelled out, "Don't make an effort to disinfect this room stink body! Oh Raven, that's it, why not terminate the whole fucking house including us while you're at it! Jesus, Mary of Joseph, now you're going to desecrate the entire sewer system with your toxic filth! Out fucking standing! Don't make an effort to hold it in Raven, you stinky bastard!" What Chief failed to realize during his tantrum was the dogs decided to piss on his leg. It served him right for locking the door. When he realized the dogs pissed on him he really blew his top. He yelled, "Your fucking dogs are convicts! You better get these criminals out of here! Just great, I can see this is going to be one fucking long day boy." "House of the Rising Sun" by the Animals played on the radio as Chief walked away in disgust. I snickered in the bathroom with the dogs.

Chief joined Wolf for breakfast. Wolf made some eggs, hash browns, bacon and toast. Chief said, "That smells damn good, looks even better." Wolf said, "I removed all the grenades this morning except on the doors." A few minutes later the dogs and I came running down the stairs. I said, "I see you removed the traps." Chief mumbled, "I see you've been setting a few of your own traps." Wolf and Chief both laughed. With sincerity I said, "I am sorry about last night, guys." Wolf replied, "Have some breakfast then feed the dogs the leftovers. I will remove the basement and back door traps first. Pack what you can for food and water then let's get a move on."

Cheech and Chong were right beside me at every step as I scavenged through the pantry for food to pack. The radio played "Back on Earth" By Ozzy Osbourne while I fired up a doobie. As I inhaled, out of nowhere there was a loud blast from the front. Chief ran down the stairs greeted by Wolf. The dogs took off towards the front barking like crazy. The room filled like a dust bowl. Chief threw a Winchester Rifle at me; I cocked the handle and pointed it in the direction of the door. There was ruble all over the floor. A handful of dead bodies along with body parts were strewn around the doorway which was a mess. I stepped outside to investigate; I saw a nun with her arms blown off, her face bloodied. She stumbled toward us when Cheech and Chong attacked her. I tried calling them off but she was dead anyway. Wolf said, "It looks as if the sisters were in the wrong place at the wrong time." I said, "God help us, we're condemned men now for sure." Chief yelled, "Let's get the fuck out of here!"

We packed rapidly as I made a special tea for the boys to bring with. We ran off running down a dirt road with tree stumps on both sides. We walked past a handful of gravestones. There was a couple that caught my eye as we approached another cemetery. One read, "Dead by his own hands", while the other read, "Pray it stops here." I read another one which read, "Meet me in the cemetery." The cemetery front gates were bent over as Chief read the sign. Chief said, "We are at Lagombie Cemetery. I heard the rumors of this place from the villagers. Stay alert, this place is a creep zone." Our traveling was slow because we were weighed down by carrying so much stuff. I even saddled Cheech and Chong with supplies on their backs. The weather became a problem as snow came early. Bored, I was singing out loud "Walk On The Wild Side" by Lou Reed. Chief said, "Take a break and reverse your cloaks so we can blend in with the snow." I handed the guys bottles of tea. I also gave the dogs some water to drink. Wolf said, "Jesus does this taste weird." Lagombie Cemetery was filled with green monk statues. There was also a large life-like cross statue of Jesus Christ where we rested. I asked, "Do you know where we're at yet?" Chief guzzled his tea answering, "Honestly I have no idea." We finished our break and continued on down the path. We passed some pretty cool statues and mausoleums along the way when we came to thirteen praying gargoyle statues. I asked, "Is that supposed to be us?" Wolf commented, "I sure hope not."

Journals by Chief

About 20 minutes after our break I began to feel tingling all over my body. The lights began to shine brighter. As the boys were talking to me I heard them slurring their words, we couldn't stop the laughter. The supplies no longer felt heavy to carry. I felt as if I was floating on a magic carpet. The colors today were all meshing together. I felt like I was walking on clouds free as a bird. I was expecting the clouds and colors to split open like the red sea while God walked out. At some point we must have taken another break because that was the last thing I remember before blacking out.

Later in the evening I woke up with the guys standing over me. I couldn't understand what they were saying, their voices sounded like they were muffled underwater while playing a record backwards. It was scaring the shit out of me. I remember trying to get to my feet, stumbling sideways while trying to catch my balance; it was as if someone had punched me in the temple. I was disoriented, felt sea sick, and my legs were wobbly. I was wondering if we were on the moon or something. Wolf and Raven were grabbing at me when I turned over puking. It was at that moment my hearing came back, I could hear them yell my name while the dogs barked at me with their tails wagging. I had a pounding headache. I was finally able to get my balance back. I lunged toward Raven's neck with my hands; the dogs jumped on me while Wolf tried to break things up and calm the situation down. Wolf finally pulled us apart and the dogs calmed down. I was furious as I asked Raven, "You drugged us with that fucking tea didn't you?" Raven answered, "I was trying to take the edge off you guys, bringing back peace and harmony man." I yelled, "You stupid dope head son of a bitch! Are you nuts?" Wolf grabbed us both, then pointed behind us and yelled, "Stop! Look, we are at the tri-fork. Put your heads back together, let's find the others."

As I glanced at the tri-fork there were three different directions with three totally different fronts. The path farthest to the left had a scarecrow in front of it. The center path had a white front door between two large towering trees. The path to the right had Christmas lights wrapped around all the trees. The moon in the background was bright. We were all undecided about which way to go. I closed my eyes when I saw Beast smiling pointing to the path on the right before he vanished. I said, "Let's go to the right." To our surprise the white door opened with five nuns holding lanterns walking toward us. Closest to them, Raven replied, "Tell me this isn't creepy déjà vu." Wolf said, "Maybe the sisters can tell us which path leads us to Crowley's." I answered, "I don't know about that, I remember as a kid those nun outfits gave me the creeps." The nuns walked right up to us; they were wearing makeup and red lipstick that looked hot as hell. They were also wearing spiked high heels which seemed contradictory for a nun. One of the nuns had a cigarette hanging out of her mouth. Cheech and Chong began growling as they approached. Raven turned his back to the nuns, kneeled to the dogs and said, "Easy now babies." Without warning one of the nuns stabbed Raven in the back with a sharp blade attached to a Christ-like wooden cross. The dogs immediately attacked the nuns with the intent to kill. Another one stabbed him in the upper left arm. Wolf opened fire killing three of the nuns instantly with his Browning. While falling to the ground, I fired a 44 magnum splattering one of the nuns all over the field. It sounded like a canon was fired. I shot the last trailing nun charging at me right in the belly. I walked to her as she lied on her back and asked, "Is there anything you want to tell me sister?" She whispered, "Go to hell!" I replied, "You first!" I proceeded to shoot her in the forehead. Wolf ran to check on Raven who was stumbling in confusion away from us. Cheech and Chong were licking Raven's hands. Wolf attempted to push the dogs away so he could attend to Raven's wounds; the dogs were distrustfully growling at Wolf, but Raven petted them so they would calm down. I also looked at his wounds and said, "Shit, that's serious." Wolf said, "I can patch the arm but the back wound is more serious." In a daze, Raven said, "Pull out the small bottle from my pouch of remembrance and hand it to me please." I handed him the pill bottle. Raven popped it open and began swallowing several pills then rinsed them down with a bottle of water. He then fell to his knees and Wolf attempted to patch him up. Raven said, "Get me on my feet." Wolf lifted Raven up; he grimaced in pain. Raven said, "Let's finish the journey, I'll be okay." We were worried about Raven yet there was little we could do other than hope modern day chemistry could hold him together till we found Preacher.

Wolf said, "I think we will take the path with the lighted trees." He led the way as we walked in the lighted haze only to be greeted by an old nemeses; the Tall Man stood in the pathway. There always seemed to be some hocus pocus and blue neon glowing about this wacko. I said, "I see Beast hasn't lost his sense of humor in the afterlife." The Tall Man smiled then said, "It's time for your boys' funerals." Dizzy, Raven looked at the Tall Man and replied, "Buddy, you're in the wrong place at the wrong fucking time man. I am in no mood to run." With his sinister laugh, the Tall Man responded, "I normally enjoy eating cat for dinner, but dog, just as good." The dogs were growling as Raven signaled for them to sit. Raven answered, "You know, you chased my friends around in a hearse in the cemetery, which by the way I appreciate your musical taste. You then terrorized our village, fine I can handle that because we were on your turf first. But now you insult my dogs and that hurts their feelings." Puzzled, we stayed calm. Raven said, "Apologize to my dogs and I promise you I will kill you quick." The Tall Man laughed in his reply, "You can't kill me son." Raven yelled, "I am not your fucking son, man!" Raven opened fire on the Tall Man who was hit with bullet after bullet; he finally fell backwards onto his back. I could hear screaming behind the Tall Man when I noticed the Tall Man began sitting up without using his arms, which was scary as hell. Monks came charging after us. We opened fire on them when Wolf yelled, "Let's get the fuck out of here!" There must have been over fifty of them running down the hill towards us. We all turned around heading back to the tri-fork. I sprinted through the white door. Wolf turned around watching the monks racing at him when he threw a grenade in their direction; as it hit the ground it exploded, killing half a dozen of them. Unfortunately it didn't discourage the monks. They just kept charging. Wolf opened the door, unpinned another grenade, dropped it by the outside of the doorway then closed the door. We all heard another explosion go off.

We ran through this unknown land until we tripped over one another, tumbling down a bushy hill. Each of us screamed all the way down the hilltop. As I reached the bottom of the hill the dogs were barking, wagging their tails while scratching for Raven to get up. Raven lied perfectly still on his stomach with the bags and weapons beside him. I sprinted towards him and yelled "Oh God no!" I feared he was dead. I immediately rolled him over. He began to laugh, while at the same time moaning in pain. We all laughed together in relief. Raven said, "This has been the adventure of a lifetime, man." Wolf said, "Agreed. I thought you were dead." Raven responded, "It would take an Army to kill me man." I nodded my head in agreement then said, "You're so right about that brother, it would take an army to kill you. Let me help you up." Excited, Wolf yelled, "Guys look over there, it's the ocean! Come on, let's go find the others." It was dark out, the stars shined bright; the Greek Gods must have smiled down upon us. The reflection of the water was absolutely beautiful. Walking towards the creek, across the water I could see light rising above the giant pyramid at Crowley's. Everyone became silent. I think we were all excited about seeing the others, yet at the same time reality hit us why we were there in the first place. Nobody said it out loud but everyone felt the same way, knowing this was our last stop. We knew the odds were stacked against us far worse than even the Alamo. We owed our lives not only to each other but to the Wizard as well. Without truth or loyalty, what does anyone truly have, I wondered? One by one we were dying for our own cause instead of dying needlessly for someone else's.

I noticed a small fire burning under the first bridge by the creek. Relieved, I said, "There they are!" I could hear their voices in the dark. As we got closer I heard a familiar voice call out my name. Wolf made his famous whistle noise as both tribes sprinted towards one another. Preacher and I embraced first followed by Wolf and Zombie, then Raven and Ninja. Raven asked, "What happened to your hair, man?" Ninja said, "It's a long story bro." Chief asked, "Where are the rest of the boys?" Preacher answered, "They didn't make it." Raven was devastated by the news; stunned, he fell to his knees. I think Raven was mortally wounded forever learning Ghost was dead. Both of his best friends were now dead; he never recovered from those wounds. I stood in shock, I couldn't move a limb. Zombie asked, "Where is everyone else?" I stared at Zombie. Shaking my head in shame, voice cracking I said, "They died in battle." Silence came over everyone as we all mourned our lost brothers and tried to come to grips with the reality they were gone. I could see devastation in everyone's eyes. After a few minutes I could hear rumblings of disbelief on both sides. Frantic, Zombie asked, "What the hell are we going to do now?" I threw the weapon and ammunition bags at the tribe's feet. Hesitating I answered, "We are going to war, that is what we're going to do. We are not going to take any prisoners. We are going to save Wizard if it means sacrificing us all. I am going to kill every last fucking monk before my death. Are there any more questions?" The boys became silent. Trying to break the ice, Wolf asked, "Are you boys hungry?" Preacher answered, "Starving." When Wolf showed the boys the bag of food, you could feel a bit of excitement and relief from the others.

We walked back towards the fire together; I noticed that the other tribe had no food, weapons, or supplies. Preacher and Ninja had no shoes, just duct tape wrapped around their feet. I said, "The tide is about to change in this war. I want you to fill your bellies tonight, enjoy, and celebrate each other's company." I pulled a couple bottles of wine out of the dog's bags and passed them to the boys. I reached in Raven's pocket, grabbed a couple joints, and passed them around. I said, "Let's party tonight with each other celebrating our fallen brothers. They have traveled in honor to the next place." I could hear short lived happiness from the boys as they were pleased to see me relax and smoke a big fatty with them. I instantly restored the guys' morale and faith with the exception of Raven. One thing about Raven: he was no dummy. So that night, sitting around the campfire I left him alone as we drank, filled our bellies, exchanged war stories, and got high as kites. I realized the journey wasn't over nor the war but we were going to enjoy being reunited. How sweet it was that night. As for Raven, Preacher worked on his wounds. Raven sat by the campfire and said, "God, I hate drugs but they sure love me." The boys chuckled. I asked Preacher later, "How are Raven's wounds?" Preacher answered, "Not sure yet. I think he is dying of a broken heart."

CHAPTER THIRTY ONE: FRUITION

Journals by Chief

I was the first to wake up under the bridge. I watched snowflakes hit the ground only to melt. The weather was actually pretty warm out. I stared at everyone as they slept yet I focused on the voices of those who were no longer here. A deep sadness came over me. I also anticipated the loss of the ones that were still to come. I didn't know if we had days, hours, or even minutes left with each other. I knew we were about to unleash hell on Crowley's Tomb. In life there is always a flipside to every coin. There was no doubt in my mind the druid monks were a last stop to hell. I knew I was going to die: it was just a matter of when, how, and by whom. I just wanted to rain on their parade. I walked in the distance alone trying to get my thoughts together. It seemed like we had been through hell and back, yet I also knew we were just scratching the surface for what was to come. I wanted to make sure I had my wits about me. If I were to die today, I wanted to free the Wizard and die with honor. Most people on earth are terrified to die, not me, the truth is I was scared of living. If I lived after graduation I would be just another working stiff. Here the adrenaline rush could never be duplicated. In the cemetery we had more lives than a cat. We had defeated at this point everything in our paths and what we didn't, we avoided with reckless abandon. I think we all felt the same way in that regard, nobody just came out and said it. Each one of us was as ready as the next to die especially for Wizard. The guys were the best of an elite tribe. Each one put themselves on the line day after day. We became used to living our lifestyle in an hourglass which gave us all a greater appreciation for one another. If we were all to die young, I can tell you, we were taking Crowley's Tomb and his filthy henchmen with us. They had to go down and we all knew it. It is so weird when you know your time is almost up, I mean the way you look at life on the way out is so much different than the way you looked at life on the way in.

I walked back to the tribe, everyone was up except Raven. Preacher woke Raven up to examine his wounds. Raven's face didn't look good. He seemed pale; I knew he lost a lot of blood. I wanted to send him home but Raven refused to get in the canoe; he would never leave us. Raven was a tough son of a gun. He was a dirty fighter, but man he could shoot a bow better than Robin Hood, that's for damn sure. He came from a broken home like most of us. He was a party animal, loved rock music and had a giant soft spot in his heart for animals. The dogs loved him and there was no doubt he loved those damn dogs. Raven always said he wasn't scared of any man; if he was to lose the fight, the other person would be sorry they ever tangled with him. Down deep I knew he was heartbroken over Ghost and Maverick's deaths. All three lived right next to each other. The love for his friends, dogs, and drugs kept him going somehow. The way he looked physically I would be surprised if he made it through the next day. I had to turn away to wipe my tears. Preacher worked on Raven's wounds, attending to them the best he could. Preacher was gravely concerned by the look on his face. Walking up to me while fighting back tears, Preacher said, "I don't think he's going to make it much longer. It's a miracle he has made it this far." I asked, "What do you want me to do? We have no way of getting him home. Even if we did, you know as well as I do, Raven would never go home and nobody could make him either." Preacher said, "It's a miracle. I guess the drugs are the only thing keeping him alive. He is a modern day walking chemical." I replied, "He is a drug store cowboy."

I gathered everybody around me. I opened the bags from the clowns then began to disperse handguns, ammunition, and assault weapons to the boys individually. Each weapon was different, some new, some old. I gave Zombie the Winchester, an assault rifle, and the 44 Magnum. Nobody was happier than he was. Wolf meanwhile handed each person six grenades. Each member also was given a bonus of one combat knife along with one boot knife. I then divided the rations of food among everyone, maybe two day's rations at best. I said, "These were a gift from our fallen brothers. When you shoot, you shoot to kill. Make every bullet and grenade count. If you have any questions about your weapon, see me, Zombie, or Wolf." Wolf said, "Most would call this a suicide mission, my hope is Wizard's still alive; we must save his life no matter the cost. With that being said, we cannot go the same way we did before. They will probably be expecting us to do that. Hell, they might even have that area booby trapped." Preacher asked, "So what are we going to do?" I answered, "After talking to Wolf we think the best way would be to travel past the creek entering the quarry from the rear. By doing so we can use the element of surprise possibly." Preacher asked another question, "What if they have that area booby trapped or are waiting for us there?" I answered, "That is a distinct possibility but I doubt it. They apparently don't think we're that smart or willing to go the extra couple of miles. My guess is they think we will come from the same way out of desperation. Before you ask me about Wizard being alive, I can't say. He might be dead, we have to expect that. If he is alive it's a bonus; if not, prepare for heartbreak and death. Either way I am going to kill every last one of them regardless. So you all know right here and now; I am not planning on returning for that is my destiny. I have an appointment with death. My intentions are to embrace him along with the other jokers. Are there any other questions?" The meeting went silent. Coughing, Raven said, "Let's go kill them all leaving no prisoners behind." We all laughed. I said, "Okay, if there are no questions take five minutes to pack your gear up, get your thoughts together and then let's move out." With sarcasm Wolf remarked, "Don't forget to bring your balls along." Everyone broke out in laughter. Wolf grabbed most of Raven's gear and said, "Let me make it easier for you." Raven replied, "Thanks, man."

I walked up the creek leading the way while Wolf watched from the rear. We walked about three miles before we came across a small wooden bridge that crossed over the creek. I kept moving along to the other side of the creek where Wolf and I traded places. We walked another half mile before Wolf stopped, turned to us all and said, "I believe this is where we want to head up the field." I noticed a collection of bones that made a walkway. Ninja shook his head as we continued down the path of bones. The day started out bright with clear skies but was now turning to a red glow. We traveled several more miles before the path ended. As we all caught up to Wolf we finally saw what he did: an open field covered in bones. The sun looked as if it was just on the other side of the field. The sky was glowing reddish orange. It was as if it burned the flesh right off the bones. On each end of the field there was a mound of bones stacked as high as a tall building. The rest of the field was flat covered in bones. Beginning to panic, Zombie asked, "What the hell happened here? It looks like the killing field." Wolf answered, "I have no idea; it appears more like Armageddon." Ninja disagreed, "No, it looks more like a death march from a Nazi concentration camp." Preacher commented, "Looks like an atom bomb was dropped here." Zombie asked, "Who could have done this?" Raven answered, "Only Crowley's sick misguided monks could've done such a fucking sickness." I said, "I'll go first. Stay close and keep up."

I walked towards the burning sun as the others followed behind. I was busy humming the song "Heroin" by The Velvet Underground when I realized Raven had lagged farther behind the tribe. He had sweat pouring down his face and stopped in the middle of the field to give the dogs some water. I heard a loud violin playing sad music. Zombie said, "That sounds like the song 'Moonlight Improvisation' by Vadim

Kiselev." Suddenly I could feel the ground trembling as if it was moving. Wolf pointed to one of the bone piles, we all looked up at the same time to see what it was. The sun was so bright, so blinding I didn't know if it was a beast or a man. The closer I strained my eyes, the more evident it became that it was some type of ghoul. The skin was grayish-white in color, it had strange pointed ears. His body was extremely skinny. What I remembered most was his eyes. Those eyes could have killed you with his glare. It was ranting on the bone hill pointing at us, stomping on the top of the bones; the ghoul then blew some horn that sounded like a Viking horn. My God was it ever loud. Wolf yelled, "He is calling for reinforcements! Run, get out of here!" We all sprinted for the other side of the field to get off the bone yard. As we were running we could feel something grabbing at our feet and ankles. Ghouls were coming out of the ground. We were all screaming as there was a lot of commotion going on. The ghoul on the hill wouldn't stop blowing his horn. I wanted to shoot him, but I couldn't stand still long enough to get a shot off because of what was going on beneath us.

Wolf and I made it to the other side when Zombie got tripped up by a ghoul beneath him. Ninja and Preacher lifted Zombie back up. Wolf and I were picking off the ghouls coming up from the ground near Zombie. The boys made it to the other side when Wolf noticed Raven was stuck behind us as he screamed, "Noooooooo!" As Zombie, Preacher and Ninja turned around, Raven and the dogs were stuck in the field fighting off ghouls. Zombie took aim at the ghoul on top of the hill then fired one shot, hitting the ghoul in the head as he watched his body roll down the hill. Meanwhile, Cheech and Chong were bravely fighting off the ghouls trying to protect Raven with all the energy they had left in them. We were picking off as many ghouls as we could in an attempt to save them. Raven was a maniac killing several, but there were just too many. It was like watching a rerun of General Custard in his last stand. The more shots that we fired from a distance, the more they multiplied. The ghouls had now tackled Raven and the dogs. Preacher yelled, "Zombie, kill them for the love of mercy!" Suddenly an explosion rocked the area, dirt and bodies flew in all directions. Apparently Raven had stolen some of the dynamite from my bag; he used the grenades to set off the dynamite. There was no way he was going to let the ghouls take his dogs or himself for that matter. He took as many of those bastards as he could with him down to hell. Before leaving the earth, Raven made sure that neither his dogs' bodies nor his own were going to be left in vain for a free meal. I was hysterical as Wolf and Ninja had to hold me back from charging back onto the bone yard. Preacher fell to his knees as tears flowed from us all. It was hard to watch our friend die so helplessly yet valiantly. Wolf yelled, "God damn! Raven is one heroic son of a bitch!"

As the smoke cleared what appeared to be hundreds now seemed like thousands of ghouls forging ahead after us. Wolf yelled, "Come on, we gotta go!" We raced into the woods running up a rocky hill. The ghouls were still chasing behind us. Ninja asked, "What are these fucking things? What do they want?" Zombie yelled, "To eat us!" We took off running only to find a ledge at the end of the hill; there was nowhere else to run. I looked down saying, "Oh shit!" Wolf also peeked over the ledge yelling, "We need to jump!" Though I feared no man, I was not thrilled of heights. I yelled back, "Are you fucking suicidal? That's crazy, let's stay and finish the fight here." Wolf replied, "That is sure death. Jumping is the only way. It's 70 or 80 feet from the water." Preacher yelled, "We will all die for sure!" Zombie, who is a math genius, quickly answered, "Wolf is right; we can survive the fall without major injury." The ghouls were closing in when Zombie, with a running start, jumped off the ledge. Ninja grabbed Preacher then jumped off the ledge next. You could hear them screaming on their way down. Wolf grabbed me and said, "It's our turn big boy, let's do this thing." I yelled, "Wait a minute! I need a song." Wolf asked, "Are you crazy? We gotta jump!" I replied, "I'm thinking 'Do You Feel Like We Do' by Peter Frampton." Wolf responded, "Great fucking tune! Now let's go!" Running hand in hand, Wolf and I jumped off the ledge. I screamed, "Jesus Christtttttttttt!" We screamed all the way down when we both plunged in the water like a thunderbolt.

CHAPTER THIRTY TWO:
THE BLACK MASS MASSACRE

Journals by Preacher

As we all flowed down the river I could see pure relief in Chief's face. It took guts to face his fears, but then again the alternative wasn't so appealing either. From somewhere in the distance I could hear the song "Lonely is the Night" by Billie Squire. Zombie was the first to shore trying to fish everyone out with a long tree branch. Eventually I got ashore; I think we all had aches and pains from the fall. We were damn lucky to be alive. Reality was hitting us hard with Raven's death along with those brave, crazy ass loyal dogs of his. My heart ached like everyone else. I could see it was going to refuel the fire of rage in all of us. Wolf found a cave so I knew we were getting closer to the quarry. Wolf immediately had Chief and Ninja gathering branches so we could get a fire started. We needed to get warm, get our clothes dry and gather what supplies and weapons we had left. Zombie got busy checking, cleaning, and attending to the weapons. We lost a few from the fall.

Later that night, we sat around the fire naked waiting for our clothes and supplies to dry. We ate whatever food was left out of boredom. As I stared at everyone it was apparent we were not going back home, death was inevitable. What gave me motivation was thinking about what those bastards did to Medicine Man, Wizard, and the others. The more I thought about the others whose lives were lost, the angrier I became. I wondered how many innocent people the monks tortured and killed. I couldn't get the image out of my head of those valiant dogs and Raven fighting a battle of insurmountable odds; I will never forget their sacrifice the rest of my days. The fallen tribe members, Raven, and the dogs were not heroes in my eyes, they were Gods. Their story will be legendary; they reached the pinnacle of being immortal. Was this not the real reason we were all really here? Yes, we all wanted to save Wizard, but our cause ran so much deeper than that. I think deep down, we all wanted to be that of Greek Gods, we all wanted to be Zeus or Achilles. We wanted everyone to remember our names forever. I guess we were guilty of vanity among other things. Maybe the detectives were right, maybe we were crazy. As I reminisced of our lost brothers the song "Fly to the Angels" by Slaughter kept replaying in my head, yet when I thought of Crowley' Tomb "Faceless Man" by Creed would play instead. I could hear these songs struggling back in forth in my head. It seemed so long ago when we lost Medicine Man. Through our journeys I know we all had that same burning question that nobody wanted to ask because of superstition: "Who's Next?"

Later that night our clothes were mostly dry, I was not crazy about them being damp. I kept thinking to myself *"we are all our own devils here on earth walking in the footsteps of hell".* I believe the chambers of Crowley's Tomb were the ultimate evil and we let Satan trick us into thinking there was only one devil in the world, when in reality there are many, including ourselves. We eventually fell asleep cuddled together like a sleeping pack of dogs. When morning came Chief was standing over us and said, "The time for revenge is upon us. It is time to send Lucifer back to that bitch of a mother. There is no time for mercy, only time for killing. From here on out leave your conscience behind, it will serve no purpose moving forward." Zombie asked, "What time is it?" Chief replied, "Who gives a shit. It's time to make a house call to the Devil himself. It is time to unleash murder on the Devil." Zombie responded, "Great! Just what we need a breakfast of champions." Chief was losing his grip with reality. I believe Raven's death broke him.

We walked through the rock tunnels before climbing our way uphill. My muscles throughout my body seemed numb. I just wanted to get up this fucking hill. Every bone in my body hurt. I knew everyone else felt the same because we all had the giggles as our way of trying not to cry from the pain. Eventually we all made it up as I immediately laid my back on the ground. I stared at the sun as if I were saying my last goodbyes to the sky and mother earth. I saw three ravens fly by in the sky. I knew it had to be Raven and the dogs. It was just too symbolic for it not to be. I could hear the winds cry, which was horrifying to listen to. It was like a blurry scream of souls passing by in pain. We walked for awhile through large rock walls when I came to a black door in the rock. Phrases etched in the door read, "He that committeth sin is of the God; for the God sinneth from the beginning. For this purpose the Son of the Devil was manifested, that he might destroy the works of the God." Zombie remarked, "That is fucked up." I answered, "Yes it is. It is all reversed from the scriptures of John 3:8. These people are sick demented bastards for sure." Chief warned, "Be mentally prepared to see shit you have never seen in your life. From here on out you have to get angry but don't let fear creep inside you. Use your hate as your strength for revenge. The Devil will be preying on weakness. Once I open this door there is no turning back." You could see everyone was anxious to translate their fear into bravery and anger.

Chief opened the door leading us down a dark stairway. Ninja said, "Damn, my legs feel shaky." We came to another black door with writing that glowed in the dark in red. It read, "And the great God was cast out, that old serpent, called the Christ, and God, which deceiveth the whole world: he was cast out into the earth, and his angels were cast out with him." Wolf said, "Man do these monks ever have it wrong. These people are really confused and twisted." You could see everyone holding their breath as Chief opened the door. What we saw next was enough to make you want to go back up the stairs. Blood flowed down the walls like a river. The light underneath it made it terrifying to watch as it streamed down the stairway edges like a waterfall. The blood never entered the stairway: a very dark, sinister, and symbolic event for sure. It was creepy watching it continually flow downstream next to you. I could hear the famous song "Cry" by Michael Ortega being mocked coming from the walls, while also hearing a female voice singing opera. It gave me shivers. From behind, Zombie yelled, "Hurry up Chief! This place is spookier than hell!" Chief answered, "That's because we are on our way down to hell." Zombie yelled back, "You guys scare me more than the devil himself! How in the fuck did I ever let you talk me into this?" We all laughed at Zombie. I knew that was his way of fighting off his own fears with whining and complaining.

As we got deeper into our descent inside the Devil's nest I just couldn't help but think how nuts these people were and yet how crazy we must have been as well. Another door emerged with a glowing yellow and orange color with more nonsense. It read, "Submit yourselves therefore to Satan. Resist the temptation of God, and he will flee from you. Lest God should get an advantage of us: for we are not ignorant of his devices." Ninja asked, "What is he talking about?" I answered, "Pay no attention; that is Satan attempting to warp the words of the Bible." Zombie asked, "Don't you think we should be worried?" Chief answered, "Whatever our translations, thoughts or opinions, it will make no difference or outcome in the war of murder between God and Satan. While they play their games, we will play our own games. They can all burn in Heaven or Hell; it makes no difference to me. Now let's keep moving."

Chief opened the door; the path became very narrow so we had to walk single file. In my first breath, it felt as if I swallowed depression and despair. It was pitched black, you could hear the cries coming from the walls. As I looked up there was no cover over us, just a dark sky. I could see ancient stars but the sun had been removed by black skies of darkness. As I walked down the stairs I could hear the roar of thunder and the sight of lightening. Rain began to fall on us. I could see the moon experiencing the lunar eclipse. Wolf asked, "What the fuck is going on?" I answered, "I think we are in what the monks consider their purgatory. This is where the soul must be stripped naked. This is where the soul lives most of the time. This is where our souls are most vulnerable and where all suffering must occur. The soul must be burdened with suffering in order to be forgiven in someone's demented mind." The rain felt like fire drops as it burned your skin. Zombie spouted out, "I think the Catholics believe your soul is forgivable under God's judgment waiting to be burned by fire or something like that." I replied, "Not exactly." Chief said, "I don't give a God damn what the Catholics think. They have started more wars than anyone. They rape children and get away with it. In my opinion they are sinners of greed for the love of money and the servants of Satan. They are behind the occult." I commented, "Well Chief, tell us how you really feel."

While leading the pack Chief answered, "Think about this: Christ told Peter not to build churches yet after Christ died they built them anyway. Look who goes to church, mostly the weak, right? Who does Satan prey on the most? The weak! Strong characters don't allow him in to begin with. They have a relationship without a fellowship. The word of God should be preached anywhere with no money involved. Do we always need to talk to Mr. Profit Man in order to go to church? I mean, how much money do the churches expect to get from one's family in order to witness their show? Money and greed: that is the church's masochistic drive. It's how Satan works on the leaders. Look at their leaders, they either fall from grace through the greed of money or sex. Go listen to these evangelists then look at their pocket books. Anyone could sling words for that kind of money. Do the Popes really need that big of a palace to live in, in order to preach God's word? Why does the Pope not shelter the homeless there? Why do they have the cloak-and-dagger library? Aren't they supposed to share information, shedding light on things instead of hiding in darkness like shadow governments do?" I began to rebut Chief's ideas when we heard Chief yell out, "Another door!"

I began profusely sweating as the halls got hotter. I leaned over to read the etching on the door which read, "And the God that deceived them was cast into the lake of fire and brimstone, where the angel and the false prophet [are], and shall be tormented day and night forever and ever." I think everyone was speechless so Chief went to grab the door handle only to burn his hand. He wisely used his cloak jacket to open the door. Immediately a heat wave hit us: the walls were on fire. Chief ran down the stairs with us following behind. We covered ourselves with our jackets to avoid burning. I could feel the flames under my feet; it was hot as Hell! It was like walking on the top of a fire pit. I heard screams of tormented, tortured souls. Hell was punishing souls while unleashing its fury. We came to the bottom of the stairs only to be at another door. I felt like I was being cooked alive. Exhausted and sweating from the heat, I wasn't sure if I had any energy left. Writing was etched in fire on the door which read, "Welcome to Hell." Chief said, "It's my pleasure."

Chief rushed out and almost fell off the ledge. You could see fiery lights down below. The breeze was at least very refreshing. Chief had to walk carefully around the ledge, as did everyone else. Again Chief had to face his demon: the fear of heights. We eventually found a cavern area where we sat looking down into the quarry. I was stunned by what I witnessed. Across from where we sat on the top of the quarry I could see fire all around. For a minute I thought we were inside the mouth of a large volcano. There was a familiar ghost ship that was hanging off the ledge. The people on the ship's top deck had the appearance of Klu Klux Klan members. The red hoods and robes gave me the willies. It made my hair stand straight up. The ship appeared to be falling down into the quarry, as if the world was not round, yet it was very stationary and bolted down. All around the middle edges of the quarry were built-in stone balconies as if you were at the opera. Glancing further to the bottom there was a large city that seemed to be on fire. There was a large watch tower that glowed in blue light with fire around it. You could see a cemetery with reverse crosses in an open field burning. There was another field of people screaming in what appeared to be a pool of fire. You could see monks pushing people off a cliff into the fire pool while others were being dangled over the fire pit like pigs being roasted. It was gruesome to watch, the screams of pain were torture to listen to. Witnessing people melt right before your eyes into skeletons was horrific and unbearable. On another cliff monks were pushing people off the ledge only to land in a large pit of serpents. In a fenced-in area you could see weird creatures and Satan's dark knights annihilating defenseless slaves. They were being butchered for the feast. Other slaves were shackled in chains while being tortured by sadomasochists wearing leather masks. I heard the sounds of whips and witnessed the flesh being torn off their bodies. The more I scanned the area the more gruesome it got. There was a caged arena where you could see a free-for-all as hell-hounds, war-hogs, humans, unicorns, ghouls, and beasts that I can't even describe were fighting and killing one another. Wolf pointed to an area in which people were being boiled in large pots like soup. As they screamed the monks would just hit them in the head with a paddle and keep stirring the pot. The scene was beyond horrendous.

I watched deformed creatures jousting with Hell's warriors. The warriors all had the same gold plated armor with giant swords and spears. Long horns came from each side of their head. The helmets were intimidating while the army's numbers were frightening. I watched a woman shackled in chains being pulled by the four horses of death. I watched Hell's warriors rape her as her screams resonated through us all. She screamed God's name only to fall on deaf ears. Apparently God was just the usual spectator with the balls of a coward. Chief said, "I can't take this. Let's go kill these fucks!" Wolf wrestled Chief to the ground and yelled, "This isn't the wild west Chief! These nuts play for keeps! We can't just go rush down there. They will torture and slaughter us as they're doing now. Use your head! The peoples' fates down there are sealed already. Keep a lookout for Wizard. Let everything else fucking go!" All of us were sickened by what was going on down there. We were expecting to fight monks but this was beyond all comprehension. This was truly a war we could not win. We were in way over our heads, outmatched and outnumbered. Ninja said, "Chief, we are good, but this is out of control, it's getting ridiculous." Chief answered in a coy voice, "The bigger the army the harder the fall." Everyone kind of shook their heads thinking maybe Chief had lost his mind. I realized we were all a little crazy to begin with, unfortunately in Chief's world he was losing his grip on reality. I think the losses were becoming more than he could bear. God's hypocrisy and Satan's cruelty finally broke him.

There were all kinds of doors throughout the quarry walls. Some of the doors were covered in skulls. There was one door that seemed so out of place. It had green ivy growing all around the quarry walls with vines wrapped around the gated entrance. But the one doorway that stood out the most was a stairway that went halfway up the quarry. Giant reapers with laser red eyes in dark blue cloaks guarded the entrance. Their swords were three times the size of anything we ever used. There was a large platform next to them. The large golden throne was surrounded by candles guarded by creatures with horns and spears in black robes. Babies were being sacrificed by monks who tossed them into a stoned quarry pool as if they were trash being discarded. We could only watch helplessly as the babies struggled in the clear water, drowning one at a time over and over again. The monks were getting a kick out of it; you could see them laughing and celebrating after each toss of a child. They were high fiving each other as if they were participating in a sporting event. It was disgusting and we couldn't do anything about it. If we charged in we would only be part of the slaughtered for the feast.

We were growing restless in our frustration when Ninja asked, "When is the killing, infliction of pain and suffering enough for these people? When does it ever end, God damn it? These are babies for Christ sake!" Lowering my head in shame, I answered, "It doesn't end. Every time I tried to get closer to God I only came away feeling betrayed by a cowardly dictatorship. I am sure if that was God's son being thrown into fire or water he would come to his rescue. He certainly had no problem with revenge for the death of his son. He was rewarded with Heaven. What are these people rewarded with? Is their suffering not the same?" Chief interrupted, "You're wrong! You're so fucking wrong! It is going to end with us here tonight! We might not be able to kill all of them, but I promise you we're going to kill all the leaders, disrupting this evil empire of fucking retards! I never did like bullies. These people are cowards. Unlike Christ, we need no rewards!" Staring down again I could see midgets in a line being slaughtered like cattle, thrown for everyone to eat at the main table. Zombie walked away shaking his head in utter disgrace yelling, "Jesus fucking Christ this is so bad, this is so bad! This is pure genocide!"

I had seen enough. I hurried further down the edges of the quarry when a loud bell went off as organ music began to play. From below people ran towards the stage area as if they were running to get the best seat at a concert. Then all the madness stopped, at least for the moment. No one noticed us because we pretty much blended right in. The bell stopped only to be followed by horns and bugles. The heavily guarded door opened near the stage, parading out of it walked nine killer elite monks wearing their green cloaks. A few minutes later Father Blackwell walked on stage pumping his fist followed by the President of the Shadow Government waving to the crowd. Manson strutted out along with his psychotic side show partner Hitler. I was stunned to see government officials involved in this. It gave me the creeps. Not to mention the twin psychos; I could feel my blood boiling at the mere site of those idiots. Hate is an incredible force when used for fuel. The roar of the crowd went into a complete frenzy when Satan himself popped out in his circus red cloak. Wolf said, "Speak of the Devil." Now I was beyond pissed off. I wanted to kill them so bad I could taste it. We were all so far lost in our own souls that hate and killing were the only things that could satisfy us at this point. The anticipation of revenge was greater than the taste of good, there was no turning back. No matter what, we planned on destroying the evil that God had created. His most beautiful angel had to go down. I no longer cared if God didn't want to take responsibility. I think being imperfect is a way of life, even for God. He might wish to tell the world he was perfect but that was a lie, simple as that. I had reached a point where I couldn't tell the difference between God and Satan anymore; they seemed to be the same. Maybe God was a coward or maybe he just lost control of the situation. I didn't have the answer and I certainly didn't give a shit! Those psychos were going down with or without God's blessing. God sitting on the sidelines watching this madness was a sin in itself. I thought Jesus Christ died for our sins, I was wrong. Every time I wanted to run to God it was shit like this that stopped me.

The freak put his hands up looking up in the sky as if he was the Pope or God. I was fucking appalled by this arrogant fool. I was trying hard to remain calm. I needed to keep my revenge in check so I could think with all my wits. Satan threw out reverse crucifix necklaces with himself nailed to the cross to the crowd. Insecure women who starved for attention flashed their breasts as if Satan was throwing them golden beads. Self respect was lost in this evil pit. The Devil's Rejects and his Demonic Choir began singing creepy songs as everyone chanted, "Hail Satan!" I could hear the haunting bell go off followed by creepy wind chimes. Yippy, we were now at the same place we ran from, another form of hypnotic church. It was so disturbing to watch this charade. The midnight odyssey was just beginning. The killer elite monks stood circled behind the throne while Hitler and Manson stood on opposite sides of the Devil. Satan began his speech, speaking in reverse Pig Latin in a deep monstrous voice. Pentagrams lit up on the stage floor and all along the quarry walls. As we continued to witness and listen to this mumbo jumbo the boys were getting a bit hostile. I could see in Chief's demeanor he was a ticking time bomb. I almost admired his carefree insanity. My courage was no more than burning rage. Satan's sermon was nothing more than gibberish. This place was the chronicles of the plague and there were no halos to be worn. Obviously sleeping Jesus was sleeping the night away.

The Black Mass had become silent when the mark of the witch strutted out with nothing on but high heels. She had nun servants by her side. The Pagan Queen was beautiful and extraordinarily tempting yet evil all in one breath. Music played to her every move. On both sides of the stage nuns began pole dancing. The vanity was so self-worshipping I wanted to puke on the audience; apparently the people craved attention and were willing to sell their souls to the Devil. The dark ages were upon us as Satan sat on his throne when the Pagan Queen came up, kissed his hand then kneeled before him. On her knees she enjoyed performing a sex act on Satan. Finished, he pointed out towards the crowd when she stood up, lit her hair on fire then simply walked off the ledge backwards landing in a pool of fire. Zombie yelled, "No way! What a waste." I guess she was somehow offering herself as a sacrifice in honor of him. It was creepy shit to sit and watch this nonsense. People were going crazy cheering. It was at that moment a trap door opened behind the killer elite monks. Out came some black cloaked monk thugs pushing Wizard to the stage floor. There were also four kids dragged onto the stage that appeared to be our classmates. They set Wizard on a floor pentagram, put candles around him then without warning nailed him to it. Before we could react our classmates were made to kneel in front of Satan. By the quick glance we got of Wizard he looked badly beaten. Wizard was suffering yet you could see he was defiant. I am sure his wisdom and sarcastic nature along with his riddles didn't sit so well with the impatient monks. Nonetheless, I felt a sense of relief and happiness just to see the Wizard was still alive. Of course, it only took seconds for fear to come crashing down on my party.

Satan stood up, everyone below bowed to the prick. I kept wondering to myself, '*how were we going to save the Wizard against Satan's Army?*' I knew all hell was about to break loose. Satan grabbed the first classmate by the neck then threw him off the ledge as his body hit the snake pit. The crowd went crazy as their sick sporting event continued. Satan was savoring every moment of his twisted party. The next classmate was chosen by the killer elite monks who dragged him by his hair, tying him to a post. Hitler ripped off the kid's shirt then gutted him like a pig. Zombie pointed his gun at Hitler when Wolf pushed his gun down. Hitler was enjoying pulling out his intestines while the kid was still alive. I can't imagine the pain that poor soul went through. These sick bastards had no mercy or compassion for life. All they knew was torture and death. These monks were psychotic killers with empty souls. The kid was thrown off the ledge for Satan's beast to finish him off. The third classmate had his throat cut then was kicked off the ledge to the audience who again went into a frenzy of cheers. I figured he at least went quicker without much suffering. I was so mad I wanted to burn this whole place to the ground. Manson grabbed the last classmate, punched him a few times in the face then tied his ankles. Obviously the other end of the rope was fastened to the ledge. Manson pushed him off the ledge as people stoned him to death while he hung upside down; I was fucking speechless. I noticed the other guys had their heads down in shame, hands covering their faces. I couldn't help but wonder: did our classmates get kidnapped or did they get caught while trying to explore Crowley's Tomb? Regardless, I felt responsible somehow, yet we did nothing to save any of them. The guilt was very hard to burden, let alone process in my mind. I think we were in complete shock.

Satan walked up to Wizard. You could see Satan telling him something; we regrettably couldn't hear the conversation. Satan yelled out to the crowd, "Where is your God? Where are the Cemetery Boys? I am sure both are witnessing your devotion. Why does no one help in your time of need?" The crowd yelled obscenities at the Wizard. Hitler sliced Wizard a few times in the face. Wizard did not cry out in pain or for help. Chief aimed his gun at Hitler when Wolf restrained him from doing so. Hitler slowly inserted the knife into Wizard's stomach. He walked to the bottom of Wizard's feet then stabbed both feet from the bottoms. You could see Wizard was in tremendous pain yet he would not cry out. He refused to give those sick bastards the satisfaction. Wolf quietly said to Chief as he put his hand over Chief's mouth, "If you shoot one of these pricks now, we will never get our revenge. I am telling you, they will slaughter us in far worse ways. One kill is not worth the many kills to come. Remember that. Now compose yourself. We are all pulling our guts out here over this tragedy."

Whispering in Wizard's ear, Satan yelled back out to the crowd, "Tell the Cemetery Boys to come out kneeling before me and I will end this quickly." Wizard relented, shaking his head yes. You could see in his face the pain was killing him. Satan yelled to the crowd, "The traitor who worships before me has words to speak." I could tell Wizard was dying and we helplessly watched our mentor who we loved being slaughtered because of our own sins. There was no torture that Satan or his monks could do to us that would be worse than this: and I mean nothing. Wizard yelled out in a stern voice, "Boys avenge meeeeee!" In disgust, Satan closed his eyes, shook his head then gestured to Hitler, who suddenly cut Wizard's heart out. With no time to react at what happened, it took all of us to hold Chief down. Tears flowed down all of our faces. Hitler handed Satan Wizard's beating heart. Satan held it up to the crowd then the sick fuck began eating it as the demented crowd cheered out, chanting Satan's name. Confetti simultaneously rained down on the crowd. Before my own eyes, I watched Satan shape-change into something I'd never seen before. He turned into a beast, then back into human form. I said, "I'll be God damned, he really is Satan!" This place had to be far worse than hell! Our dreams came to a crashing end with Wizard's death. I don't think we were prepared for it, let alone to witness it. I never really considered the obvious; we were oblivious to failure because our own vanity got in the way. Hope was lost forever and we were responsible for it. Not even Chief's own words earlier in the day could have prepared us for the cruelty and the savagery of Crowley's Tomb. It was a nightmare that went unthinkably wrong. Wolf yelled to everyone, "Get up, we have to kill these fucking murderers!"

The celebration below us was in full blown pandemonium. It was a rerun of Sodom and Gomorrah happening before our eyes. It was just shameful: the killing, torturing, suffering and sinful bloody orgies taking place down below - there was no way to describe what had just taken place or what was still going on. It's a party that I guess never ends here. We obviously got on the wrong fucking train coming here in the first place. Satan waved at the crowd then yelled in an enthusiastic deep voice, "Indulge in the feast in my name." The crowd went wild. Satan whispered to the killer elite monks, "I know those boys are here. Find them! Bring the Cemetery Boys to me alive if possible." A monk asked, "What if we kill one?" Satan answered, "The dead cost nothing. Now move!" Satan, Hitler, and Manson vanished through the trap door.

We found a secluded area where Wolf took over the leadership of the tribe. Chief had too much anger and hurt to make rational decisions. He never wavered or cared about the decision we made. Chief was a team player, no different than the rest of us. He was just waiting to unleash his revenge on those twisted fucks. Chief was like a thoroughbred horse waiting for the gates to open. Whatever hope was in his eyes left with Wizard's death. His demeanor was now that of a man on fire with death behind him. Wolf drew in the sand as we huddled going over the plan. We didn't have much time. I remember staring at one another knowing this was possibly the last conversation we'd have together. Wolf looked at us impersonating Dirty Harry, momentary laughter broke out. Wolf said, "A laugh is worth dying for and there is no one I would rather die with than you guys. Take a damn good look at each other, watch each other's back till your very last breath. Now let's get the fuck out of here and go kill them all!" That small speech helped bring a little life back into each one of us. It was like a halftime speech when you're down by three touchdowns.

CHAPTER THIRTY THREE: THE SHAFT

Journals by Preacher

I sprinted down the quarry ledge when Zombie said, "I will cover your asses, I can hit a tick off your nose from here." Wolf instructed Ninja to go deal with the ghost ship. It was very loud at the bottom of the quarry. We ran halfway down the quarry when two killer elite monks ran towards us. Within the blink of an eye both monks fell off the ledge. I knew Zombie had just put bullets in their heads. You couldn't even hear the shots fired because of the loud party noise. Even if you screamed you would have to assume it was coming from down below with all the killing still going on. As we ran further down the quarry, I could see monks, beasts and warriors being picked off by Zombie's rifle. Nobody even noticed. There was just way too much commotion going on. Out of nowhere a thunderous blast shook the quarry. The night sky lit up like the Fourth of July as debris dropped from the sky. Wolf yelled, "Get down!" Laying down I said, "Looks like the apocalypse is here." The explosion got everyone's attention. The ship had vanished from the ledge. The loud explosion echoed in the quarry. I think many thought it was just part of the festivities. Another killer elite monk pointed up in the sky only to be dropped where he stood. Zombie continued his assault, picking off the elite monks one by one. Suddenly chaos reigned if that was even possible; people were running in all directions confused by what was transpiring. Wolf pointed to the ledge where people were still being thrown into the pool of fire when we opened fire on about ten monks. They never knew what hit them. By the time we let our fingers off the trigger there were no monks remaining on the ledge.

Our assault was in full swing, Chief threw a stick of dynamite at the bottom of the quarry followed by the rest of us unleashing a few grenades. In my mind Christmas came early. The dynamite was much louder and even more destructive than the grenades. The quarry became a dust bowl. I couldn't see a thing. We kept assaulting the quarry with gunfire along the way until we neared the stairs that led to the stage that Satan and his goons had been on. Every time monks approached us we just filled them with bullet holes. The Devil's Army had never seen the ultimate hell being unleashed from the Rebels of Heaven. We had brought the fight to Hades as Death enjoyed the buffet. Approaching the stairs we greeted some of Satan's warriors with bullet holes. Wolf yelled, "This certainly beats target practice!"

Chief yelled, "I love the murder of rapture!" Chief was rapidly losing it. He put blood on his face from one of the dead monks, which scared me.

Zombie's vision was blocked by all the dust so he high-tailed it out of the crawlspace making his way down when he heard his name being called by a familiar voice from behind. Ninja caught up with Zombie as they continued racing down the walkway to find the tribe. Ninja asked, "Did you see that ship explode?" Zombie answered, "Yeah that was incredible! Let's go find the others." Running down the quarry hill we were shooting anything in our path. The monks were spread out all over the place, they seemed confused. For whatever reason, the monks had hate in their heart, especially for us. The best thing about Satan's Army was their weapons were outdated. We now had the upper hand, or so we thought. The giant guards were actually no match for us. Chief killed them before we could even pull the trigger. The masochist ran up the stage stairs where Wolf appreciated shooting them first in the balls with the first shot while we finished them with the second. I guess Wolf enjoyed watching them suffer. It immediately took their manhood away from them that's for sure.

With Ninja and Zombie catching up we walked through the trap door where Wolf quickly booby trapped it with a few grenades. With the death of Wizard we no longer had anything to lose. The hallway inside the quarry was mostly red with a mix of black stone. I swear if felt like it was revolving when we heard an explosion. I could feel the trembles from the blast as my ankles hurt running down the pathway. The continued circular movement from the walls was making me dizzy as we came across a giant elevator door. The elevator had candles all around it. The door looked as if it was on fire (although it wasn't); it also had skeletons engraved on it with a human skull above it. "Highway to Hell" by AC/DC played from the elevator speakers. Wolf said, "Well the music's fitting." Zombie, trailing behind everyone else in a panic asked, "This place really is hell, isn't it?" I answered, "No it's not hell. Hell is here on earth. This is just the murdering psychos twisted minds' interpretation of what hell is. We are in Crowley's hell, not hell itself." Zombie replied, "I have to admit this is the first elevator that I can relate to the music. Usually elevator music plays that shitty stuff in an attempt to kill you slowly." Wolf, who stood standing in front of the door, pushed the button for the door to open asking, "Well, are you ready to take the elevator to hell?" Within a second of that question the door opened up. A large beast with the body of a lion and face of an ape with large fangs attacked Wolf before we could react; Wolf's body was hanging out of the beast's mouth. The beast's eyes were darker than the ace of spades. Wolf screamed as the jaws closed down on his body. I started shooting at the beast, but it had already run down the hall with Wolf's body hanging from it. The beast turned around towards us from a distance; I could see Wolf pull the pin from one of his grenades. Chief yelled, "Get down!" The beast charged towards us when an explosion went off. Blood spewed out all over the place. I remember looking up; I couldn't see any semblance of Wolf anywhere. I began to weep when Chief said, "There is a time to cry; this isn't the time." If we didn't feel like we lost the battle already this put an exclamation point on the war. I could feel the interior of my heart shattering with blood pouring from it. My soul was crushed.

The elevator made a dinging noise when Chief yelled, "Come on! Get in!" We got up and ran into the elevator. The elevator had see-through glass in the rear. On the way up I witnessed the eternal prison rooms that glowed in red lights where half-man, half-beast creatures behind red bars screamed at you like maniacs. I could see strange creatures I had never seen in my life, some deformed, others in the shapes of wild beasts, all locked up. Ninja said, "It looks like hell's asylum." I didn't know what waited for us above, I just knew I was scared. Seeing those things locked up in a cage staring at us with the thirst to kill was terrifying. Wolf was here one minute and gone in the blink of an eye. Wizard was gone forever as were our dead classmates. We may have felt immortal before, but this was a wakeup call on mortality. I had flashbacks of everyone we had lost. We no longer had the time to mourn our lost brothers. My head was spinning. I think that's when I was most scared knowing my time was about up. The elevator doors opened; we all ran out except Chief who took all the dynamite we had left, lit the fuse then sent the elevator down. We took off running for our lives down the hall, just as we got outside on the lawn a massive explosion went off. The building we came from was the Bell Tower. I got up stumbling forward only to fall back to the ground watching the tower behind implode as it fell like a brick. My ears were ringing. The explosion scared the living shit out of the monks who were scattering like cowards outside. I continued firing at anything that moved. There was no sight of the hierarchy. There was dust in every direction. Between the darkness and the aftermath of the explosion, it was nearly impossible to see anything. Chaos surrounded us like the plague. We ran toward the pyramid when all of a sudden Zombie fell to the ground screaming. Ninja turned backed only to see an arrow sticking out of Zombie's right calf. Ninja managed to help Zombie to his feet with me helping him make it toward the pyramid. I could hear arrows hitting the outside of the building and the trees as we neared the pyramid. Luckily Chief knew how to get inside the secret door of the pyramid.

Zombie was in a lot of pain as we ran down the halls of the pyramid. We made it to the giant pentagram floor surrounded by the gateway entrances. I said, "What a creepy place." I heard voices in the distance so we ran into the first gateway door. The doorway was guarded by a boned goat statue that resembled a warrior of some kind. It was obvious we were in what appeared to be a torture chamber. There were deformed women living in small bird cages with their mouths sewn shut. The walls were covered with dead people hanging in chains and straps. I opened the iron maiden only to be met with a dead body mutilated by spikes inside the door. Zombie yelled, "Jesus Christ, the bastards murdered detective Parks!" Ninja replied, "The whole police force must be looking for him." Chief said, "Certainly not the best way to go." Zombie yelled, "Fuck, this sucks! So much for the God damned cavalry coming to our rescue!" Another dead police officer was dangling from the ceiling, hanging from his arms behind his back. I can't imagine what pain he suffered from his own weight. Ninja said, "I thought torture chambers went out of style a long time ago." Chief answered, "Apparently nobody told the druids about it." In the corner a female officer's body had been tortured by a rack device; her arms and legs looked like spaghetti. On a small table next to her there was a bucket of blunt torturing instruments used to insert in the officer. I pushed the body aside so we could put Zombie on the table to examine the wound to his calf. Frightened, Zombie said, "Please, let's just get the fuck out of here! It's a butcher shop in here! If I am going to die, please not here." I answered, "You're not going to die but the pain is going to be unbearable for a few minutes." Chief held Zombie down covering his mouth while Ninja held his legs down, I quickly broke the end of the arrow off as Zombie squirmed around in pain. I proceeded to pull the arrow through, using my belt as a tourniquet then covered the wound with bandages from my medicine bag. I gave Zombie the last of the pain pills. The injury looked gruesome.

Chief said, "We have to keep moving", so Zombie got between Ninja and I as Chief led the way through the torture chambers. We walked by the chair of torture when Chief yelled "Oh my God!" I recognized the Wizard's brother Zoe in the chair. We were shocked at the painful discovery. Ninja yelled, "Those mother fuckers. I don't think I will ever sit on another chair again." Walking through the chambers there were so many cruelty devices it became unspeakable. Just when I thought the madness ended we ran into Pusher. Chief said, "Oh man, these crazy sadistic fucks really have no mercy!" Pusher was tied down on a table where a rat cage was strapped to his abdomen. The open side of the cage was placed on his stomach. Apparently a heating element was placed on top of the cage. The rat's natural instincts led them to flee from the heat. With fatal results the rats burrowed through Pusher's body. I had seen enough ghastly devices, but seeing them used was disturbing. I felt like we stepped back into medieval times. Knowing that Parks and the cavalry were slaughtered off sucked, to say the very least. It just seemed as if no stone was unturned by the monks. We may have caught the evil empire by surprise; unfortunately it didn't seem to matter because Satan always seemed to be one step ahead of us. With the death of Wolf, Satan once again got the last laugh while we got the shaft.

WOLF

CHAPTER THIRTY FOUR: THE EXORCIST

Journals by Preacher

We kept moving down a stairwell when we heard voices. Chief slammed open a door downstairs that startled the enemy and himself. To our surprise we were met by the familiar faces of Deacon Brownstone, Bishop Benedict, and two creepy monks. Before the monks could respond, Chief fired two shots, killing both. Bishop Benedict dressed like the pope yelled, "You just murdered two holy monks!" Chief replied, "Well you're right, they are more holy now. Murder I think not, they had it coming. Now I am going to kill you two rat fucks!" Pleading, the Pope said, "Please I beg you, my work is not finished." I asked, "Your work? What the hell kind of work do you do exactly?" Benedict answered, "We cleanse out the souls of those in need by purification." Chief knocked off the white cone hat of the Bishop then yelled, "You people are fucking insane! You dress like the pope, you sick bastards get off on torturing helpless people, and you have the nerve to call yourself a Bishop. What the fuck is wrong with you?" Benedict answered, "His Holiness will cleanse all your souls as well. You will be free at last to live a life of riches." Speaking softly I said, "Well let me cleanse your soul first Bishop. Have a good trip to never-never land." A shot rang out as I shot the Bishop in the balls; he fell to his knees in excruciating pain as I walked up to him pressing the gun to the Bishop's head. Deacon Brownstone yelled, "Don't do it! You will be condemned in darkness for eternity." I replied, "We are already condemned and so are you. Betrayal is a bitch, have a safe trip to Hell." I pulled the trigger as blood stained the wall. Chief stood over the Bishop's dead body and said, "You got off easy, pal." Brownstone yelled, "You're all crazy!" Ninja laughed then responded, "You should be more careful who you trust Deacon; even your boy Lucifer was once upon a time an angel." One shot rang out as Zombie shot the Deacon between the eyes. Zombie said, "Exactly."

We walked back upstairs to the gates trying to hunt down the Hierarchy. I could see Chief was getting anxious; the smell of blood was in the air. The taste for killing was becoming an addiction for us. We were beyond revenge. It was just like Wizard said it would be. We had brought evil to ourselves; there was no way of turning back the clock. We had become judge, jury and executioner. We finally experienced the complexity of becoming God, Death and Satan all in one. We were now as guilty as they were of murdering the world and everything in it. Chief reveled in it. Life is so precious, no one, not even the holy Creator has the right to take the life of another. I knew now more than ever our moments were fleeting. It was just a matter of when, where and how. How we would be remembered was an afterthought when facing death directly in the eyes. Our responsibility, consequences, and even our own karma were coming back for vengeance to rule the roost. Frankly, I didn't give a damn anymore. We were past the point of no return for forgiveness. I could not only hear the song from Kansas "Point Of No Return" playing in my head, I could clearly see the writing on the wall. All that was left was to finish the game.

All of a sudden monks charged out of the gates only to be met with bullets from our guns. The taste became more rotten with each bullet. Bodies were piling up like walls but the stupid bastards kept coming. When the charging stopped there was no one left to kill. It became eerily silent. There was still no sight of the Hierarchy. None of us had any ammunition left in our assault weapons. We were down to our handguns and knives. Chief said, "Let's finish these mother fuckers! I don't want Satan or his misfits to get away. Pick the door of your fate." Ninja said, "I don't think we should split up." Chief, pissed off, answered back, "We have already covered one gate; it will take us way too long to search each gate together plus it gives them every chance to bail and escape." Limping, Zombie barked at Chief, "If we are all going to die here today, let's die together!" I said, "I have to agree with Zombie and Ninja. There are nine gates; we have already been in the first one. Let's go counter clockwise and hunt them down. I promise they have no intentions of running." Chief was out-voted and he knew it. Chief answered, "Have it your way." Ninja replied, "I assure you, Satan's army will be coming to hunt us down."

We charged in the ninth gateway - it wasn't like anything we expected. We went through lush rooms with different colored neon lights. Music played from room to room. I heard "Girlschool" By Britney Fox and Shot Gun Messiah's "Shout It Out." There were nuns performing rituals in locked cages throughout. They ignored us as if we weren't even there. The nuns appeared to be in a trance. Surrounded by chaos the nuns acted as if nothing was wrong: just business as usual. I could hear music in the distance more to our liking by Dokken, the song was "It's Not Love." When we walked into the music room we were met by a beautiful woman who looked like Elvira, she was not scared of us and said, "I have been expecting you." Still limping, Zombie asked, "Who are you?" The woman replied, "I am the oracle; my name is

Madalaine." Chief asked, "Oracle? Where is Satan hiding?" Madalaine answered, "Your anger blinds you from the truth. His Highness is all around you. What song would you like me to pleasure you with?" Ninja belted out "Madalaine" by Winger. Giving Ninja a dirty look, Chief said, "What the fuck is that supposed to mean, he is all around us?" It was too late; this little hot she-devil was dancing on one of the poles. She was the most beautiful woman I had ever seen. Madalaine motioned her finger for Ninja to come to her. Zombie warned, "Watch it Ninja, this is all wrong." Ninja went to the woman as she dangled her long hair over his face shoving her large breasts in his mouth; she then pulled out a knife. Before she could stab Ninja, Zombie shot her right in the face killing her instantly. Ninja turned to Zombie yelling, "Holy shit!" Zombie said, "Armageddon is here Ninja, get your head out of your ass. We're not on a trim hunt you selfish prick!" I rolled my eyes in a sigh of relief said, "Let's go, Satan's crew is not here." The nuns awoke from their trance when they began acting like psychos in their bird cages. They yelled obscenities at us. I walked out of the room as the song "Don't Close Your Eyes" by Kix played.

Out of the blue from the ninth gate Chief ranted, "Do you know what really killed Rock 'n Roll?" Ninja answered, "Fucking grunge music." Chief answered, "Nope, what killed rock was bands turning on each other. There was plenty of money to go around. Bands' jealousy, greed, deceit and selling out to the Devil for pop songs to be a hit ultimately killed rock. Headliner bands were jealous by other bands' musical expressions. It was sad. Corporations took over, pimping the bands out like cheap whores. Look at the greed of bands and what they started charging to go see a concert. They priced themselves right out of the market. They took advantage of the fans like us. While they were all killing themselves with alcohol and drugs, not to mention the almighty pussy, they deserted the male listeners that bought the albums and merchandise. I used to play air guitar and worship them like Rock Gods. Their biggest sin of all was they believed in their own hype versus supporting one another in the rock community. That, my friends, closed the coffin not only sealing their fates but that of the loyal fans. Now in Hell I suffer for it with the shit music of today. I think I would rather commit suicide than listen to another bubble gum female singer who can't write her own music, can't play a musical instrument, or her only stage show is to act like a whore onstage. What a rip off! I only hope one day as a whole the Rock Gods learn from their mistakes and make a comeback with a vengeance. They need to take back what was and will always be rightfully theirs and the fans to begin with." Zombie replied, "Chief, I agree with you a hundred percent! Not to worry, a band like the Beatles or another will come again to rise from the ashes putting rock music back in its rightful place one day soon." Chief said, "Well, I fucking hope sooner rather than later. This new music of today is pure shit! It's such an embarrassment to the history of music. At least Pearl Jam's grunge music was just another form of rock music." Ninja said, "Well I am glad you got that little rant out, maybe we can get back to the task at hand." Zombie sarcastically replied, "I would keep quiet if I were you after your little pussy debacle."

I could hear the song "Heaven's Trail (No Way Out)" by Tesla in the distance. I said, "Trust me on this; let's go to the sixth gate. I have a hunch we will find them there." Without argument we approached the sixth gate. It had demon artwork on the door. A cow statue stood in front of it. We walked down a painted red and black hallway towards an intersection. On one side I could hear grandfather clocks going off while music jammed the song "Turn up the Radio" by Autograph. In the other direction I heard "Bang Your Head (Mental Health)" by Quiet Riot. I said, "Chief it's your call." Chief yelled, "Let's go bang our heads!" We ran towards the music when Chief opened the door to a red strobe light in the room. At last we met with the entire Hierarchy. The evil empire was accompanied with human beings full of metal parts throughout their bodies. The half-man, half-machines had to be created by Satan himself; there could be no other explanation for such a disturbing creation. Suddenly sirens rang out and the lights went off as the duel between the Rebels from Heaven and the fallen angels kicked out of Heaven exploded.

The fracas erupted with gunfire, swearing, and screaming in the red room. I couldn't see in front of myself except when a shot rang out. I could see sparks in the air along with a strobe light atmosphere. It was the Wild West of anarchy in the dark. When the lights suddenly came back on it was my worst nightmare. Chief sat against the wall with a metal pipe sticking out of his left shoulder. I had been struck with a deep wound to my abdomen. Dead bodies were all over the floor. The sight of human machines made of metal parts terrified me. These people were mutilated freaks with metal spines, arms, and legs. There was no sign of the hierarchy. Chief yelled, "God damn it, they got away again! Somebody please help me up." The room had three doors to exit from. Ninja tried observing my wounds when I said, "Let me be! Chief's right; sooner or later we all have to face our destiny. This is where mine begins and ends. I am going through the door on the left by myself." Chief replied, "I'll take the door on the right. You boys take the door in the middle. Let's finish this sick game!" Nobody argued this time. I watched Chief pull out the pipe as blood splattered out. God, it looked awfully painful yet he never made a sound. I was choked up with emotion; I knew this time had to arrive sooner or later, it was inevitable. Ninja, not known for goodbyes, bolted with Zombie through the middle door. We all had pretty much gotten accustomed to not saying goodbye to one another. We just didn't like to say it. Maybe we were superstitious or we just didn't want to show our emotions. I nodded to Chief without saying a word. Chief said, "I know amigo, I know, there are no words to say it." Within seconds we vanished through the doorways.

Worried about Chief I turned back around chasing after him. I tried catching up to Chief who was determined for revenge. He opened the door running down a narrow stone path that led outside. Chief looked up at the early morning blue sky. He was in the courtyard where the cement walls were 15-20 feet high. I watched as he walked down the grass aisle staring at a dead end. As I glanced in the other direction the four horsemen rode towards him. Chief had no more bullets so his gun was useless. He threw the handgun to the ground. He drew out his once-proud Kama's then took a deep breath and stood in meditation waiting for his last wish of embracing with the Pale Horse known as Death, which was leading the charge galloping towards him in slow motion. I yelled, "Nooooo!" Chief took a deep breath then raised his Kama's high above his head standing motionless. The Four Horses of Revelations were no longer galloping towards him, Death raced to the finish line for the taste of blood and the victory of another soul. You could hear the Horses' breathing and the sound of their hooves pounding on the ground getting louder and louder when at the moment of impact Chief struck the Pale Horse; a loud terrifying scream came from the horse. It was the first time Death had a taste of its own medicine as Chief, in one mighty blow, delivered what he promised all along: the embracement of what is said could not be done. The Four Horsemen, along with Chief's body, disappeared in a flash. Black rain fell from the early morning sky. Mother Earth was soaking in the sins of her maker while Chief rode into the afterlife embracing Death; his rage waged on to embrace that of Angels, Demons, Satan, and even God himself. He did what no sane person would ever do: he conquered the Pale Horse known as Death. His remembrance is much higher in the annals than that of the Greek Gods; his name lives on for all of eternity. He finally got his wish as his chronicles live on. I get goose bumps thinking of the kid who faced Death then rode into Eternity to kill the one who was responsible for creating this mess in the first place. I not only respected Chief for what he stood for, I loved the vain son of a bitch. I know one day Chief will embrace his maker delivering death to his kingdom so that he can finally take responsibility for his own actions and that the almighty one can experience his own death. Maybe then he could understand true loss.

As I went back inside I was greeted by the peeping tom better known to us as the Boogieman. He walked down the stairs toward me as I slowly pulled my knife out with my left hand. He stood silent a few feet away from me when I said to myself, 'Who am I kidding?' I quickly drew out my handgun, simultaneously firing the first shot as he charged after me with a knife. The bullet hit him in the shoulder yet he still managed to stay on his feet. I fired a second shot hitting him in the chest as he lifted the knife but the bastard wouldn't go down. I yelled, "Fuck you!" This time I aimed for his head and fired again, this time hitting the Boogieman in the forehead. I pulled the mask off his face, which was unrecognizable from burn marks. I walked up the stairs surprised I lived this long.

CHIEF

Journals by Zombie

We ran past a bloody hallway before entering a large forum that reeked of death. Limping to hide behind some wooden crates I said, "What a psycho circus." Ninja replied, "You're not kidding brother." There was an incinerator burning in the corner. Along the walls stood hundreds of starving animals in cages that appeared abused including dogs, cats, birds, raccoons, goats, lambs, and even a cow. It was a fucking sin to witness. I saw the Tall Man tossing a body in the incinerator like it was a rag doll. I spotted Manson talking to four weird gothic-like beings on stilts, their faces painted like out of a bad horror movie. The circus atmosphere of this place just kept getting weirder by the second. Animals cried out loud for help. It didn't take a rocket scientist to tell they were frightened. It was too hard to ignore; I had to help the poor things. We slowly crept forward hiding behind some boxes when the Tall Man left through the back door. Manson turned briefly staring around the room. Cages were stacked one on top of the other. Ninja said to me, "I've got a plan. I want you to create a diversion. Distract the freaks with noise while I free the animals." I said, "I've got a better plan." Ninja asked, "What's that?" I answered, "Watch and see." I limped out from behind the boxes singing "Working Man" by Rush when I shot the first freak on stilts. Before the next one approached, Ninja fired a few shots missing the freak before I shot him in the head. Manson yelled to the other freaks, "Kill them!" As usual, the coward ran out the back door. Ninja yelled, "I am going after Manson!" He tossed me his handgun and said, "You're more dangerous with this than I am. Now give them hell!" As the other two gothic freaks wobbled towards me I began singing the song "Tom Sawyer" by Rush. Toying with them, I cut them in half watching the stilt freaks come crashing down. They were no match for me as the confrontation was short lived. For fun I walked up to them as they tried crawling to escape; I shot them in both hamstrings and the buttocks then lectured, "Now you can reap what it's like to suffer, you degenerate freaks." I opened a few bags of animal food spreading it all over the floor. I went to the cages and freed the animals. The dogs rushed over attacking the gothic freaks. It wasn't a pretty sight as the pit bulls shredded them for breakfast. I guess they liked their meat rare.

Meanwhile, Ninja chased Manson all over creation. At full speed, Ninja gained on Manson when Manson stopped on a dime tripping Ninja, who fell to the ground. Manson charged after Ninja who made it to his feet only to be tackled by Manson; Ninja flipped him over his body. They both immediately got back up on their feet when Manson said, "I am going to make you suffer before killing you." Ninja responded, "You talk too much." With a front round-house kick Ninja hit Manson right in the jaw with a lethal blow. Manson was stunned as Ninja delivered several kicks to the face knocking Manson backwards. Manson had no answers for Ninja's assault. With a strong sidekick Ninja busted Manson's left knee cap. Manson fell to the ground in agony. Ninja yelled, "Get up! I am just getting warmed up you son of a bitch!" In anger, Manson somehow made it to his feet only to have Ninja this time kick and break his right knee cap. Manson fell to the floor head first. Ninja sat on Manson's back, lifted his head up and said, "This is from Medicine Man you piece of shit! See you in the afterlife. Now enjoy the flash of light." Ninja broke Manson's neck.

Exhausted, Ninja got up on his feet then turned around only to be met with a knife to the abdomen from Hitler's skeleton knife. Hitler whispered, "Shhh! Take your medicine well." Hitler stabbed Ninja again while whispering in his ear, "Go ahead now cry out, it's gotta hurt you fucking gook bastard." Ninja fell flat on his back. To his surprise, Hitler stared down the barrels of my duel handguns. Hitler said, "Now that's not fair. Why not settle this like honorable men?" I replied, "You bring a knife to a gunfight, kill my friends then ask for fairness. Don't you know there are no fair fights in war?" In anger, Hitler yelled, "You don't have the balls to murder me in cold blood!" I answered, "You don't know me very well. This is the end of the line for you. Fuck you!" I fired several shots, hitting Hitler in the knee, hand, groin, and shoulder. I stood over him as he lay on his back dying and said, "Checkmate!" Using my last bullet, I shot Hitler in the head, sending him where he belonged.

I leaned over Ninja, who thankfully was still alive as I helped him to his feet. I could see Ninja's wounds were fatal as blood flowed out of his belly like a river. I said, "Let's get out of here." In bad shape, we limped down a hallway towards a door before Ninja collapsed. Lying on his back with blood coming from his mouth, Ninja said, "You know the first movie I ever saw was "Butch Cassidy and the Sundance Kid" with my father. This is a fitting end to my life. I want to die in the daylight. Give me my gun back." I asked, "Why? We're out of ammo." Ninja answered, "I always wanted to die a cowboy." I handed him the pistol then said, "We might as well give those bastards one last dance." I started singing "Blaze of Glory" by Jon Bon Jovi when Ninja interrupted, "Help me to my feet; let's finish the game for the last time." I replied, "You know, I am no longer scared to die. I have seen this in a vision." Both of us ran out the door with our guns pointing in the air when we were met with an ambush of arrows falling from the sky.

ZOMBIE

CHAPTER THIRTY FIVE: FINAL BENEDICTION

Journals by Preacher

Somewhere on my way back from killing the Boogieman I took a wrong turn and got lost. I panicked running down the hallway when I turned a corner, without looking I crashed into Gabriel. I heard someone yelling his name when he ran off. I also yelled, "Gabriel, come back it's me, Preacher!" I spotted someone jogging towards me when out of the shadows I saw the face of the man I distained most, Father Blackwell. He stopped dead in his tracks as I pointed a .38 pistol at him and said, "Blackwell, you are one slippery sick prick!" Father Blackwell said, "You got it all wrong. Be reasonable, it wasn't my fault about your father." I replied, "Blackwell some things are better left unsaid." Blackwell yelled, "Nooo!" I replied, "I'll see you in Hell!" I fired one shot to the head killing Father Blackwell. I tried searching for Gabriel when I spotted my old nemesis the Tall Man. It was time I faced my fears. I needed to kill the Tall Man so I checked the chamber of my .38 special. I had two bullets left and a knife, not very encouraging for what I was about to walk into. I chased after the Tall Man when I saw Gabriel go down another hall. I chased after him when I saw him go in a doorway.

When I reached the door I took a deep breath then slowly opened it. The room had a red mist to it. I had a hard time keeping my balance as the room had a 3D feel to it. My vision became blurry from the mist inside it when out of the haze the Tall Man stood laughing. I had no more energy to run. The Tall Man said, "Last but not least boy, we have been waiting for you." I asked, "For what?" The Tall Man replied, "For your soul to keep." I responded, "Let's embrace at last old man." The Tall Man ran towards me when I shot him in the heart; he stopped in hesitation. With my last bullet I aimed carefully and shot the Tall Man between the eyes; he fell flat on his back. Within seconds he rolled over and got up. I said, "Oh Shit!" He stood there laughing when his demeanor changed to anger as he yelled, "My turn you little filth!" He charged right at me as I drew out my knife. Just before he reached me a force knocked the Tall Man into the wall. He got up again and the same thing happened. He was flung into the opposite wall. I watched as the shadow figures came into focus. It was my lost brothers the Cemetery Boys! I watched Medicine Man, Animal, Beast and Shadow do a number on the Tall Man. Their bodies would appear and then disappear much like the Tall Man. Magic waved for me to go down the hall; as I ran past I turned around to get one last look at the boys when the room went dark. I couldn't see in front of me when I noticed a bright light coming from under a door.

I quietly opened the door; the room was entirely white with the exception of a large colored global sphere that lit up. Satan sat in a plush red chair staring at the sphere; the Tall Man hung from a giant mirror behind him as if he was hanging on a clothes hook. I pointed my gun towards Satan who stood up as the Tall Man made funny faces at me. Bluffing with an empty gun I yelled to Satan, "Move and I will kill you where you stand!" Satan said, "We meet again Preacher. I have been expecting you for some time. If I wanted you dead you would be dead already." I replied, "That's bullshit! The best man lost and you don't like it!" Satan answered back, "I have to admit, I underestimated how well you boys would play the game. You boys have been a real pain in the ass, you resilient little shit!" In anger I asked, "Where are Hitler and Manson?" Satan replied, "Oh, that's good. That is really good. I can feel the boiling of your anger and the salty taste of the kill. I admire that quality. I love revenge, for my revenge has been sweet as hell should I say." Irritated with the mind games, I said, "No, I wouldn't say or even agree. Let's just say for the sake of it that you really are Satan; your wiring is all wrong!" Satan replied with laughter, "Please let us whisper to each other dear boy before we kill one another." Unfortunately with an itchy trigger finger and no bullets I said, "Make no mistake, I promise you I am going to kill you before I leave the earth. Take a seat on your fucking perch and keep your hands where I can see them. If you make any sudden moves I will knock you on your prissy ass." I continued pointing the gun back and forth watching intently at every movement of Satan and the Tall Man in the mirror.

Satan sat back on the chair with his hands on the arm rests. I sat in a white chair across from Satan and asked, "Why all the propaganda and charades? You people are crazy! I don't understand, revenge against whom?" Satan answered, "My dear boy, your maker has deceived not only me but the world he built. He has taken no responsibility for it and he wants me to take the fall because I questioned his judgments. God underestimated my abilities: that of being a God. Have you ever wondered why you were told Jesus came from Heaven, which by the way is a very big advantage to have when you ask humanity (who has never seen his face or kingdom) to have faith in your precious God? Jesus came from Heaven to pay for your sins. He then rose from the dead then poof went back to Heaven. God also broke commandments using murder as his revenge on those who persecuted his son. Yet I ask you, why does he not take your revenge? Why are you not in Heaven? Why are you still paying for sins if Jesus paid for your sins already?" Looking befuddled I answered back, "Satan, I have many questions here on earth. No priest or church has ever been able to answer my questions but my own conclusion is he is the maker of all things. He doesn't work on our time or your time. God created time but is not from time. He made you, he made the dinosaurs, all the angels of Heaven; unfortunately the human race which you are so jealous of and hell bent on destroying, shit, God has made it all for that matter! I give him all the power and glory. While I sympathize with you I can actually agree with you that God has not taken responsibility for making such an evil piece of shit like you. I also agree he murdered the world from the fate of the dinosaurs to the drowning at the great flood. You both have taken the lives of innocent people and animals. I think it's hypocritical to say 'thou shalt not kill' yet God killed and murdered. He made you then cast you out of Heaven for wanting to be God. Ultimately the way I see it, you killed for him. In my mind God is an accessory to murder. He has let religions which take his name start wars using murder as a weapon of excuses. Most wars started over religion. He did take revenge for his son. What father wouldn't? In the end, for me the reason we have never seen God's face is because we as humans are incompatible with him. God is of fire, how could you embrace what is not compatible with flesh? You, Adam and Eve fucked that one up in the Garden of Eden. While again, I can see your point, God made the tree of life; that alone should be a sin. Look, when I play with my plastic soldiers I get to say who lives and dies because I am the maker. Ultimately God is the maker and he has the right of passage to be the dictator of life. It's his world, we only live in it. If God truly chooses to make the world suffer then so be it. Karma comes to us all, even him, but today it has come for you."

Laughing, Satan said, "Wow I am impressed Preacher, you do know something of the Bible. You are so right, your God made the Heavens, the world, and everything in it. I questioned God, yes. I wanted to be that of my own God. God set the bar through his own actions; I only mock them, you can see that right? Killing is in God's blood, God made the dinosaurs yet they killed one another. Killing has been in God's nature for eternity. What makes it right for him and wrong for me or anyone else? God murdered the dinosaurs because he knew he made a mistake yet he continues to have humans preach that he is perfect. He kicked me out of Heaven because of his own jealousy and control issues. God is a control freak, a dictator who has always had a taste for killing. God worried that I might actually do a better job than him. This notion since the beginning of time, that he kicked me out of Heaven with my angels, who God refers to as demons, is a lie. We chose to leave. I have tried to give man a better life to live; only to witness God preach fear and hypocrisy. God does not love anyone; if he did you would all be in Heaven with the angels already. God plays games with humans like an experimental toy. He seeks perfection yet he is not. Humanity is being deceived!" I asked, "What have you done to make this world better? Your own actions speak louder than words as you have set out to destroy mankind, right Satan? For whatever sick reason, God has let you wreak havoc here on earth for far too long. Well today I am going to do what God apparently doesn't have the balls to do, that's to end you. I am not waiting for the apocalypse. I don't give a shit about the horns, the trumpets, or the horsemen of revelations. Your end is today my friend: that is a fucking fact!"

Satan smiled while the Tall Man stared at me. Satan replied, "You are the last Cemetery Boy, Preacher. All your friends are dead. Soon you will join them." With anxiety I asked, "What the fuck are you talking about?" Satan slowly got up, touched the sphere then calmly sat down laughing as he asked, "I love watching a good rerun, don't you?" The sphere played back the deaths of Chief, Ninja, and Zombie. I could feel the steam coming out of my ears. I looked directly at Satan and said, "Well it looks like they took your friends with them." Satan remarked, "Well, all things are replaceable. I learned that from God. You humans only know of sin. You thrive on sins and you justify it in one way or another in your own minds. Go look at the housewife who justified sleeping around or those who make more money than they know what to do with yet they do not share with the world. Sure, anyone can give a small portion while sitting on billions. You humans are greedy, shallow, and hurtful to your own kind because of their height, weight, skin color and countless other reasons. You continually pray to your God about 'wanting'; that is all you humans ever do, want, want, want, need, need, need. If you get what you prayed for then you'd say you were blessed and if you don't get it then you curse God. I told God a long time ago if he would stop giving to humans they would have no need to worship him. They are selfish beings. When is it ever enough? Now that is God's biggest sin of all. You humans preach fear that the end of the world is coming. Where is your precious God? Maybe he enjoys watching mankind suffer, just a thought. I have a news flash for you: he is never coming. Suffering on earth is forever.

Ask the Jews at Auschwitz if God came to their rescue. Governments and dictatorships have more power and control over you than God. Humans are slaves to a form of government and corporate dictatorship. God cannot take what is rightfully mine. The only Revelation you will ever witness is me squashing mankind's greed. I have had no hand in selling books that make promises or threats to mankind. God only watches from his comfy cowardly sidelines of human's own greed. He created imperfection. Revenge was for his screw-ups and for that of his son's, not yours. Give onto me your revenge. 'Revenge is mine' said the Lord, oh really? Your God is a coward that murders from above. I am your God because I face you for I am not a coward. I don't make promises I can't keep. Look around you, my monks want for nothing." Trembling with fear and anger while pointing the gun at Satan, I said, "You're off your fucking rocker, Satan. Talk about calling the kettle black. You twist things to play in your favor. God said he would come down and lock you away only to let you out one last time for a thousand years. I am afraid I can't allow this to happen so you can have free reign again. Humans have had enough of you; I certainly know I am way beyond sick of all your bullshit. Maybe Chief was right, maybe you really are God's brother. No matter, your time is finished today because I am going to pull the plug on it. You and God are wrong about a lot of things. I don't give a shit about Heaven, Hell, or even Purgatory. You and God couldn't promise or buy the Cemetery Boys' souls. Neither of you are worthy of your own worlds. Whatever happens to me and my tribe let it be, but you're coming with me. Now get up out of that fucking chair! I am tired of listening to you or the Bible for that matter. God is the maker and he can have it all, I don't give a damn about vanity. You betrayed God. I am here to tell you that even Heaven has rebels! Let me give you something to think about: even the Devil can be betrayed. I have no interest in you, God, wars, or even greed, but I have a tremendous interest in killing you today. You are not a God!"

Satan stood up staring directly into my eyes and replied, "Go ahead Preacher pull the trigger and find out for yourself. Come on, try to kill me you little heathen!" The radio suddenly played "holy diver" by Dio. Startled, I stared back at Satan and said, "I am going to do what God apparently couldn't do." Satan asked, "And what is that?" I threw the gun and my knife on the floor; hesitating I answered, "I am going to offer you the other cheek." Before I could finish my sentence I felt a painful stab in my back. I fell to the floor only to see Gabriel standing over me with a dagger in his hands. Satan yelled in my face, "You filthy little shit, all of humanity serves me, for you are all worthless and weak!" I replied to Satan, "I wasn't finished what needs to be said to you." Satan yelled, "Then finish already!" I continued, "Satan, I forgive you of your sins and I love you as a brother." The mirror behind Satan instantly shattered in thousands of pieces as the Tall Man vanished. Out of nowhere Satan's body was struck by electricity then suddenly transformed into an ugly worm that fell to the floor. In my final moments I tried killing the worm but Gabriel quickly picked the worm up and ingested it. I saw his eyes turn into that of the Devil's when I yelled, "Noooo!" I knew I needed to kill Gabriel so out of desperation I tried crawling to grab him, but he immediately ran off. I heard the radio playing "The Way It Is" by Tesla, when in failure I rolled over on my back in severe pain to accept my fate. Suddenly I could see a light coming toward me. I heard the song, "The End" by The Doors. I saw shadow figures walking towards me when I exhaled my last breath; then without warning a flash came over my eyes. In a bubble I watched myself die with my eyes open. I had a look of peace on my face.

PREACHER

CHAPTER THIRTY SIX: RESURRECTION

Narrated by Sheriff Langley

The National Guard along with the local authorities arrived too late to help the Cemetery Boys; they did however crash the party at Crowley's Tomb. Whatever monks were left either escaped or died that day, no one was taken into custody. The Cemetery Boys' and Wizard's ashes were placed in a mausoleum in the Labyrinth. Unfortunately, the government and authorities came up with some wild concocted story of how Detective Parks and Bloom were the heroes, along with the local police department and National Guard. By all accounts, apparently the governments saved the day at Crowley's Tomb. The Village wasn't buying what the government was selling, they knew better than that. Weeks went by as the Police Department and various government departments took their time making a spectacle of it all. The story was so twisted from the truth of what really happened; they took all the credit through the media with very little notation of the Cemetery Boys. The whole story smelled like a pile of shit. Something didn't add up.

The following summer rumors still circled the wagon when one day a big story hit the media like a bombshell. An unidentified person stumbled upon journals locked away in the police archives and sent them to the media. The media outlets told a whole different story of what really happened at Crowley's Tomb. Hot off the press, the report multiplied like wildfire all across the country. Several local authorities and SG officials were fired. Ironically, that summer at a baseball game, reporter Marilynn Jenner was caught on TV taking a homerun ball away from a third-grader who had caught the ball in centerfield; she was fired the next day. Over time the SG crumbled while authorities confiscated the land; the new government peddled it to the highest bidders. In time the government sold Crowley's Tomb to the Village. The Village turned it into a museum and tourist attraction. Statues were made to honor all thirteen of the Cemetery Boys in a circle surrounding the pyramid with Wizard in the middle of the park. My daughter was a driving force behind that. Later, another monument was built in front of Crowley's Tomb with the Cemetery Boys' faces and famous story etched in stone.

IN ANOTHER PLACE AND TIME

New Journals by Preacher

I wish I could tell you we all ended up in Elysium to meet God but that never happened. Is there a God? Absolutely! Just nothing like mankind manipulates him to be. Apparently our luck is still running about the same in the next place. I guess if it wasn't for bad luck we wouldn't have any luck at all. I really can't tell you what transpired between bodies. I learned we travel through bodies and who we really are is somehow connected in the blood. I don't want to bore you with the scientific details, I just remember waking up in a very dark place listening to a song by The Doors called "When The Music's Over". I could hear talking with laughter echoing from familiar voices in the background. I also smelled a familiar scent from a tobacco pipe. I rose out of bed wearing my shoes, pants, shirt and cloak as I always had. I checked my body: there were no wounds. I felt as alive as ever. When my vision finally became clear again I looked around the room and saw thirteen beds with each member of the tribe standing at the end of their beds. I got up and walked to the end of the bed where I was met by Wizard standing in the middle of the room. Wizard said, "We have been waiting for you to awake my son." Next thing I knew I was being hugged by each member of the tribe. The room was full of electricity and excitement. I couldn't believe we were all united again. Suddenly Magic began singing "United" by Judas Priest and before long we were all singing along. I felt so alive and peaceful. I could feel goose bumps while singing. When we finished singing I asked Wizard, "Am I dreaming? Is this a dream?" Wizard yelled in his reply, "A dream to some but a fucking nightmare to others!" I asked Wizard, "Am I dead?" Wizard answered, "We are now in the afterlife where the fight goes on kid, only this time we have the proper weapons to take the fight to them. Remember, in the afterlife, there is no such thing as time. We are free to roam the world like God."

The guys interrupted Wizard as I watched each tribe member shape-change in and out of their bodies. It freaked me out. Everyone now had some sort of special powers of their own. I was still a bit confused as I looked around the room. Scratching my head I asked, "Where are we?" Zombie answered, "We are in the Labyrinth Mausoleum. We have been waiting for you so we can continue the fight with evil." I asked everyone, "Do you expect me to believe we are dead and now reunited with each other in the same room? This is from way out in fucking left field man." Chief smirked then answered, "Yep, mind blowing. Go check the mirror over there and take a long hard look for yourself." I walked over to the mirror where I could hear "Strawberry Fields Forever" by the Beatles as I stared straight into the mirror. I didn't see anything. I waved my hands, I made faces, yet I still couldn't see a fucking thing. I turned to everyone and said, "I don't understand. I can see you as clear as day. I saw you shape change. I can feel and hear all of you. For that matter I can feel myself." Ghost asked, "Isn't it cool? You're going to love it bro." I replied, "Not really, it's freaking me out!"

My best friend Medicine Man said, "Think of it as being in the spirit world more or less." I could sniff the smell of pot in the air so I glanced over at Raven and asked, "Even in death you're still smoking that shit and doing drugs. Why?" Smiling, Raven answered, "Personally, I don't like drugs but drugs for some reason or another sure love me." The room erupted in laughter. Animal asked, "Are you ready to fight them?" I asked, "Fight who? There is no one left to fight, we're dead." Beast answered back, "You're wrong, dead wrong. It's just the beginning." Shadow said to Wizard, "Show him." Wizard pulled out a see-through crystal ball from his pocket. I could see images of Delilah leading our girlfriends dressed in Cemetery Boys jackets walking through the Cemetery. I could also see a familiar foe of ours in a black hearse coming towards the girls, along with Gabriel smack dab in the middle of them both. I yelled, "Oh Shit!" Chief said, "Exactly!" Maverick said to Wizard, "We should be going now." I asked, "Going where?" Ninja answered, "To do what we always do. It's time for round two. Ding, ding!" Panicking as usual, Zombie interrupted, "Maybe we should stay here for awhile and let things blow over." Chief rolled his eyes, asking Zombie in a very unpleasant tone of voice, "Please tell me you're not going to start this shit all over again, are you?" Zombie pointed at Chief yelling back, "Screw you creep-o!" Zombie walked away whining to himself, "I hate this fucking guy!" The guys just laughed at Zombie when Wolf hugged me and said, "Welcome back brother, you look great." I answered back, "Thanks bro, I missed you guys." Wolf glanced around the room then said, "Before our journey begins I need to remind you of one thing." Everyone asked at the same time, "What's that?" With a big old smile, Wolf answered, "Don't forget to bring your balls." The room erupted in laughter. With a grin on his face, Wizard yelled, "It's our time to kick some ass!" The room went in an uproar. It felt just like old times.

Suddenly I heard a door open down the hall of the mausoleum. I heard loud familiar footsteps walking in slow motion. Cheech began to bark as Chong growled. The footsteps got louder when a blue glow crept in. Zombie yelled, "Oh shit, not again!" Chief yelled, "Shut up!" Around the corner the footsteps got louder and louder when our old nemesis the Tall Man appeared in front of us and with a smile yelled, "Let the games begin!" He ran toward us with that ugly face of his while stretching out his long arms when within the blink of an eye we, along with the Tall Man, vanished into thin air. For once, we were on a level playing field to fight the enemy. The door of the mausoleum again opened as it made that old creaking noise. Again eternity heard footsteps but this time much softer coming from the hall. An old man walked in the room holding a lantern and wearing a top hat. He walked over to the mirror rubbing his mangy beard and said out loud while staring in the mirror at his own reflection, "You can check out anytime you want, unfortunately you can never leave." Snickering, the Night Man began whistling "Hotel California" by the Eagles as he closed the mausoleum door and disappeared.

Preacher's Afterlife Journals

With the song playing "Knockin' On Heaven's Door" by Guns N' Roses; Heaven had locked us out. As for us we arose from above the ashes bound in the never ending battle with evil. We were banned from Heaven. That was our punishment from God for lack of faith. Much like the loyal servant Moses who was punished by God for loyal service; our boundary lines were set within the cemetery gates and that of the afterlife. We could be seen in the cemetery but not outside of it, yet the ultimate evil had no boundaries. I guess God had a sick sense of humor after all. At least we were given a license to fight evil for eternity from the cowardly, political, and vanity leaders in Heaven. Truth be told, we're all just puppets on a string regardless on earth or in Heaven. If we had just killed in the name of God and had more faith; would we have been punished I wondered? Hypocrisy/killing has no end, especially in the afterlife. At best we were given an equal killing field with evil and just like the good book (Bible), our names were simply remembered. As it turned out the great "Apocalyptic War" in the book of Revelation was nothing more than our everyday life. So in the end, our journals on earth became a legendary "Rock-N-Roll Fable" and that I can live with my friends. With our story told I will leave you with this song for thought: "Imagine" by John Lennon. May you live FOREVER!

ABOUT THE AUTHOR

A lifetime of experiences- from growing up in the foster care system and seeing the system fail kids who were born into unfortunate circumstances, to my own struggles with religion, surviving divorce and infidelity, as well as the many profound friendships over the years - helped shape me into the person I am today: honest, unafraid to speak the truth, compassionate, and someone who truly enjoys the simple pleasures in life! My journey has led me to my true passion: writing, which I look forward to sharing with you in many different genres.

I reside in the beautiful Sarasota/Bradenton area of Florida, where I enjoy many passions: cooking, making new friends & developing relationships through FaceBook, football, dogs, meditation, motorcycles and working out. I am especially passionate about all things nature related, including spending time exploring the gulf beaches, boating, snorkeling, kayaking, camping, wildlife exploration and feeding the birds & squirrels. My biggest passion is writing while overlooking the serene Manatee River from my window.

I was born in the Chicago area and lived in many states during my childhood. I spent many years living in Las Vegas, NV as an adult, where I owned popular Italian Restaurants/Pizzerias before returning to my true home - the incomparable Gulf Coast of Florida. I am 49, active, young at heart and embrace aging, which has helped fuel my passions!

CONNECT WITH CASEY

Visit the Crowley's Tomb Website at www.crowleystomb.com to enter contests, order merchandise, poster giveaways, fan participation, vacation giveaway, Q&A, fan feedback along with an opportunity to be a patch member of Crowley's Tomb and much, much more. I love to interact with my fans and encourage you to share your thoughts with me through my website, FaceBook page or Twitter.

Please scan the code below to be directed to my website for details:

www.ingramcontent.com/pod-product-compliance
Lightning Source LLC
Chambersburg PA
CBHW061129200626
46817CB00016B/441